COA

KU-525-153

WITHDRAWN

Cove Library
Tel : 245350

....

**PLEASE RETURN TO THE ABOVE LIBRARY, ON OR BEFORE
THE DUE DATE. TO RENEW, PLEASE QUOTE THE DUE DATE
AND THE ABOVE AUTHOR/NUMBER.**

 Aberdeen City Council Library Services

X000 000 039 8751

ABERDEEN CITY LIBRARIES

THE TURBULENT YEARS

Margaret Pemberton titles available from
Severn House Large Print Books

UNFORGETTABLE DAYS
THE FOUR OF US

THE TURBULENT YEARS

Margaret Pemberton

Severn House Large Print
London & New York

This first large print edition published 2008
in Great Britain and the USA by
SEVERN HOUSE PUBLISHERS of
9-15 High Street, Sutton, Surrey, SM1 1DF.
First world regular print edition published 2005 by
Severn House Publishers, London and New York.

Copyright © 1990, 2005 by Margaret Pemberton.

All rights reserved.
The moral right of the author has been asserted.

British Library Cataloguing in Publication Data

Pemberton, Margaret
    The turbulent years. - Large print ed.
    1. Vietnamese Conflict, 1961-1975 - Missing in action -
    Fiction 2. Military spouses - Fiction 3. Female friendship
    - Fiction 4. Saigon (Vietnam) - Fiction 5. Large type books
    I. Title II. Pemberton, Margaret. White Christmas in Saigon
    823.9'14[F]

    ISBN-13: 978-0-7278-7700-0

Except where actual historical events and characters are being described
for the storyline of this novel, all situations in this publication are
fictitious and any resemblance to living persons is purely coincidental.

Printed and bound in Great Britain by
MPG Books Ltd, Bodmin, Cornwall.

CHAPTER ONE

It was two-thirty on a Wednesday afternoon when the official-looking black sedan drove up and stopped outside Abbra's home. She had spent the morning writing, and her chapter was going well. At twelve o'clock she had taken a coffee break and had decided to go for a short walk before resuming work. She had driven across to Golden Gate Park and had strolled by the edge of the lake, mentally plotting out the end of her chapter. Satisfied that all she now had to do was to transfer the words in her head onto paper, she had driven back home, not thinking about Lewis, thinking only of the imaginary world that had become so real to her. And then, as she turned into the driveway, she saw the sedan.

The occupants didn't wait for her to turn off the Oldsmobile's engine before they stepped from the car, slamming the doors behind them. She froze, her hands tight on the wheel. Both men were in army uniform. Both were officers. And one of them was a chaplain.

They returned, beginning to walk toward her, and the instant she saw the expression on their faces she knew that Lewis was either dead or captured.

"Mrs. Ellis?" the unordained officer asked her as she forced her hands numbly from the wheel and clumsily opened her car door.

She stumbled out onto the drive, facing him. "Yes. I'm Mrs. Ellis." The sun, which only a few minutes before had been so pleasurable, was now sickeningly hot, so searingly bright that she had difficulty in focusing on the man's face.

"Could we speak to you inside for a few minutes, Mrs. Ellis?"

She nodded, her throat dry, her heart pounding. *Please don't let him be dead!* she was screaming silently. *Please, dear God, don't let Lewis be dead! Don't let him be dead!*

She walked across the drive and slipped her key into the lock. She couldn't ask. If she asked, and if he were dead, there would be no going back. Every second that they didn't speak was a second longer of hope, a second longer of being able to pretend that everything was still all right, that perhaps it was a welfare visit. That perhaps Lewis had been injured and was being flown home, that perhaps...

"Your husband has been taken prisoner, Mrs. Ellis," the chaplain was saying to her gently.

They were in the living-room. Lewis's photograph was in a small silver frame on one of the side tables. She had planned to write to him that evening. It would have been one of her last letters, for in another four weeks he would be coming home to her.

"He and his companions were ambushed on one of the canals after they had searched a village for North Vietnamese forces." It was the other officer speaking now. He was mature and grizzle-haired and his voice was full of regret. "One of your husband's fellow officers managed to escape. He saw your husband taken prisoner. As he was captured in the South, it may be impossible to receive official confirmation for some time—"

"Was he hurt?" she interrupted harshly. Her hands were balled into fists. He was alive. He was alive and that had to mean that he would come home to her again eventually.

"It is the opinion of the officer who witnessed the incident that he was not seriously injured."

"Thank God." She was crying. The tears were streaming down her face. She tried to stop them. She tried to be as courageous and as dignified as she knew Lewis would want her to be, as befitted an army wife, but no matter how hard she tried she couldn't stop the tears.

"You will receive an official telegram tomorrow, Mrs. Ellis," the middle-aged and fatherly officer was saying to her, "and if there is anything that the army can do..."

He handed her a card. She didn't even look down at the piece of paper. There was only one thing she wanted the army to do. "Just bring my husband back to me," she said, her tears splashing onto her dress and the card in her hand. "Just bring Lewis home."

They wanted to stay with her until her parents returned home from the art exhibition they were visiting, or until a friend or a neighbor could be telephoned to come and sit with her. She vehemently refused all such offers.

"No. I want to be alone for a while." It was the truth. She didn't want solicitous comfort. She wanted to be alone with her thoughts of Lewis.

Reluctantly, sensing that it might be best, they took their leave. Slowly she crossed the sun-filled room, picking up his photograph from the table.

"Where are you?" she whispered brokenly, and then, to her horror, she was drowned by another emotion as well as grief. She was overcome with anger, anger that he should have promised her he would be home within a few short weeks, and now wouldn't be home with her for perhaps years and years, anger at the awful, terrible loneliness that she knew lay ahead.

"*Oh, Lewis!*" she howled in agony to the empty room. "*Where are you? When are you going to come back to me?*"

By the time her parents returned, her face was still wet and streaked with tears, but her voice was steady.

"If he's a prisoner of war, then you'll be able to write to him, communicate with him," her father said gruffly when he had recovered from the worst of the shock.

"But I thought only pilots who were shot down over the North were prisoners of war?" her mother asked bewildered. "Lewis was in the South, wasn't he? How could he possibly have been captured by North Vietnamese forces? It

8

doesn't make any kind of sense. We are *winning* the war, aren't we...."

"It isn't as cut and dried as you seem to think," Abbra's father responded somberly. "It isn't a game between the Rams and the Redskins. It's far more complicated than that."

When her father mentioned the Rams, Abbra said quietly, "The army will break the news to Lewis's father, but they won't contact Scott. I'll have to do that."

"Nonsense!" her mother retorted despite her distress. As far as she knew, for the last month there had been no contact between Abbra and Scott Ellis, and she didn't want contact to be resumed. "His father will telephone him. There's absolutely no reason for you to do so. You are far too upset."

"No. Abbra is right," her husband interrupted. "Abbra should call him. It would be awful if he heard about it on the news or read it in the papers."

"Colonel Ellis will contact him!" her mother insisted.

"I'd rather he heard the news from me," Abbra said in a quiet, inflexible voice, and as her mother broke out into further protests she walked out of the room. The telephone in the hall was too public, and she went past it, crossing the hall and entering her father's study, closing the door behind her.

She hadn't seen or spoken to Scott for four weeks, ever since the day when she had last lunched with Patti Maine. Since then she had told the household help that if Scott telephoned, she was not at home.

A week before she had received an affectionate letter from him. He was assuming she was away on another research trip, but as he hadn't received so much as a postcard from her he was getting worried. Would she please telephone him the instant she returned home?

She had put the letter to one side, not knowing how to reply. The more she had thought about what Patti had said, the more she had realized the kernel of truth behind it. She and Scott had been spending too much time together. People were beginning to speculate about the nature of their relationship. And Abbra had been too self-absorbed to notice. A tiny piece in a gossip column a week after her lunch with Patti showed her how very visible they had become as a couple.

Rams star Scott Ellis attended a charity game at La Jolla High School on Wednesday evening, and was *not* accompanied by his sister-in-law, the pretty and vivacious Mrs. Lewis Ellis. Could this sudden rift in family relations stem from Scott's involvements in antiwar demonstrations? His brother, Captain Lewis Ellis, is at present on a year's tour of duty in 'Nam. It could be that sister-in-law Abbra isn't the only one to have taken offence at Scott's antiwar stance. His father, Colonel Thomas Ellis, a highly decorated Second World War veteran, is also likely to be displeased.

10

It was an unpleasant little piece, but Abbra knew that if she had read it before she had lunched with Patti, she would have focused on the references to a possible rift between Scott and his father. She certainly would have missed the sexual insinuations completely. But they were there. She could see that now. Even worse, she knew that there were seeds of truth in the insinuation. She admitted it. She *was* physically attracted to Scott. He was so magnificently Adonis-like, so tall and powerfully built and golden-haired, she didn't see how any woman could fail to be. Yet until Patti had pointed it out to her, she had not realized how dangerous the situation was, how dependent she was on him emotionally, and how dependent he might be on her...

She knew that she needed him now. Her parents could commiserate with her, her friends and neighbors would be sympathetic, but she didn't need commiseration or sympathy. She needed someone who understood her, someone who would understand her anger as well as her grief. She needed someone who would realize just how monstrously obscene the prospect of not seeing Lewis again for years and years was.

After she had dialed his number, the telephone in his apartment rang for so long that she thought he must be out. Just as she was about to hang up, he answered, and at the sound of his familiar, zest-filled voice, her hard-won composure abandoned her.

"It's Abbra," she said, her voice breaking. "Oh, Scott! Lewis has been taken prisoner by the North Vietnamese!"

There was a second's stunned silence, and then he said, "Hang in there, sweetheart. I'm on my way."

She put the telephone back on its rest and leaned back against the wall, her eyes closed, her tears falling fast and free. It was what she had wanted to hear. He hadn't asked any of the questions anyone else would have asked, questions which she could not possibly answer. He had simply said that he would come to her. And when he did, she knew that he would give her the strength to be able to face the next few days, and the days that would follow those.

She didn't want to talk to him in the house. Despite the dreadful circumstances, she knew that her mother's attitude toward him had not changed. So as the time approached when she expected him, she waited in the hall, prepared to run out to his car the second she heard its engine.

"Do you think you should leave the house?" her father asked, a worried frown furrowing his brow. "What if there is a telephone call from the army? What if there is further news of Lewis?"

"I have to talk to Scott, Daddy. And I have to do it away from the house."

He nodded unhappily, understanding her reasons. There would be plenty of time for her to sit waiting for the telephone to ring. Too much time. "I think I hear a car turning into the drive," he said gruffly, wondering how long it would be

12

before they heard any further news, until they learned exactly where Lewis was being held. And under what conditions.

She ran out of the house toward Scott's approaching Chevrolet. He drew to a halt, leaning over and opening the door for her, and then, as she tumbled into the passenger seat, he turned the car around, driving back down the drive and out into the wide, tree-lined street.

He drove to the Botanical Gardens on South Drive and parked in a quiet corner. Not until he had done so, and the Chevrolet's engine was switched off, did he speak.

"Who came to tell you?" he asked gently, turning to face her. "What did they say?"

Her news had already marked his face. The lines around his mouth had deepened, and his eyes, usually so full of laughter, were dark.

"Two officers, one was a chaplain." Her voice was unsteady but her tears were drying on her cheeks. She had been crying since she had called him, and now she could cry no more. She was exhausted both emotionally and physically, drained with shock. "They said that Lewis and his companions had been ambushed on a canal after they had been searching a village for North Vietnamese forces. One of Lewis's fellow officers managed to escape and he saw Lewis being taken prisoner."

"North Vietnamese? Not Viet Cong?"

"No. They definitely said that he had been captured by North Vietnamese." She pushed the dark fall of her hair away from her face, asking,

13

"Do you think that means they will take him north, to Hanoi?"

He shook his head. "I don't think so. I think the North Vietnamese who captured him probably came from Cambodia. It's much closer."

"Would your father know?" Her voice was beginning to break again. "I can't bear not knowing where he is. What if the North Vietnamese weren't taking Lewis prisoner? What if they simply took him away and shot him?" Her voice cracked.

He clenched his hands in order to physically prevent himself from reaching out and taking hold of her. He wanted to rock her against his chest. To soothe and comfort her. To lie to her if necessary. Instead, he said, his knuckles white, "If the army thought that was likely, they would have told you that Lewis was missing in action, not that he had been taken prisoner. They've probably had other incidents exactly like this one. Maybe it's the policy of the NVA to take prisoners. Did they say anything else to you?"

"Yes." His words were helping her put aside her worst fear ... that Lewis had simply been led away and shot. She was beginning to feel a little better, a little stronger. "They said that since Lewis had been captured in the South, it might be some time before there is official confirmation that he has been taken prisoner."

"Which has to mean that this has happened before and that confirmation is usually forthcoming," he said, trying to reassure her further.

She nodded, and then said with great hesita-

14

tion, "There's something else, Scott. Something that no one knows."

He looked down at her, puzzled, wondering if the strain was already beginning to prove to be too much for her.

Her face was ivory pale, her eyes tortured with anxiety. "Lewis isn't as fit as everyone thinks he is." She had promised Lewis she would never tell anyone about his petit mal attacks. But it was a promise she could no longer keep. She had to be able to tell Scott. If she did not do so, he would never understand how terrible were her fears for Lewis's physical and mental health.

"Lewis is as strong as a horse," Scott said gently. "He's always been proud of his physical fitness."

She shook her head, tears glittering on her eyelashes. "No," she said, praying that Lewis would forgive her. "He suffers from petit mal. A mild form of epilepsy."

If she had said that Lewis suffered from St. Vitus' dance, he couldn't have looked more skeptical.

"*Epilepsy?* That's crazy, Abbra! Lewis is an army officer! He's never had a fit of any kind, ever, in his entire life!"

"Not the kind of fit that you are referring to. No, he hasn't, and I pray that he never will." Her voice was choked with tears. "But he suffered a head injury shortly before we were married, and ever since he has suffered from moments of disorientation."

"Maybe, but it couldn't be called *epilepsy,*"

15

Scott persisted.

"Lewis went to a private neurologist in Los Angeles. The form of petit mal he suffers from is so mild that in the majority of people it would not be worth mentioning. But Lewis is in the army. He couldn't risk having the words on his medical record. And so the army doesn't know. No one knows."

Scott's face was nearly as white as her own. "Are you telling me that this thing could develop? That imprisonment could make it worse? Could he develop the types of fits where people thrash on the floor?"

"I don't know. But I'm so afraid for him, Scott, so terribly afraid." Her voice broke completely. After a few minutes, when she had regained control of herself, she said, "My father says that as a prisoner of war Lewis will be able to write to me and receive letters from me. If that happens, then I will be able to bear it. I just need to know that he's still alive, Scott, that he will be coming back to me. Eventually."

They had gone for a short walk through the rock garden and then he had driven her back home, promising to call her the following evening to see if there was any further news, and saying that he would drive up to see her again on the weekend.

"Tom telephoned," her father said as she re-entered the house. "I think he has taken the news quite badly, but is trying not to show it."

"I'll phone him back." Abbra desperately

16

wanted to talk to him. As a military man, her father-in-law would be able to tell her what was likely to happen next, what steps would be taken for Lewis's release and when she might be able to expect word from him.

"—we don't have much information about Americans who are being held prisoner in the South," he told her, destroying her hope that he would know the location and name of the prison camp that Lewis might be sent to.

"But what about the Red Cross?" she asked. "Surely if they arrange for letters and parcels to be delivered to prisoners, they must have details of where prisoners are held."

There was a small, uncomfortable pause on the other end of the line, and then her father-in-law said gently, "You mustn't raise your hopes that there will be contact with Lewis through the Red Cross, Abbra. It's true that there is some contact with Americans being held in Hoa Lo, but—"

"Where is Hoa Lo?" she interrupted. She prayed it was in the South. If it was in the South, she could still hope.

"It's an old French colonial prison in the center of Hanoi."

She closed her eyes, leaning against the wall, a feeling of dread rising. He didn't know any more than the officers who had visited her with news of Lewis's capture.

"I'm very sorry, my dear," he said awkwardly, "but I'm afraid there is nothing we can do but wait."

* * *

17

The official telegram notifying her of Lewis's capture came the next day. She read it over and over, searching for any clues that she might have missed as to his whereabouts or his physical condition. There were no clues to be found.

The brief description of Lewis's capture was identical with the accounts she had already been given. The telegram then went on to say:

In view of the above information your husband will be carried in a captured status pending receipt and review of a full report of the circumstances. You may be certain that you will be informed of any information received regarding your husband or any action taken regarding his status. Your great anxiety in this situation is understood and I wish to assure you of every possible assistance together with heartfelt sympathy at this time of heartache and uncertainty.

The last line read:

Inasmuch as your husband is presently being carried on a captured status it is suggested for his safety that you reveal only his name, rank, file number, and date of birth to inquiries from sources outside your immediate family.

She stared at the curt, brief words. *Why?* Why was she being instructed to be careful about who

18

she spoke to and what she said? What possible difference could it make to Lewis's safety? The words puzzled her.

She put the telegram away in her bureau drawer, wondering when the army would be in touch with her again, when she would be told what was being done to effect Lewis's release.

That weekend Scott drove up to San Francisco and they drove together out to Lake Tahoe, walking for miles through the forest north of the lake. The mountain air was crisp and clean and she found the mindless exertion of placing one foot ceaselessly in front of the other hypnotically soothing. For the most part they walked in silence. She had no new information for him, and his own thoughts were too dark and too troubled to be shared.

Ever since she had called him with the news, he had been agonizingly reliving his first dreadful instinctive reaction. He had wished he could have Abbra to himself. Maybe for good.

He had murdered the feeling at its birth, overcome with horror and self-loathing so crushing in intensity that he had been scarcely able to breathe. Even if it meant never seeing Abbra again, he didn't want his brother dead and he didn't want him to be imprisoned in a filthy, godforsaken Vietnamese prison. He could not forgive himself that his reaction, however fleeting, had been so obscene.

Almost as difficult was the knowledge that just when Abbra needed him most, self-preservation demanded that he see very little of her.

"Did I tell you about the trip I'm taking to Mexico next week?" he asked, not looking across at her as he spoke, but riveting his eyes on a distant peak of the High Sierras.

She gave a small shocked gasp, swinging her head toward him. "No ... I ... will you be away long?"

"Until the season starts," he lied, self-hatred making his voice curt.

She stumbled slightly and he dug his clenched hands deeper into the pockets of his jeans, his fists clenched. He couldn't reach out for her now. If he reached out for her now, he would be lost.

"I'm sorry, Abbra," he said, his eyes still fixed firmly ahead of him. "I know it couldn't have come at a worse time..."

"No." Her face was set and pale, her jawline firm. "Perhaps it's better that you are going away, Scott."

He was so certain that at last she had realized the true nature of his feelings, he halted in his long, loping stride, his eyes meeting hers. There was no new agony in her expression, no terrible understanding, only fierce determination.

"I must get used to being on my own," she said quietly. "And the longer you are with me, giving me companionship and comfort, the harder it will be for me eventually."

They had stopped walking, and as they stood in the shade of the redwoods, looking across the glittering lake toward the High Sierras, it seemed to Scott that everything unspoken between them was being silently acknowledged. He had been wrong to assume that she didn't know how he felt about her. She did. Probably had known for a long time.

He replied thickly, knowing that they would meet only seldom in the future, and that their easy, happy-go-lucky camaraderie was over. "I love you, Abbra."

She was standing a yard or so away from him, her dark hair blowing softly around her face, the white silk shirt she wore tucked loosely into the waistband of her jeans.

"I know," she said huskily, not trusting herself to say anything more.

She didn't turn to face him. She couldn't. She was too terrified of what might happen.

He was silent for a long time and then he said, his voice taut and strained, "I think it's time I took you home, don't you?"

She nodded, turning away from the lake and the mountains, walking with him, ravage-faced, back toward the Chevrolet.

The loneliness that followed was crushing. She knew no other army wives, no other women who could identify with what she was suffering. She waited daily, expecting a communication from the army, some information about what was being done to effect his release, or even get in touch with him, but nothing came. At the end of the month, feeling as isolated as if she were alone on another planet, she called the telephone number on the card that she had been given.

The voice on the other end of the line was sympathetic and understanding and regretted that Abbra had not realized she had been assigned a personal casualty assistance officer who would keep her abreast of whatever development affected her or her prisoner husband.

It was the first time she had heard the expression "prisoner husband" and she hated it. "My husband's name is Lewis," she said stiltedly. "Lewis Ellis."

She was transferred to her personal casualty officer, who said he was sorry that he had not previously been in touch with her, and who also referred to Lewis as her "prisoner husband". There was no news regarding Lewis. It was too soon, he said.

Her novel became her life support system. She withdrew into a world of imagination, writing from early morning to late at night, deriving a certain wry amusement from anticipating Patti's amazement when she received, so quickly, a novel she was not expecting for several months.

She didn't tell Patti that Lewis had been taken prisoner. She didn't want to have to endure more well-meant sympathy that would inevitably fail to comfort. The only person who could have given her comfort was Scott, and after his terrible admission to her at Lake Tahoe, she knew that she could never turn to him for comfort again.

Sometimes, at night in troubled sleep, Lewis and Scott seemed to merge into one person, and when she woke, the sense of loss and loneliness that she felt for both of them was indistinguishable. As the weeks passed, she found that she could fight her loneliness for Lewis a little by writing an ongoing letter to him in the form of a daily diary. The simple act of writing down his name, telling him of the way she was spending her day, what she was doing, what she was thinking, how she was missing him, seemed to bring him a little closer to her.

Where Scott was concerned there was no such comfort. She couldn't think about Scott. She dared not think about Scott. The football season had begun again, and according to the media, he was playing brilliantly.

He did not write to her, and he did not telephone her, nor did she expect him to. His three words in the depths of the Tahoe forest had made it impossible for him to do so. She knew that he was thinking of her, and that he shared her suffering as she waited for news of Lewis.

She started paying attention to the news.

At the beginning of October it was reported that U.S. planes had attacked the city of Phu Ly, thirty-five miles south of Hanoi, and that all homes and buildings there had been destroyed.

Abbra wondered what the military objective had been at Phu Ly. The brief news reports gave no indication. That afternoon she went out and bought herself a large map of Vietnam and a copy of Bernard Fall's *Street Without Joy*. Scott had once told her that if she wanted to understand what had led up to the U.S. presence in Vietnam, and the rights and wrongs of U.S.

involvement, then Fall's was the book she should read. Over the last few weeks she had become acutely aware of how little she knew about the place her husband had been sent. She was also becoming angry and disillusioned at the army's seeming complacency over Lewis's capture.

The casualty officer who had been assigned to her continued to be sympathetic, but he never had any new information. He seemed more concerned in reminding her that if interviewed by the press, she was to give no information over and above Lewis's name, rank, serial number, and date of birth, than he was about the complete silence about Lewis's whereabouts. In January she finished her novel. She had put everything she had into it, adding all the pain and uncertainty of her past few weeks, but whether it was what Patti was expecting, she had no way of knowing. She was too close to what she had written to be able to judge it herself. She knew only that finishing it had given her a sense of achievement so great, it had been almost orgasmic. She telephoned Patti's office, intending to tell her that the novel was finished and that she was putting it in the mail, only to be told by Patti's secretary that Patti was on vacation and wouldn't be back until the end of the month.

She sent it off anyway, almost relieved that it would be at least another three weeks before Patti could read it, and before she would be coming back to her with an opinion.

A week later, in his State of the Union address,

President Johnson announced somberly: "Although America faces more cost, more loss, and more agony in Southeast Asia, we will stand firm in Vietnam."

Abbra was filled with an overwhelming sense of despair. The war would continue. But for how long? How long would it be before prisoners were exchanged? Before there were true negotiations?

On February 2, just as she was beginning to wonder if Patti had returned yet from vacation, her telephone rang. She lifted the receiver, not imagining for a moment that it would be Patti, and Patti's husky voice said ebulliently, "Congratulations! I came back from Argentina yesterday morning and spent all last evening reading *A Woman Alone*. It's even better than I had hoped it would be, and I'm sure that both the British and American publishers are going to love it. They took quite a gamble with you, and it's a gamble that will, in my opinion, pay off handsomely."

Abbra was flooded with relief. She still had to wait to hear from the publishers, but if Patti was pleased about the book, then it meant she had succeeded in what she had set out to do. She had written a full-length novel with commercial possibilities. And if she had written one, then she could write another, and another. She was so ecstatic that she had nearly finished dialing Scott's number before she realized what it was she was doing.

She replaced the telephone receiver with a

shaking hand. It had seemed so natural. He had given her so much encouragement; he had given her confidence. He had believed in her. Without him she doubted if she would ever have had the temerity to write more than the first page. And now she couldn't pick up the telephone and tell him that Patti thought the book was wonderful. They couldn't meet in the Polo Lounge to celebrate the news, laughing and talking as they had laughed and talked so often in the past. He couldn't read the manuscript.

"I wish you hadn't said it, Scott," she said to the empty room, feeling as if her heart were breaking with longing. "Oh, how I *wish* that you had never said it!"

Four weeks later, at the beginning of March, Patti telephoned her to say that the American publisher had already responded to her about *A Woman Alone* and that he was delighted with it.

"You'll be getting a long letter from the person who has been assigned as your editor, detailing what revisions they think are necessary. From what they say, no major surgery on the manuscript is needed, so don't worry. It's all very normal. I hope to be hearing from the British publisher by the end of the week, and I have absolutely no worries as to what his response is going to be. He's going to be thrilled! All you have to think about now is what you're going to write about next!"

In April she visited her father-in-law for a few

days. Lewis's capture had done nothing to diminish Colonel Ellis's conviction that the only thing wrong with American military intervention in Vietnam was that it wasn't hard-nosed enough.

"We shouldn't only be bombing the North; we should be fighting on the ground in the North, where *everyone* is the enemy," he said fiercely. "Not pussyfooting around, worrying whether or not we're shooting so-called friendly civilians! If we invaded the North, no holds barred, Ho and his cronies would be groveling for peace within days!"

He was equally emphatic in his views on the antiwar activists who were demonstrating in increasingly larger and larger numbers.

"They should be shot as traitors," he said vehemently. "They're not fit to call themselves Americans!"

Abbra disagreed. Some of the antiwar activists were veterans, men who had fought in Vietnam and who had been so appalled by their experiences that on their return they had publicly burned their uniforms and tossed their war medals into the garbage.

Instinctively she had always felt it was wrong for Americans to be in Vietnam, but out of loyalty to Lewis she had tried to view American intervention in a different light. To see it as necessary for world peace. She no longer held that belief. The reading she had done in the past few months had convinced her that her initial instincts had been correct and that she should have held to them. As far as the antiwar activists

27

were concerned, she was in total sympathy, and the days she spent with her father-in-law, fond as she was of him, were a terrible strain.

In May she began work on a new book, and even though there was still no shred of information regarding Lewis and where he was being held, or even if he was still alive, she continued to write her daily journal to him.

In June she was contacted by the army, but not with the news that she had been praying for.

In light of the circumstances of Lewis's capture, and the dearth of information since, his status had been reviewed. He was no longer being classified as a prisoner of war, but as being missing in action.

She didn't leave her room for three days. She knew what the army was trying to say to her. They were trying to tell her that Lewis was dead, but she didn't believe it. He was alive. She *knew* he was alive. She couldn't have lived through the past months believing him to be alive if he had been dead. It wasn't possible.

Two days later Scott telephoned her. "I'm sorry," he said simply. "But you shouldn't fear the worst, Abbra. Just because there's no hard information about the men who have been taken prisoner in the South doesn't mean they aren't still alive."

"I know," she said brokenly. "And Lewis *is* alive, Scott! I know he is!"

He hesitated awkwardly. It was the first time they had been in contact for over ten months.

"Would it help if I came up to see you?" he asked, not knowing what he wanted her answer to be.

If he saw her again, he knew that nothing would have changed, that he would still want her as fiercely and hungrily as he always had. And nothing could come of it. Nothing could ever come of it. She loved Lewis, and as long as there was the faintest hope that Lewis was alive, she would never love anyone else.

And if Lewis were dead?

His jaw clenched, white lines edging his mouth. He didn't want Lewis to be dead. No matter what the price, he didn't want Lewis to be dead.

"No," she said huskily, her voice sounding as if it were choked with tears. "No, I don't think so, Scott."

His disappointment was so devastating that he had to lean against the wall behind him for support. Of course he had known what he wanted her answer to be. And she had not given it.

"Bye, sweetheart," he said thickly, wondering how she was managing without friends who could understand her position, without a supportive family, without anyone to lean upon or confide in.

All through the summer she worked on her new idea. There was still no news of Lewis, still no real reason for her to believe he was alive apart from her own unshakable conviction.

In September she decided that she had been a

compliant army wife for quite long enough. She had done everything that the army had advised her to do. She hadn't spoken about Lewis to the press or to casual friends. She hadn't involved herself in the antiwar movement. She hadn't made a nuisance of herself, or been an embarrassment, in any way whatsoever. And her passivity had gained her nothing. She still didn't know if Lewis was dead or alive. If he were alive, she still didn't know where he was being held. In over a year she still hadn't met, or spoken to, another woman in the same situation. She had had a bellyful of passivity, and she was going to be passive no longer.

In October, when the antiwar movement announced it would be holding an enormous rally in Washington, its aim being the closing down of the Pentagon, Abbra locked her manuscript away in her desk and bought herself an airplane ticket.

She was going to abandon her compliant-wife role and become a fierce antiwar activist. Helping to close down the Pentagon seemed as good a way as any in which to start.

CHAPTER TWO

Serena turned off the main road into the cobbled mews at suicidally high speed, tires screeching as she came to a stop. She was late. She had less than half an hour to bathe and change before Rupert arrived. They were going to have dinner at Quaglinos and then go on to the Colony in Berkeley Square. She slammed the front door behind her, wondering whether to wear her new Mary Quant dress, or her Louis Feraud.

As she slipped her key in the lock she could hear the telephone begin to ring. "Damn," she said beneath her breath, pausing for a moment to enjoy the fragrance of begonias and fuchsias spilling from a hanging basket. "If that's Toby, he can jolly well wait." Despite her open involvement with Rupert, Toby was as persistent as ever. Because she was fond of him in a completely asexual way, and because she had known him for what seemed to be forever, and because all his friends were also her friends, she still continued to see him. Whenever there was a function where all her old cronies would be gathered, and where the behavior was likely to be infantile, such as a hunt ball, where champagne could be expected to be sprayed with gleeful abandon over ball gowns and dinner

31

jackets, or a debutante party where guests were likely to be thrown into a swimming pool, then she spared Rupert's dignity and was to be seen, instead, with Toby.

She stepped into the tiny hall and picked up the ringing telephone.

"I'm sorry, Toby my sweet," she said, not sounding remotely sorry. "But tonight is an impossibility, I'm..."

"It isn't Toby. It's Daddy." Her father's voice was heavy and strained. "I'm afraid it's bad news, darling. Sorry to break it to you like this, over the phone, but thought it was better you heard it from me than from anyone else."

"Lance?" she said immediately, her voice cracking. "It's Lance, isn't it? What's happened to him? Has he been arrested? Is he hurt? Where is he?"

Wherever he was, she would go to him. She would leave a note for Rupert. He would understand. Her hands tightened around her car key. "Where is he, Daddy?"

Her father's voice sounded weary. "It isn't Lance, darling..."

She leaned back against the wall, ashamed of the relief she felt. It was her mother. Her mother had been taken ill. She would drive to Bedingham early in the morning and stay there as long as necessary.

Her father cleared his throat. "I'm afraid that it's Kyle. His father telephoned me a few minutes ago. He's been shot down. A colleague says he saw him alive on the ground after the crash, but it was in a heavily infested Viet Cong area and there's been no news of him since." He paused uncomfortably and then said, "He's been officially listed as missing in action. I'm sorry, my dear, I'm most dreadfully sorry."

For a second she didn't feel anything at all. She couldn't. She was beyond feeling.

Her father's voice sharpened. "Serena? Are you there? Can you hear me?"

"Yes," she said at last with a great struggle. "Yes, I can hear you, Daddy." She couldn't think of anything to say, anything to ask. Incredibly, all the time Kyle had been in Vietnam, it had never occurred to her that he would be killed or injured or listed as missing. Other men might be, were being every day, but other men weren't Kyle. Kyle was too exuberantly alive, too fiendishly lucky, too arrogantly *sure* of himself, to come to grief. It was unthinkable to think of him as a loser. Inconceivable.

"Would you like to come home for a few days?" her father was asking. "Bedingham is at its best, the walls are half drowned in roses and honeysuckle."

Her eyes closed, she thought of Bedingham. The roses had been out on their wedding day; pale Ophelias and dark purple Reine des Violettes. What would have happened if Lance hadn't returned that day? There would have been no hideous scene for Kyle to walk in on, no need for him to have sped away from Bedingham and back to America. In all probability he would never have enrolled at helicopter school, never

33

have been sent to Vietnam.

"No, Daddy," she said thickly. "No, I don't think I'll come back to Bedingham. Not just now."

If Lance hadn't returned that day, she and Kyle might have been at Bedingham now, together. To be there without him would be unbearable. Slowly she hung up the phone. She remembered someone, somewhere, saying "if" was the smallest, most terrible word in the English language. Whoever had said it was right. *If* only she hadn't left Kyle's side and hurried to the nursery to meet Lance. *If* only Kyle hadn't grown impatient and followed her. *If. If. If.*

Rupert arrived twenty minutes later, looking elegant in a gray silk suit and with a carnation in his buttonhole. He took one look at her white, ravaged face and said, "My God! What on earth is the matter, Serena? What's happened?"

She was holding a large vodka and tonic tightly in both hands. She made no move to put it down or to walk toward him. Her eyes met his, their smoke-gray depths so dark they seemed almost black. "Kyle has been shot down," she said with devastating simplicity. "He's missing in action."

He stood without moving for a moment, realizing instantly the changes and strains that were about to be put on their relationship, and then he walked across to her, gently taking the glass from her hand. "Tell me," he said with exquisite tenderness, drawing her toward him. "Tell me everything you have been told."

Dry-eyed and still in shock, she haltingly repeated what her father had said to her. He was appalled at the scant amount of information.

"When did it happen? How long ago? Why didn't the army contact you as Kyle's next of kin?"

"Presumably because Kyle never gave them my name as next of kin," she said with unflinching candor. "When he joined the army, he believed we were going to divorce. We were reconciled only hours before he left for Vietnam. I suppose it's only natural that he should have given the army his father's name as his next of kin, and not mine."

"And have you spoken to his father yet?"

"No." A tremor ran through her.

"Don't you think you should?" he persisted. "You need to know whether Kyle was shot down in the North or in the South. If he was seen alive on the ground after he crashed, you need to know why he has been listed as missing in action when he could very possibly have been taken prisoner."

"I need something else first," she said unsteadily. "I need to be able to believe that it's true, that it has really happened. I need to be able to cry."

Even after she had spoken to her father-in-law the tears refused to come.

"*It's all your fault!*" he had shouted at her savagely. "*If it weren't for you, Kyle would never have joined the army! He would never have gone to 'Nam!'*"

She believed him. She had known it the instant her father had told her what had happened. She was responsible. No one else.

For the next few days she still went into the antique shop, but she did so out of robotlike habit. She was no longer the ebullient, kooky personality that had so fascinated customers and gossip columnists alike. She was pale and withdrawn, and though she responded gratefully to Rupert's sympathy and support, she did not sleep with him. And she did not sleep with anyone else either.

She broke the news to Lance in his Chelsea *pied à terre*, standing with her back toward him, staring out over the gray, rolling expanse of the Thames.

"He was shot down near the Cambodian border," she said bleakly. "He was trying to pick up a reconnaissance squad that had been cut off and who were surrounded by Viet Cong. One of the other pilots, a friend of his, swears that he saw him scramble out of the helicopter alive, but the Viet Cong were everywhere and—"

She turned, about to tell him how Kyle's buddy had flown under suicidal fire time and again in an effort to land beside Kyle's blazing Huey.

He had been silent while she had been talking, and she had taken for granted that despite his virulent dislike of Kyle, and his fierce opposition to the war, he would be as shocked and as horrified as Rupert had been. No doubt if she hadn't turned around so unexpectedly, he would have made a hypocritical effort to sound, and seem, suitably sympathetic. She was never to know. She swung around, catching him unaware, and saw the expression on his face.

He was smiling, sheer pleasure written clearly on every feature. It was then that the frozen dam within her broke. "*You bastard!*" she howled, springing forward and raking at his face with her nails, the tears pouring down her cheeks. "*You miserable, mean-minded, pitiful, bastard!*"

It had been Rupert who had hauled her off him. He had been waiting for her in the street, in his Lagonda, and had heard her howl of rage. By the time he had sprinted into the block of flats and up the stairs, Lance had half fallen across a sofa and Serena was raining blows on him, sobbing hysterically, calling him names that would have made a stevedore blanch.

"*For Christ's sake!*" he had said, striding across the room and physically separating them, relieved to see that Lance had made no effort at retaliation. "What's the matter with the pair of you? Can't you behave like reasonable human beings?"

Serena was still sobbing, the tears spilling down her face and on to her minidress, her hair streaming wildly over her shoulders and down her back. She tried to speak and couldn't. Now that she had at last begun to cry, she was unable to stop. She was crying because she felt so wretchedly guilty, crying because Lance had been so stupidly insensitive and because things had once more gone wrong between them, and above all she was crying, at last, for Kyle.

Lance slithered into a sitting position on the sofa, his tie pulled halfway around his neck, a button torn from his shirt. "It was my fault," he said tersely to Rupert, dabbing at the scratches on his face with a handkerchief. "Serry thought I was pleased about Anderson being declared an MIA."

"You *were!*" Serena gasped convulsively. "And he isn't *Anderson*, he's *Kyle!*"

"Were you?" Rupert asked him tightly.

Lance looked up. From where he was sitting, Rupert seemed very tall indeed. And very threatening.

"Yes. No," he said undecidedly, springing to his feet so that he wouldn't feel at a disadvantage. "Hell! I wasn't pleased in the way Serry thinks I was pleased! I wasn't pleased just because it was her husband who was missing!" He began to pace the room furiously. "*If* I was pleased, then I was pleased because the Americans have to learn they can't win in Vietnam, and it seems to me they're going to learn that only when the great American public finds the loss of American life in Vietnam unacceptable. As far as I'm concerned, the sooner they do *that*, the better!"

Serena had finally stopped crying. She pushed her hair away from her face, wiping her cheeks with her fingers, saying in a flat, tired voice, "I should have known better than to have come here with such news. Will you take me home please, Rupert?"

Lance stopped pacing abruptly, his eyes flying to hers. He didn't want her to go. He didn't want there to be another rift between them, but he was damned if he was going to apologize to her in front of Rupert. He said instead, "If Kyle is alive and if he's been taken prisoner, then you'd better start looking at things from my point of view, Serry. You'd better start getting involved and demonstrating for an end to the war, because until it ends, no one outside Vietnam is going to see Kyle Anderson again."

She hadn't replied. She, too, had wanted to make things right between them, but somehow she felt that to do so would be disloyal to Kyle. And loyalty to Kyle suddenly seemed very important. It was all that she could give him, all that she could do for him.

Over the next few days she read everything that she could about the war. She read about the way Americans were treated by the Viet Cong if they fell into their hands, how they had been found with steel rods rammed up their penis and anus, of how some had even been skinned alive.

The war was no longer an event of no concern to her, and the more she read, the more she began to think that perhaps Lance's point of view wasn't so extreme after all. Three weeks later she received a letter, via her father-in-law, from Charles Wilson.

"...Kyle is alive, I'm sure of it," he had written. "I saw him scramble from the Huey, but there was no way anyone could land and pick him up. The ground fire was unbelievable." He gave her

39

the exact position where Kyle had gone down and then wrote, "He was my best buddy, the best I've ever had, and I'm going to do my damnedest to try to have his status changed from MIA to POW." He had signed the letter Chuck, not Charles.

She read and reread the letter and then put it down thoughtfully. It hadn't occurred to her that there was such a vital difference in status between MIA and POW. Until Kyle's disappearance, she had hardly been aware that there *was* a difference. She had thought there was nothing she could do for Kyle, but she had been wrong. She could campaign for his status to be changed. And to do that, she would first have to inform the United States Army that she was an army wife.

It was a decision she had almost made before she had read Chuck's letter. Although her father-in-law had forwarded that particular piece of mail to her, she couldn't rely on him. If she wanted to be sure of receiving every bit of possible information about Kyle, then she had to inform the correct authorities that she was his wife, and that she was entitled to receive it.

Two weeks after she had written to the army, enclosing her birth certificate and her wedding certificate, she received an official reply. For the first time she was given an official account of Kyle's last mission and the way in which he had been shot down. And she was told of how Chuck Wilson had flown through enemy fire repeatedly in an effort to land beside Kyle's blazing Huey, and of how, in doing so, he had sustained near fatal injuries.

She had reread Chuck Wilson's letter again. He had written merely that "the ground fire was unbelievable." There was no mention that he had been injured in his attempt to rescue Kyle. No mention that he had, apparently, been writing to her from a hospital bed.

The letter from the army also apologized that Kyle's personal belongings had been sent to his father and not to her, but assured her that there had been no personal mail among the items. It finished by asking her to treat all information regarding her husband as confidential.

"What information?" she had said aloud, bewildered. She had written back asking why, if her husband had been seen scrambling from his Huey alive, he was being listed as MIA and not as a possible prisoner of war. She also asked for the name of the hospital where Charles Wilson was being treated so that she could write to him and thank him for his brave rescue attempt.

At the beginning of October, she received her next official communication from the United States Army. She opened the buff-colored envelope without any premonition that it might contain news other than the information she had asked for.

"—your husband's name has been included in a list of names recently released by Hanoi. It is believed that he is being held in Hoa Lo prison, Hanoi. In view of this information, your husband's status has been changed from MIA to

41

POW. You may be certain that you will be informed of any further information received regarding your husband. Inasmuch as your husband is now being carried in a captured status, it is suggested, for his safety, that you reveal only his name, rank, file number, and date of birth to inquiries outside your immediate family—"

He was alive. She began to tremble, and then to laugh and cry at the same time. He was in some ghastly prison, but at least he was alive.

"I *knew* you wouldn't be dead!" she exulted aloud, as if he were in the room with her. "You're too damned *hip* to be dead!"

Rupert was intensely relieved by her news. He knew how guilty she felt, and though he believed her guilt to be irrational, he had been unable to convince her.

"Nothing you did was responsible for Kyle haring back to the States and becoming a pilot," he had said gently when she had told him why she felt so guilty. "You can't imagine for a moment that if *I* had been in Kyle's shoes, and if I had walked in on that odious little scene in the nursery, that I would have imagined you were a willing party to what was taking place. The fact that Kyle did so only proves to me how little he knows about you." Or loves you, he had been tempted to add, but hadn't.

Looking across at her as they sat on the sofa in his elegant Knightsbridge home and she finished telling him about Kyle's official change of status, he hoped that the news would enable her

42

to shed some of her guilt, and that their relationship would at last return to normal.

His arm was around her shoulders, and he pulled her closer to him, sliding his free hand up a long, slender, smoothly naked leg. "I've missed you in my bed, lady," he said, his voice thickening. "Welcome back."

Despite the brisk weather, beneath her minuscule skirt she was wearing only the briefest of panties. He pulled them low, her honey-gold pubic hair brushing springily against the palm of his hand as he began to caressingly separate the lips of her labia, sliding his fingers into her hot moistness.

She gave a deep moan, stiffening and contracting against him. It had been nearly two months since she had made love. And Kyle was now no longer missing in action, feared dead, but a prisoner in Hanoi. She closed her eyes as Rupert lowered his mouth to hers, his thumb circling arousingly over her clitoris, his fingers continuing to move and probe. She had not made love and Kyle was safe. Very gently she pushed her hands up against Rupert's chest, pushing him away from her.

He looked down at her queryingly, his hand still moving rhythmically, loving the slippery, excited feel of her.

"No," she said, her eyes apologetic. "I'm sorry, Rupert. I can't."

He frowned slightly, his penis so engorged it was straining painfully against his trousers. "Don't be silly," he said, his voice dark with

43

need. "There's no reason in the world for us not to make love now."

"There is." She was so excited she was nearly screaming, but she stilled his moving hand with hers. "I didn't make love and Kyle is no longer missing in action but a prisoner of war. If I continue not to make love, then he'll be released, I know it."

He stared at her. "You are joking, aren't you?" he asked at last.

Smoke-gray eyes, wide-set and dark-lashed, held his. "No," she said, wriggling slightly and freeing herself from his hand. "I know it isn't very logical, but..."

"It isn't logical at all!" Rupert said, thwarted desire trying his patience to the limit. "It's sheer primitive superstitious nonsense! How on earth can your making or not making love affect what happens to Kyle in Hanoi? And when you talk of not making love until he's released, how long have you got in mind? The war has been going on for years already. It's hardly likely to come to a sudden halt just because you've taken a vow of celibacy! Kyle could be in Hanoi for years!"

She stood up, smoothing her miniskirt down over her thighs, her hand trembling slightly. "Kyle couldn't endure captivity for years," she said unsteadily. "It would kill him."

He rose to his feet slowly, facing her, bitterly regreting his ill-chosen words. "Maybe he won't be there for years," he said quietly. "A war does not have to end for prisoners to be exchanged."

"No," she agreed, slipping on her shoes. "It

44

doesn't."

She was going, and he knew that she would not be coming back. He regarded her with loving affection, and pity, and regret.

"If he *is* exchanged, it won't be because you have been behaving like a nun,' he said, resigned.

Despite the hideous images his words had conjured up, of Kyle being immured in Hoa Lo prison for years on end, an amused smile quirked the corners of her mouth. "I don't see why not," she said with a return of her old jauntiness. "After all, going without sex is the greatest sacrifice I could possibly make!"

At the end of October her father telephoned her to say that he and her mother were going to Barbados for the winter. Although his domestic staff was quite capable of looking after his aging spaniels, he said the dogs would prefer it if a member of the family was also there and would she kindly oblige?

She obliged quickly. Bedingham was at its best in the autumn, and she had been away from it for far too long. She drove north out of London, beneath a pale apricot sky, feeling as if a physical burden were being lifted from her shoulders with each mile she traveled. At Bedingham she would be able to see the future more clearly. Her affair with Rupert was over, although he was still the first person she turned to if she needed advice, or sympathy or support. He had offered her a partnership in the antique shop in an effort to both retain her services in the shop and to ensure that contact was maintained between them, but she had turned it down.

She didn't want any encumbrances, however pleasurable. Kyle's capture had changed her life. Though she couldn't imagine what the future held, she was certain it was going to be something far different from anything she had experienced in her past. And when it came she wanted to be ready for it.

Lance had left several messages on her answering machine, but she had not contacted him. It was as if denying herself the relief of a reconciliation with him was yet another of her voluntary penances.

In November, during his weekly telephone call, Rupert rather ruefully informed Serena that he had become the regular escort of Lady Sarah Mellbury, the seventeen-year-old daughter of an old school friend.

Serena had been vaguely amused and not the slightest regretful. If she had wanted to resume her old relationship with Rupert, she knew that Lady Sarah would have been no obstacle. But she didn't want to resume their old relationship, at least not yet. She wanted to remain at Bedingham, tramping the grounds and the beech woods with the dogs and returning to drink Earl Grey and to eat piles of buttered crumpets before a roaring log fire.

The army had forwarded her the name of the military hospital in Japan where Chuck Wilson was being treated and she had written to him, thanking him for his brave attempt to rescue Kyle.

Just before Christmas she received a reply. It was an odd letter, brief and curt and indicating that he saw no reason why they should enter into further correspondence with each other. She wondered why. As a buddy of Kyle's, it was impossible to imagine him as being anything other than outgoing and extrovert, and his first letter to her, though full of pain, had been sympathetic and friendly.

He had been transferred to a hospital in the States and she decided not to be deterred by his almost formal reply. She wrote again, asking him when he expected to be discharged, saying that she would like to meet him, so that she could thank him personally.

When the New Year arrived, Serena was convinced that Lance was, for once, correct. Anti-war demonstrations were necessary if the war was ever to be brought to an end. She drove up to London to take part in a demonstration.

It was bitterly cold, and there was snow and ice underfoot as she merged with an amazingly large group of stalwart marchers, tramping with placards held high from Trafalgar Square to the American Embassy in Grosvenor Square.

She marched along near the front of the procession, linking arms with a bearded hippie carrying a banner with the words I HATE WAR on it, and a fierce-looking girl who said she was a student at the London School of Economics.

47

As they entered Grosvenor Square, chanting "Ho-Ho-Ho Chi Minh, Americans *out*! Ho-Ho-Ho-Chi Minh, Americans *out*! Americans *out*!" they joined an advance group of protestors already in the square. A number of mounted police were gathering in the adjoining side streets. A grin touched her mouth as she saw Lance's distinctive silky-gold shoulder-length hair. It had been over four months since he had reacted so horribly to the news that Kyle had been shot down, and she had long ago forgiven him. She had also decided that after such a long time, a reconciliation would no longer be an act of disloyalty toward Kyle.

In an effort to negate the effeminacy of his hair, Lance had grown a Che Guevara style mustache. He was smoothing it with his forefinger, casting an assessing eye over the numbers entering the square, when he saw her. At first there was only blank amazement on his face and then, as her grin deepened and she waved exuberantly in his direction, relief flooded his eyes and he began to shoulder his way through the crowd toward her.

"Serry! What the devil are *you* doing here?" he shouted to her as the chanting around them became louder and more vitriolic and the police horses began to edge their way into the square.

"I thought I'd come and give you a little sisterly support!" she yelled back, hugging him tight, insanely happy to be back on the old footing with him again.

"Then stick with me and keep away from the

horses! Christ alone knows why they're being used for crowd control when it's so slippy underfoot. One of them is sure to go down!"

"I hope not," Serena said passionately, "We're not such a large crowd. They don't need to use horses to keep us in control."

Lance gave a snort of derision. "You've a lot to learn," he said darkly, grateful that she was making it unnecessary for him to apologize to her, that she knew that he was sorry, that his hideous little display of glee need never be mentioned between them again.

He took hold of her arm, forcing a way through toward the front of the crowd. "What have you been doing with yourself all winter? Did you know that the parents have fled to Barbados?"

She nodded, squeezing after him, narrowly avoiding being hit in the eye by a placard declaring BRING THE TROOPS HOME. "Yes, Daddy phoned me before they went and asked me if I would look after the dogs. I've been at Bedingham ever since."

"Alone?" The words were out, and the implication that if he had known he would have joined her there, before he could stop them.

She tactfully avoided his eyes. "Yes," she said as a scuffle broke out on the edge of the crowd between one of the demonstrators and a foot policeman. "I've been doing some reading, and thinking, and I've been bombarding the United States Army with letters." She kept her eyes firmly averted from his. "Kyle's status has been changed from MIA to POW. He's in Hoa Lo prison, in Hanoi. What I want to know from the army is what the hell they're going to do to get him out."

"And have you had much success?" he asked, knowing damn well that she couldn't possibly have.

"No," she said grimly. "But they haven't heard the last from me. Not by a long shot."

In March her parents returned from Barbados to Bedingham and she reluctantly returned to her mother's *pied à terre* in London. She began to be seen at parties and discos again, but she felt as if she were attending them merely out of force of habit. The more fun everyone around her was having, the more acutely she was aware of what Kyle must be suffering. When she went out to dinner with Rupert, and he sent back the wine because it wasn't chilled enough, she wondered whether Kyle was receiving clean water to drink, whether water was there for him when he needed it. If he was manacled and shackled for large parts of the day. If he ever thought of her, and of the precious hours they had spent together at Bedingham.

In April she received another letter from Chuck Wilson. He had been discharged from the hospital and was going to stay on an uncle's ranch in Wyoming for the summer, to recuperate. He still made no mention of his injuries, and he barely mentioned Kyle or his incarceration in Hoa Lo. The letter seemed hardly worth the bother of

50

writing, unless, as there was no mention of his Wyoming address, it had been written to let her know that he would not be contactable for several months and to dissuade her from corresponding with him further.

"But I will, Mr. Wilson," she said to herself. The paper was stamped with what she presumed was his home address in Atlantic City, and she put it away carefully in a bureau drawer. She was beginning to have a shrewd suspicion as to why his letters were so out of character for a man who had been Kyle's best buddy, and she had every intention of finding out if her suspicions were correct. She would make contact with him when he returned from Wyoming, and it wouldn't be by letter. It would be in person.

All through the summer, her letters to the United States Army, and to the casualty assistance officer who had been assigned to her, continued. She asked if she could be given the addresses of other wives with husbands imprisoned in Hoa Lo, so that she could write to them, and introduce herself to them, but no addresses were ever forwarded. By the end of the summer her patience was wearing thin.

"They won't release any information to me," she said exasperatedly to Lance as they shared a punt on the upper reaches of the Thames. "I don't even know how many other men are being held in Hoa Lo. If I had the names and addresses of some of the other wives, I could at least write to them. They are probably just as frustrated by

51

the American government's policy of discouraging inter-POW-family relationships as I am. We could form a pressure group of sorts. Hell, we have to do *something*. Some men have been held prisoner since 1965!"

"Write an open letter to *The Washington Post*, appealing for any other wives in the same situation to contact you," Lance said practically, punting around the low-lying tendrils of a willow tree. "And go to the States. There's a massive demonstration being planned for October in Washington. Dr. Benjamin Spock is going to speak and a vigil is going to be held at the Pentagon. It's supposed to be the biggest antiwar demo yet held."

"And it's at the end of the summer," Serena said cryptically.

"What does that remark mean?"

Serena lay back against the punt cushions, a white silk shirt open at her throat, her long legs encased in a pair of pale blue jeans. "It means that someone who has spent the summer in Wyoming will no longer be there," she teased.

Lance didn't rise to the bait. Instead of asking her who the devil she knew in Wyoming, he said instead, "Are you going to go to Washington for the Pentagon demo?"

She nodded, her eyes gleaming with fierce determination. "Yes. And I'm not going to come back until I've made contact with other women whose husbands are being held in Hanoi. I can't be the only wife frustrated by the American government's attitude toward the prisoner issue. There must be other rebellious waiting wives. And I'm going to find them."

CHAPTER THREE

After the dizzying success of the open-air concert, life had been so hectic that Gabrielle scarcely had time to draw breath. The group had been inundated with offers from agents, all wanting to assume dictatorial control of their affairs. Radford had rebuffed all the offers no matter how extravagant the promises.

"Hell," he had said to her with his crooked grin. "I ain't come so far to hand myself over body and soul to some motherfucker who does not really give a shit. When the right agent comes along, I'll *know* it!"

The right agent finally came along in the shape of Marty Dennison, an Englishman with a formidable reputation where black music was concerned.

"And despite having a white lead singer and two white guitarists, your music *is* black," he had said when Radford had introduced him to the band. "That's its main strength. Your other strength is your singer. Anyone that sexy could take an audience by storm without your even having to play a note!"

Contracts had been drawn up, record contracts had been signed, a tour of England in November had been planned, new songs had been endlessly discussed and even more endlessly practised. By the time she realized that Gavin's last letter had not been followed by any others, it was the end of August.

At first she did not worry too much. The mail delivery to and from Vietnam had always been erratic, as she knew from years of correspondence with her aunt. And probably Gavin was not in a position to write to her. The newspapers were full of reports that United States air force jets had mistakenly attacked two South Vietnamese villages eighty miles south of Saigon, killing 63 and wounding over 100 civilians. It was likely that Gavin was down there, covering the story.

At the beginning of September, just as they were embarking on the first of their gigs, one of their pianists was found dead from a drug overdose.

Radford was almost beside himself with fury. "That *son* of a bitch!" he raged. "Why *now*, for Christ's sake? Why did the stupid bastard have to *spoil* everything right *now*!"

They had another pianist, and they could still make music, but their unique sound came from their ability to sound like an inflated studio band ... three guitars, two basses, and not one piano, but two.

"Let Michel stand in," Gabrielle had suggested, and because Michel knew backward every number they had ever practiced, and because he had very little choice, Radford had bad-temperedly agreed.

His bad temper had faded the moment he heard Michel play. "Jeez! Why didn't you *tell* me he was this good?" he berated Gabrielle. "He may not look the part, but that boy has *soul!*"

By the second week in September, Gabrielle's thoughts were no longer centered on her new singing style but on the lack of mail from Saigon. By the end of the month, when there was still no letter from Gavin, she was concerned. Then, on the first day of November, two letters, neither from Gavin, arrived simultaneously.

One envelope was postmarked Saigon and was in Nhu's handwriting. The other envelope was franked with the name of Gavin's press agency.

She picked them up from the mat slowly, sensing disaster. In his last letter he had not said what his next assignment was to be. He had been ragingly angry about the human cost of the Americans' free fire zone policy, and enthusiastic about his meeting with Nhu, saying that he was "looking forward to meeting the rest of her family quite soon". Was that what had happened? Had he met Dinh? And if so, why hadn't he written since?

She opened Nhu's letter, her hand trembling as she smoothed out the wafer-thin paper. It was written in the manner of all Nhu's letters. No names were mentioned. Dinh was merely an "uncle". Gavin was a "mutual friend". The real content of the letter had to be guessed at from

55

seemingly innocuous information.

—your uncle was insistent, and as it was what our mutual friend wanted too, I thought there could be no possible harm...

...I think your uncle wants to show off his skill as a craftsman, and certainly our mutual friend seems eager to learn...

...so they are traveling together at the moment but I unfortunately have no address for them...

He was with Dinh. She didn't know whether to feel jubilant or appalled. Dinh had once again come south and had asked to meet Gavin. And they were now "traveling" together, and Dinh was "showing off his skill as a craftsman" to him, which meant that Dinh had taken Gavin deep into Viet Cong territory and was showing him the war from a Viet Cong point of view.

Her first recognizable reaction was relief. If Gavin was with Dinh, then he was safe. She tried to remember everything her mother had ever told her about him. "He was fiercely intelligent, even as a little boy," she had said once, "and because he was the only son he had a very, very strong sense of family." Her voice had trembled slightly. "And even though we have all been separated for so long, I know his sense of family is something that he has never lost. When he came south on his undercover mission for General Giap, he risked his life by entering Saigon and making contact with Nhu. He is still our brother. Still the head of our family."

Remembering her mother's words reassured Gabrielle. Even though she had never met Dinh, even though there had never been any communication between them, he *was* her uncle. Gavin was his nephew by marriage, and, despite his nationality, would be treated as family.

Taking a deep breath, she opened the letter from Gavin's employers. At least it didn't contain any new or shocking information. Gavin wasn't dead or injured. He had gone off on an assignment of his own, no one knew where, and he had not returned. Enormous efforts had been made to trace him. He had been seen leaving the bureau with a Vietnamese woman and had then entered a shabby Renault, alone. The driver, a Vietnamese, had driven off in the direction of Cholon.

That was the last anyone had seen of him. Because of the nature of the note he had left behind, a copy of which was enclosed, no immediate alarm had been raised. Although absenting himself from Saigon without first conferring with his bureau chief, Paul Dulles, was highly irregular, it had been assumed that he was working on a story which had warranted the action he had taken.

His continuing silence, however, had given the agency no other option but to presume him missing. His salary would continue to be paid into her account for the next six months, after which, if there was still no news of him, the situation would be reassessed. They were very regretful and hoped most sincerely that their fears for Gavin's safety would prove to be false. If they could be of any further help she had only to telephone.

She walked into the kitchen with both letters and sat at the scrubbed wooden table, looking down at them thoughtfully. The Vietnamese woman who had been seen talking to Gavin in the bureau only minutes before he disappeared was obviously Nhu. Had the Vietnamese driving the car been Dinh? She had no way of knowing. Whether or not it had been, Gavin was most certainly with Dinh now. Her problem was whether to reveal her information to the press agency.

She reread both letters. If Gavin had wanted to reveal the identity of his informant, and the identity of the person he was going to meet, he could, presumably, have done so. And he hadn't. He had said merely that "something huge had come up" and that he would "explain all" when he returned. But he hadn't returned, and the only person who could explain, even in part, was herself.

And if she did so? She rose from the table and put the kettle on in order to make some coffee, grateful that her mother was out visiting Madame Garine. Nhu would be questioned, possibly by the Americans, possibly by the South Vietnamese police, maybe by both. She would be clearly marked as having links with the Viet Cong, and it was more than likely that she would be arrested, which was precisely why Gavin had not revealed her name to his superiors. And why she could not do so either.

She poured the boiling water on top of the

58

freshly ground beans. There were no decisions to make. Gavin had made them all for her. All she could wait patiently until he resurfaced in Saigon with what she knew was going to be the biggest news scoop of the war.

Despite the grimness of the weather, England in November was frenetic and fun. The band began their tour in the North, working the plush, giant-size, workingmen's clubs that attracted entertainers of the stature of Tom Jones, the Righteous Brothers, Georgie Fame, and the Blue Flames. As their tour progressed and they moved farther south, the traditional clubs gave way to a string of enormous, recently opened Mecca nightclubs. At both types of clubs they received thunderous ovations, and by the time they reached London, all of them, including Michel, were riding on a permanent high.

"Baby, this is one buzz that isn't going to die away!" Radford had said to her with his wide, lazy grin. "We are really *going* places this time around!"

When they reached London they made their first ever studio television performance.

"What is the program called again?" Gabrielle asked Michel as they piled into a black taxicab that was to take them to the studios.

"Ready, Steady, Go," Michel said in execrable English, and then, reverting to French, "It's networked all over the country and this is the first time, ever, that a group without a hit record has been asked to appear. God alone knows how

Marty managed it."

"He managed it because clips from the open air concert have been televised over here and because everyone in the country wants to know who the hell we are," Radford said, holding one leg by the ankle across his knee, his free arm flung out across the top of the rear seat, brushing the back of Gabrielle's shoulders. "And because when we *do* cut a record, it's going to go *straight* to the top, like a *rocket*, baby!"

Michel squeezed himself onto the jump seat with angular clumsiness, resenting the easy, careless manner in which Radford had made bodily contact with Gabrielle. His initial enthusiasm for the American had cooled the instant he had become aware of the almost palpable sexual attraction that existed between him and Gabrielle. He knew very well that Gabrielle had not physically capitulated to the attraction, but he was always painfully conscious of Radford's apparently innocent touchings, both on- and offstage, and as the tour had progressed and they had all been thrown into one another's company for at least eighteen hours out of every twenty-four, his disquiet had increased.

"When *do* we cut the record?" he asked tersely, staring out the window at the dark wet London streets so that he wouldn't have to see Gabrielle's fiery red hair brushing against Radford's leather-jacketed arm.

"The morning after we arrive back in Paris," Radford replied, his eyes dancing in amusement. He knew damn well what was bugging Michel and he wondered, not for the first time, just what Gabrielle saw in him that she valued his friendship so much.

Michel fell silent. There had been many discussions between Radford, Marty Dennison, and their record company about the song they were to launch with. The deal was that they would cut a single, which would be released quickly, and that they would then immediately begin work on an album. It had been agreed early on that the album would include at least one song written by Gabrielle. With a backing arranged by Radford, it was the best song in their repertoire, and Michel knew that there was a good chance that it might also be the choice for the single.

If it was, then he knew that in the future Radford would be working even more closely with Gabrielle, and that musically she would have less and less need of him. He wished that Gavin would return from Vietnam. At least his jealousy of Gavin wasn't touched by fear for her. With Gavin he knew that her happiness and the happiness of *le petit* Gavin was secure. Their happiness would certainly not be secure if she had an affair with Radford James.

Michel's large, ungainly hands hung impotently between his knees as the taxi drew up outside the television studio. He had known right from the very beginning that she would never turn to him as a lover, but at least he was her friend. And if Gavin Ryan didn't return soon from his mysterious assignment, then he had a

61

dreadful feeling that, as a friend, he was going to have to give her some serious advice, advice which he was terrified she might not take.

Except for Christmas Day, the entire month of December was spent in a recording studio. After her long absence from *le petit* Gavin while she had been in England, Gabrielle hated that she could not take him to the studio with her, as she had taken him to rehearsals. He was growing into such an interesting little person, holding his head quite steady and following her around the room with his eyes, gurgling with delight whenever she approached him to pick him up. She wanted to be with him when he said his first word and took his first step. *She* wanted to be with him, and she was determined that once the mammoth recording session was over and they were back on the road again, wherever she went, *le petit* Gavin would go too.

She knew her relationship with Radford intrigued the rest of the band. The feeling of *rapprochement* between them was so total that it was impossible for anyone not to notice. Onstage, instead of merely backing her with guitar and vocals, he had begun moving forward to share center stage with her, turning several numbers into such highly charged, erotic duos that audiences had been brought stamping to their feet, howling for more.

But the sexual attraction was given rein only onstage. She wasn't in love with Radford. She was in love with Gavin. And although she was well aware that it was within her nature for her to enjoy sleeping with someone she wasn't in love with, she knew that it wasn't in Gavin's nature. Wherever Gavin was, she was certain that he was being faithful. And so for his sake, and because she knew that it mattered to him, so was she.

Wherever Radford was, there were girls. He treated them all with insolent carelessness, barely even remembering their various names. When she had teasingly chided him about his cavalier attitude, he had simply given her his dazzling gypsy smile and had said, "Honey, if you would only come across, like you *know* you should, and be my old lady, I wouldn't have no *need* of anybody else!"

She had been standing and he had been sitting down, drinking a beer, and she had laughed and run her hand tightly over his tight, crinkly hair before turning and walking away from him. Despite his smile, his eyes had been hotly serious and a flush of heat had surged down into her vagina, so ragingly insistent that it had taken her nearly all her power to have been able to laugh and walk away.

All through January and February there was no word from Gavin. He had now been officially listed as MIA. He wasn't the only journalist to be so. Members of the press corps who eschewed the news briefings at the Follies and instead hitched lifts on whatever air transport was available to far-flung battle sites risked their lives just as much as the soldiers in the field.

Gavin's salary was no longer paid directly into their joint account. Instead, she had received a sympathetic letter from the Paris office and an ex gratia payment to cover her immediate needs. She had also received a letter from Paul Dulles and had agonized about how to reply to it.

She knew so much more than his employers did. She knew the identity of the woman who had visited Gavin at the bureau office. She knew who he had been going to meet. She was nearly one hundred percent sure of what had happened after that meeting, of the proposition that Dinh must have put to Gavin and that Gavin had been unable to turn down. She knew that he wasn't dead, that at any moment he was likely to emerge from the jungle several pounds lighter but triumphant. He would be able to give the agency a story that no other Western reporter could give, a story of the war as seen through Viet Cong eyes by a man who had lived with them for months.

But she couldn't tell Paul Dulles what she knew. If she did he would immediately seek Nhu out and question her rigorously. She would be unable to answer his questions, and this contact would bring her to the attention of the South Vietnamese authorities. So Gabrielle had replied to his awkward letter of sympathy by saying that she was confident Gavin was still alive and that fear for his safety was groundless.

Sometimes, in the long, dark hours of the night, doubt would assail her. If he were alive, surely he would have managed to get word to her via Nhu? She would toss and turn, trying to imagine circumstances under which such action was impossible. Even if Gavin couldn't make contact with Nhu, surely her uncle could do so.

She remembered the long years in which Nhu had heard nothing from Dinh. For men who had gone north to join the NVA, or who had stayed south and joined the Viet Cong, lack of contact with their families was normal. Gavin had been out of contact with his family for only seven months. Her uncle would regard that period of time as unimportant. But what if he weren't with Dinh? What if her aunt Nhu's assumptions were wrong? What if Gavin had been killed months before, on the day that he left Saigon?

It was then that she would slip out of bed and pad softly across to the crib that held her sleeping son. Gently, so as not to wake him, she would lift him up in her arms, holding him tight, tears glittering on the long, curling sweep of her eyelashes.

All through spring and early summer, letters continued to arrive from Nhu, but they contained no further information. Nhu's distress at being a party to Gavin's disappearance was obvious, though carefully concealed in her wording in case eyes other than theirs should read the contents.

In the bright light of day, Gabrielle continued to be fiercely optimistic. Gavin couldn't be dead. If he were dead she would *know*. Every instinct she possessed would be telling her so. "He isn't dead," she said repeatedly to Michel. "But oh! I wish that he would get word to Nhu! Just one little word and I would be able to live on it until he returned!"

Workwise, her life was frenetic. The single had been released, and though not shooting to the top of the charts, it had entered them at a position that had pleased even Radford. Marty Dennison had asked for more songs from her, eager to capitalize on the success of the record and their British tour. He had arranged gigs for them all through the summer in places as far away as Stockholm and Dublin.

"You can't possibly take *le petit* Gavin with you!" her mother had declared, aghast, when Gabrielle had announced her intention of doing so.

"Yes I can," Gabrielle had said stubbornly. "Michel will help me look after him."

"But what about when you are onstage? Who will look after him then?"

"I will find someone," Gabrielle had said with immovable firmness. "I'm sorry, *Maman*, but he's coming with me. It's hard enough living without Gavin. I'm not going to live without my baby as well."

It had not been easy. Maids, in the hotels they had stayed in, had looked after him for her whenever they could, as had some of the fans she attracted, but baby-sitters on such an ad hoc basis were not an ideal solution. When she was in Dublin, the young Irish girl who had offered

66

to care for him while she was onstage was so likable and so enamored with *le petit* Gavin that Gabrielle asked her if she would like to become his nanny, traveling with them wherever they went.

She had accepted immediately and Radford, who had been left on more than one occasion literally holding the baby, was extremely grateful. "Every band should have a nanny," he had said laconically when she had asked if Maura could be put on the payroll. "Man, it's what *this* band has needed all along!"

When the LP was released it was even more successful than the single had been.

"America next stop," Radford had said triumphantly. "Marty is fixing up a tour for the fall. From now on there ain't going to be no stopping us. This time we're *really* on our way!"

It was the end of the summer when the crucial letter from Nhu arrived. Gabrielle was in Paris because they were rehearsing for the fall tour and her mother brought it into the kitchen with a troubled face.

"It is much heavier than usual, *ma chère*," she said as *le petit* Gavin tried to walk toward her on chubby legs, holding onto the edge of a chair. "Do you think there is news?"

Her eyes flickered over the envelope; Gabrielle knew that there was news, and that it wasn't good. She tore open the letter, reading slowly, her heart racing.

"I am very distressed to have to tell you that a

visitor came to see me yesterday in order to inform me that we can expect no further news of your uncle, or of the friend who is traveling with him. Nor should we seek for such news. I am terribly sorry, dear niece, but it seems that at the moment nothing further can be done..."

She passed the letter silently across to her mother. Vanh read it slowly and then raised her eyes to Gabrielle. "Perhaps..." she began quaveringly.

Gabrielle shook her head. She knew that her mother was beginning to believe that both Dinh and Gavin were dead. But *she* didn't believe that they were dead. They couldn't be dead. "No," she said fiercely, her hands balling into fists. "Don't say it, *Maman*. They are alive. I *know* they are!"

Gabrielle had never really spoken to Radford about Gavin, but he knew the brief outline. Her husband was in Vietnam and was officially listed as missing. Now she told him about Nhu's dispiriting letter.

"That's pretty bleak news, baby," he said sympathetically.

"My mother thinks that both he and Dinh are dead—"

He put his arm around her shoulders, hugging her tight. "Hey steady there. No news is good news, isn't that what they say? And this letter from your aunt is a no-news letter. All it's saying is don't hound them. They'll get in touch in their own good time. Don't say one damn thing about

68

either of them being dead."

She had been grateful for his reassurance. She didn't want him as her lover because she didn't want anyone as her lover, only Gavin. But she did want him as a friend.

His eyes sharpened as he looked down at her. "You're not going to do anything silly, are you?" he asked with sudden, terrible intuitiveness.

Her eyes were blank. "I don't know what you mean," she said truthfully.

He gave an inward sigh of relief. For once he was way ahead of her. She hadn't yet taken it into her head to hotfoot it to 'Nam herself. He hoped to God she never did. The band would certainly not survive without her. Thinking of the American tour that was soon to start, he said, "I'm going to take time off when we're in Washington to march with the brothers. Why don't you join me? You might even meet up with other chicks in the same position as yourself."

"I'm sorry," she said, wondering how on earth she was going to survive the American tour when her mind would focus on nothing but Gavin. "I don't understand."

He tossed a foreign edition of *The Washington Post* across to her.

"A pretty uptight-sounding English chick isn't too pleased at the line the American government is taking toward POWs. Her husband is a chopper jock being held in Hanoi."

Gabrielle took hold of the newspaper, reading the letter that had caught his attention. "I'm going to write to her," she said immediately.

69

"I'm going to write to her today."

"And the march on the Pentagon?" he asked. "The Black Muslims are taking part in a march on the Pentagon in a couple of weeks time." He grinned and gave a black clenched fist power salute, raised high. "I thought my old friend Malcolm X might like a little support from me."

"Are they going to protest the war?"

"They sure as hell ain't going there to enlist!" he said, laughing down at her.

Despite her fearful anxieties for Gavin's safety, a small smile touched her mouth. An anti-war demonstration in the heart of Washington would be an event Gavin would certainly not want her to miss. And the English girl who had written so angrily to *The Washington Post* might also be going.

"I'll come with you," she said decisively. "The brothers won't mind, will they?"

With great difficulty he resisted the urge to scoop her off her high-booted feet and crush her against him. "Hell, honey," he said, wondering how much longer it would be before she finally shared his bed. "The brothers ain't going to mind having you with them. They're going to be de-*lighted*!"

CHAPTER FOUR

The pain in Lewis's shoulder was excruciating, and blood was pouring down his arm and his chest. To evade being captured he knew he had to act. Immediately. Before he even left the water.

"*Duoc!*" The North Vietnamese screamed at him. "*Di di!*"

His left arm was useless. It was a heavy blood-soaked weight that felt as if it had been ripped from its socket. He had to hurl himself at the North Vietnamese; he had to knock the Kalashnikov from his grasp. From far behind him, from the other bank, there came a high-pitched scream and then a silencing blast of machine-gun fire. He staggered in the waist-high water. It wasn't Duxbery. Duxbery had been killed in the first barrage of shots to hit the boat. It was Drayton. They'd killed Drayton and now they were going to kill him.

The water around him was carmine with blood. He steadied himself on the mud and slime of the canal bed and then, as the North Vietnamese, losing patience, moved angrily toward him, he summoned up all his strength and hurled himself forward.

He knew as he moved that he stood no chance

of escaping. Even if he disarmed and killed his potential captor, there were swarms of other North Vietnamese on both banks who would immediately open fire. He couldn't escape, and he knew it, but he sure as hell wasn't going to flounder to dry land at the point of a gun only to be shot like an animal at his captor's leisure.

The grin of triumph on the North Vietnamese's face vanished as Lewis dived upon him. At the same instant as Lewis's right arm made contact with the Kalashnikov, knocking it upward, it blasted into life, bullets plowing into the air. There would be other bullets soon, bullets far more lethally directed, but Lewis didn't care. His right hand was on his victim's throat as they fell together, rolling and tumbling under the surface of the filthy water.

He never knew why he wasn't shot there and then. His initial advantage, that of taking his enemy by surprise, was lost almost immediately. Blood was still pumping from the wound in his shoulder, pain was still searing through him, and his left arm was as useless as a piece of dead meat. It was only seconds before his opponent had the upper hand, and only a fraction of a second longer before other hands laid hold of him, dragging him half drowned and semi-conscious toward the bank.

He expected to be shot. Never for one minute did he imagine that he was going to be taken prisoner. He was thrown facedown, a half a dozen Kalashnikovs pointing at his head.

The officer in charge gave a brusque order, and

instead of the expected blast of automatic fire smashing him from this world and into the next, hands were laid on him once again and his sodden clothes, right down to his khaki shorts, were savagely stripped off him. His boots were next, yanked from his feet and handed over, the spoils of war, to the officer in charge.

Still with the Kalashnikovs aimed at his head, coughing and spluttering up fetid canal water, he rolled himself onto his knees. The wound in his shoulder was now clearly visible, and he saw with relief that it was a flesh wound and that though nerves and tendons to his arm had been severed, no bones had been smashed.

The officer nodded to one of the soldiers standing guard over him, and the next minute his right arm and his injured left arm were yanked behind his back. He cried out in agony, falling and blacking out. When consciousness returned, he was still on his knees and still in excruciating pain. His arms had been tied behind him with vine rope, and a pad made from the shirt they had stripped him of had been tied across the gaping wound in his shoulder.

It was the first hopeful thing that had happened to him since he had hit the water. Their action made no sense unless they intended to keep him alive. And if they were going to keep him alive, then he would be able, at some point, to make an escape.

He was gestured to his feet, and he rose with difficulty, towering over the smaller Vietnamese soldiers like a captured Gulliver over the inhabitants of Lilliput.

There was no noise from the river behind him, no sign of life. The bodies of the men who had traveled out from Van Binh with him floated facedown on the water, or lay sprawled on the far bank. He saw no sign of Duxbery or Drayton.

He was almost grateful for the pain. At least it dulled the rage he felt at being herded along like a tethered bull. They didn't make for the village he and his men had so recently searched. Instead, they forged a path westward, through the bush. With no boots, Lewis's feet were soon as bloody as his shoulder. He tried not to think about snakes, about red ants. Instead, he tried to recreate a map of the area in his head, to anticipate where they might be heading, and for how long the hideous march would last.

It seemed to take forever. At one point the North Vietnamese came to a halt, and water from a plastic bottle was poured into a tin pannikin and passed around, but he was given none and he would have roasted in the fires of hell before he would have lowered himself to ask. He wondered why he'd been selected to be a prisoner. Perhaps they were a regular unit of the North Vietnamese Army, and they were trying to emphasize the difference between themselves and the local Viet Cong. Perhaps they had a tradeoff in mind. Perhaps they thought he was a colonel or a bigwig in the CIA. Perhaps they wanted information from him.

He winced as he stumbled in the wake of the soldiers. He'd always believed he was mentally

74

prepared for torture, but he had imagined himself facing it in the peak of physical fitness, not with a half-severed arm. He was burning up with the beginnings of a fever, and though his feet never stopped moving forward, he knew that he was slipping in and out of semiconsciousness. At the next halt he was given water. His near-naked body was tormented by feeding mosquitoes and leeches. He tried to distract himself by thinking of Abbra, of how the news that he was missing in action would be conveyed to her, and failed. He couldn't think of Abbra. He would fall apart. Think about Tam. Pretty Tam, who had begged him not to leave on the morning's mission. Tam who had so devastated him by telling him that she was in love with him.

He plodded on, pain from his injured arm and shoulder raging through him, the fever intensifying. What would Tam do when she heard the news? Who would tell her the news? Presumably the bodies on the riverbank would be found. Duxbery and Drayton would be verified as being killed in action. What about him? Would it be believed that he was dead as well? Somehow he had to escape. He had to inform someone that he was alive, that there was no need for Abbra to be contacted, no need for her to worry.

When they finally came to a permanent halt it wasn't in a village. It was a campsite deep in the bush. Half a dozen thatched bamboo and straw huts circled blackened rice pots and a mud-baked oven. Green and black nylon sleeping hammocks were slung between the surrounding trees. The soldiers immediately in front of him rounded on him, yelling at him to squat, Vietnamese fashion. He did so with relief, swaying dizzily, and then, unable to balance himself for his bound arms, toppling over. As he struggled back into a crouching position the wound in his shoulder began to bleed profusely again.

"*Ten yi?*" the officer demanded, standing over him. "What is your name?"

His name at least he could give them. His name, his rank, his service number, and his date of birth. But nothing else. Section five of the Code of Conduct for Members of the Armed Forces of the United States, the oath he had sworn when he first joined the army, was categorical. "When questioned, should I become a prisoner of war, I am bound to give name and rank, service number, and date of birth. I will evade answering further questions to the utmost of my ability. I will make no oral or written statements disloyal to my country and its allies or harmful to their cause."

If his captors had not shot him because they thought he would give them information, then they had made a grave error of judgment. Section six, the final part of the Code of Conduct, was in his blood and his bones. "I will never forget that I am an American fighting man, responsible for my actions, and dedicated to the principles which made my country free. I will trust in God and in the United States of America."

"Captain Lewis Ellis," he replied curtly,

wishing to God that he didn't feel so faint, that the blood streaming hotly down over his chest and arm would once more begin to congeal. He gave his service number and his birth date and then felt himself beginning to lose consciousness.

There was a sharply rapped order from the officer, and two of the soldiers who had trekked behind him all the way from the canal ran forward and physically supported him, hauling him to his feet. Still bound, with leeches feeding on his blood-soaked body, he was dragged toward one of the huts and thrown inside. Seconds later a young boy entered. He was in uniform and over his shoulder he carried a small box. He put the box down, regarded the wound in Lewis's shoulder without moving forward to physically examine it, and then turned abruptly on his heel, leaving the box behind him.

Lewis struggled into a half-sitting position, leaning against the wall of the hut. He tried to focus on the box that the young boy had left behind. Was it a first aid kit? Was the boy a paramedic? He summoned up all his remaining strength and began to edge himself toward it. He was saved having to attempt near-impossible contortions by the return of the boy. This time he carried an aluminum bowl of steaming water. Lewis began to tremble with relief, then was suddenly consumed by fury at the thought that his trembling would be seen as a sign of weakness.

His face impassive, the boy put the water down

while two other soldiers remained at the doorway of the hut, rifles in their hands. The vine thongs tethering his arms were released.

With cloths that had obviously been used many times before but which had been boiled clean, the boy began to swab his arm and shoulder. Looking down, Lewis could see the wound clearly and he knew he had been lucky. The bullet, no doubt aimed at his heart, had scored a near miss, hitting no vital organs. But the way his arms had been wrenched behind him and tethered had caused the real damage to the severed nerves and tendons.

With a pair of stainless steel tweezers the boy began to dig into the wound for the bullet. With his jaw clenched tight, and his teeth clamped together to prevent himself from crying out, Lewis stared with fierce concentration through the open door of the hut, fixing his gaze on the mud-baked oven. Food was being prepared. Rice was being cooked in one of the large blackened pots. He fixed his eyes firmly on the pot as the boy prodded deeper. Once the bullet was out and the wound was cleaned, it would heal. And then he would be able to think of escape.

The bullet was retrieved and the boy began to swab his shoulder with a ball of cotton soaked in alcohol. The sooner he made an escape attempt, the better. Statistically, early escapes were the most successful. And he wanted to put a quick end to the mental agony ... for him and Abbra.

The boy began to work the alcohol-soaked swab into the wound, and a nerve ticked convulsively at the corner of Lewis's jaw. Finally, just when he thought he could bear it no longer, the swab was withdrawn and discarded and fresh swabs, soaked in a solution he could not identify, were plugged into the gaping hole. His upper arm and shoulder were then bandaged with strips of green cloth.

"Thank you," he said automatically when the boy had finished.

The boy picked up the aluminum bowl and the medical box and looked at Lewis directly for the first time. There was a faint gleam of surprise in his eyes but nothing more. He still did not speak. He merely gave a slight shrug of his shoulders and then turned, walking out of the hut, past the soldiers who were still standing guard.

Now that he was no longer in danger of dying from loss of blood, Lewis became aware of how ravenously hungry he was. He could smell the rice that was being cooked and hoped fervently that he would be offered some.

That he had been captured by a small group of North Vietnamese Army troops instead of Viet Cong was surely to his advantage. If he had been captured by the Viet Cong, he knew he would have been a short timer indeed.

The general pattern of Viet Cong captures was for the prisoner to be tethered by the neck and then hauled around Viet Cong sympathetic villages in order that the peasantry could observe how inferior and animal-like the Americans were. When the fun and games of baiting the helpless American were over, he would be shot, preferably by one bullet and by a very young boy just to emphasize to the onlookers how easy it was to kill a large, apparently invincible, *khi dot*. A big monkey.

Americans who were captured by the NVA were generally pilots shot down over North Vietnam. There, after being paraded through the streets like circus animals, they were imprisoned either in the huge Hoa Lo prison complex in Hanoi, or a smaller prison known to the Americans as the "zoo", at Cu Loc.

But he wasn't in North Vietnam, he was in South Vietnam, and here there were no prison camps. He would just have to put his trust in the fact that the NVA were disciplined soldiers, soldiers that he, and the majority of his colleagues, had always regarded with respect.

The boy who had treated his shoulder, though no more than sixteen, had been competent. He wondered why they were so far south. It was possible that they were a splinter group from the large contingent who had been attempting to ferry supplies in from Cambodia, the group he and his men had engaged earlier in the month. But if they were, why hadn't they headed immediately back to their Cambodian sanctuaries?

The two soldiers on guard moved toward him, one of them bending down to pick up the vine rope. As he approached with it, obviously about to retether him, Lewis said abruptly in Vietnamese, "If you wrench my arms behind me again, tying them at the elbows, I will lose my injured arm. It will die. Drop off."

For a second both men hesitated. They knew that many Americans knew some Vietnamese words. Words for "go" or "come", or words that were blasphemous. But they had never encountered an American who spoke their language.

Their hesitation was minimal. His arms were seized and yanked behind him, and Lewis knew, through a sea of pain, that in the next few seconds blood would once more begin to trickle stickily down his chest. He was protesting vociferously when the young paramedic walked quickly into the hut.

"No," he ordered his comrades. "Tie him by the neck and feet. Not the arms!"

The vine rope was put around his feet, anchored on his right wrist and then looped around his neck. It was then run up to the bamboo rafters. If he tried to move more than an inch or two in any direction, the rope tightened around his neck, threatening to strangle him. While he was being tied like a hog, the paramedic was placing his left arm in a makeshift sling, which looked like a piece of dried banana leaf. Whatever it was, it served its purpose. He immediately felt better.

Outside the hut the soldiers were beginning to gather, bowls in their hands, around the huge rice pot.

If he were given a share of the rice, it would be a fair indication of the kind of treatment that lay ahead of him. He waited tensely. He needed food. The fever that had washed over him in waves on the trek to the camp was now subsiding, though he was damned sure it wouldn't have done so if his shoulder hadn't been so thoroughly cleaned.

At the first opportunity he intended making his escape, and the fitter he was, when that moment came, the better it would be for him. He wasn't daunted by the forests and swamps he would have to negotiate. He had been trained in jungle survival, and he had lived long enough in Van Binh to have come to terms with the water-logged, leech- and snake-infested terrain.

The officer who had appropriated his boots entered the hut. Looking at the small size of his feet compared to his own, Lewis wondered how he would ever find them comfortable to march in.

"You will come with me," he said brusquely. "You will answer questions."

The two guards at either side of the doorway moved forward, releasing the vine rope that tethered him from the rafters.

Lewis abandoned all hope of a share in the rice. He certainly wouldn't be fed immediately before an interrogation, and sure as hell would-n't be afterward, when he had refused to tell them whatever it was they wanted to know.

It was dark now, and he was led across to a table shielded by a protective awning of green camouflage parachute silk. On the table was a tiny oil lamp made of a small glass bottle with a wick stub sticking out the top.

The officer sat behind the table, the two soldiers flanked Lewis, who stood before it, and the interrogation began.

"Your name?" he was asked again. "Your rank?"

Lewis told him. He was still half naked and the evening chill struck through him, bringing goose flesh out on his arms and his legs.

"Your company?"

"Under the Code of Conduct for Members of the Armed Forces of the United States I am required to give only my name, rank, service number, and date of birth!"

The officer's face tightened. "You will answer all questions or you will be given correctional period."

Lewis had no need to ask what he meant. Correctional period was a euphemism for torture.

He repeated obdurately, "I am required to give only my name, rank, service number, and date of birth."

Some of the questions he was asked, and which he refused to answer, were oddly personal ones. Was he married? Did he have children? Whereabouts did he live in imperialist America?

Despite everything he could do to prevent it, he began to sway on his feet as he repeated, time and time again, his name, rank, service number and date of birth. His arm and shoulder were hurting like hell. He was freezing. He was hungry. And his cut and bloody feet were attracting the attention of ants and land leeches and God only knew what else.

Before he disgraced himself by fainting, the interrogation came to an abrupt end, and with no violence. He was marched back to the hut and then, before he was retethered, one of his guards threw a pair of black pajamas toward him and a sleeping mat. As he struggled one-handed into the pajamas, another soldier entered and placed a bowl of rice and a bowl of leaf tea down on the floor beside him. The rice was flavoured with salt pork soup and was surprisingly appetizing. He wolfed it down, uncertain whether to expect such treatment in the future, or if it was merely the calm before the storm.

He was retethered, a loop of the rope again going around his neck, making it nearly impossible for him to sleep. As he lay on the sleeping mat, shivering violently in the thin cotton pajamas and with mosquitoes clustering on his unprotected feet, he wondered why the officer had accepted his noncooperation with comparative good grace. It had been almost as if he had not been really interested. And if that were the case, why on earth had he taken him prisoner?

He was in torment from the mosquitoes, and he tried to think about Abbra, Abbra, who had so naively wanted him to tell her all about his life in Vietnam so that she could feel a part of it. It suddenly occurred to him that he didn't know if Abbra had ever traveled out of the United States. If she had, it would have been only to Canada or to one of the more sophisticated Mexican beach resorts. Nothing she had ever experienced could possibly give her any idea of what Vietnam was like. It was beyond anyone's imagination.

He found himself thinking of Tam. Tam would

know exactly what he was suffering. He hoped to God whoever was sent out to Van Binh to replace him would keep Tam on as cleaning girl. If she returned to her father, she would inevitably face beatings.

Despite his agony a smile touched the corner of his mouth. He recalled how hostile and defiant she had been when he had first met her. She had hated him so passionately she had fairly sparked with animosity. Later she had cared for him with all the diligence of a devoted wife, laundering his clothes, cooking, cleaning. He was going to miss Tam. She had brightened up the last few months immeasurably.

He had slept intermittently, waking at dawn to the sound of men drilling. The NVA's reputation for rigid discipline was obviously one that was well deserved. About ten minutes later the paramedic entered the hut, two guards in attendance. He didn't remove the dressing from Lewis's wound but bent his head toward it, sniffing it. It smelled clean, no sign of gangrene, and he gave Lewis an imperceptible nod before turning and walking away.

Later, a dish of leaf tea was brought to him and held for him to drink.

"I need exercise," he said to the guard who held the dish to his mouth. "I need to move or my blood will stop circulating."

His body felt as if his blood had stopped long ago. The method by which he was tied was fiendish, the slightest movement causing pressure of his neck. The guard didn't respond by releasing his bonds, but to Lewis's even greater surprise, he took out a packet of Ruby Queens from his shirt pocket, lit one, and then gave it to him to inhale. It was the best cigarette he had ever tasted and one he knew he would never forget.

When the drilling was finished, the officer who had interrogated him the previous evening entered the hut. "Good morning, imperialist American," he said almost affably. "You are to prepare to meet your new escorts." As he was speaking to him, the guards were freeing his bonds.

Lewis stretched his cramped muscles gingerly. Escorts? Then he wasn't just being held prisoner. He was being taken somewhere. But where? Cambodia?

When he was led out into the morning sunlight, he groaned inwardly. Twenty or so black-clad Viet Cong were milling with the small group of NVA troops. He was going to be handed over. And in the hands of the less-disciplined Viet Cong there was no telling what might happen to him.

He tried to follow the conversations taking place around him. The NVA troops were continuing westward, back to their Cambodian sanctuaries after apparently bringing in a convoy of supplies. He was unable to discover where the VC were heading, though it was obvious from their behavior that they were in transit and that they were not going to remain long in the makeshift camp.

In an agonizingly short space of time he was

86

rebound though this time his arm was allowed to remain in its sling. His right arm was wrenched behind him, and tied to vine rope that was threaded through over his bent left elbow. His left wrist, lying flat against his chest, was also tied so that he could not slip his arm out of the sling and ease the pressure of the rope. Then, as before, the rope was passed around his neck and down and under the right arm rope. It was an ingenious method of bondage, making his neck answerable to nearly every movement that he made.

There were no formal farewells as the troops divided and went in two different directions, the NVA westward, the VC heading toward the densest part of the U Minh forest. The ground was so waterlogged that it became impossible to follow any land trails, and a kilometer or so from the camp Lewis was ordered at gunpoint into one of a half dozen waiting sampans.

Traveling on a web of narrow canals, hemmed in by dense vegetation, they penetrated deeper and deeper into the U Minh. It was hideous, swamp-infested terrain, thick with snakes and poisonous spiders. Escaping, without a weapon of any kind, would be no picnic.

Lewis wondered again why he was being kept alive. Presumably it was believed he would give them information. And even when they found he wouldn't, he would still retain a certain value. Prisoners were highly prized commodities at peace negotiations, though not all prisoners were given their freedom when negotiations were complete. He remembered being told at West Point that thirteen French prisoners captured at Dien Bien Phu were not released by Hanoi until sixteen years later.

As the late afternoon merged into dusk a flight of B-52 bombers screamed overhead. They were probably from Guam. He wondered what their mission was, where they were heading.

Homesickness, strong and pungent, caught him by the throat. He'd been trained in jungle survival techniques and had been prepared both mentally and physically for captivity. But the reality was far worse than anything he had anticipated. The loss of dignity affronted him the most. He couldn't go for a pee or a shit without having a VC standing over him with a loaded AK-47, and the salt pork soup had affected his bowels adversely.

It was dark when their journey at last came to an end. He could discern small huts on stilts, their numbers indicating that this camp, unlike the previous one, was semi-permanent. He was given a half coconut shell of sickly-sweet palm sugar juice to drink and a minute portion of rice to eat. Then he was tied for sleep as he had been tied by the NVA.

The pain in his shoulder had begun to ease slightly, but his left arm had swollen to alarming proportions. He wondered if infection had set in and hoped to God that it hadn't. If it had, a couple of penicillin shots would be an easy cure, but he wasn't going to be given any penicillin shots, and he had a suspicion that the VC answer to the problem would be swift, and amateur, amputation.

He had been given a mosquito net for protection, and despite the numerous bugs that managed to circumnavigate it, he slept, lightly and restlessly. At dawn he was awakened by having the muzzle of an AK-47 prodded against his chest. He was taken to a latrine trench to relieve himself, and then marched back to the hut.

During the short journey he was able to verify his suspicions ... the camp had been in existence for some time. He wondered how often US aircraft flew over it. Or if they did? If helicopters flew that way, he might be able to attract their attention. Even as the thought came to him, he knew that any such chance was minimal. The camp would not have survived as long as it apparently had without being skillfully camouflaged. He knew there wasn't a hope in hell of foot troops penetrating so deep in to the U Minh. It was an area that the Saigon military left alone. So as rescue seemed to be out of the question, the only alternative was escape.

He pondered how escape in such a hellish region might be achieved, when the two Viet Cong who had been standing guard at the door of the hut ordered him abruptly to his feet. He was led out into the heat of early morning and marched to the center of the compound, where a Viet Cong officer, the black material of his pajamas of much better quality than those of the guards, stood waiting.

Lewis took a deep breath. It looked as if he

was about to suffer his first interrogation at the hands of the Viet Cong. And he doubted if it would bear much relation to his brief interrogation with NVA.

He was right. All the information demanded of him was military. No one in the U Minh was interested in whether he was married or not, or where he was born.

He replied to the questions as he had to the previous ones. He gave his name, rank, service number, and date of birth and claimed that under Article 17 of the Geneva Conventions, no other information could be demanded of him.

The Viet Cong officer disagreed. "You will be punished," he said, and his eyes flicked toward the banana-leaf sling.

Lewis felt his stomach muscles contract. It was what he had expected from the first moment he had been captured. From the number of Viet Cong standing in a semicircle around the edge of the compound, everyone else had expected it too. The officer nodded toward two of the guards, and they approached Lewis, lengths of nylon cargo strapping in their hands. Lewis gritted his teeth. Damn his injured shoulder. Damn, damn, dammit!

"Have you changed your mind?" the officer asked him in Vietnamese. "Do you wish to cooperate?"

Lewis swallowed hard and repeated his name, his rank, his service number, and his date of birth.

"And that is all?" the officer said when he had

finished.

"Under Article 17 of the Geneva Conventions and under the Code of Conduct for Members of the Armed Forces of the United States, that is all."

The officer did not seem disappointed. He merely nodded toward the guards and then stepped back a yard or two. In the few seconds before the guards laid hold of him, Lewis realized the officer had moved so that he would be well clear of any splattering blood. And then the banana-leaf string was ripped away and he didn't think of anything else except agonizing pain for a very long time.

Before the torture began he had been determined not to let even a groan of pain pass his lips for the onlookers' enjoyment. He didn't groan. He screamed. His shoulders were lifting out of their sockets, his chest was exploding, his ribs projecting like drawn bowstrings. Unconsciousness was a black pit he hurtled into gratefully, only to be wrenched back into agonizing consciousness by having cold water thrown over him.

The pressure was relieved. He was asked if he would answer the questions put to him. With his jaw clenched so tight that it felt permanently locked, he gasped out his name, rank, service number, and date of birth. And then he remained silent.

The pressure not only resumed, it intensified. He began to vomit and choke on his vomit. He lost control of his bowels and his bladder. He

91

was no longer Lewis Ellis, West Point graduate, captain, husband of Abbra. He was an animal. A thing. A creature with no control over his bodily functions.

Each time he was asked a question he gaspingly told his questioner to go to hell. He told him in English, in French, and in every Vietnamese dialect he knew. And his suffering continued.

He didn't know whether the officer in charge finally ordered him to be released from the straps because of the possibility that he would die, and never be of any use, or because he had grown bored with the proceedings. Either way, the end finally came. Lewis couldn't walk back to the hut. He had to be dragged, leaving a trail of blood, bile, and feces in his wake.

He knew it would happen again. It would happen again and again until he was broken and until he not only gave them all the military information he possessed, but until he also agreed to sign statements admitting that he was a war criminal, and that his country had perpetrated war crimes against the Vietnamese people.

He had to escape. Even if he just crawled away to die in the swamps. He had to escape and he couldn't even move.

All through the rest of the day he lay on the floor of the hut. At one point someone brought him water and a bowl of rice. He tried desperately to eat, but he only gagged and brought back every mouthful that he succeeded in swallowing. The wound in his shoulder had crusted over with

92

dried blood. His left arm was useless. Unlike the rest of his body, he couldn't feel pain in it. He sniffed at it, wondering when signs of gangrene would begin to show, wondering what would happen to him when they did.

The guards at the door of his hut had changed. Dusk fell. He heard a radio. Over a roar of static, Radio Hanoi's "Hanoi Hannah" was describing how massive U.S. forces had been "decimated", how innumerable U.S. ships had been sunk and aircraft shot down.

As Lewis listened to the two obligatory American pop songs that followed the news item, included in the hope of persuading American servicemen to tune in to Hanoi, Lewis became aware that the new guards had moved some distance from the door of the hut, presumably to listen to the radio better, and that he was unmanacled. He was being given his chance, and even though his limbs were swollen and racked with pain, he had to take it.

He forced himself onto his knees and inched toward the door of the hut. As far as the Viet Cong were concerned, it was obviously recreation hour. They were all gathered around the radio, listening intently. The men who had been standing guard over him were only a few yards away, but their backs were to him. Could he do it? Could he simply crawl away? Even if he wasn't spotted, it would be only a matter of five or ten minutes before his disappearance was discovered. They would know almost immediately. But it was dark. And the forest was dense. It might be possible. And he had nothing to lose. Stealthily, hardly able to believe that he could have even gotten to the door of the hut without attracting attention, he lay flat on the ground and wriggled outside. Every movement was unspeakable agony. It was impossible for him to lift his right arm above his head in an effort to haul himself onward. He had to be content with clawing at the ground, one-handed, and digging his toes into the earth for leverage. But he was moving. He was heading away from the hut, away from the compound and the gathered, listening men, and toward the pitch-black immensity of the forest.

Over the radio's static Elvis Presley gave way to Joan Baez. "Christ Almighty," he said to himself as he cleared the beaten earth of the camp and burrowed into waist-high vegetation. "Don't they know she's singing an antiwar song!"

The ground beneath him was becoming less firm. Moisture oozed through his fingers. Cautiously he raised himself to his knees, and then to his feet. He could no longer see the camp; he could no longer be seen. He headed off in a northeasterly direction, his feet sinking ankle depth into mud at every step. A snake that he could not see, but only sense, slithered across his feet. And then he heard commotion behind him.

He began to run, his left arm hanging uselessly at his side, his swollen ankle and knee and elbow joints screaming out in protest. He was sinking deep into the mire with every step. The ground was pulling him downward, drawing him back.

He could hear the Viet Cong bursting into the forest behind him and he forced himself to go on, knowing that he had a lead of about fifty yards maximum. Water gleamed dully in the darkness. He headed toward it, floundering into its depths. If he could submerge himself, breathe through reeds, then he still might escape.

The water was a mere sheen covering swampland. Something hideous and nameless coiled itself around his legs and began to tighten its hold, dragging him downwards. He twisted and turned to free himself, and as he did so he began to sink down into the morass. He was embroiled up to his waist, and then his armpits. *"No!"* he yelled out hoarsely, knowing that the creature wrapped about his legs was about to be the victor. *"For Christ's sake, no!"*

The Viet Cong surged from between the trees. Hands grasped hold of him. He was being torn apart at the waist. One of the black-pajama-clad figures leaned toward him and then thrust his AK-47 beneath the surface of the water and fired. The threshing, unseen weight around his legs was stilled. Like a beached whale he was dragged, bleeding and broken, onto firm ground.

Early the next morning he was transferred from the hut to a bamboo punishment cage. It measured a bare four feet by six feet and was just high enough for him to sit up in it.

And there he stayed. He wasn't taken out for exercise. He wasn't taken out to go to the latrine. There was no shade from the sun by day, and no shelter from the cold by night. His wound stank with putrefaction, but to his everlasting amazement the arm did not turn gangrenous and did not have to be amputated.

Day followed day, and week followed week, and month followed month. When he was taken out of the cage, a little while before Christmas, it was so that he could once more be questioned. And tortured. That was the first time he broke. Not outwardly but inwardly. They tied up his elbows again until they touched; they ruptured an eardrum; they beat him with bamboo rods. And when at last they threw him, more dead than alive, back into the cage, he closed his fingers around the bars and he thought of Christmas in California. He thought of turkey and hot showers and soft beds. And he thought of Abbra, and how it was going to be years before he'd see her again. If he ever saw her again. And he lowered his head to his hands, and wept.

CHAPTER FIVE

The Huey never made it to the ground. It smashed into the jungle canopy, hanging vertically, a bomb just waiting to detonate. Kyle pushed himself bloodily away from the control panel and yelled at his copilot to get the hell out. There was no reply. One of the bullets had smashed the Huey's Plexiglas bubble and hit him between the eyes.

Kyle didn't hang around. He had only seconds to escape before the Huey exploded and he did not waste one of the them. He was out of his harness, out of the crippled ship, falling and tumbling through the thick foliage to the ground.

When the Huey blew the blast rocketed him for thirty yards. His helmet had been torn off and his hair and his flak jacket were on fire, he felt as if he had broken every bone in his body, and as he rolled in hellish agony on the ground he was aware that half a dozen North Vietnamese Army regulars were running forward toward him. He struggled to reach for his pistol and failed.

His hand wouldn't move. His arm wouldn't move. He didn't know if it had been broken, or if it had been shot off or ripped off. He knew only that the flames were no longer picturesque and that he was in danger of becoming the barbecue dish of the day.

He rolled on the ground, struggling to reach for his pistol with his left hand, but where his pistol should have been there was nothing. Blaspheming viciously, expecting a round of machine-gun fire to blast him into eternity at any moment, he beat at the flames engulfing his head with his good arm.

No machine-gun blast came. He was surrounded. The flames leaping from his flight suit were extinguished. His scalp felt as if it were leaving the top of his head, but his hair was no longer on fire. High above him, coming under a slaughtering barrage of artillery fire, a Huey circled desperately. He knew who was at the controls. Chuck, risking his own neck in a suicidal attempt at rescue. He could see the Huey take fire, veer and dip.

"Get the hell out, you dumb bastard!" he yelled skyward as his boots were yanked from his feet and he was searched for weapons.

For the first time since he had hurled himself from his ship he could take mental stock of his injuries. His right arm was still attached to his body but was broken, the bone projecting unnaturally at the elbow. His back was burned, but he had no way of knowing how badly, and his scalp and face were also burned.

He was alive though. He clenched his teeth as he was ordered to his feet, wondering how the hell he was going to survive the pain of his burns without proper medication. He was alive, but he was also injured ... God only knew where on the Cambodian-Laos-'Nam border ... and a prisoner. He was, in short, in the biggest crock of shit he'd ever been in in his entire life.

The ground was littered with the bodies of the reconnaissance party, shot down as they had tried to board the Hueys. Kyle could see a couple of ARVN soldiers being herded away from the site at gunpoint, but he could see no other American survivors.

"You're on your own, baby," he told himself grimly, fighting against waves of pain and faintness and nausea. And in Saigon, Trinh would be on her own too.

Long before they had cleared the scene of carnage he collapsed. When he fleetingly floated back to consciousness he was aware of being carried on a stretcher. For a crazy moment he thought it was a regulation U.S. army stretcher and that he was on his way to a blissfully civilized, sanitized U.S. army hospital. And then he saw the khaki-uniformed pith-helmeted Asians carrying him and he wondered why they were going to such lengths to keep him alive, and what it was they intended doing with him.

The burns on his back were unbearable and for nearly two weeks he was able to think of nothing else. The NVA treated him by coating the burns with a mixture of leaves and gunge. When he weakly protested that the leaves would cause infection, he was told that the leaves possessed a special healing quality. What was in the gunge he never found out, and looking at the sickly mess, he thought it better that he didn't know.

His arm was bound tight against his chest and though awkward was the least of his troubles. His main concern, once his flesh began to heal, were the puckered scars on his forehead and temples. Would Trinh find them physically repulsive? He thought not. Serry would, but then, he wasn't in love with Serry anymore. He wondered how she would react to the news that he had been shot down. Her asshole of a brother would probably leap so high for joy he'd hit the fucking moon.

Since his capture, they'd rested only at night. The NVA kept on moving, traveling north. They were in a high mountainous area, and he suspected that they were in Laos, not 'Nam. Wherever they were, there were no U.S. troops on the ground and the farther they traveled, the less chance there was of them running into any, and of him being rescued by them. Occasionally planes would fly over, but the Viet Cong had ears like dogs and were always in deep cover before aircraft were directly overhead.

"For Christ's sake!" he said exasperatedly as they plowed on through another long, hot, insect-ridden day. "Where the hell are we *going*?"

It was a question he had asked a hundred times before. For the first time he received a reply. "Hanoi," the Vietnamese at his side said succinctly. "We go to Hanoi."

Kyle stumbled and nearly fell. "We're *walking* there?"

The Vietnamese grinned. "We walk from north of Vietnam to south, and from south to north many times," he said in commendable English. "Walking to Hanoi on Ho Chi Minh trail is holiday. Vacation."

"Not for me it isn't," Kyle muttered grimly. He knew now where he was being taken. To Hoa Lo prison, North Vietnam's main penitentiary.

The ARVN troops who had been taken prisoner with him had been left in one of the Montagnard villages that they had passed through. Now he knew why. Their status didn't warrant the long march to a prison used primarily for shot-down and captured U.S. fighter pilots.

"And how long is it going to take us to walk to

100

Hanoi?" he asked, sweat pouring down his face as they threaded their way through terrain thick with rotting vegetation.

"Twelve weeks, thirteen weeks," the Vietnamese replied. He had a Soviet Kalashnikov AK-47 slung around his neck, and Kyle knew that if he made one false move he would be in the rifle's sights and it would be good-bye world forever.

All of the soldiers were Russian armed. The AK-47 was their basic weapon, but there was also a scattering of Type 56 assault rifles and one man even carried an RPG-7 antitank missile launcher.

Kyle thought constantly about overpowering one of the North Vietnamese and fighting his way free with a captured weapon. So far he'd had no chance, but he was constantly on the watch for one. He certainly didn't want to find himself incarcerated in Hoa Lo. Once in there, he might never see the light of day again.

Although the trail ran through rugged, mountainous country, they quite frequently met with parties of soldiers and peasants ferrying supplies south. The sacks of rice and crates of military hardware were strapped to bicycles, some of them modified with a length of bamboo attached to the handlebar and seat column, enabling the bicycle to be controlled by a man walking alongside it, even over the roughest ground.

Whenever such a party was sighted, his captors would slip a rope around Kyle's neck and lead him, animal-like. "Why the hell is this necessary?" he fumed, hating the humiliation of if. "You have AK-47's and Type 56 assault rifles leveled at my head all the time! You don't need to tether me as well!" He was never answered, but he knew why the rope was considered necessary. It wasn't enough for him merely to be their prisoner. He had also to be cowed and subjugated, and though he felt very far from being either, the rope around his neck gave him the appearance of being so.

As they climbed higher the terrain changed, the vegetation thinned, the dense foliage giving way to forests of pines. Their only food, apart from fruit and berries gathered as they trekked, was rice. Every soldier carried his own supply in a cotton tube slung over one shoulder and under the opposite arm. At night they slept on hammocks slung between the trees. They passed through no more villages, but the traffic on the trail grew heavier. There were carts and trucks as well as bicycles, as bombing raids by U.S. aircraft became frequent.

He had been exultant when the first F-4 Phantoms screamed overhead, raining down orange-sized incendiary bombs. The bomblets were packed inside a canister and burst open immediately after release from the aircraft, seeding a large area. They were impossible to hide from, the only defense against them being to pray like the devil that they wouldn't drop on his patch of ground.

After he had spent a half dozen heart-stopping occasions waiting for a raid to come to a conclusion, his reaction became far less enthusiastic. Apart from human victims, the damage they caused was minimal. The trail was still roadworthy. Trucks, even if they were hit, were always miraculously repaired. Traffic on the trail continued with a dogged persistence that Kyle could only reluctantly admire.

Intermittently, as the altitude began to decrease and as they crossed the border into North Vietnam, there were antiaircraft units and supply dumps and maintenance depots by the side of what had now become a recognizable road.

"Soon there will be antiaircraft units and maintenance depots all the way into the South," one of his guards told him proudly. "Soon Ho Chi Minh Trail become a three-lane highway, just like you have in America."

They began to travel only at night, though even then U.S. planes flew overhead. Sometimes the planes were Phantoms, but more often they were air force gunships, converted transport aircraft fitted with low-light-level television, infrared sensors, ignition detectors, night observation scopes, and other electronic detection devices. But despite all their technological hardware, the traffic on the trail continued, ammunition, guns, and rice traveling in a near continuous flow from north to south.

"What is going to happen to me when we get to Hanoi?" Kyle asked the most talkative of his guards. He had a pretty good idea, but conversation of any sort was a relief to the constant monotony of walking, walking, walking.

"In Hanoi you will be very well treated," the guard said with a confidence that Kyle didn't share. "Vietnamese people realize you are not vicious imperialist aggressor but only a dupe of the imperialist American government. You will be educated to understand better."

"And then?" Kyle asked, mildly amused.

"And then you will be given your freedom. You will be able to tell other American soldiers of how they, too, are dupes of imperialist American government."

Kyle groaned. He had heard rumors about pilots tortured in Hanoi until they made confessions of "war crimes" that could be used by the North Vietnamese for propaganda. He needed to escape before he reached Hoa Lo prison, and his time was running out fast.

Nighttime would be best, he plotted as he plodded on under his captor's watchful eyes. The greatest handicap to a successful escape was the impossibility of merging among members of the local population. If he had been in France or Italy in the last war, then once he had initially escaped there would at least have been a chance of his staying free because, suitably dressed, he would have been indistinguishable from the natives. There was no such cover in Vietnam. In Vietnam, no matter how he dressed, he was immediately recognizable as a big white American. In daylight he would not be able to move twenty yards before the alarm was given and he was recaptured.

The risks were colossal but Kyle was determined to take them. He planned to make an attempt that very night. He would wait until the rest period, until he was taken into the vegetation at the side of the road to relieve himself. Then he would take his guard by surprise and overpower him, grabbing his weapon. What he would do after that, whether he would shoot it out with the remaining dozen or so soldiers or whether he would be able to steal off into the undergrowth undetected, he didn't know. He would play it by ear.

He was never given the chance. They had been on the trail only for an hour or two that night when two trucks, traveling south to north, drew up beside them. Seconds later he was being ordered at gunpoint into the rear of one of them. Some of the soldiers clambered aboard with him, grinning euphorically, while others boarded the second truck.

Kyle could have wept. There would be no more rest stops in the dark and at the side of the road. No more crazy, virtually impossible chances of escape. From now on escape was hopeless. He was traveling at high speed towards Hoa Lo, and there wasn't a damn thing in the world that he could do about it.

He closed his eyes and leaned his head back against the tarpaulin, wondering how he could get a message to Trinh, how he was going to survive incarceration, how long it would be before he was once again free.

Although the tarpaulin covers were still down

early the next morning, he knew that they were now driving over asphalt instead of the rough road surface. Obviously they were very close to Hanoi, possibly even in Hanoi. At what he took to be a roadblock, they stopped for a few minutes. A uniformed figure flicked back the tarpaulin and gazed at Kyle in hostile curiosity. Then the tarpaulin was replaced and the journey continued. He could hear the sound of other motor vehicles. Jeeps and motorcycles.

They halted again, and this time the soldiers who had escorted him all the way from the Laos-Cambodia-'Nam border were gestured out into the road and two impassive-faced soldiers he had never seen before took their place, their rifles cocked. Kyle felt a pang of regret at his abrupt separation from his erstwhile companions. At least he had come to know what to expect from them. He didn't know what the hell to expect from his new guards, or the guards who awaited him Hoa Lo.

The tarpaulin hadn't been securely replaced, and he glimpsed the embankment of a large river and the houses and streets of a city. The truck began to slow down. There were trees and then a high concrete wall topped with shards of broken glass and a triple strand of barbed wire. The truck came to a halt. He had arrived. He was at Hoa Lo. And in another few minutes he would be inside. Perhaps for years. Perhaps forever.

The truck halted for a second and there was the sound of massive gates creaking open. Slowly the truck rumbled forward again for a few yards and then came to a halt. Behind them the gates grated and slammed shut.

It was the most terrible sound that Kyle had ever heard.

Minutes passed and then the tarpaulin was lifted back by a Vietnamese wearing the uniform and insignia of an officer. He spoke sharply to the two soldiers in the truck, and they leapt to their feet, prodding Kyle out of the truck at rifle point.

His first impression was of how cold it was. Ever since he had arrived in Vietnam he had sweltered in almost unbearable heat. Now, in Hoa Lo, he shivered in the damp, chill air. He was at the entrance of what looked to be a long tunnel. The officer turned, leading the way into it, and Kyle saw that it was an underpass running beneath part of the great, gaunt building that stood above it.

At the end of the underpass were yet more gates. They were double gates made of heavy iron. Kyle had never heard of any captured Americans escaping from Hoa Lo, and the reason was obvious. Hoa Lo was escape-proof.

Beyond the gates was a bare courtyard about a hundred feet long and sixty or seventy feet wide, paved with worn cement. The buildings surrounding the courtyard were of grimy white stucco and the windows were few and high. Looking upward, Kyle could see that they were glassless and barred with double steel grating. He clenched his jaw. Being imprisoned in Hoa Lo would be awful, but he had to survive it. He had to think of Trinh and of what she would be suffering, not knowing what had happened to him or where he was.

He was marched to the far end of the court-yard, where there was yet another high double gate. It remained shut. Instead, he was led into the right-hand cell block, down a concrete-floored corridor, and through two sets of steel doors. There was no sign of other inmates, no noise except for the echoing resonance of the guards' booted feet. A cell door was thrown open and he was shoved inside.

It was then that his heart really sank, then that he experienced his first real wave of panic. The cell was barely seven feet by seven feet, and it was totally empty except for a sleeping pallet and a slop bucket. Ever since he had figured out where he was being taken, he had anticipated at least being with other Americans. He knew what his own strengths and weaknesses were. He could fly into the jaws of hell if necessary, with crazy, daredevil defiance, but he couldn't face the thought of being locked away alone.

He gritted his teeth, knowing damn well that if the bastards suspected how much he hated solitary they would keep him in it permanently. As it was, he would be alone only until after he had been questioned. Such a tactic was routine. A nerve began to tick at the corner of his jaw. What might not be so routine was the method of questioning. He had been captive now for over three months and he had suffered nothing worse than shouted insults and the prods of rifle butts.

He had been lucky. Unless he was very much mistaken, his luck was fast beginning to run out.

He was ordered to strip out of the remnants of his uniform and was given two pairs of well-worn and well-washed shirts, two pairs of khaki trousers, two pairs of athletic shorts, two sets of underwear, and a belt. He sat on the edge of the low pallet, looking at the clothes in mild surprise. It was better than he had anticipated. At least the clothes were clean and the spare set indicated that they would be kept laundered.

He wondered if there was anyone in the adjoining cells and tapped experimentally on the wall behind him. Immediately a guard screamed at him through the inspection grate in the cell door. Kyle shrugged, seemingly unconcerned. He had achieved his object. His tap had sounded hollow and he was sure that the cells on either side of him were empty, which meant that the many pilots who had been shot down over the North, and imprisoned in Hoa Lo, were in another section of the prison, probably in the section beyond the double gates at the far end of the courtyard. The area he was in, then, was merely a reception area. His spirits lifted slightly ... perhaps his eventual cell might not be quite so small or so spartan ... and then immediately fell at the realization that he would find out only after he had been interrogated.

The questioning began the next morning, shortly after dawn. He was taken out of his cell and down the flaking whitewashed-walled corridor to a nearby room. In the center there was a table, behind which sat the officer who had led him from the truck into the prison. There were steel hooks in the ceiling of the room and ominous dark brown stains on the walls and on the concrete floor. Kyle tried not to imagine what the hooks might be for and what the stains had been caused by, and concentrated instead on feeling nothing but contempt for the diminutive Vietnamese who had him so totally in his power.

"Your name?" the officer asked curtly in heavily accented English.

"Anderson."

"Your full name?"

"Kyle Royd Anderson."

"Your rank, service number, and date of birth?"

Kyle answered equally curtly. There was a moment's silence. He had given all the information that the Code of Conduct allowed and his interrogator was obviously well aware that he had done so. When he spoke again there was a more menacing tone in his voice.

"The name of your division?"

"I'm not obliged to answer that question."

"I ask you again, the name of your division?"

Kyle eyeballed him. "Under the American Code of Conduct I'm not obliged to answer that question."

There wasn't a flicker of emotion on the officer's impassive face. "The American Code of Conduct is not recognized in the Democratic Republic of Vietnam," he said stonily. "Please answer the questions you are asked. The name of

110

your division?"

For a fleeting second Kyle was tempted to avoid what was obviously going to happen and to tell him. After all, he wasn't a duty, honour and country West Point grad. He hadn't been flying helicopters out of patriotism. He had been flying them for kicks, for the sheer hell of it. What difference would it make if the obnoxious bastard questioning him learned the name of his division? It was hardly information that would enable Hanoi to win the war. If he had been a fighter pilot with a knowledge of future targets, then he could understand the importance of keeping what he knew to himself. But he wasn't a fighter pilot. He was a chopper jock, and nothing he knew could be of the slightest help to the North Vietnamese war effort. The temptation came and went. He was also an American and he had never yet been shit scared of anyone or anything.

"The name of your division?" the officer repeated.

"I'm not obliged to answer that question," Kyle said again.

"But you will answer my question. You will answer all my questions," the officer said, rising to his feet. For a disbelieving moment Kyle thought the interview had come to an end, and then the officer continued. "Many Americans before you have stood where you stand now. They, too, have always said that they would not answer my questions." He paused and gave a shadow of a smile. "They always have. Eventually." He began to walk toward the door. "I am going to let you think about what I have just said. When I come back I will ask the same question again. It will be in your best interests for you to give me an answer."

The door closed behind him, the guards remaining in the room. Despite the cool dampness of the walls a bead of sweat trickled down the nape of Kyle's neck. He had never been a coward, but he could think of better ways of spending his time than sitting in a room where blood had obviously been spilled, waiting for the moment when his own blood would, in all likelihood, mingle with the stains on the walls and the floor.

His interrogator was gone for what Kyle judged to be thirty or thirty-five minutes. When he returned he sat once more behind the table, resting his clasped hands lightly in front of him. "You have now had time to think," he said, his voice bereft of any inflection whatsoever. "I will ask you again. What is the name of your division?"

Kyle knew that if he told him, it wouldn't end there. There would be other questions, hundreds of them. "I'm not obliged to answer that question." Contempt and defiance oozed from his every pore.

The officer smiled thinly. "You are very foolish," he said and nodded toward the guards at the door.

Behind him Kyle heard the door open and two sets of footsteps approach. He clenched his knuckles until they were white. The bastards could do whatever they wanted, but he wouldn't give them the satisfaction of seeing him break. He would die before allowing them to gloat over him.

His arms were wrenched behind him and his mouth tightened. His broken arm had mended while he had been on the trail north, but he was still protective of it. His elbows were strapped together and then his wrists. He gritted his teeth against the pain as his chest was forced outward. He had expected something different. He had expected them to make play of the barely healed skin on his back and head. Shackles were fastened around his ankles and then his legs were splayed out and a bar was run through the shackles to keep them that way.

Trinh, he thought. *I must think of Trinh.*

The strap was brought down and beneath the bar and then pulled, yanking the bar upward and forcing him into a contorted ball. He closed his eyes, fighting the cries that rose in his throat. He thought of Trinh, gentle-eyed and tender; he thought of her mischievous sense of fun, her beguiling naïveté.

His bones were being wrenched from their sockets, his muscles and tendons were being torn apart. He couldn't think of Trinh any longer. He thought only of wanting the excruciating agony to end.

It didn't end. It grew worse. Time no longer had any meaning. Periodically the straps would be released and his circulation would start to flow again, the pain as it did so almost as intense as that of the torture. He would be asked if he would now answer the questions put to him. Each time he refused, his interrogator would take another cigarette from the packet on the table and nod to his henchmen to restrap and shackle him and the agony would begin again.

At one time he thought the room was getting darker, as if night were approaching. Perhaps it was. Perhaps he had been in hell the whole day. Or perhaps the room seemed dark because his eyes were full of blood.

He had vowed that he would die before allowing his torturers to gloat over his capitulation. He knew now that they weren't going to allow him the luxury of death. The agony he was suffering would not kill him, it would simply continue for ever and ever and ever. And he couldn't endure it. No one could. Now, when he was restrapped, eyeball to eyeball with his ass, he was also beaten. Bamboo clubs rained on his shins and elbows and knees. Rubber-strip whips cut into the barely healed flesh of his back. Fists smashed into his face. He vomited and kept vomiting and when he could croak out a sound other than a scream of pain, he pleaded with them for the pain to stop. And he promised to tell them anything that they wanted to know.

Afterward, alone in his cell, he wept. The bastards had broken him. The information he had been able to give them had been minimal. But it would have made no difference if it had been top secret. He would still have given it. And the knowledge filled him with self-loathing.

For a week he was virtually ignored by his guards, and in that week something cold and rocklike entered into him. He had given into the bastards once, but he would not do so a second time. And there would be a second time, he was sure of it. It wasn't only military information that the North Vietnamese wanted from their prisoners. It was propaganda. The day would come when a uniformed figure would enter his cell and demand that he make a tape recording proclaiming how he repented of his war "crimes", and admitting to being a "Yankee imperialist aggressor". At the thought of his father, or Serry, listening to any such babblings, his resolve became obsessional. He wouldn't do it. He had sunk as low as he was going to sink, and he would be damned to hell for all eternity before he would sink any lower.

At the end of seven days he was removed from his cell and taken once more down the corridor and out into the courtyard. The double gates at the inner end of the courtyard were opened and he was led through them into yet another underpass. This time it wasn't a tunnel, but a roof between two one-story buildings. There was a further courtyard, slightly smaller than the first one, and to his intense relief he could see hands at the bars of the windows that looked out onto it.

He was marched across the courtyard and into the right-hand cell block. He could physically sense the nearness of other Americans and

115

nearly sobbed with disappointment when he was led into another empty cell. Within minutes of his being left alone there, there came a tapping on the wall. He answered it eagerly, euphoric at making contact. Was it a fellow G.I.? The tapping continued in carefully spaced out rhythms. Kyle listened intently. Was it Morse? Was the guy in the cell next to him tapping out the Morse code? Whenever a guard was in the vicinity the tapping stopped, only to be continued later, in the same insistent rhythms.

Over the next few days tapping came from the cell on the other side of him as well. It wasn't Morse, he had worked that out nearly immediately, but it was obviously a similar code by which his fellow prisoners were communicating with each other. An alphabet code. And in order to participate, all he had to do was crack it.

He was still trying to fathom it out when he was moved from his cell and put in with another prisoner. His initial delight was slightly tempered by the fact that his fellow prisoner, a radar intercept officer who had been shot down in an F-4 Phantom, was sullen and uncommunicative and obviously suffering from some kind of mental breakdown. He had been a prisoner for eighteen months, and though Kyle could not get him to talk about himself, he did manage to get from him the key to the wall-tapping code.

The code was called the Smithy Harris code, and was named after the prisoner who had devised it. It was based on a crossword puzzle of letters, five lines down and five across. The first line across was A-B-C-D-E. To spell out a word containing one of these letters you made a tap on the wall to indicate that it was in the first line across, then paused and quickly tapped out one for A, two for B, and so on. The second line was F-G-H-I-J. Two taps indicated that the letter was in the second line, and then the taps followed the same pattern as for the first line. The letter K was not used at all, the letter C being used as a substitute in order to keep the letters to twenty-five, and not twenty-six.

The code transformed Kyle's life. Information could be passed and received around the prison. Conversations could be conducted via the walls. He discovered that as a helicopter jock he was a rarity in Hoa Lo, but that he wasn't alone in having capitulated to torture. The knowledge came as a kind of relief, but did not alter his fierce determination to withstand anything in the future rather than become a propaganda tool.

Tapping messages out, and receiving them, took painstaking time. Y-O-U A-R-E N-O-W I-N H-E-A-R-T-B-R-E-A-C H-O-T-E-L, his neighbor in the next cell tapped out to him when he first understood and began to use the code. T-H-E P-R-I-S-O-N A-S A W-H-O-L-E I-S C-N-O-W-N A-S T-H-E H-A-N-O-I H-I-L-T-O-N. T-H-E S-E-C-T-I-O-N W-H-E-R-E Y-O-U W-E-R-E I-N-T-E-R-R-O-G-A-T-E-D I-S N-E-W G-U-Y V-I-L-L-A-G-E. T-H-E-R-E A-R-E T-W-O M-O-R-E M-A-I-N S-E-C-T-I-O-N-S T-O T-H-E P-R-I-S-O-N. O-N-E O-F T-H-E-M I-S F-O-R W-H-E-N W-E M-O-V-E O-U-T O-F H-E-A-R-T-

117

B-R-E-A-C, W-H-I-C-H I-S U-S-E-D A-S A R-E-C-E-I-V-I-N-G S-T-A-T-I-O-N. T-H-E O-T-H-E-R I-S L-A-S V-E-G-A-S A-R-E-A.

W-H-A-T I-S L-A-S V-E-G-A-S A-R-E-A? he tapped back, none too happy at the thought that if he was still in the receiving area, there were still, presumably, question sessions to undergo.

L-A-S V-E-G-A-S I-S A C-I-L-L-E-R came back through the wall. I-T I-S U-S-E-D F-O-R P-E-R-I-O-D-S O-F L-O-N-G A-N-D B-R-U-T-A-L I-N-C-A-R-C-E-R-A-T-I-O-N. Y-O-U A-R-E B-E-T-T-E-R O-F-F H-E-R-E O-R I-N N-E-W G-U-Y T-H-A-N I-N V-E-G-A-S.

Kyle found it hard to believe that treatment anywhere in the Hilton could be worse than what he had received in New Guy Village. A chill ran down his spine. His decision not to cooperate if asked to make statements that could be used by the North Vietnamese for propaganda purposes would very likely lead him, eventually, into Las Vegas. It wasn't a prospect to look forward to, and he tried hard not to think about it, concentrating instead on culling every little bit of information he could via the wall taps.

He was asked to memorize the names of every man known to be imprisoned, so that if he were sent to another camp he could pass on all the names that he knew, and add new ones to the list. That way, if anyone escaped or was unexpectedly released, he could carry the names back to the States. There were over three hundred names and he memorized them all, in alphabetical order.

118

It came as a surprise to him to learn that some-where on the route north Christmas had come and gone without him being aware of it. He wondered how Trinh had celebrated it, and remembering the family ancestral altar he had seen in her home, with candles flickering beside it, he wondered if she was perhaps more Buddhist than Catholic, and if she would have celebrated it at all.

Serry would have celebrated it. Serry would have been at Bedingham. He only had to close his eyes to imagine every aspect of Serry's Christmas. There would be a huge, decorated tree in the yellow and white formal living room. There would be log fires, holly and mistletoe, mince pies and mulled wine and carol singers. And if it hadn't been for her brother's stupidity on their wedding day, he would probably have been there, sharing it all with her. And he would never have met Trinh.

Despite his physical discomfort a smile tugged at the corner of his mouth. Trinh. God, but he loved her. When the present nightmare was over, he would track her down, wherever she might be. He would take her back to the States with him. Trinh was the only good thing to have come out of his time in Vietnam. Trinh, and his friend-ship with Chuck.

He sat on the low pallet in the cell, smoking one of the three cigarettes a day that were given them in Heartbreak. Chuck would tell Trinh that he had been shot down, and that he had not simply abandoned her. Chuck knew how serious they were about each other. He knew that their affair was not just the usual easy-come-easy-go arrangement enjoyed by the vast majority of Americans in 'Nam. He would have contrived a two-day pass to Saigon and would have gone straight to the International to tell her what had happened.

She would be waiting for him. She wasn't Serry, who he couldn't imagine waiting faithfully for anyone for even twenty-four hours. She was loyal and steadfast, and he was certain that she would wait years for him if necessary.

His body never recovered from the severity of the torture he had undergone on his arrival, and all through the long, tedious, pain-filled days of spring, the knowledge that Trinh was waiting for him sustained him.

He wasn't taken for questioning again for a long time. He knew the reason. New prisoners were being processed through New Guy Village and into Heartbreak thick and fast. America was obviously escalating the air war and the information to be obtained from shot-down B-52 and F-4 Phantom pilots was far superior to any that could be extracted from a mere helicopter pilot.

When they came for him again, it wasn't to try to extract further military information. It was to force him to make a written "confession" that Hanoi could use for the purpose of anti-American propaganda.

It was just the beginning of the end for him, and he knew it. J-U-S-T D-O Y-O-U-R B-E-S-T fellow prisoners had tapped through the walls to him. T-H-E B-A-S-T-A-R-D-S W-I-L-L B-R-E-A-C Y-O-U. T-H-E-Y B-R-E-A-C E-V-E-R-Y-O-N-E E-V-E-N-T-U-A-L-L-Y. J-U-S-T D-O-N-T G-I-V-E I-N T-O T-H-E-M R-I-G-H-T A-W-A-Y. T-A-C-E A-S M-U-C-H A-S Y-O-U C-A-N F-I-R-S-T.

Kyle had no intention of giving in to them at all. He was taken to Room 19. It had been christened the Knobby Room by men unfortunate enough to have been questioned there. The nickname came from the fist-sized knobs of plaster on the walls designed to absorb the sound of screams.

The routine was exactly the same as it had been at his earlier interrogation. He was asked to write a statement confessing to war crimes. He refused. He was asked again, and at his second refusal his arms were once more yanked behind him and strapped tight and high at the elbows, almost separating his shoulder blades. His legs were forced into spurlike shackles, and a pipe and strong rope were used to lock his ankles into place.

As the pain intensified he struggled against it with mental strength. He would not write a statement that could be broadcast by Hanoi Radio. He would not. He would not. *He would not!*

When they returned him to his cell he was unconscious. His mute cellmate shook and shuddered, doing nothing to help him, terrified that he himself might be subjected to the same treatment.

The next day they came for him again. And the

next. And the next.

T-H-R-O-W I-N T-H-E T-O-W-E-L C-I-D came the instructions via the tap code. Y-O-U H-A-V-E D-O-N-E Y-O-U-R B-E-S-T. D-O-N-T L-E-T T-H-E B-A-S-T-A-R-D-S C-I-L-L Y-O-U.

He couldn't throw the towel in. He was obsessed with shame at how easily he had capitulated when first under torture. He wouldn't give, in to them again. He would endure all the fires of hell, but he vowed not to become a coward or a traitor.

Y-O-U C-A-N-T D-O A-N-Y M-O-R-E C-I-D the tap code repeated time and time again. N-O O-N-E I-S G-O-I-N-G T-O T-H-I-N-K A-N-Y L-E-S-S O-F Y-O-U F-O-R M-A-C-I-N-G P-R-O-P-A-G-A-N-D-A S-T-A-T-E-M-E-N-T-S F-O-R T-H-E-M. T-H-E W-H-O-L-E W-O-R-L-D W-I-L-L C-N-O-W I-T W-A-S O-B-T-A-I-N-E-D U-N-D-E-R T-O-R-T-U-R-E.

Kyle was no longer able to tap messages back. His fingers were broken, his nails wrenched from their beds. Somewhere in the part of his mind that was still functioning he knew he was being a fool. They were killing him by inches. He would never see Trinh again, never be able to take her to America. The knowledge made no difference. He was obsessed by his vow. Consumed by it. He would not be paraded before the world at large as a groveling, humiliated traitor. He would die first. And he knew he was going to die soon.

They threw him in a cell in Vegas. He was

deprived of sleep, deprived of food and water, and no comforting messages came through the walls. The scar tissue on his back had been sliced open by rubber whips and was festering and crawling with worms; he was covered in boils; every joint in his body was dislocated.

Then they took him into Room 18. The Meathook Room. He knew what they were going to do to him, and he knew he couldn't survive it. He thought of Trinh, of how her world would collapse when he did not return for her.

He was no longer screaming. He couldn't scream anymore. He could barely whimper. He thought of Serry as she had looked the day they had met at Bedingham, her pale gold hair falling water-straight to her waist. Serry, tall and high-breasted and magnificent, her crystal-gray eyes alight with joyous recklessness.

From a far distance he could hear the sound of Mick Jagger singing, and feel the warmth of the sun on his face as it filtered through the heavily laden branches of the beech trees. Then there was nothing. No music. No sunlight. He was flying. Flying higher than he had every flown before.

CHAPTER SIX

Gavin's emotions were in turmoil the five days that he spent with Dinh in the tunnels of Cu Chi. His main worry was Gabrielle. Somehow he had to let her know that he was alive and safe, yet he had no reliable means of doing so. Nhu would certainly write Gaby that he had been going to meet Dinh, but he was convinced that Nhu did not know Dinh planned to abduct him, and that she would be as alarmed and perplexed by his continuing absence as Gaby.

Dinh promised him that Nhu had been told about the mission, and that he was alive and well. Gavin hoped and prayed that he was speaking the truth.

"Because of the urgency with which my report is being awaited in Hanoi, our trek north will not be as arduous as it has been for me in the past," Dinh said to him in a moment of rare confidence. "Once we leave the Iron Triangle we will travel most of the way by jeep."

Tingles prickled down Gavin's spine. He had heard the phrase "Iron Triangle" before, on American lips. The area was rumored to cover sixty square miles, and ever since World War II it had been a refuge for antigovernment forces. The area was cut by marshes and swamps and

124

open rice paddies, and huge stretches of forest so thick that only foot trails could penetrate them, making penetration by American and South Vietnamese forces nearly impossible. It was in this area, to the northwest of Saigon and bordering the Cambodian border, that the Office of South Vietnam was rumored to have its headquarters. Was that where they were going? To COSVN? To Viet Cong headquarters?

He knew better than to ask. Vietnamese were secretive by nature, and asking would end Dinh's quite extraordinary candor. The mystery of the COSVN's location obsessed the Americans. Jimmy Giddings had spoken of it as if it were a miniature Pentagon buried deep in the jungle, though when he had done so, Paul Dulles had corrected him, saying that in his opinion COSVN wasn't a place or a building, but that it was people.

Whatever it was, the Americans had gone to enormous lengths to find it and to bomb it into oblivion. So far, unsuccessfully. And now Gavin was probably going to walk right into it. If he had to wait a year before he could file his story, it would be worthwhile. He would have the scoop of a lifetime.

In the five days he spent in the tunnels, the area came under American surveillance three times. The first time, as U.S. troops swarmed over the ground above them, they were so near that Gavin could smell their aftershave lotion.

"How can they not sense our presence?" he whispered to Dinh as the troops moved away, oblivious that they had been within feet of a North Vietnamese Army platoon, and an entire regiment of Viet Cong.

A slight smile touched Dinh's hard, straight mouth. "Americans are not attuned to the earth as we Vietnamese. They look for the obvious. Even when they do stumble onto a tunnel entrance, it does not occur to them that it is anything but a short, underground bolt-hole. The trapdoors leading into the main complex are rarely discovered." He paused, his eyes gleaming in the light from the makeshift oil lamp. "And when they are, the discoverer does not usually live to tell the tale."

Two days later Gavin saw first-hand what happened when a tunnel entrance was discovered. He and Dinh, and the handful of NVA men who were with Dinh, had been moving steadily through the tunnels in a northwesterly direction. The other occupants of the labyrinthine tunnel system were all Viet Cong. Their numbers staggered Gavin. Entire platoons were moving with ease beneath ground that was rigorously patrolled by South Vietnamese and American forces.

At one point they rested near a conference chamber where a small group of black-clad figures were in urgent conversation. On seeing Dinh, the leader of the group immediately approached him with slightly awed deference. Gavin could hear words that sounded like the name of a village, and then the Vietnamese name for Americans, but very little else. When the

126

men had returned to his waiting companions, Dinh turned toward Gavin with a slight shrug of irritation.

"We are going to be delayed. The man who just spoke to me is the political commissar of the local defence force. The Americans swooped on his village a little less than an hour ago and in their search they found a tunnel entrance. They have blown the trapdoor away and are at the moment waiting for reinforcements before attempting to explore it further."

"What will happen when they do? Will they simply lob dynamite down here?" Gavin asked, trying to sound casual about the prospect of being blasted into eternity.

"Our tunnels are too cleverly made for them to be able to cause much damage to the main complex from an entrance," Dinh replied, a glimmer of amusement in his voice. "We will go a little nearer and I will explain to you the steps that are being taken in order to turn events to our advantage."

They were back to wriggling, bellydown, through the narrow communication tunnels. Above him, vibrating through the dark red earth, Gavin could hear the *whump-whump-whump* of helicopter rotor blades. They went up a three-foot shaft and into another communication tunnel and then Dinh motioned for him to crawl into a side alcove. Ahead of them Gavin could dimly discern the dark shape of another figure, a Viet Cong with his back toward them, crouched and waiting.

127

Ten minutes passed and then, as the sweat began to run into Gavin's eyes, there came the vibration of voices and feet above them. No matter how many Americans had been brought in by helicopter, only one could enter the tunnel at a time. And when he did, the waiting Viet Cong would kill him.

Gavin began to shake. The situation was pure nightmare. He had to remain hunched and silent as an American slid into the tunnel to his death. If he called out he would probably be able to save him, but his own life would be forfeit.

There was the sound of a small earth fall, and Gavin knew the American was beginning his descent into the entrance shaft. All entrance shafts were shallow, little more than three feet in depth, and now Gavin saw why. The American had entered feet first, and as his feet touched the bottom of the shaft, and while his head and torso were still above ground, the Viet Cong several yards ahead of them fired at point-blank range into his undefended lower body.

Gavin clenched his nails so tight into his palms that he drew blood. At that moment he knew he had lost any innocence remaining to him. From now on he would feel, and be, old beyond his years.

There were cries of terror and agony from the wounded man, shouts of alarm from his comrades as they struggled to pull him free.

The Viet Cong in front of them had now turned toward them and was wriggling rapidly back down the tunnel toward the shaft leading into the lower communication tunnel. He paused, his hand flying once again to his pistol as he neared the side alcoves and he saw Gavin's pale, distinctly western face.

"*De ve nha,*" Dinh said softly. The Viet Cong stared hard at him for a moment and then continued his rapid retreat.

Gavin and Dinh followed hard on his heels. Behind him Gavin could hear the wounded American yelling desperately, "*For Christ's sake get me the hell outta here before that goddammed gook cuts off my balls!*"

Gavin knew damn well that when they did get him out, a barrage of firepower would be directed down the tunnel at their rear, and he propelled himself at top speed down the next, slightly deeper shaft, and into the second communications tunnel.

The Viet Cong had inserted himself into an alcove near the trapdoor above the shaft, and Gavin and Dinh wriggled past him like eels, not pausing until they had reached the trapdoor leading down into the main tunnel network.

"What happens now?" Gavin spat at him.

"If we are unlucky, they will throw gas canisters into the entrance shaft. The zigzag of the tunnels and the ventilation system will prevent the gas from poisoning the central complex, but there is not much chance that we would escape the fumes. If we are lucky, the Americans will do what they usually do. They will enter the first tunnel with the intention of rooting out whoever it was who injured their comrade."

From Dinh's words Gavin realized with shock that it was possible the Americans still had no idea the tunnel could be anything other than a small, localized hiding place big enough to give shelter to one or two guerrillas.

In the darkness he could sense rather than see Dinh's rare smile. "You will see that though we are now at a trapdoor leading down into the main tunnel system, this particular tunnel does not stop here. It continues on for another twenty-five yards."

"Where does it lead?" Gavin whispered, listening fearfully for sounds of action from the first shaft.

"It leads nowhere. And if my comrades' plans are successful, it is all the Americans will ever find."

There came the sound of first one pair of booted feet dropping cautiously to the floor of the first shaft, and then another.

"We must retreat to the main tunnel network to give my comrade room to maneuver. I will tell you what it is he is doing as he is doing it," Dinh said, opening the trapdoor and slithering down into the black hole beyond.

Gavin followed quickly. As far as he was concerned, Dinh could have explained the entire exercise verbally, without having risked both their lives by bringing him along to watch.

Gunfire reverberated from the first communications tunnel down into the tunnel in which they were lying. Earth showered over them and Gavin was gripped by a new fear, a fear so terrible it almost made him lose control of his bowels. What if hand grenades and dynamite were thrown into the tunnel? What if the earth fell down in a wall both behind and in front of them? What if they were buried alive?

"The Americans are now entering," Dinh whispered unnecessarily. "My comrade will have removed the trapdoor to the second shaft and will be crouched in it, waiting for them."

"And the gunfire?" Gavin whispered back, the blood pounding in his ears, his heart hammering so fast he thought it was going to give out.

"The Americans, firing down the tunnel ahead of them."

Gavin wiped dry red clay from his face. The bullets would not find their mark. Their target was not hiding in the darkness ahead of them, but was concealed in a shaft leading downward.

"What happens when the Americans crawl so far along the tunnel that they come to the shaft?"

"Wait," Dinh said, his voice tense. "And you will find out."

A split second later the roar of an AK-47 blasted Gavin's eardrums. The whole earth shook around them as first one clip was let off and then another. Screams tore through the dank, enclosed darkness, and Gavin could feel his self-control galloping away from him. He didn't know if the screams were from the Viet Cong or the Americans, and he didn't care. He was bathed in pure terror. He wanted out. He wanted out as he had never wanted out before.

Dinh had begun to move again, wriggling fast

and furiously deeper and deeper into the main tunnel network. When at last he reached an alcove and paused, he gasped out, "That moment, as the Americans approach the second shaft, is the most dangerous moment of all. If they had rolled a hand grenade ahead of them and it had fallen into the shaft, then our comrade would have been killed. As it was, he waited until they were nearly on top of him and then he jackknifed out of the shaft in front of them, taking them by surprise."

There came the sound of someone wriggling with practiced ease toward them, away from the hell of the continuing screams.

"It will be a long time before the Americans are able to remove their dead and wounded," Dinh said comfortably. "When they do, and when they pluck up the nerve to investigate again they will find the tunnel empty. The trapdoor to the second shaft will have been replaced, and will be indiscernible to them. They will simply crawl along the tunnel and into the decoy tunnel. At the far end of it they will find an escape hatch, assume that the guerrilla who inflicted the damage on them has escaped by it, and very thankfully regard their mission as complete. The dummy tunnel they have found will be dynamited and destroyed, and there will be no damage to the main network."

The guerrilla who had, single-handed, inflicted such horrendous damage on the Americans slithered abreast of them.

"*Khong xau*," Dinh said to him warmly.

Behind them, beyond the closed trapdoor, dull cries could still be heard. As Dinh and his comrade began to wriggle back toward the main complex of conference chamber and kitchen and sleeping chambers, Gavin followed them, consumed by horror and relief. He no longer felt like a journalist. He felt like a traitor. Not until he experienced an American bombing raid on Phu Hoa village some five days later did his sense of balance return.

They had left the tunnels behind them and their small party, consisting of himself and Dinh and two of Dinh's aides, had been traveling north westward at night, by bicycle.

"We will be able to replenish our supplies and rest at Phu Hoa," Dinh said to him as the night sky began to pearl to gray, presaging dawn. "I will also be able to renew some family contacts. A second cousin of mine is married to the local village chief and I have not seen her since we were children."

Gavin was trying to work out what the relationship between Gaby and the village chief's wife must be, when dawn broke in a blazing crack of yellow and orange and crimson-rose, and the planes came.

There was no warning. There had been no sounds of gunfire, no indication that any engagement was taking place in the vicinity between Viet Cong and ARVN or U.S. troops. In the early dawn light the countryside looked spectacularly beautiful and peaceful.

They were bicycling through a plantation of

133

banana and mango trees and there was very little low vegetation to hamper their progress. After the claustrophobia of the tunnels, the long night ride with humid air blowing soft against his face had been paradisiacal. In the light of the rising sun, Gavin could see a cluster of straw-thatched houses ahead. There would be breakfast of sorts. Eggs, if they were lucky, and almost certainly fruit. He was happy. He had survived what had to be the worst part of the ordeal, the tunnels at Cu Chi. He had established an amazingly close rapport with Dinh. And he had a news story that, when it was told, would establish his reputation as a war reporter.

It was Dinh who heard the planes first. "B-52s!" he yelled, throwing himself from his bicycle headlong onto the ground, his hands over his ears. Almost simultaneously the two young NVA officers riding with him followed suit. Gavin crashed to the ground a mere split second behind them. The planes never broke the early morning cloud cover. They could have been B-52s as Dinh averred. They could also have been Phantoms or F-105s. Whatever they were, they were unloading everything that they carried onto the unsuspecting village.

Even with his hands pressed tight over his ears, Gavin could hear the whistling of the bombs as they fell. "*Jesus, Mary and Joseph,*" he whispered beneath his breath, and then he was rocked almost senseless by the sound of the explosions. The ground heaved and kicked beneath him, giant fissures cracking wide. He dug his elbows and feet into the earth to gain some kind of purchase, but it was impossible. His body wouldn't adhere to the ground. He was plucked from it as if he were a dry leaf and carried amid a maelstrom of felled trees and gouged earth. When at last his body slammed back onto the ground he was fifty yards from where he had dived from his bicycle. There was no sign now of the bicycle. There was no sign of Dinh or the accompanying NVA officers. There was only a choking cloud of thick dust, the crackle of leaping flames, and the terrified screams of women and children.

He tried to crawl to his feet, but his legs wouldn't support him. Twice he stumbled and fell before managing to stay upright and run swaying toward the village and the flames and the screams. Through the dust and still-falling debris he saw Dinh and veered pantingly toward him.

"*Why?*" he shouted to him, unable to hear his own voice. Unable to hear anything. "*What was the provocation? The reason?*"

Dinh was shouting back at him, and like a lip-reader he read the words, "No reason! There doesn't have to be a reason! Perhaps a U.S. platoon is held down some miles from here and called in air support! Perhaps it is a matter of confused targeting! Perhaps it is a matter of the pilots merely off-loading their bombs! This, Comrade, is the war as suffered by the peasants. This is why you are here. To see and experience it."

While Dinh had been shouting across at him, they had been running in the direction of the village. The two young NVA officers were also on their feet and running. Their small party had miraculously sustained no injuries, but then, they had been on the periphery of the attack. It was the village that had sustained the full blast of the bombs.

They ran past the dead and dying buffalo, past terrified children running out into the banana and mango plantations away from the engulfing flames.

"Christ! What do we do when we *get* there!" Gavin yelled desperately. "We have no medical kits! No plasma! We can't get these people to a hospital!"

Dinh turned his head toward him and smiled. It was a terrible smile. "War is a different game without dust offs and quick evacuation to a military hospital, eh, Comrade?"

Gavin did not reply. They were among the injured who had managed to escape from the flames. A girl of about ten years old was laid on the ground, hideous gurgling noises coming from her throat. Her chest had been stoved in, the skin burnt and withered. One arm had been blown off just above the elbow joint, and though the upper portion of her face was still recognizable, the lower half was a nightmare of charred flesh.

Gavin fell on his knees beside her. He had nothing with which to ease her agony. There was not one damned thing that he could do for her.

"Oh God, oh Jesus!" he sobbed as Dinh grabbed hold of his arm, pulling him away, dragging him onward.

The dead and dying lay scattered over a wide area. Although dawn had only just broken, several of the men had already been making their way toward their rice paddies. A small boy whose task was to care for the family buffalo lay dead beside it in a dike, the rope with which the animal had been tethered still held tightly in his hand.

A Vietnamese wearing only a loose pair of cotton trousers ran through the mayhem toward them.

"See what they have done?" he cried to Dinh. "See what they have done to my village!"

He was weeping, beating his bony chest with his fists. "They have killed Sang! They have murdered the mother of my children!"

Dinh had his arms around him, hugging him tight, and then he was saying, "Where is she? Take me to her."

Gavin stumbled after them, aware that the distraught Vietnamese was obviously the village chief and that Sang must be the second cousin Dinh was so looking forward to seeing again.

She had been dragged clear of the flames engulfing the straw-thatched houses and lay on her back on the dusty ground, two small children clinging to her lifeless hand, sobbing fiercely.

Dinh knelt down beside her, his face a carved wooden mask. He felt for a pulse, a heartbeat, and then, his shoulders slumped, he slowly rose once more to his feet.

Gavin looked down at the dead woman. She had been no longer young and had the old, worn look of every peasant woman who was no longer in her early twenties. But her hair was still beautiful. Long and glossy-black, it lay spread around her like a fan.

Gavin felt his throat tighten. Somewhere, however distant, there had been a blood link between this woman and Gaby. Crazily, as he stood in the middle of the bombed and burning, obliterated Vietnamese village, the words of the seventeenth-century English poet and churchman John Donne came into his mind. "No man is an Island, entire of itself; every man is a piece of the Continent, a part of the main; if a *clod* be washed away by the sea, Europe is the less, as well as if a promontory were, as well as if a manor of thy friends or of thine own were; any man's death diminishes me, because I am involved in Mankind; And therefore never send to know for whom the bell tolls. It tolls for thee."

There was nothing more that could be done for Sang, but there were scores of other villagers who needed whatever primitive treatment could be given them.

For the rest of the morning he worked with Dinh, bathing wounds with freshly boiled water, bandaging with makeshift lengths of torn cloth, fixing splints with sawn-off lengths of bamboo. It had been countless hours since he had last slept, and as he wearily helped the villagers to bury their dead, Dinh said to him again, "This is why you are here, Comrade. To see and to report."

Gavin nodded and wiped the sweat from his eyes. The question Dinh would never answer was when would he be allowed to file his report.

They worked all through the long, hot day and then rested briefly with the still-dazed survivors. No one showed surprise that the attack had taken place. No one offered a reason for it. It was possible that the village had been destroyed by criminal accident, and it was equally possible that it had been destroyed because it was reported to be a Viet Cong stronghold. Gavin had no way of knowing which was the truth. He knew only that where the village had existed there was now only a charred crater. And that Sang and dozens of her neighbors had died a hideous and violent death.

At night he, Dinh and the two accompanying NVA officers set off once more, their bicycles freakishly unscathed, heading northwest, toward the Cambodian border and the Ho Chi Minh Trail.

During the following arduous days and nights his rapport with Dinh deepened. Dinh told him why he had decided to go north, and what life had been like for him in the first painful years away from his family.

"I am a southerner, Comrade. A Saigonese. Even after all these years of living in the North, I am still a Saigonese."

"Then what made you leave?" Gavin asked, excitement gripping his stomach muscles.

Dinh's conversation was almost always conducted in official Communist jargon. The words *comrade, imperialist*, and *puppet regime* peppered his every sentence. His present friendly simplicity indicated that confidences might be about to be shared.

"I left in order to be able to fight the French under the only man who appeared to me to be capable of doing so. That man was Vo Nguyen Giap. At Dien Bien Phu we achieved our success. When we raised our flag over the shattered French command post, all of us who had fought so hard to rid our land of foreign domination were euphoric. We thought that Vietnam would now be governed by officials of our choosing. But then came the Geneva agreement."

He paused for a long moment. They were sitting around a small campfire after a hard day's traveling. The two TVA officers had gone down to a nearby lake to try their luck at catching fish, and the only sound was that of insects in the surrounding undergrowth.

Gavin remained silent, waiting. At last Dinh said heavily, "Vietnam was to receive independence, but she was also to be temporarily partitioned at the seventeenth parallel until elections were held. The prime minister in the South, Ngo Dinh Diem, reneged on his promise to hold elections, knowing full well that if elections were held, Ho would be in and he would be out."

The flames crackled and spat. A small lizard ran across Gavin's booted foot. "Under Diem the government in the South became increasingly

140

oppressive. Men who had valiantly fought to free Vietnam of the French were regarded by Diem as rivals for power. They were hunted down and murdered. And it wasn't only those who actively fought the French who suffered. Very soon even his mildest supporters were herded into prison camps."

Gavin remembered the countless U.S. statesmen who had declared that South Vietnam was the model of a "free world democracy" which America was committed to defend against the "Communist threat". Had they known the truth? When President Kennedy had made his inaugural address and charismatically stated, "Let every nation know, whether it wishes us well or ill, that we shall pay any price, bear any burden, meet any hardship, support any friend, oppose any foe to assure the survival and the success of liberty," had he known what kind of government he was supporting in South Vietnam? Had he known the kind of "democracy" it was that he was calling on his countrymen to defend and to perhaps lay down their lives for? Gavin hoped passionately that he had not.

"It was then I knew that I could not return to Saigon," Dinh continued, staring broodingly into the flames. "As I had been active in fighting the French, it was only a matter of time before I would have been rounded up and killed. And so I gave my loyalty to the only man worthy of it, Ho Chi Minh."

There came a sound of leaves being crushed underfoot as the two NVA officers returned from

141

their fishing trip.

"It must have been very lonely for you," Gavin said quietly, knowing how important family was to him.

Dinh nodded, but the two officers were now within earshot and he said merely, "From that time on my overriding aim has been the reunification of Vietnam under Communist control. To that end I have relinquished family, personal ambition, and personal happiness."

The two NVA officers were sitting down beside them, triumphantly displaying their catch. Before he congratulated them, and before he began to help in skewering the fish in order to roast them, Dinh turned his head. His eyes met Gavin's. "And I have no regrets," he said simply. "None at all."

For the next two weeks they continued north-westward toward Cambodia, traveling only at night. They were heading toward the Fishhook area, where Cambodian territory bulged down into Vietnam like a gigantic teat.

The trail ended on the enormous Mimot rubber plantation. A wooden gate barred the way across the trail and there was a control point manned by half a dozen guards. As Dinh spoke with the guards, discussing him Gavin was sure, he felt dizzy with relief and euphoria. He was at COSVN, the famous Central Office of South Vietnam. No reporter had ever gained entry before him, and he doubted if any would after him. He had scored a momentous first and he burned with the longing to file his story.

"Come," Dinh said to him. The heavy gate was lifted and they were escorted down the trail beyond by two of the guards.

The jungle vegetation on either side of them was thick and lush. Wild orchids ran riot, their wax-white cups stark against the dark green foliage; vines and creepers covered the trees so thick overhead that the sunlight fell through them in bright, slanting bars. Away from the trail, half hidden under the jungle canopy, were houses built peasant-style, and half a dozen long, low buildings with entrances to a tunnel system clearly visible.

They were taken to one of the houses nearest to the trail, and it became clear that only Gavin, under guard, was to be left there.

"Take this opportunity to rest, Comrade," Dinh said as a look of unease flashed across Gavin's face. "I and my companions must make our reports to our superior officers. There is much for us to discuss, and it may be some time before I see you again."

It was three days. He was fed sparingly on boiled rice, a small hunk of salt, and dried fish. It was a diet he was becoming accustomed to. Looking down at a frame that was becoming increasingly gaunt, he wondered what Gaby would say when she saw him. In the loneliness of his temporary isolation he could almost hear her husky, unchained laughter.

His throat tightened and he clenched his fists. He must not allow his thoughts to dwell longingly on Gaby. If he did, he could become completely unstrung. The only way of surviving the tremendous opportunity that he had been given was by suppressing all thoughts of normality. Like an alcoholic, he had to live one day at a time.

However impressive Dinh's rank had been at Cu Chi, at COSVN it was dwarfed by the men of real power. Later, when they were in the jeep traveling northward again, he learned that not only was General Tran Nam Trung, the commander-in-chief of the National Liberation Forces, one of the senior officers that Dinh had to report to, but that he had also had to make his report to Pham Hung, a Politburo member and first party secretary, and General Hoang Van Thai, commander-in-chief of all northern forces in the South. It was a thunderingly impressive lineup.

"And now it's straight ahead for the North," Dinh said to him with satisfaction as they vaulted into the jeep that had been provided for them. "And think yourself lucky, Comrade, that you are traveling now and not ten years ago when I first made the journey. Then it was nothing but a near-impassable foot track snaking down from the North over the Truong Son mountain range."

"Is the route still the same as the original?" Gavin asked curiously, deeply thankful to be exchanging the discomfort of his bicycle for the relative comfort of the jeep.

Dinh nodded as one of the NVA officers took

144

the wheel. "Yes, though now it is not just one single track but a network of routes running roughly parallel with cross-links at strategic intervals."

"And for the moment we travel through Cambodia?"

"For the moment," Dinh said, flashing one of his rare smiles.

There were times, in the nights that followed as they bumped and swayed over cratered tracks, when Gavin almost longed to be back on a bicycle. Without a map he had only a hazy idea of where they were, and sometimes he was not even sure which country they were in, Cambodia, Vietnam, or Laos.

One night they only narrowly avoided being spotted by enemy planes as they crossed wide fields of thatch near Pleiku. For a little while after that he was able to judge where they were because Pleiku was a name that meant something to him. In February 1965 the Viet Cong had attacked the U.S. base at Pleiku and he remembered it being referred to as a traditional market town in the central highlands.

From then on the route became increasingly mountainous and the amount of heavily camouflaged traffic on the trail continued to amaze him. After crossing the Ben Hai River they had descended into the foothills of the Truong Son. The massive mountain range ran like a backbone through North and South, but now there were no more perilous passes to negotiate. Instead, they were soon in thick forest and it was then, when for the first time attack seemed unlikely, that invisible B-52s bombarded the stretch of trail on which they were traveling.

As before, there was no warning. The world simply erupted around them in an apocalyptic frenzy. Although Gavin learned afterward that the center of the bombing had been over a mile away, the sonic roar of explosions tore at his eardrums, reducing him once again to total deafness. The jeep was lifted in the air by the blast and thrown yards off the trail, landing on its side. A blow to his head left him with no memory of how he crawled from the wreckage. He could only remember, as the attack continued, pressing himself into the earth and losing control of both his bladder and his bowels.

When at last it was over, he couldn't believe that he was alive. He forced himself to his knees, and then to stumble to his feet. "Dinh!" he shouted into a ringing silence. "Dinh!"

Fifty yards away two figures moved slowly, lifting themselves cautiously from the ground. Neither of them was Dinh. A new fear gripped Gavin, even worse than the mind-bending fear he had just experienced. "Dinh!" he shouted, his voice cracking. "DINH!"

"I am here, Comrade," a voice said from behind him.

Gavin spun around, nearly sick with relief. "Christ! I thought you were dead. I thought we were *all* dead!"

Dinh flashed him one of his rare grins, brushing debris from his uniform. "Fear is debilitat-

146

ing, Comrade. You will have to learn not to capitulate to it so easily." There was no censure in his voice, only amusement. "Let us see if the jeep is still roadworthy. If it isn't, we have a long trek ahead of us."

Together the four of them managed to rock the jeep back onto its wheels.

"The gas tank is still intact," one of the NVA officers said optimistically. "I don't think we're going to have a problem."

They didn't. Ten minutes later, with freshly hacked saplings camouflaging the hood, they were trundling northward again.

"In another few minutes we shall be on a very safe section of the trail," Dinh said to Gavin in confidence.

Gavin looked across at him suspiciously. "We're not going underground again, are we?"

Dinh grinned again. He was beginning to enjoy Gavin's company. "No, Comrade. For the next few miles we are going to travel by stream."

They didn't take sampans. Instead, the NVA officer at the wheel simply drove into the shallow water, using the bed of the stream as if it were a road, constantly changing gear as he moved from sandy stretches to pebbled beds or to deeper portions.

"These sections of the trail are difficult to spot from the air," Dinh said, visibly relaxing. "The bushes on either bank give natural camouflage and the water erases all traces of movement immediately. Deeper streams are used to good account as well. Supplies are packed into

147

waterproof containers and floated downstream from one supply post to another."

Gavin believed him. He was beginning to think that there was nothing that he now would not believe about NVA ingenuity.

The next day, at a busy supply post, they exchanged their battered jeep for a six-wheel-drive ZIL army truck.

"In which we will drive into Hanoi," Dinh said, highly satisfied at the progress they were making. "There is no more jungle to negotiate. From here on we should experience no more delays."

He was overly optimistic. Within an hour they came under attack again, this time from three F-4s. They survived the attack unscathed, but those traveling in trucks ahead of them were not so lucky.

It was dusk the next day when Dinh prodded him lightly in the side and said, "You've been asleep for the last hour, Comrade. If you sleep any longer, you will miss our entry into Hanoi."

Gavin shot upright in his seat, his heart beginning to beat in thick, short strokes. Hanoi! Whatever he had envisaged when he had left Paris for Saigon, it had not been this. To be riding in a Russian truck, accompanied by three NVA officers, into *Hanoi*! It was incredible! Un-believable!

The shanty houses of the suburbs gave way to gracious stone-built mansions. On their right-hand side the broad, deep waters of the Lake of the Restored Sword gleamed dully. On their left-hand side, as more houses came into view, Gavin could see that despite their original grandeur, their facades were now crumbling, their paint-work peeling.

"Your first night in Hanoi will be one of comfort," Dinh said, watching Gavin's reactions to everything with interest. "The French built a splendid hotel in the city center, the Metropole. A room has been booked there for us. You will excuse me this evening if I leave you almost immediately. I have to report to my superiors."

Gavin nodded, unable to drag his gaze from the somber streets. They drew up outside a huge, grandiose building that looked unutterably drab. But still Gavin was overwhelmed at his good fortune. He was in Hanoi. *Hanoi*. With luck he would soon be interviewing General Giap. Possibly even Ho himself.

CHAPTER SEVEN

As she sat on the plane, flying from San Francisco to Washington, Abbra knew that she was on the verge of permanently alienating herself from her father-in-law. He regarded all antiwar demonstrators as traitors, and she knew that when he discovered she'd been involved in the march on the Pentagon, he would be both bewildered and outraged.

She gazed out of the window at banks of cloud

and an autumn sun and wondered what Lewis's reaction would be. He had always believed implicitly that American involvement in Indochina was both a moral and a political necessity. Would he still think so? She had no way of knowing.

The plane began to descend through the clouds toward Washington's National Airport. She had no friends in the city; she knew no one who would be participating in the march. Scott would have come with her if it weren't football season but she was no longer able to ask Scott to accompany her anywhere. Their days of easygoing camaraderie were over.

She clenched her hands tightly in her lap. She would not think of Scott. Thinking of Scott was almost as painful as thinking of Lewis. Instead, she would think of the days ahead of her in Washington. She would need to check into a hotel, to find out where the meeting point for the beginning of the march was to be, and she would need to keep an eye out for other women who were in the same position as herself, women whose husbands were also either prisoners of war or missing in action in Vietnam.

In the first class cabin of a Boeing 707, Serena slipped on eyeshades and stretched her long, suntanned legs out in front of her. There were another six hours before the plane was due to land at Washington's Dulles International Airport, and she intended spending the time asleep.

A stewardess asked her quietly if she would

like a blanket and she nodded. It was the 19th of October. As the planned march on the Pentagon was to take place on the twenty-first, it meant that she would have to wait until the twenty-second before traveling on to Atlantic City and visiting Chuck Wilson.

She had not communicated with him since April, when he had written to say that he had been discharged from the hospital and was going to his uncle's ranch for the summer to recuperate. For all she knew, he could still be in Wyoming. If he was, she had no address for him, and if his uncle's last name wasn't Wilson, tracking him down would be impossible.

She began to drift off to sleep, wondering why his letters had been so curt and odd in tone, wondering if the antiwar demonstration in Washington was going to be similar to the one she had participated in in London, wondering what the French girl would be like who had written to her in response to her *Washington Post* letter, and wondering if they would manage to meet, as they had arranged, at the Lincoln Memorial before the march began.

Gabrielle drove into Washington on Route 46 with the same nonchalant expertise with which she drove in Paris. Their gig the night before had been in Baltimore, and though Radford still planned on making the march, there had been problems with the sound system and he had been forced to stay behind, ironing out the kinks.

It was a year and one month since Gavin had

dropped so precipitately from sight. Since then there had been not a word about him, not even a rumor. Nhu's letters still arrived, strained and distressed, but she never mentioned him. Gabrielle did not believe he was dead. Why was she so *certain* that he was still alive?

However hard she tried, she could find no logical reason. Her conviction was based on instinct, nothing more. Her hands tightened fractionally on the wheel. Instinct was something that had never failed her, and she was willing to stake her life that it was not failing her now. Gavin was alive. All she could do was live through the time until he returned home.

She turned left, heading toward the Lincoln Memorial. Was that true? Was passively living through the intervening time all that she could do? She was half Vietnamese. Saigon had been her home, was, in her heart of hearts, still her home.

"*Mon Dieu*," she whispered softly under her breath. She began to slow down, no longer able to concentrate on her driving, her heart racing.

Why hadn't she thought of it before? Merciful heaven, how could she have been so *stupid* as to not have thought of the obvious months earlier? She would go to Vietnam. She would make contact with whoever it was who had told Nhu that there would be no further news of Dinh and Gavin. She would follow the route that they had taken, and she would find Gavin herself!

The crowds were enormous. Abbra had never

seen so many people all gathering together with one purpose in mind. The crush had been so dense that it had taken her over an hour to walk from her hotel in N Street, close by the White House, to the rallying point of the march, the Lincoln Memorial, a little over a mile away. The lawns around the memorial were black with people camping out. The majority of them were long-haired, and outlandishly dressed in Afghan coats and love beads, but a surprising number were no longer young.

There were middle-aged and middle-class protesters among the throng. The angular, silver-haired figure of Dr. Benjamin Spock, the baby expert, was clearly visible, as were other notable personalities. Abbra caught a fleeting glimpse of both Arthur Miller and Norman Mailer before the throng closed around them and they were lost to view amid a sea of waving placards.

Some of the placards had pictures of President Johnson on them, and were headed with the words WAR CRIMINAL in scarlet print. Others bore the words OHIO STATE, GET U.S. OUT OF VIETNAM, BRING OUR BOYS HOME, MAKE LOVE NOT WAR, and STOP KILLING, STOP IT NOW.

A large contingent jostling near her was carrying red and white flags with yellow stars on them. She stared at the flags for a moment, puzzled, and then understanding dawned. They were Viet Cong flags. Horrified, she began to push through the crowd away from them. She was against the war, and didn't care who knew it, but that didn't mean that she had become a

Viet Cong supporter, and she didn't want to be mistaken for one.

As the crowd began to move off, heading toward the Arlington Memorial Bridge, Abbra saw a girl who looked as bemused as she herself felt. Elegant and willowy, with pale blond hair falling straight down her back, she stood nearly a full head taller than most of those milling around her. A sumptuous wolf-fur coat protected her from the October chill, and because she wore it negligently thrown open, with her hands thrust deep in her pockets, Abbra could see that the dress beneath the coat was white and ravishingly short, barely skimming her thighs. Knee-high snakeskin boots and a distinctive silk Union Jack scarf completed the ensemble, and looking at her, Abbra wondered if the day would ever come when she, too, would be as stunningly, as effortlessly, sophisticated.

As the chant "Hell no, we won't go" was taken up by the thousands around her, Abbra began to squeeze her way across to the girl who, despite the very British scarf, she was sure was Scandinavian.

"It's amazing, isn't it?" she said when she at last reached her. "I never imagined so many people would be here. There must be 40 or 50,000 at least."

"More, probably," the girl said with a grin. Her voice was low and attractive, the accent not Scandinavian but decidedly English.

"Do you mind if I walk with you?" Abbra

asked a little shyly. "I was nearly swallowed up a few moments ago by a group carrying Viet Cong flags, and though I'm against the war, I don't want to be seen as a Viet Cong supporter."

"Oh?" the girl queried, falling into step beside her. "Why not?"

Abbra paused for a second. She very rarely spoke of Lewis, and never to strangers. Now she heard herself saying with surprising ease, "My husband is an MIA."

Eyes the color of smoked quartz held hers. "And mine is a POW," Serena said, holding out her hand. "My name is Serena Anderson, and I'm very pleased to meet you."

Abbra shook her hand tightly. For an insane moment she wanted to cry.

"I'm Abbra, Abbra Ellis," she said thickly, knowing that at last she had found someone who understood her suffering, someone with whom she could share her grief and her hopes. "Have you been at antiwar demos before?"

Serena nodded. "In London. Outside the American Embassy." She flashed Abbra her wide, dazzling smile. "I thought the numbers there were enormous, but this is incredible! I was supposed to be meeting another POW wife here. A French girl whom I've never met before. If you see anyone wearing a silk scarf replica of the French flag, let me know. It will be Gabrielle."

They had reached the bridge and a crisp, chill wind was blowing off the waters of the Potomac. Abbra was wearing a bright red jacket over a

155

dove-gray turtleneck sweater and dark gray trousers, and she pulled the collar of the jacket up high around her throat.

Serena plunged her hands even deeper into the pockets of her coat. "My husband, Kyle, is being held in Hanoi. In Hoa Lo prison."

All around them the chant "Peace now, peace now" had been taken up and Abbra had to shout as she replied, "My husband's name is Lewis. He's a captain and was serving with a four-man mobile advisory team deep in the Delta. He and his men were ambushed on one of the canals shortly after searching a village that was suspected of harboring North Vietnamese troops. A survivor said that he saw Lewis being taken prisoner by North Vietnamese who had attacked them. That was a little over a year ago." Her eyes were suddenly overbright, "There's been no news of him since," she finished tightly.

"Jesus," Serena said. For a moment she didn't say anything else. She couldn't. In coming to the march she had hoped that she would meet another woman in the same situation as herself, and she had met one whose situation was worse. At least she knew where Kyle was. There was even the faint hope that he was receiving her letters. Abbra had no such hopes. At last she said simply, "I'm sorry, that's really tough."

The words were trite and inadequate, but as their eyes met, she knew that Abbra understood the depth of feeling that was behind them.

"Do you think there's going to be any trouble?" she shouted across to Abbra as she caught

156

her first sight of the thousands of U.S. army troops and state marshals and national guardsmen who surrounded the Department of Defense.

Abbra had no previous experience of antiwar demonstrations, but she shook her head. "No. David Dellinger is the main organizer of the march, and he's a lifelong pacifist. The purpose is simply to seal off the Pentagon through sheer numbers so that no one can get in or out. Because of the scores of different groups of people taking part ... women's groups and church groups and war veterans and civil rights pacifists, as well as students and black militants and left-wing intellectuals ... Dellinger figures that the government will *have* to recognize how widespread opposition to the war is."

They were near enough now to see the rifle barrels being held at half guard by the soldiers, and Serena, remembering the violence that had taken place at the much smaller demonstration outside the American Embassy in London, hoped that her conviction was well founded.

"What would your husband think of all this?" she asked curiously over the roars of chants of "Johnson *out*! Johnson *out*!"

Abbra hesitated for a telltale second, and her cheeks colored slightly. "I guess he wouldn't like it, but when he comes home, I think that he will understand why I did it."

They were no longer moving forward, and the crowd around them were so tightly packed that it was impossible to move more than a few inches to either the left or right.

"The enemy, we believe, is Lyndon Johnson!" one of the organizers of the march declared ringingly from the Pentagon's main entrance as the vigil began. "He was elected to the presidency as a peace candidate and within three months he has betrayed us!"

"Do you think those things are loaded?" Serena asked Abbra, her eyes once more focusing on the half-raised rifles.

Abbra shook her head, a smile of amusement quirking the corners of her mouth. "No. How could they be? This is America, Serena. Not some third world dictatorship!"

As Serena saw some of the young women at the front of the crowd flirting with the soldiers and placing flowers in the rifle barrels, she laughed at her idiocy. "Sorry, I have a brother who always suspects the worst where authority is concerned, and some of his paranoia must have rubbed off on me."

A wave of singing rippled through the vast throng. "All we are saying, is give peace a chance," thousands of voices sang in unison. Serena and Abbra sang with them, Abbra deeply grateful that she had not asked how her parents and her father-in-law would react when they knew of her participation in the march, and Serena far more moved than she had expected to be by the sight of so many Americans demonstrating against a war that their country was committed to.

"*Can't we go any further forward?*" Serena

shouted across the roar of voices. *"Can't we get inside the building?"*

Abbra shook her head, blue-black hair swinging silkily against the upturned collar of her jacket. *"No. The permit for the demonstration allows us to assemble on the blacktop parking plaza outside the Pentagon's main entrance, and on the nearby lawns, but though public visitors are allowed into parts of the Pentagon, none are being allowed in today."*

Serena was disappointed. Even Lance would have been impressed if she'd been able to enter the American government's military headquarters.

An Indian summer sun had broken through the clouds, and all around them coats were being shed. The unmistakable sweet-sweet odor of pot drifted over their heads and, looking around her, Abbra realized for the first time that they were no longer amongst a mixed section of the crowd ... women's groups and church groups and middle-aged intellectuals ... but that they were deep in a crush of hippies and left-wing activists.

She was just about to suggest to Serena that they edge their way back into a more moderate flank, when scuffles broke out a few yards away from them.

As the singing around them changed to shouting and the crowd began to sway disruptively she shouted, *"What's happening, Serena? Can you see?"*

"Dellinger!" a long-haired student in front of her yelled back before Serena could reply. *"He's*

been arrested for sitting in front of troops who ordered him to move on!"

From that moment the tone of the demonstration changed. The left-wing activists surrounding them began to taunt and jeer the military police who were standing on the wall that separated the lawns from the parking plaza.

To the left of Abbra a youth wearing a Viet Cong flag tucked into his headband, picked up a stone and threw it at the nearest MP. Other left-wing demonstrators began to follow suit.

"I think it's time we made a discreet retreat," Serena shouted. "If Dellinger is the pacifist you say he is, this is the very last thing he would want to have happen."

Abbra agreed whole heartedly. The left-wing activists carrying Viet Cong flags were only a tiny fraction of the crowd, but they were an ugly minority and were obviously eager to cause trouble.

The trouble came quickly. As she and Serena tried to force their way toward a woman's group who were carrying a twenty-foot banner with the words SUPPORT OUR GI'S. BRING THEM HOME! emblazoned on it, full-scale fighting and arrests broke out.

It seemed to Abbra afterward that none of the activists who had actually caused the disturbance were the ones being hit on the head with federal marshals' nightsticks. As the marshals launched into the sea of protesters, it was students and hippies who bore the full brunt of the attack.

She was aware of Serena grasping her hand tightly to prevent herself from falling, of the blinding sting of tear gas, and then, as she fell against him, the long-haired student who had shouted to her that Dellinger had been arrested, was seized by a federal marshal. In horrified disbelief she saw the marshal raise his club, saw the student cover his head with his arms and his hair fly as the club made contact with his head and he sank down onto his knees.

"No!" she screamed, wrenching herself away from Serena's grasp, throwing herself onto the marshal, dragging hold of his arm as he raised the club again. *"No! No! No!"*

The marshal threw her off as if she were an irritating fly. His club came down again, and this time the force of the blow knocked the student's black loafers from his feet. As Abbra scrambled hysterically to her knees, she could see the blood pouring down from his hair onto the cement surface of the plaza. "Bastard!" she screamed at the marshal, using a word she had never used in anger ever before in her life. "You pathetic, cowardly, *bastard!*"

The marshal turned toward her, his arm rising again. All around them fellow demonstrators, male and female, were being clubbed and hauled off to police vans. Serena grabbed hold of a discarded coat that was being trampled underfoot and hurled it over the marshal's head. *"Quick!"* she shouted to Abbra. *"For Christ's sake, run!"*

Abbra tried to, but the crush was too dense. With Serena once more grasping tight hold of her, she pushed and shoved in Serena's wake, away from the marshals and their crucifying billy clubs. As tears from the gas poured down her face she was aware with surprise that she was not remotely frightened. She was angry, angry at the troublemakers who had betrayed the demonstration organizers and turned what had been a peaceful, dignified antiwar protest into a bloody brawl, and furiously, blazingly angry at the brutality of the federal marshals.

As arrest after arrest took place, a voice in the crowd began singing "The Battle Hymn of the Republic", and more and more voices joined in. Singing lustily, almost resigned to the fact that they, too, would eventually be grabbed hold of and dragged off into one of the waiting police vans, Abbra and Serena tried to remain on their feet and to push through to the rear of the crush. As they did so, fresh localized spots of fighting between troops and demonstrators erupted.

"Oh, God," Serena said resignedly. "Here they come again."

They had reached the fringes of a large contingent of black demonstrators. Abbra could see one placard with the words OLD SOLDIERS NEVER DIE ... YOUNG ONES DO being carried by a uniformed black army veteran. Another placard bore the words NOT WITH MY LIFE YOU DON'T.

From somewhere in the distance Abbra was aware that "The Battle Hymn of the Republic" had ended and that "America the Beautiful" was now being sung defiantly. As she lustily launched into the second line, a half dozen of the black demonstrators were knocked to the ground by nightstick blows. Shielding her head with her arm in an attempt to avoid a similar fate, she suddenly saw a petite, red-headed girl go sprawling down amid the melee.

Serena had seen her, too, and together they instinctively rushed forward to drag her clear of the danger.

Their action brought them in front of the military police. As Abbra caught hold of one of the girl's wrists, hauling her to her feet, a stunning blow hit her head. Dazed, she could hear Serena screaming her name, but she couldn't see her; she couldn't see anything but scarlet flashes scoring dense blackness.

"I'm all right!" she gasped, lying. "I'm all right!" Blood, hot and sticky, was trickling down the side of her face and onto her neck. Incredibly, she still had hold of the girl's wrist, was still on her feet helping Serena pull the girl free of the demonstrators who had fallen on top of her.

Slowly, as the three of them staggered back into the main body of the crowd, her vision cleared. She could see Serena's face, white with anxiety, could see the face of the girl they had pulled clear of the military police nightsticks, her green eyes full of indignant outrage, a silk tricolor tied around her throat.

"We need to sit down," Serena was saying. "We need to bandage your head."

Dizzily Abbra nodded and allowed herself to be led to the fringe of the crowd and the grassy lawns of the mall.

"*Mon Dieu!*" the girl they had rescued was saying as she staunched the flow of blood with a handkerchief. "I thought things were more civilized in America! No one told me I should have come with a crash helmet and a baton!"

For no reason at all Abbra began to giggle. "No one told me either," she said, grateful that the pain in her head was beginning to ease.

"Are you okay?" Serena asked her tightly.

Abbra didn't venture to nod her head. To do so would have brought a roar of fresh pain. Instead, she said, her voice sounding strangely thick, "I think so. I don't think I've got a concussion."

The redheaded girl suddenly saw Serena's scarf and her eyes widened. "*Alors!* Are you Serena Anderson? Are you the girl I was to have met at the Lincoln Memorial?"

Serena nodded. She had noticed Gabrielle's scarf, but had been too concerned by Abbra's wound to take time to introduce herself.

Gabrielle, too, returned her attention immediately to Abbra. "*Je regrette*," she said, distressed. "It would not have happened if you had not stayed to pull me free."

"It wouldn't have happened if we hadn't had troublemakers at the front of the crowd, and unnecessary thuggery from the federal marshals and the military police," Serena responded tightly. She took a close look at Abbra's head and said with relief, "You're right, Abbra. I think you're going to be fine. The bleeding has stopped, but you're going to have a God almighty

164

bump there for a few days."

"And a God almighty headache," Abbra said ruefully.

Serena looked around her. At the parking plaza and the grassy triangle of lawn beyond it, running battles were still taking place. Above the shouting could be heard a valiant rendering of "We Shall Overcome".

"Let's get away from here," she said. "This thing is going to go on all night, and you're in no condition to risk another run-in with the troops. If we make it back as far as the traffic circle at the Virginia end of the bridge, we should be able to pick up a cab."

"And go where?" Abbra asked weakly as the French girl slipped her arm supportingly around her waist.

"My hotel would be the best bet. We can call a doctor up to put some stitches in your head. It's no use going to any of the hospitals. They're going to be overrun."

Abbra felt too weak to protest. Serena was obviously eminently capable, and she was quite happy to go along with anything that she said. As they began to edge their way through crowds both arriving in the vicinity and attempting to leave, Serena said to her, "Sorry, I haven't introduced you, Abbra. Gabrielle, Abbra Ellis. Abbra's husband is an army captain being held somewhere in South Vietnam. Abbra, Gabrielle Ryan. Gabrielle wrote to me after seeing a letter I wrote to the *Washington Post*. Her husband is Australian, and a journalist. He's been missing for just over a year." She raised a hand, flagging down a taxi. "We'll talk more when we get to my hotel, and after you've been seen by a doctor."

Abbra willingly allowed herself to be helped into the taxi, smiling despite her violent headache when she heard Serena direct the cab driver to the Jefferson Hotel.

The Jefferson. Of course. Where else had she expected Serena to be staying? The Jefferson was one of the most prestigious hotels in town. Situated only four blocks away from the White House, its rooms were decorated with fine antiques, the laundry was hand ironed and delivered in wicker baskets, and the manager personally greeted guests at the front door. And with the Jefferson as an address, any doctor called would most certainly come. Knowing that she had nothing further to worry about, Abbra leaned back and closed her eyes for the duration of the short cab ride.

When the doctor had duly stitched the wound in her scalp and had given her a pain reliever, Abbra began to feel a great deal better.

"What are you doing in America?" she asked Gabrielle as a bellboy wheeled a trolley of food and drink into the room. "Are you here just to see Serena?"

Gabrielle sat in a deep-buttoned armchair, her legs curled beneath her. "No. I am a singer," she said as Serena poured coffee for Abbra and two glasses of Château Latour, Grand Cru for herself and Gabrielle.

Serena handed Abbra the cup of coffee and Gabrielle her glass of wine. "What kind of a singer?" she asked, interested.

Gabrielle grinned, her eyes full of mischievous laughter. "At this moment in time, a rock singer."

"Oh, God! I wish I'd known you when Bedingham had its pop festival! You would have been a sensation!"

"Bedingham?" Gabrielle had written to Serena at her London address. "What is Bedingham?"

"Bedingham is my family home," Serena said, a new note entering her voice. She put her wineglass down and, sitting on the end of the canopied bed, she began to tell Abbra and Gabrielle all about Bedingham.

Abbra lay back against the pillows. Serena had insisted that she go to bed the minute they had entered the room, and she had reluctantly obeyed. Now she was glad that she had. The pain reliever had made her feel slightly woozy and as Serena spoke of Bedingham she felt so relaxed that she was almost asleep.

"And you, Abbra?" Serena said at last, when she had told the story of the pop festival and how she had met Kyle. "What do you do? Where do you live?"

"San Francisco," Abbra replied, easing herself up against the pillows. And she told them of how her mother had asked Lewis to pick her up from a party, and of how they had fallen in love, and then she told them about her novel, and of how it was soon to be published, and of how she had

167

already started on a second book.

Outside in the darkness, police sirens could still be faintly heard, but none of them paid any heed to them.

"And so what happens to us now?" Serena asked when Abbra had finished telling her story. "Do you return to San Francisco, Abbra? To finish your novel? And do you finish your tour of America, and then return to France, Gabrielle? If so, when are we going to meet again? Because we *have* to meet again, that is obvious."

"I am not returning to France," Gabrielle said quietly. "Or at least not for more than a few days." She paused and they waited expectantly. "I am going to Vietnam," she said with devastating simplicity. "I am going to look for Gavin."

For a long moment even Serena was rendered speechless. It was Abbra who spoke first, her voice incredulous. "But you can't! The country is at war! Where will you go? Where will you stay? How can you possibly find out any more than the Australian and the American authorities can find out?"

Gabrielle's kittenlike features were determined. "I can go, Abbra, because Vietnam is as much my country as France is. My mother is Vietnamese. I lived in Saigon until I was eight years old."

There was a sigh of understanding from Serena. It had been obvious to her almost from the first that Gabrielle was of mixed blood. Why hadn't she realized she was half Vietnamese?

"I speak Vietnamese," Gabrielle was saying. "I

168

have family in Saigon." She paused again, opened her mouth to say more, and then changed her
mind.

"What is it?" Serena demanded, sensing her
discomfort. "What is it that you don't want to
tell us?"

Gabrielle said awkwardly, "This is difficult for
me. Your husband is a prisoner in the North, and
Abbra's husband is probably being held in terrible conditions by the Viet Cong in the South,
and..."

"And?" Abbra prompted her gently.

Gabrielle gave a helpless Gallic shrug of her
shoulders. "And my uncle is a colonel in the
North Vietnamese Army. Gavin wanted to meet
him. To find out what the war was like from an
NVA point of view. My aunt in Saigon arranged
the meeting. Gavin went off with my uncle and
nothing has been heard of them since. That was
over a year ago. If he could have gotten in touch
with me, I know that he would have. But he
hasn't, and so..." Her voice faltered a little. The
admission she was about to make was one she
had never before put into words. "And so I think
that perhaps he is a prisoner. As Lewis and Kyle
are prisoners."

For a long time no one spoke, and then Serena
shook her head slowly, as if to clear it to be able
to think clearly. "Jesus," she said in a stunned
voice. "That is one *hell* of a story!"

Gabrielle rose to her feet in the lamplit room.
"You see why I hesitated before telling you.
Perhaps now that you know about the loyalties

of some members of my family, you would prefer it if I had never contacted you? If I now left?"

"Nonsense!" Before Serena could respond, Abbra sprang from the bed, ignoring the fresh waves of pain that her action occasioned. "Your husband is missing just as mine is missing," she said fiercely, taking both of Gabrielle's hands in hers. "And I know that I am speaking for Serena as well as myself when I say that all that matters is that the three of us are friends, and that we are all suffering the same kind of agony."

"She's right," Serena said. "She is speaking for me."

"*Ça va*," Gabrielle said, her eyes suspiciously bright.

Reassured that Gabrielle was no longer going to take flight, Abbra let go of her hands and returned a trifle unsteadily to the bed, sitting down on it Indian-fashion and saying with a smile, "So that's it, Gabrielle. There is no more to be said."

"Oh, but there is," Serena corrected her. While Abbra had been talking so passionately to Gabrielle, she had walked across the room to the window and had stood, looking down into the neon-lit darkness of 16th Street. Now she turned around, her eyes holding Gabrielle's. "There's something very important still to be said. I want to come with you to Vietnam, Gabrielle. Can I?"

If it had been anyone else, even Abbra, Gabrielle was sure that she would have said no.

But Serena was different. She could sense a recklessness beneath the English girl's capably cool exterior that matched the recklessness in her own nature.

"Yes," she said unhesitatingly. "Of course you can come."

"I have something to do first," Serena said, adrenaline racing through her veins. "I have someone to see in Atlantic City. Chuck Wilson. He was Kyle's buddy and he was seriously injured trying to rescue Kyle."

"And I have something to do as well," Gabrielle said, not looking forward to the scene that lay ahead of her. "I have to tell Radford, the leader of the group that I sing with, that I'm taking off for Saigon. After doing *that*, anything that happens to me in Vietnam will be a walk-over!"

"What about me?" Abbra exclaimed indignantly. "You surely don't expect me to return to San Francisco while you two fly off to Saigon! If you're going, I'm going too!"

"No," Serena said emphatically. "No, you're not, Abbra. Listen to me for a moment. Gabrielle's situation and my situation are very different from yours. You are an army wife in a way that I, for instance, am not. Your husband is a professional soldier. When he returns home he will return to a career in the army. And he won't thank you if you ruin his future prospects by upsetting the military."

"But..." Abbra began stubbornly.

"But nothing," Serena said gently but firmly.

"You have your book to promote, your second novel to write, and your father-in-law to appease. From what you've told us, if he thought for one minute you were going to fly to Vietnam, he would have a cardiac arrest!"

Abbra felt her throat tighten. Serena was right. Abbra knew it, but she didn't *want* her to be right. She wanted to go to Vietnam. She wanted to do something positive to find Lewis. And she couldn't. Lewis's career in the army was his life. She couldn't jeopardize it, no matter what the cost.

"Okay," she said thickly. "But write to me. Write to me every damned week."

Serena grinned, relieved Abbra had been practical. "We will," she promised, and turned toward Gabrielle. "So when do we leave?"

"Our American tour ends in two weeks. I'll return to Paris with the band and speak to my parents, and I'll meet you there. Don't bother about a hotel. As long as you don't mind sleeping on a sofa, you will be very welcome in Montmartre."

"That's it, then. It's all settled," Serena's satisfaction was bone-deep. "But if you don't mind, Gabrielle, I won't accept your very kind offer of hospitality. I'll book into my usual haunt whenever I'm in Paris, the George V. I might as well enjoy what comfort I can while I can!"

A second bottle of Château Latour, Grand Cru stood uncorked on the trolley, and she picked it up, topping up both her own glass and Gabrielle's, and pouring a glass for Abbra.

"Here's to us," she said exuberantly as they raised their glasses high. "And to our husbands; and to the day when we shall all meet again!"

CHAPTER EIGHT

The next day, on the flight back to San Francisco, Abbra planned her immediate future. Although, as a loyal army wife, she knew she couldn't accompany Serena and Gabrielle to Vietnam, she had no intention of continuing with her present life-style. The advances from her book, though not enormous, had given her financial independence and she was determined to do at last what she had longed to do for months. She was going to move out of her parents' home and rent a small house of her own.

Not in San Francisco. Not anywhere where there would be distractions. She wanted a beach house on a lonely part of the coast where she could write without interruption, and where her surroundings would give her mental solace as she continued in her long, agonizing wait for Lewis's return.

Remembering the weekend, she felt a glow of comfort. Talking to Serena and Gabrielle about Lewis, knowing that they understood implicitly everything that she was suffering, had been the best kind of therapy she could possibly have undergone. And in talking about Lewis, he had seemed closer than ever to her. Optimism, fierce and strong, surged through her veins. She knew he was alive. All she had to do was wait for him.

Serena rented a car for the trip to Atlantic City. She had no idea what to expect when she arrived there. The address she was driving to was the one that had headed Chuck Wilson's last letter to her, the letter in which he had said only that he was going to Wyoming for the summer to re-cuperate, and the letter in which he had implied that there was no need for them to correspond further. The address could be his family's home or his personal one, or even, if the stationery had been borrowed, that of a friend.

As she approached the coastline and caught her first glimpse of gray, surging, Atlantic break-ers, she hoped that her suspicions were not correct. If it were, then she did not know how she would react, what she would say.

She turned off the highway, driving through the suburbs into a quiet residential area. In an-other few moments she would be able to do what she had wanted to do for so long. She would be able to thank the man who had risked his own life in an effort to save Kyle from capture.

The house was an old white wooden-framed house with clapboard siding, set in a large plot thick with shrubs and bushes. She parked the car and picked up her full-length wolf coat from the rear seat, then, slipping the coat on, she walked up the pathway toward the front door.

She rang the bell and heard it jangle, but there was no response. She rang again, a slight frown creasing her brow. She couldn't possibly leave without making contact with either Chuck or with someone who knew where he was. There was no sign of life from the front of the house, and so she dug her hands into the pockets of her coat and began to walk around to the rear.

Flowers edged the pathway, asters and chrysanthemums and black-eyed susans, calendulas and marigolds. In the distance were more unexpected delights: bayberry and sumac and wild beach rose. She wondered bemusedly who the imaginative gardener was, and then turned the corner.

Dominating the rear was a big glass-enclosed porch furnished with a wooden table, presumably for summer meals, and several upholstered, cane-framed chairs. There was also another chair there, facing away from her, with an occupant in it. A wheelchair.

"Oh, God," she whispered beneath her breath, her worst fears confirmed, and then as the figure in the wheelchair remained oblivious of her presence, staring broodingly out over the carefully tended lawns and shrubbery, she stepped resolutely forward and into the porch.

"Hello," she said, her hands clenching in the depths of her pockets, the nails digging deep into her palms. "I'm sorry to disturb you like this, but there didn't seem to be anyone in the house to answer the bell and..."

The wheelchair spun to face her.

"And so I thought I'd walk around and see if I could find anyone," she finished inadequately.

He was about twenty-three or twenty-four, but his eyes were ages old. They were so old that she felt chilled just looking into them. And they were blazingly angry.

"Now that you've done that, would you kindly leave!" His voice was a whiplash in the mild fall air.

"No," Serena said, regaining her usual cool self-possession with difficulty. "I'm Serena Anderson, and I presume that you are Chuck Wilson." She stepped toward him and held out her hand. "I've wanted to meet you for a long time, Chuck."

He ignored her outstretched hand. He knew who she was. He had known the instant he had set eyes on her. "I don't encourage visitors, Mrs. Anderson, and I would prefer it if you left!"

She regarded him long and intently. He had light brown hair worn a trifle long, high cheek-bones, a slightly aquiline nose, gray eyes, and a finely chiseled mouth. There was something about him that reminded her very strongly of Kyle. He was Kyle's build, tall and lean, and even though he was in a wheelchair, she could sense the same restless, reckless energy.

"I've no intention of leaving," she said unperturbedly, her decision made.

She walked over to the nearest of the cane chairs and sat down. "Now," she said, swiveling her long legs in their over-the-knee derring-do boots, to one side and crossing them at the ankle, her fur open to reveal her lemon minidress, "Why don't you stop behaving like an embittered child and tell me all about it?"

He drew in his breath between clenched teeth, his knuckles white on the wheels of the chair. She opened her shoulder bag, taking out a couple of joints and a cigarette lighter. "Keep me company," she said, passing one across to him.

He hesitated for a long moment and then at last one hand uncurled and he accepted the proferred joint.

"What exactly is it you want to know?" he asked curtly when they had both lit up and inhaled.

She didn't ask any of the questions he had been expecting, questions about Kyle's shooting-down and capture. Instead, she said matter-of-factly and with a stunning lack of pity in her voice, "Are you going to be in that obscenity for a lifetime, or is the day going to come when you can throw it away?"

A ripple of shock ran through him, and then he blew a plume of sweet smoke into the air, saying a trifle unsteadily, "Kyle told me you could be a pretty surprising lady. You are. And the answer to your question is that I'm probably stuck here for life."

She didn't say she was sorry. She didn't say any of the trite, banal, meaningless phrases that he was sick to the gut of hearing. Instead, she said with almost casual brutality, "Then you had better start getting used to it, hadn't you?"

Before he could recover his power of speech

she rose to her feet. "If you point me in the direction of the kitchen, I'll make some coffee. Or perhaps wine and a few beers would be a better idea. Do you have any in, or shall I drive down to the local store?"

"You're staying, then?" he asked with what he intended to be cutting sarcasm, knowing even as he spoke that he wanted her to stay. She was doing what no woman had done since his Huey had been riddled with tracer fire. She was treating him without pity. And she was making him feel as if he still retained a shred of masculinity.

"Oh, yes," she said with a lazy smile, her perfectly smooth blond hair swinging glossily straight almost to her waist. "I never pass up a party. Of course I'm staying."

A little later she made omelets for them both. They ate them at the table on the porch, remaining there, talking and drinking until it was dark and then, when it became too chilly, they retreated into a room that Chuck described as his "den", taking their third bottle of wine with them.

His mother had returned home from a family visit at the end of the afternoon and had been at first surprised, and then delighted, and finally disconcerted by Serena's presence. Now, as they settled themselves in the den, Serena curling up in a battered armchair, and Chuck propelling his wheelchair so that he was within arm's reach of the coffee table and his glass, she knocked on the door and hesitantly entered.

178

"Is there anything I can get either of you?" she asked a trifle awkwardly. "I know that Mrs. Anderson has already cooked a light supper, but if the two of you would like something a little more substantial..."

"We're fine," Chuck said sharply, and at his graceless response Serena saw a spasm of pain cross his mother's face.

She could well imagine the hell it must be, living with a son so embittered, and she also knew how deeply shocked Mrs. Wilson must be by her own behavior. A POW wife, drinking heavily with her husband's crippled buddy, a buddy crippled because he had tried to save that self-same husband.

She smiled warmly at her, saying with all her considerable charm, "Thank you so much, Mrs. Wilson, but we really don't want to put you to any bother. Perhaps later we could all have some coffee and sandwiches together?"

"I'll do some chicken and ham," Mrs. Wilson said gratefully and then, remembering the omelets and Serena's obvious unconventionality, added hurriedly, "But perhaps you are a vegetarian? If so, I could..."

"I'm not a vegetarian," Serena said firmly, aware of Chuck's glowering countenance, "and chicken and ham would be fine."

Appeased, Mrs. Wilson thankfully withdrew and Chuck said tightly, "There's no need for you to endure supper with my mother."

Serena tilted her head slightly to one side and regarded him quizzically. "Were you always such an obnoxious bastard toward her, or is it something you've worked hard at cultivating since 'Nam?"

He said obliquely, "You'd be damn obnoxious, too, if you were trapped in someone's company twenty-four hours a fucking day."

"But you're not," Serena said. "Cars can be adapted so that you can drive. I don't know what pension you get from the army, but it must be enough for you to hire whatever nursing help you need and to live independently if you want to."

She made everything sound so easy that at that moment he hated her. He thought of the last letter Kyle had written to her, the letter in which he had told her about Trinh and of how he wanted a divorce. The letter which he had not handed over to be given to her along with Kyle's other personal effects. The letter was still in his possession, and for one vicious moment he was tempted to spin his wheelchair toward his desk, get the letter and hurl it into her lap. The moment came and went and he didn't move. He didn't want to hurt her. He didn't want to shatter all her illusions.

He said tersely, "Let's change the bloody subject. Tell me what happened yesterday in Washington. The headlines in this morning's *Post* said, '55,000 Rally Against War; GIs Repel Pentagon Charge.'"

She told him about the demonstration, about the peaceful gathering that had taken place at the Lincoln Memorial and that had been attended by at least 50,000 people, and she told him about the march and the peaceful way the demonstration had begun at the Pentagon, and how it had disintegrated and broken up into a series of vicious battles between troops and demonstrators.

She had no idea whether he would sympathize with antiwar demonstrators, as so many other war veterans did, or whether he would resent them. Even after she had finished telling him about the demonstration she was no wiser. He merely grunted, turning the conversation back to her again, asking her about her life in England, about Bedingham.

Her face took on an inner radiance as she began to tell him about her home. He watched her, tormented by so many conflicting emotions that he could barely contain them.

When Kyle had first told him about the blond-haired, long-legged, sophisticated, wild and reckless English aristocrat that he had married, he had been intrigued. And envious. She had sounded like a girl in a million. A girl out of a storybook. And she was. She was incredible. Her hair was so pale in the lamplight that it looked almost silver; her features were a perfectly carved cameo, her eyes crystal-gray, her mouth wide and full-lipped and passionate. It was a face he could look at for a lifetime and never grow tired of. And he couldn't contemplate making even the slightest sexual overture to her. To do so would be to risk seeing pity in her eyes. Even horror.

Rage and frustration and bitterness roared through him. He wished he were dead. He wished he had died in his Huey, not been whisked by his terrified copilot to the nearest aid station and then flown on to a superbly equipped military hospital.

Kyle had been luckier than he. Wherever Kyle was, he still had the use of his legs. When freedom came for him, he would still be able to flirt and screw and stagger with his buddies from bar to bar on all-night drinking sessions. A paraplegic didn't have drinking buddies. He would be only waist-high as they crowded round a bar. Conversation would flow over his head. He could imagine the bartender asking them if he, the cripple, would like something to drink. But he wouldn't ask him directly. People never spoke to cripples in wheelchairs directly. They always addressed their questions and comments to whoever else was there, as though the person in the wheelchair were handicapped mentally as well as physically.

It was a scenario he had assiduously avoided. He had contacted no old friends, no fellow veterans, no fellow war maimed. He had hidden himself away, first at his uncle's ranch in Wyoming, and then in his mother's house. And though she did not know it, Serena was the first person to have broken through.

He found his mouth crooking into a smile as she described her father's horrified reactions to Bedingham's pop festival.

Serena saw the smile and knew that she could

182

give herself a small congratulatory pat on the back. The man she had encountered earlier that afternoon had quite obviously not smiled for a long, long time. She said quietly, knowing that now it was safe to talk about it, "Tell me about Kyle. Tell me about your time together in 'Nam. Tell me of how he was shot down, and of what happened immediately afterward."

His smile died, but the rapport between them remained unbroken. "Kyle was one hell of a buddy," he began, his eyes clouding with reminiscence.

He didn't tell her about their mutual whoring. He didn't tell her about Trinh. He told her about the good times. How the two of them had flown their Hueys as if they were souped-up Mustangs, flaring their birds into hot landing zones through clouds of pink smoke, loading on wounded, kicking out some answering ammo, and then half an hour later coming back and doing it all over again. How, when they were contour flying, they had flown so low they had been practically skiing over the treetops and tall grass. And then he told her about their last mission. Of how Kyle had been shot down. Of how he had seen Kyle hurl himself from the blazing ship to the ground and how he had flown into dense fire in an attempt to pluck him to safety.

"What happened?" she asked gently as he paused, unable to continue.

He looked away from her, his face suddenly closed and shuttered. "First of all we took a burst through the cockpit. I was temporarily blinded by the debris. Then we were hit again, and this time a bullet hit below my chest protector and went right through to my spine. End of story."

The bitterness was back in his voice, and this time she didn't try to jolt him out of it. She said instead, regretfully, "I'd better tell your mother we're ready for supper now. In another half hour I shall have to leave."

He kept his face averted from hers so that she could not see the sudden panic that had filled his eyes. "It's too late for you to drive back to New York. Why don't you stay here the night?"

It was an invitation she had known that he would make. "No," she said, wishing that things were different, wishing that she could stay. "Sitting smoking pot and drinking wine with you all afternoon and evening is reprehensible enough behavior for a POW wife. I can't ruin my reputation completely by suggesting to your mother that I stay the night."

He turned his head, his eyes meeting hers, and a new emotion flooded through her. "Kyle told me you were a girl who didn't give a damn about what people thought of you, and as far as your reputation is concerned, it's more than safe enough with me. Now."

She ignored the last savage barb and forcing a smile, rose to her feet. "Nevertheless, I can't stay," she said, her voice a little unsteady. "I'll go and tell your mother that we're ready to join her for supper."

"Then where will you stay?" he persisted, his

184

eyes holding hers unrelentingly.

"I have a hotel room booked," she lied, and appalled at the realization that had so suddenly hit her, she walked quickly out into the hall and across into the living room.

Jesus! Why hadn't she been prepared for such a reaction the instant she had realized how similar he and Kyle were? When he had turned his head, his eyes meeting hers in the lamplit room, the emotion that had flooded through her had been one of overpowering physical attraction. And he was confined to a wheelchair, for God's sake! He probably couldn't even function in bed. Even if he could, he was Kyle's best buddy. And she had vowed to remain celibate until Kyle was freed from Hoa Lo.

Her hand was trembling as she knocked on the living room door and entered. The whole thing was too farcical to be true. She was probably just feeling gratitude toward him for what he had done for Kyle. Or she was overcome with admiration for his bravery. Another alternative came to her, this time repellent. Perhaps she was one of those sick freaks who was sexually turned on by deformity. She dismissed the possibility almost as soon as it occurred to her. She knew herself better than that. The simple truth was that wheelchair or no wheelchair. Chuck Wilson was a damned attractive man with whom she had felt and immediate rapport.

"We're ready to join you for supper now, Mrs. Wilson," she said with all the graciousness she was capable of. "Chuck has told me all that he can about my husband, and I'm very grateful to him. And for what he did for Kyle." She paused and then said, knowing how inadequate the words were, and knowing that there were no words adequate enough, "I'm terribly sorry about the injuries Chuck sustained on Kyle's behalf. If there is anything I or my family can do..."

"There is nothing anyone can do," Chuck's mother said bleakly, her eyes harrowed.

Serena hesitated. What she was going to say next could, if it were misinterpreted, sound appalling, but it had to be said. "I don't want you to take offence, Mrs. Wilson, but my family is reasonably wealthy and..."

To her intense relief she saw that no offence had been taken.

"I understand what you are saying, Mrs. Anderson," Mrs. Wilson said with exquisite dignity, "and I am appreciative of your offer. But it isn't a question of money. It is a question of Chuck's own attitude about what has happened to him. He has never, ever, said that he regretted what he did and he has never blamed your husband for what happened to him. But he can't accept what happened; he can't even begin to learn to live with it."

There came the sound of the wheelchair speeding out of the den. There was nothing more that they could say to each other. At least nothing that mattered.

"I'll serve supper, then," Mrs. Wilson said as her son propelled himself into the room. "It's so

186

nice to have company for a change. Perhaps you'll call on us again, Mrs. Anderson?"

Radford stared at Gabrielle as if she had taken leave of her senses, "Do I hear you *right*, baby? You're walking *out*? You're giving up everything we've sweated for to go to *Vietnam*? You're going to make *me* and the *rest* of the band give up everything we've sweated and bled for just when everything is good?"

She nodded, her eyes holding his unflinchingly. She had known what it was going to be like. She had known that she wasn't only turning her own back on fame and fortune, but that by her defection, leaving them without a lead singer, she was in all probability forcing the entire band to turn its back on it too.

"Yes. *Je regrette*, Radford. I know how crazy this must seem to you. I know what terrible timing it is, just when the band is on the verge of the really big time and the new recording contract has been signed, but it is something I *have* to do, *mon ami*. You will be able to find another singer, someone far better than me..."

They were standing backstage amid a tangle of electric cables and amplification wires. Up front, on the piano, Michel was experimenting with a new arrangement. The notes tinkled softly, stopped, began again, this time slightly differently.

In the dull light Radford's skin had a sheen to it. Beads of pure rage clustered on his brow. He had been checking the readjusted lighting system, still convinced that the physics were all wrong, the beams focusing eyes away from Gabrielle's spot and not on her. He was wearing a T-shirt, hip-hugging jeans, and sneakers, and he was mad enough to murder.

"You walk in here. You tell me you're going to fuck up everything I've worked for since I was knee-high to a grasshopper, and you tell me you're *sorry*! What kind of a dude do you think I am? Do you think I'm going to say, 'Oh, that's all right. Miss Anne. Sure ain't no bother for me', because I ain't going to *do* that, baby!"

Everything that had always smoldered between them was rising to the surface, seeking its outlet in frustrated anger.

"You *are* this band!" he spat out at her, "just as much as *I* am. There ain't no way you going to walk out on everything now. No *way*, baby!"

The piano had ceased to tinkle. From somewhere a long way away Gabrielle could hear the faint sound of *le petit* Gavin squalling lustily. Maura would be with him. Maura would pacify him.

She could see the blinding, white-hot fury in his eyes and she knew it was completely justified. She was fucking him up, fucking the entire band up. She said a little unsteadily, "I said I was sorry, Radford, because I know of no other word to use. I *am* sorry. I know exactly how damaging my action is going to be for everyone, but it is something that I *must* do. I must try to find Gavin. I can't remain, waiting impotently, any longer."

188

"*Jesus Christ!*" He covered the distance between them in one stride, grasping her shoulders so hard that she cried out in pain. "Forget about him! He's dead! Gone! Finished!" Passionate fury had merged into other feelings too long suppressed. "This shit has been going on for too long, Gabrielle! You want what I want. You want to be the number one attraction in the *world*! And we can be that! We can be that *together*. Do you understand what I'm saying to you? Not only together onstage, but *together*, baby! *You* and *me*! An *item*!"

The skin was taut across his cheekbones. She could smell the perspiration sticking to his body and the faint lemon tang of his cologne. She could feel his hardness as he pressed her against him and sexual longing screamed through her, demanding satisfaction.

"You want what I want," he said again, no longer shouting at her, his voice harsh and full of need. "I want *you*, baby. And you want me. You always have. You always will."

Through the thin silk of her blouse his touch was scorching her skin. She couldn't move. A sob of shame and despair rose in her throat, and then Michel was saying tautly, "*Le petit* Gavin has fallen and grazed his knees. I think you had better come and comfort him."

The sob turned to one of gratitude, and she pushed herself away from Radford, not looking at him, not daring to look at him. "*Merci*, Michel. Where is he? Take me to him."

* * *

It was a long time before she felt calm again. She had been on the verge of betraying Gavin's trust in her and only Michel had saved her. The knowledge left her feeling drained and sick at heart.

When she next faced Radford, both of them knew that the personal Rubicon they had reached would not, now, be crossed.

"I will fly back to Paris the morning after our last American concert," she said to him, deep circles carved beneath her eyes, her kittenish face, usually so full of impishness and laughter, white and grave.

He had known that nothing he could do or say would persuade her to stay. "I'll get another singer," he said raspingly, a nerve ticking convulsively at the corner of his jaw. "But she'll only be a temporary. You're still a member of the band." Knowing another moment of her nearness would unstring him completely, he pivoted on his heel and strode away.

She watched him, slim and supple in his blue jeans, his strong shoulder muscles rippling beneath his cotton T-shirt, and she hated herself for the regret knifing through her.

She was still feeling quite subdued two weeks later when she walked into the lobby of the George V to meet Serena.

Serena had arrived in Paris the day before. She had telephoned, announcing her arrival and saying that she was in possession of a Vietnamese visa, a fact that didn't surprise Gabrielle. She had known that a 'minor' difficulty such as obtaining a visa for a country at war would pose no problem for a girl who obviously had friends in high places.

She smiled to herself as she crossed the sumptuous lobby. If Serena had told her that her father was Britain's Home Secretary, she wouldn't have been surprised.

"*Gabrielle!*" Serena called out, striding to meet her, head-turningly stunning in a raspberry-pink, miniskirted wool suit.

They hugged in the center of the lobby, oblivious to the masculine attention they were attracting. Serena suddenly pulled away from Gabrielle, regarding her still-strained face quizzically, "My God, Gabrielle. What on earth has happened to you since we last met? You look as if you've been through the wringer!"

"I have," Gabrielle responded with a grin, suddenly feeling her old, bubbly, bouncy self again. "And you? You are looking a little strained too, *n'est-ce pas?*"

Serena gurgled with laughter. "Life has certainly had its moments since Washington," she said, thinking of Chuck. She slipped her arm through Gabrielle's and as they stepped out of the George V and into the Parisian streets and the pale November sunshine, she said confidingly, "Let me tell you all about it."

CHAPTER NINE

The house Abbra rented looked out over the beach a half mile or so north of La Jolla. Her parents had been appalled when she told them she was moving, but she had been adamant.

"I need isolation in order to work, Mom," she had said, slipping her arm through her mother's and giving it a loving squeeze, willing her to understand.

"You have all the isolation you need here! Why, you spend *hours* in your room writing. I'm sure it can't be natural for anyone to spend so many hours cooped up all alone..."

"All writers spend hours cooped up alone, Mom," Abbra said, laughing. "If they didn't, they would never get any work done."

"You won't be able to spend hours cooped up alone when Lewis returns," her mother retorted tartly. "All this writing nonsense will have to stop then."

Even though Lewis was MIA and not a POW, Abbra insisted that he be spoken of as though his eventual safe return were a certainty.

She sighed, knowing that now that her mother had brought her resentment of her writing into the conversation, there was absolutely no point in continuing.

Her mother had thought her writing a harmless occupation until the day that her book had been published. Then, seeing it in the bookstores, faced with tangible evidence of an achievement she didn't understand, she had regarded it as harmless no longer.

Though Abbra had been thrilled when she first saw her finished book, and was elated each time she saw it in the store her name boldly printed across the jacket, she was aware of her mother's consternation over her daughter's new stature. Now she said, not wanting to get into a futile discussion with her mother over Lewis's approval or disapproval, "I'm going shopping for some sheets and tablecloths this morning. Why don't you come with me? We can lunch together and then stroll around an art gallery or a museum."

Her mother had been slightly mollified. The conversation had changed course. And a week later, with her car packed to capacity with clothes and household items and books, and her typewriter safely wedged in the front seat beside her, Abbra had driven south to the new home she had chosen for herself, by herself.

Abbra's life soon took on a routine. In the morning she reread her previous day's work, and then wrote a minimum of twelve hundred words. The novel she was now working on was far more ambitious than her first novel had been and totally different in style. "A novel about North Beach in the fifties and the burgeoning beat generation!" Patti had said doubtfully when she had first spoken to her about it. "It doesn't sound commercial, Abbra."

Abbra doubted that it was commercial too, but her first novel wasn't selling as many copies she, Patti, or her publishers had hoped, so she didn't see that she had anything to lose by attempting something more ambitious.

In the afternoon she would walk on the beach, and when she returned she would write her daily diary, the diary that she mailed each week to Lewis, care of the North Vietnamese government.

There was never any reply. There was never any news of him. His name never appeared on any official list of prisoners being held. There were times, when she was overtired, or when it all seemed too much for her to bear, when she wondered if there was any point in continuing with the letters. They seemed to merely disappear into a black hole, a limitless void. The despair would pass, and the following week's letter would be sent, but the loneliness and the longing remained, and were never eased.

In the third week of December she returned to San Francisco for a few days to spend Christmas with her parents. There was a card for her from Scott, but there was no letter enclosed, only his signature, big and bold and achingly familiar.

She put the card back in its envelope quickly, aware of her mother looking speculatively in her direction. Although nothing had ever been said, it was almost as if her mother had guessed at the reason he no longer visited her or telephoned. She had put no letter in her Christmas card to him, either, and she had not told him that she had moved. If there were news of Lewis, then she would contact him. Until then, she had to stay out of his life.

There were cards and letters from both Gabrielle and Serena, and she drew enormous strength from them. They were both in Saigon. Gabrielle was making as many contacts as she could with people who had known her uncle, and Serena was working as a volunteer in one of the local orphanages. Abbra had been amused by the last revelation. It was hard to imagine Serena, so carelessly soignée, feeding and changing tiny babies and clearing up the kind of mess that tiny babies were apt to make.

On the first of February she turned on the television to listen to the morning news as she made her breakfast, and was stunned to hear the news of the Viet Cong's Tet offensive. It was the Vietnamese New Year and all across South Vietnam hundreds of towns and cities and U.S. bases had come under simultaneous attack. In Saigon, Viet Cong guerrillas had blown a hole in the embassy wall and entered the grounds. There were reports that the embassy had been seized and was under Viet Cong control, that the war in all its fury had finally reached the heart of Saigon.

All day she listened to every newscast, fearful for Gabrielle and Serena, wondering if they were

195

safe. The evening news programs had live coverage of the events. At the embassy four GIs had been killed and another had been critically injured. The initial news flash, that the embassy had been seized, was denied, but the situation was still one of terrifying confusion. Dead Viet Cong lay sprawled on the embassy grounds as heavy automatic gunfire continued. Six and a half hours after the attack, the embassy was declared secure again, the last of the assailants being shot by a senior embassy official as he crept up a flight of inner stairs.

The American Embassy wasn't the only "secure" building to come under attack. A small group of Viet Cong, a woman among them, had tried to break into the Presidential Palace. There were live pictures of American and South Vietnamese troops engaged in a pitched battle with the attackers, their dead still lying in the street where they had fallen.

Saigon's main radio station was seized. Roads were blocked to prevent American and South Vietnamese reinforcements from entering the city. General Westmoreland's headquarters were attacked. There were reports from outlying towns of foreign doctors, nurses, missionaries, and schoolteachers being slaughtered by the insurgents, and Abbra's fears for Serena and Gabrielle increased.

For a week, newscasts reported running battles in Saigon between the Viet Cong and American and South Vietnamese forces.

Abbra knew that she could expect no news of

Serena and Gabrielle until order was restored. The often sunless February days passed with agonizing slowness. As normality returned to Saigon, there were horrific news reports of the fighting further north, in the old imperial capital of Hue.

The fighting in Hue continued for twenty-four murderous days, and at the end of the fighting, when the recently raised Viet Cong flag was ripped from the flagpole of the ancient fortress that dominated the town and the South Vietnamese red and yellow banner rose again, one hundred and fifty U.S. marines lay dead. Four hundred South Vietnamese troops also died in the often hand-to-hand fighting, and it was estimated that thousands of civilians, some victims of Communist death squads, other victims of American air and artillery strikes, had also died. The city itself, the most historical and the most beautiful in the whole of Vietnam, was devastated.

It was while she was reading a newspaper report in which an American officer was describing paradoxically how "we had to destroy the city in order to save it", that a telegram arrived for her from Gabrielle. She and Serena were safe. Tet had been *"très grisant"*, very exhilarating. Rocket and mortar explosions had trapped them in their hotel room for three days, but now they were okay. She would write soon. And she sent much, much love.

Abbra's relief was colossal. She was able to concentrate on her novel again. She had

197

promised Patti that it would be finished by Easter, and she wanted to be professional and meet her self-imposed deadline.

For the next few weeks, television news coverage was all of the fighting at Khe Sanh, a marine base in the northwest corner of South Vietnam. The marines' mission was to cover North Vietnamese infiltration routes from Laos, eight kilometers away from them, to the west.

At the end of January they had found themselves besieged by two crack North Vietnamese divisions, one of them the same division that had, fourteen years before, led the assault on Dien Bien Phu. All through February and March the newspapers were full of harrowing reports of the fighting. Day after day, eighteen-, nineteen- and twenty-year-olds were being slaughtered. Looking at the photographs, Abbra's antiwar convictions solidified.

On March 31, tired and looking ill, President Johnson went on nationwide television to announce that he would not be seeking re-election. Abbra felt a surge of hope. A new presidency would mean new political decisions. Both Eugene McCarthy and Robert Kennedy, the two men seeking nomination as Democratic candidate, were antiwar. If either man became president, then the war would surely end. She began to root for Kennedy.

On April first, she finished her novel and on the third she delivered it to Patti, and they went for a celebratory lunch. On the fourth she felt as if she would never be able to celebrate anything again. Dr. Martin Luther King was shot dead in Memphis. The assassination of a man who had always advocated peaceful resistance no matter how violent the provocation was so monstrous that Abbra felt as if a member of her own family had been murdered. There was worse to come.

On June 6 Robert Kennedy, the man she had hoped would be the next president, was gunned down in the Hotel Ambassador in Los Angeles minutes after triumphantly winning the California primary.

Two weeks later, when the black limousine slid to a halt outside her pastel-painted house, she knew that the saying "Death comes in threes" held true. She never remembered going to the door or opening it. She only remembered facing the army officer and the accompanying chaplain, and the army officer saying gently, "Do you have a friend we could call, Mrs. Ellis?"

She shook her head, overcome by a dizzying sense of déjà vu. She had been here before. Another army officer had asked her if she could call a friend before breaking his news to her, and that news had not been news of Lewis's death. She clung to a remnant of hope. There was no reason why the news this time should be of Lewis's death. It couldn't be. She would have known if he had died. She wouldn't have to be told. She would have *known*.

Looking around him and realizing that there was no neighbor within easy reach who could be called on to sit with her, the officer said unhappily, "May we come in, Mrs. Ellis?"

She tried to say yes, but no words would come. Her throat was so tight that she felt as if she were being strangled. Mutely she opened the door wide and led the way into her little sitting room. Her typewriter was on the desk. She had been trying to get the synopsis for a new book down onto paper, and several discarded pages lay crumpled in the wastebasket.

"Please sit down, Mrs. Ellis." It was the chaplain speaking. His eyes were compassionate. She swung her eyes away from him, facing the officer, saying, "It's Lewis, isn't it? There's news?"

Taking her lightly by the arm, the officer led her to the nearest chair. Numbly she sat. "Yes," he said at last. "I'm afraid the news isn't good, Mrs. Ellis."

She waited. It was a gloriously hot day, and through the wide window of the room she could see the dazzle of sunlight on the distant surf. A half-finished page was still wound in the typewriter. She wondered what her last sentence had been and couldn't remember. She wondered if she would ever write another sentence.

"We have confirmation from a fellow prisoner, recently released, that your husband died in a jungle camp in the Ca Mau Peninsula sometime during October of last year."

October. When she had flown to Washington for the antiwar demonstration. When she had met Serena and Gabrielle and been so full of renewed hope. October. Before her first novel had been published. Before her second novel had been completed. Eight months ago. Lewis had died eight long months ago, and she hadn't known. It was impossible. Inconceivable.

She said in a cracked, harsh voice that she didn't recognize as her own, "I don't believe it."

"It's a first-hand account, Mrs. Ellis," the chaplain said gently. "There can be no mistake."

She looked into his face, and saw that he was speaking the truth. Lewis was dead. He was dead and she was going to have to live the rest of her life without him.

She rose unsteadily to her feet. "I'd like to be alone please."

"I don't think that is a very good idea, Mrs. Ellis." It was the chaplain. He was in late middle age and he looked tired and drawn. She wondered how many other wives he had broken the same news to. How he could bear to wake up each day, knowing what his work entailed.

She repeated immovably, "I would like to be alone, please."

In the end, unhappily, they left. As their limousine pulled away, churning up a cloud of dust and the fine sand that always thinly layered her driveway, she stood in the center of her sitting room. Lewis would never see it now. He would never live there with her. He would never know about the novels. Never touch her again. Never hold her and kiss her.

She was still dry-eyed. She couldn't cry. Her grief was too deep for tears. Despite the summer heat there was goose flesh on her arms and legs.

"Oh, God," she whispered, wondering how she was going to survive. *"Oh, Lewis, Lewis, Lewis!"*

Her father-in-law came to see her; her parents came, insistent that she move back to San Francisco. She refused, knowing that she could never live there again. From now on her home was the home she had made for herself when she had thought Lewis was still alive.

Scott had sent her a telegram. He was in Rome on a summer vacation. He had told her to be brave, and from Scott the words had not seemed trite.

The hardest thing of all was in believing that it was true. If there had been a body to bury, it would have been easier. But there was no body. There was no coffin, no wreaths of flowers, no funeral service, no grave to visit. There was no tangible evidence of his death at all. It was as if Lewis, and the brief days of their marriage that they had spent together, had never been.

There were so few memories. Only the platonically affectionate dates that they had enjoyed together in Carmel and San Francisco; their one-night honeymoon and their week in Hawaii. That was all the time that they had had. The paucity of it broke her heart.

She had written to Serena and Gabrielle and had received long, commiserative, supportive letters back from them. And she had told Patti, who had been exquisitely sympathetic and who had immediately driven down from Los Angeles to see her. There had been no one else to tell. Their marriage had not been long enough for them to have formed any mutual friendships. Her grief could not be truly shared with anyone. Not until Scott returned from Italy.

His father had told her that he was vacationing in Europe until the end of July, and she had reconciled herself to not seeing him until then. Without a funeral to attend there was, after all, no reason for him to return.

A week after her official visitors had arrived in their black limousine, she slipped out of the house early, just as the sun was rising, and went for a long walk on the beach. She wanted to think about the future as well as the past. A future without Lewis. What would she do? Where would she go? How would she manage to exist through the half life that lay ahead of her?

It was too early even for pre-breakfast beach-combers and she was alone. A sea gull swept inland, below eye level, the rising sun glinting rosy on its back. She would write. That much was obvious. Whatever happened, she would always write. But what else? What else could there possibly be now that she no longer had Lewis?

In the distance she saw another person on the sand. She turned and began to walk slowly back in the direction of the house. Perhaps she should think about buying the house or, if that wasn't possible, buying another house close by. After all, she would need a home, and there was never going to be a home for her on an army base with Lewis.

Wry sadness flooded through her. She was an army widow who had never experienced army life. She would never know, now, whether or not she would have adapted successfully to such a change in her life-style. She was wearing dark gray slacks and a white silk shirt, a black cashmere sweater around her shoulders. She slipped her hands into the pockets of her slacks, looking broodingly out over the pearl-gray ocean as she walked.

She didn't look toward the house until it was twenty yards away. Then, turning away from the ocean to walk across the beach to the steps that led toward it, she looked up and saw him.

He looked as if he had been standing there for a long time, watching her. He had allowed his hair to grow indecently long. Beneath the early morning sun it gleamed the color of ripening barley. She couldn't see the expression on his face or in his eyes; she didn't need to. Her heart began to beat in sharp, slamming strokes that she could feel even in her fingertips. He had come back.

"Scott!" she cried, taking her hands out of her pockets and breaking into a run. "Scott!"

She hurtled into his arms, and as they closed around her, and as she clung to him, safe in the harbor of his strength and his love for her, the frozen waste inside her thawed, and tears came in a grieving torrent.

"He died, and I didn't know," she gasped, her breath coming in great, shuddering sobs. "Oh,

Scott, how could I not have known? How could I not have been able to tell?"

He had no answer for her. He merely held her tight, stroking her hair, soothing her as best he could.

She wept as though she would never stop, and then at last she said thickly, "I loved him so much. I thought I was going to have him to love for the rest of my life."

"I know, baby. I know," he said gently, and with his arm around her shoulders, he began to lead her back into the house.

"Are you going to be able to talk to this guy who says he was in the same camp as Lewis?" he asked her as he cooked breakfast for them both.

She had cried until she could cry no longer. Now she sat with her legs curled beneath her on the window seat in the kitchen, watching him as he grilled bacon and fried eggs.

"No," she said, her eyes so dark they were almost black, her face ivory pale. "I wanted to, but in the official letter received, I was told that the soldier in question was an Australian serving with the First Battalion, Royal Australian Regiment. He has been honorably discharged and his present whereabouts aren't known."

Scott's jawline hardened. He didn't believe what she had been told for one moment. The army was simply trying not to cause waves, and perhaps trying to save her from further distress. He said, "There's a Marlon Brando film showing in La Jolla tonight. Would you like to see it with me?"

The movies. It had been months since she had been to the movies, or anywhere else for that matter.

For an instant she was too shocked by the suggestion to reply and then she said, with no doubt at all in her voice, "I'd love to."

She needed distraction. She needed to go through the motions of living until the motions once again became natural. And she needed company, Scott's company.

For four months she told no one that he had re-entered her life, and she didn't attend his games. But when he was in town he drove down from Los Angeles to take her out to dinner, to take her to the movies and the occasional concert, to discuss her work with her and to walk with her on the beach. She didn't tell her father-in-law; she didn't tell her parents; she didn't even tell Patti.

In all those months he never once referred to the words he had spoken to her in the forest above Lake Tahoe, and he never touched her, except chastely when helping her in and out of the car, or slipping her coat around her shoulders.

In October, as he was about to drive back to Los Angeles, and she was walking him from the house to his Chevrolet, he turned to her and said suddenly, his voice oddly abrupt, "Has enough time passed, Abbra? Can I ask you now?"

It was early evening and behind him the ocean

lay in indigo shadow, the surging surf milky-pale.

"Ask me what?" she said, smiling up at him with no intimation of what was to come.

There was no answering smile on his face. Every line of his body was taut with tension. "Will you marry me?" he said simply.

Time wavered and halted. She couldn't speak, couldn't move. Somewhere deep in her subconscious she had always known that this moment would come, and she had refused to think about it, had refused to think of what her reply might be.

"I love you, Abbra," he said, still not touching her, still not reaching out for her. "I always have. I want you to be my wife."

He was wearing a turtleneck sweater and jeans. Beneath the thick, sun-bleached tumble of his hair his eyes were onyx-dark. She could see white lines of strain edging his mouth and a pulse begin to beat at the corner of his jaw.

Still she couldn't speak or move. He had been her brother-in-law and for a long time, longer than she had cared to admit he had been the most important person in her life. He was also a professional football player, a pin-up, a man who could have his pick of hundreds of women. And he was in love with her. He had been in love with her for a long time.

Her heart was beating fast and light, high in her throat. Though she had known of Lewis's death for only four months, he had, in reality, been dead for a year. That was why Scott was asking her to marry him now. Because it had been a year. And because he loved her.

Suddenly it was as if a great dam inside her was at last breaking free. Loving Scott would not diminish her memories of Lewis. Nothing would ever do that. Lewis would be a part other life always. But in a moment of stunning, dizzying revelation, she knew that she loved Scott. She was deeply, irrevocably, deliriously in love with the man who was asking her to marry him.

"Oh, yes!" she said, opening her arms and stepping toward him, so sure of the rightness other answer that nothing in the world could have swerved her from it. "Oh, yes, I *will* marry you, Scott! I want to marry you more than anything else in the world!"

His return trip to Los Angeles was forgotten. Lifting her up in his arms, he turned back with her to the house, striding through the sun-filled, book-filled room in which she worked, carrying her up the narrow stairs to the bedroom he had never entered.

There had never been any physical intimacy between them beyond hugs and an occasional chaste kiss. Now he was going to make love to her, and neither of them could wait. She unbuttoned her blouse with trembling fingers, slipping her skirt down over her hips, leaving it where it fell. She stood still in her bra and panties, filled with crippling shyness. Scott was so much more experienced than she was. The models and actresses that he had dated had all, surely, been knowledgeable and unimaginably abandoned. Was he going to be disappointed in her? Was he assuming qualities about her that she did not possess?

He had thrown his turtleneck sweater to the far side of the room. Now he kicked off his jeans, looking across at her, aware for the first time of her sudden hesitancy. He didn't need to ask her what was the matter. The reason for her apprehension was blatant in her eyes. Slowly he stretched his hand out across the bed toward her.

"I love you," he said thickly. "I've never been in love with anyone before, ever." Her hand slipped trustingly into his. "I've never been to bed with a woman I love. This is my first time, Abbra. You have as much to teach me as I have to teach you."

She gave a little cry, overcome with love for him, and with gratitude for his understanding. Gently he pulled her onto the bed and into his arms. He had waited so long for her, he wasn't going to spoil everything by rushing now. "I love you, Abbra," he said again, pushing her silk-black hair away from her face, kissing her temples, her eyes, the corners of her mouth. "I love you, lady. I'm always going to love you. All the days of my life."

When he unhooked her bra and cupped her breasts in his large, strong hands, she shivered in delight. Slowly his thumbs brushed her nipples, slowly he lowered his head, kissing and gently sucking.

She had not waited for him to slide her panties down. She was so damp, and hot and eager for him, she had wriggled out of them herself, kicking them away, spreading her legs wide and pulling him down on top of her.

It had been as wonderful as he had known it would be. It had been more than wonderful. It had been the most cataclysmic, exquisite, joy-filled experience of his life. There was no ghost in the room with them. No doubt. No guilt. Only love, complete, and satisfying, and boundless.

When they broke the news that they were going to marry, her parents were so shocked they were almost catatonic. They refused point-blank to come to the wedding. They refused to meet Scott. They said that unless she came to her senses and called the wedding off, they would never have anything to do with her again.

Tom Ellis's reaction had been equally intense. At first he refused to believe it. And when they had lovingly and patiently assured him that they were telling him the truth, his rage had been terrifying. They were defiling Lewis's memory. They were shameless. Adulterous. He wished they were both dead, as Lewis was dead.

Abbra had been so distressed that it had taken nearly all her courage to break the news to Patti. What if Patti's reaction, too, was one of stunned horror? If it was, there would be no one at their wedding. They would have to pull strangers in off the street to act as witnesses.

"You couldn't have called at a better time," Patti said cheerily from the sophisticated depths of her Los Angeles office. "I was just about to

210

call to tell you Book of the Month Club has bought the book! Publication date, by the way, is *definitely* February '69, and your editor tells me that the jacket is going to be *sensational!*"

"That's great, Patti," Abbra said, barely registering it. "I have some news for you too." She took a deep, steadying breath. "I'm marrying Scott, and I would like you to be my maid of honor."

There wasn't even a fraction of a second pause. Patti let out a whoop of glee that must have been audible in the next block. "That's *wonderful* news, Abbra! I'd *love* to be your maid of honor! When is the wedding? What shall I wear? What are you going to wear? Oh, my God, I haven't been so thrilled by a piece of news in years!"

"She's pleased?" Scott asked unnecessarily when she put the telephone receiver back on its rest.

Abbra grinned. "She's pleased. And she's going to be my maid of honor."

"And a buddy from the team is going to be my best man," Scott said, pulling her lovingly down next to him on the sofa and drawing her into his arms. "So all our troubles are over, and our guest list is complete."

Despite the fact that there were going to be only two guests, they had decided on a church wedding.

It was a small, white-walled church, Spanish in style, and on the evening before their marriage she decorated it herself with small-budded pink roses and stephanotis and clouds of orange blossom.

Her dress was of pale ice-blue silk with huge puff sleeves, a tiny waist, and a softly flowing full skirt. Her bouquet was made up of the same flowers that she had decorated the church with, and although she had transferred Lewis's wedding ring to the third finger of her right hand, with Scott's blessing she still wore his engagement ring on her left hand. Instead of an engagement ring Scott had bought her a pair of delicate, antique pearl-and-diamond earrings. Apart from these, and her ring, she wore no other jewelry.

Patti was exquisite in a pale pink dress the exact color of the roses in her and Abbra's bouquets. She stood on tiptoe to kiss Scott warmly, flirted happily with the best man, and presented the bride and groom with a magnificent Lalique vase as a wedding present.

When the simple ceremony had been completed, they drove to the Hotel Valencia, overlooking La Jolla Cove, and celebrated with champagne and a lavish wedding breakfast.

They were flying to New Orleans for their honeymoon, because Abbra had never seen it before and it was a city that she had always wanted to visit.

The best man and maid of honor, by now comfortably holding hands, drove them to San Diego International Airport. At the departure lounge doors Abbra turned, her black hair swinging glossily as she tossed her bouquet toward Patti.

Patti caught it neatly with a wide smile and a naughty wink, and Scott's buddy, who was standing beside her, blushed sheepishly.

As the departure lounge doors closed behind Scott and herself, Abbra's heart was full to overflowing. She had a future again. She had someone she loved, who loved her in return.

CHAPTER TEN

Gabrielle's return to Saigon was the most traumatic experience of her life. Everything had changed. She remembered the city as being languorous and exotically sophisticated.

Apart from a few disturbingly young flower sellers, none of the sights and sounds of her childhood remained. There was nothing remotely languorous or sophisticated about the city she had returned to. It had become as tawdry and as corrupt and disheveled as an old whore. Instead of white-suited Malacca-cane-holding Frenchmen, the streets were thronged with GIs, some drunk, some stoned on drugs, nearly all of them rowdy and out for a good time.

Bicycles and pedal-cabs still thronged the streets, but they had to vie for road space with thousands of souped-up scooters and Honda 50s. Trucks and taxicabs and jeeps hurtled incessantly down the main thoroughfare. When Gabrielle had been a child it had been called rue Catinat; now it was known as Tu Do Street and all down its length, where there had once been elegant shops and boutiques and sidewalk cafés, there were girlie bars and clubs and brothels. She wasn't shocked. It wasn't in her nature. And she didn't regret the passing of the days when French colonialists dominated the city, and native-born Saigonese catered deferentially for their comforts.

Nhu had said in her letters that the American Army had simply replaced the French as an occupying force, and that the Saigonese were still second-class citizens whose primary function was to provide labor. Gabrielle could see why she thought so, but even though the main service industry was prostitution, she thought the status quo between Americans and Saigonese more equal and healthier than the unhappy status quo that had existed between the colonial French and Saigonese.

There were some things in Saigon that hadn't changed though. The stinging brilliance of the light was still the same, as was the heavy humidity and the rank aroma that rose from the Saigon River. And the Saigonese were still the same. Slim and dark and fragile-boned, they were as sassily streetwise and as quick-witted and as quick to laughter as she had remembered them to be. The years fell away and she was stunned by the realization that the Vietnamese side of her nature was far more dominant than the French. She felt as if she had never left the city, as if it were truly her home.

For Serena, adjusting to Saigon took much longer. Although it was November and there were often days when the city was awash beneath autumn rain, she found the underlying heat and humidity unrelenting and oppressive.

The first thing they had done after landing at Tan Son Nhut airport had been to drive to Gabrielle's aunt's house. The reunion between Nhu and Gabrielle had been joyfully tearful, and Serena had happily kept a low profile as the two of them caught up on family news, talking themselves hoarse. Nhu had invited them to stay with her, but Gabrielle had reluctantly declined.

"No, Aunt Nhu. We would excite the wrong kind of attention. We will stay at the Continental Palace or the Caravelle, where we will be less noticeable."

"The Continental Palace," Serena said firmly when they had said their good-byes to Nhu. "Somerset Maugham is said to have stayed there, Graham Greene *definitely* stayed there, and if it was good enough for him, it must surely be good enough for us."

Gabrielle hadn't argued. She did not care which hotel they used as a base, and as Serena was used to the comfort of hotels such as the Jefferson in Washington, and the George V in Paris, to expose her to anything less than the Continental in Saigon would have been an act of gross cruelty.

The standard of comfort and cuisine at the Continental came as a monumental shock to

Serena. The meat served at dinner was almost always buffalo meat, and *always* served with rice.

"The country is at war," Gabrielle had said to her, amused. "There is very little food, and anything other than buffalo meat and rice would be too expensive for the hotel to serve."

For a long moment Serena's beautifully sculpted face had been void of all expression. Gabrielle wondered if she was reconsidering the venture and planning to return to the luxury of her jet-set life-style in London, but she grinned suddenly, pushing a long fall of pale blond hair away from her face, saying resolutely, "I'll adapt. It's a family virtue."

She had been true to her word. By the end of the first week she had accepted the ubiquitous military presence, the armed guards in front of nearly every public building, the lethal coils of barbed wire that barricaded certain streets. She had even learned not to flinch at the sound of distant gunfire. But what she could not accept, and could not ignore, was the sight of the children, some only four or five years old, wandering the streets in misery, begging for piastres.

"Don't they have any homes to go to?" she had asked Gabrielle as they crossed the central square in front of the old French Opera House.

Gabrielle hated the sight as much as Serena, but because of her streak of Eastern fatalism, she was better able to cope with it. "No," she said, her eyes darkening. "They are war orphans. There are hundreds of them in the city. Probably thousands."

Serena was more than deeply shocked. She was horrified. Nothing in her experience had prepared her for the reality of such abject deprivation. "But why aren't they *cared* for?" she demanded incredulously. "Why aren't they in orphanages?"

Gabrielle ignored the lascivious leer of a passing GI. "I imagine that the majority of them are, but I suspect that the local orphanages leave an awful lot to be desired."

"Jesus! Do you mean that the orphanages are so badly run that these kids prefer to take their chances on the streets?" Serena asked, stunned.

"*Alors*. I do not know, Serena," she said, her cat-green eyes still dark with anguish as she thought of the plight of the street children. "I do not even know who runs the orphanages in the city. I am simply making what I think is called in English, 'an educated guess'."

They were on their way to meet Nhu, and an acquaintance of hers, a Vietnamese journalist who had been born in the South and had always lived in the South, but whose father had chosen to go north in 1954. He worked for a German news magazine, and was ostensibly loyal to the Saigon government. But he had also been a friend of Dinh's, and Nhu suspected that his true loyalties lay with the Communist North. He was certainly a man that it was necessary Gabrielle should meet, and it was important that he should be convinced, at the outset, of Gabrielle's utter trustworthiness.

Gabrielle, thinking about the meeting, lapsed into thoughtful silence. Serena dug her hands deep into the pockets of her stone-colored Burberry, her forehead puckering in a frown. No one could ever have accused her of having a social conscience. All her life she had lived a cosseted and privileged existence, and it had never occurred to her to feel a sense of responsibility to those who were less fortunate than herself. She was willful, headstrong, and selfish, and happy to be so. Charity work and good causes were a bore she had always avoided, and she had had no intention of changing the habit of a lifetime merely because she was now living in a war zone.

Her frown deepened. She still had no intention of turning into a ministering angel, rounding up the children on the streets and establishing some sort of care for them. That kind of thing wasn't her scene at all. Yet she had to do something. The question was, what?

Her frown cleared as she came to a decision. She would check out the orphanages in the city and see if Gabrielle's assumptions about them were correct. Even though Gabrielle had insisted that she accompany her to see the journalist, Serena knew that she would be a handicap. She was English, married to an American POW, not half Vietnamese and related to Dinh. Her very presence at the meeting would be enough to insure that no information of any value would be divulged.

She stopped suddenly, saying, "My going with

you really isn't a good idea, Gabrielle. And I have something to do of my own. I'll meet you later this afternoon, back at the Continental."

"Are you sure, *chérie*?" Gabrielle was wearing tight black cotton trousers and high-heeled mules. Because of the threat of rain, a short black leather jacket was slung around her shoulders, her spicy red curls brushing incandescently against the upturned collar.

Serena grinned. It was no wonder that they couldn't walk a yard down the street without being lewdly accosted. Gabrielle, quite innocently, looked every inch a pert and naughty high-class hooker. "I'm positive," she said, suddenly itching to be off on her personal investigation. "I hope this guy you are meeting proves to be the genuine article."

"*Moi aussi*," Gabrielle said with heartfelt sincerity. "*Au 'voir, chérie.*"

As Gabrielle walked away from her, her provocatively tight-fitting trousers leaving very little to the imagination, Serena turned her attention to the task of flagging down a taxi or a pedal-cab.

"My God! Will you look at *that*!" a drunken GI called out to his buddies as his eyes focused upon her. "Am I dreaming? Am I in heaven? Has Sweden suddenly entered the war and sent some women out here as a bridgehead?"

"Never mind a bridgehead, does she *give* head?" another riposted, swaying meaningfully across the sidewalk toward Serena, his buddies hooting with mirth at his wit and crowding in behind him.

"Hey, lady, is it true what they say about Swedish girls? Do they do it for free?"

Serena turned her head a mere fraction of an inch in his direction and looked at him with icy contempt, "You'd be lucky if your wife would do it with you for free," she said witheringly in her cut-glass English accent.

The GI flushed scarlet, and his buddies almost fell on the floor, laughing. Serena ignored them, turning back to her task of attracting the attention of a taxi driver. Drunken, opportunistic GIs were a constant nuisance, and both she and Gabrielle had become expert in dealing with their unwelcome attentions.

A Renault 4 taxicab swerved to a halt, and she opened the rear door, stepping inside and saying, "An orphanage, please."

The Vietnamese driver looked at her through the mirror, his eyes startled.

"An orphanage," she repeated impatiently. "A place where they take care of parentless children. It doesn't matter which one. Any will do."

The driver lifted his thin shoulders expressively, "*Không xáu*," he said agreeably. "Okay. No sweat."

They swerved away from the sidewalk and the still-whistling and appreciative GIs, and into the hurly-burly of Saigon's horrendous traffic system. A jeep blasted past them, the driver's hand firmly and permanently on the horn as he forged a way for an official Ford sedan. The taxi driver swore, swerved, regained his road space, and struggled to maintain it against a fleet of army trucks and a convoy of tanks. As they approached Cholon, the Chinese quarter, they ground to a halt as southbound vehicles plowed determinedly down both sides of a two-way street. Serena raised her eyes to heaven and fought for patience. It all seemed so senseless, and the white-helmeted Saigon police, known universally as "white mice," seemed absolutely indifferent to the chaos around them.

After an interminable length of time, and amid much verbal abuse, the traffic jam unraveled itself. Minutes later the taxi careered to a halt outside an unpromising-looking stone-gray building.

"Orphanage," the taxi driver said briefly. "You pay me in dollars, please."

Serena obliged, wondering why South Vietnam bothered with a currency of its own when the only acceptable form of payment for anything was American dollars.

She stepped out of the Renault and looked up at the building in front of her. For the first time she wondered how she was going to gain permission to wander around it at will. She didn't have a child to deliver there, and she didn't have a child to pick up, and she certainly didn't know the name of any child who was a resident. If she said she was a reporter, and if the orphanage was not well run, the staff would be immediately on their guard.

A cigarette seller approached her and she shook her head at him, pondering her problem.

She could always say that she wished to make a donation. Donations, surely, were always acceptable. And if the orphanage proved Gabrielle wrong, and was admirably well run, then she would most certainly give a donation.

Her plan of action determined, she rang the bell. A young Vietnamese girl opened the door to her, looking at her apprehensively.

"*Chào bà*," Serena said brightly, having culled from Gabrielle a minimum vocabulary so that she could at least say please and thank you in Vietnamese, and wish people good day and good-bye. "May I see your administrator, please?"

The girl's apprehension deepened into unhappy bewilderment.

"Can I see the person in charge?" Serena repeated, and then, as the girl didn't seem to understand English, she tried French. "*Je peux parler à la directrice?*"

The girl's face registered understanding, but she still made no attempt to open the door wide and to invite Serena inside.

In the shadowed hallway behind the girl Serena saw an elderly nun approaching briskly. She set a smile on her face, stepped purposefully past the unwelcoming acolyte at the door, and said genially, "*Good morning*, Sister. It was very kind of you to say that I could visit this morning. I shan't take up very much of your time, I know how terribly busy and overworked you all are..."

The nun was stern-faced, and beneath her starched white wimple her eyes were implacable. "We are expecting no visitors this morning, Madame," she said frostily. "There has been an error..."

Serena knew that if she hesitated now, all would be lost. She strode past the nun, ignoring her cries of protest, saying brightly and breezily, "I am so pleased that you are happy to accept my donation to the orphanage, Sister. The British ambassador assured me that such an amount would be most welcome and put to extremely good use."

The nun was hard at her heels, panting with the effort of trying to keep pace with her. At the mention of a donation and the British ambassador, she checked slightly. "The message to say that you would be visiting obviously went astray," she said breathlessly. "If you would be so kind as to tell me your name..."

"Lady Serena Blyth-Templeton," Serena said, reverting to her maiden name for maximum effect, "and now, if I could see the children, please..."

She could smell them long before she saw them. The whole building was heavy with an aroma of urine and feces and other substances that she could not place. She had never been in an orphanage before, never even been in a nursery, and she had not the slightest idea what to expect. As she strode into the nearest room and looked around her, the sight that met her eyes was worse than anything she could possibly have imagined.

There was row after row of white-painted

metal cots, and the occupants, some of them old enough to be attending primary school, lay docilely two and three to a bed. Nearly all of them had disfiguring skin complaints, nearly all were lying on wet bedding. Serena gagged and fought down an overwhelming tide of fury. The nun now leading the way for her obviously saw nothing reprehensible in the conditions in which the children were being kept, and to give vent to her outrage would only result in her tour being precipitately terminated.

As she slowly walked the length of the room she saw that one dark head after another was thick with lice eggs. The children stared at her dully, with no sign of animation, and she knew that what she had initially taken to be docility was apathy. God alone knew when they had last been allowed to play. Or even when they had last been spoken to. Just as they were leaving the room, one of them began to cry. A Vietnamese nurse hurried forward, giving the child a sharp smack. As Serena sucked in her breath sharply, the elderly nun at her side said quickly, "That child is always crying. He cries out of naughtiness."

"My God! How can he be naughty? He's caged in his crib like a small animal!"

The nun's face tightened. "I think that is all I can show you of our highly esteemed orphanage. In the next room the babies are being fed. A visitor would be disturbing to them."

"Don't worry, Sister. I've seen enough," Serena said grimly. "Can you give me a list of the other orphanages in the city, please?"

"And your donation?"

"A list please, Sister."

The nun didn't move and Serena said, a hint of menace in her voice, "The ambassador specifically asked me to ask for a list from you. The British Embassy's list is not as up-to-date as he would like."

"I have no written list."

"Then if you would tell me the names of the other orphanages, I will make a note of them."

"And the donation?"

"The names please, Sister."

The nun's nostrils flared and then she said curtly, "Phu My, Go Vap, Dêm Hè, Cam Hoài, St. Paul's, Ngo Thuy."

As she continued with her list, Serena wrote the names rapidly in her pocket diary.

"And now the donation, if you please," the nun finished impatiently.

Serena looked around her. No matter how large a donation she gave, she could not imagine it being spent constructively, or changing the conditions for the better.

"An appropriate donation will be sent when I have seen the conditions in the other orphanages," she said, slipping her diary into her raincoat pocket. She had every intention of giving money. A lot of money. But hopefully it would be to an orphanage that would make good use of it.

Ignoring the nun's exclamations of indignation, she strode out of the evil-smelling building and into Cholon's crowded streets. It was 1967. Vietnam was on the conscience of the world. Where was all the money being collected by European and American charities going to? How could orphanages like the one she had just visited possibly be tolerated?

She flagged down a pedicab, and beginning with the first name that the nun had so reluctantly given her, she began a day-long tour of Saigon's orphanages.

It was a day that changed her life. Not all of the orphanages were as bad as the first one. Many of them were making desperate attempts to care adequately for children in almost impossible conditions. At Phu My, older children helped look after younger children. At the orphanage run by the Sisters of St. Paul de Chartres, though there was overcrowding and the orphanage was desperately understaffed, at least it was obvious that the sisters cared for the children, and were deeply committed to their welfare. However, not every orphanage was run by the Sisters of St. Paul.

At Go Vap, a state-run orphanage, the conditions were horrendous. Food was simply put out for the children to help themselves to, and in the mad scramble, the smallest and the weakest received nothing. Serena tried to count the number of dark heads in one courtyard alone and gave the task up in despair after she had reached three hundred and twenty. There was no laughter in the orphanage, no toys, no personal care for any child. Physical chastisement seemed to be the only way that any sort of order was enforced and, as at the first orphanage she had visited, the air was redolent with the smell of soured milk and sodden bedding.

As she wearily left the misery of Go Vap behind her and told her taxi driver to take her to the last-named orphanage on her list, she felt physically sick. The scale of the problem was stupefying. There weren't simply hundreds of children in Saigon's orphanages, there were thousands.

The next orphanage was situated in a rat-infested alley not far from Tu Do Street. Serena took a deep breath, prepared for the worst, and entered.

It was like entering another world. The attendant who opened the door to her was not a nun, but neither was she an untrained peasant girl, as many of the assistants at the other orphanages had been.

"Can I help you?" she asked in a pleasant New Zealand accent.

Serena didn't stoop to the lies she had felt necessary previously. "Yes," she said, looking beyond the girl to a small courtyard where dozens of tiny babies were lying kicking their legs in the sunshine. "I'm British and I'm going to be in Saigon for quite a while. I've been trying to find an orphanage that would appreciate whatever help I could give it."

The girl's face broke into a broad smile. She was in her early twenties with a mass of thick dark hair held away from her face in a ponytail.

"Then you've come to the right place," she said zestfully. "My name is Lucy Roberts. Step right inside."

Within minutes Serena was aware that her initial instincts had been correct. The nursery was small, packed to capacity, and lovingly and efficiently run. Some of the staff were young Vietnamese girls and not trained nurses, but their attitude to the children in their care was heartening. Apart from Lucy, the girl who had welcomed her inside, there were four other trained members of staff, another New Zealand girl, an American, and a German.

"And who has overall responsibility?" Serena asked as Lucy handed her a baby to hold and feed while she began to feed another.

"Dr. Daniels. He's a New Zealander too. He isn't here at the moment, as it's his day for taking a clinic at Grall, the former French military hospital. He's an eye specialist," she added.

Serena awkwardly adjusted the tiny baby in her arms. She had never bottle-fed a baby before, and it was proving to be a far more difficult operation than she imagined.

"Why are the majority of the other orphanages in the city so badly run? Why is this orphanage, and to a lesser extent the orphanages run by the Sisters of St. Paul, the only exceptions?"

Lucy sighed, deposited the baby she had been holding back onto the rug, and picked up another little mite who was noisily demanding to be fed.

"The main problem is that there are far too many abandoned and orphaned children needing

228

to be looked after. The orphanages can't cope, and the majority of people employed in them are untrained. Hence the conditions that you have seen today."

The baby Serena was holding finished its bottle and copying Lucy, Serena lifted the baby and laid it against her shoulder, rubbing his back to encourage a burp.

"What do you mean by abandoned? Do you mean that some of these children do have parents?"

As the noise of crying babies demanding to be fed increased, Lucy had to raise her voice.

"Probably fifty percent of them."

Serena nearly dropped the child she was holding *"Fifty percent*? Then why are they in orphanages? I don't understand."

"That's because you haven't been in Vietnam for very long," Lucy said gently. "The poverty that exists here is something nearly impossible to comprehend if you have only lived in the West. Many women abandon their children because they cannot feed them. Others are abandoned because they are deformed and will be an economic liability. Others are unwanted because they are of mixed race. Many are the children of prostitutes who simply want to be free of the child so that they can return to work. And in Vietnam it is easy to be free of a child. There is no documentation of birth. The charity wards of the maternity hospitals have two and three women to a bed. It is the easiest thing in the world for a woman to walk out, leaving her baby behind her."

"And the others?" Serena asked, aware of a dizzying, fundamental change taking place deep within her.

"The others are casualties of the war. Thousands of civilians are being killed in the fighting. These pathetic scraps of humanity are the result. Babies and children without parents or grandparents. We do the best we can, here at Cây Thông. We are funded entirely by voluntary subscriptions. Mainly from the western embassies and from various military units based in Saigon. It's a very hit-and-miss affair, and we need all the help we can get."

Serena laid the baby that she had been holding back onto the rug and picked up another one. She had taken off her Burberry, and where she had been holding the baby, her lime-green Mary Quant minidress was damp with regurgitated milk stains. She did not care. For the first time in her life she was seized by a sense of mission.

"I can help you financially," Serena said, thinking of the money she had been left by her grandparents and which had always enabled her to live in comfortable ease. "But I would also like to help practically."

"Then you need to speak to Dr. Daniels. He'll be here in half an hour. Don't be put off by his abrupt manner. It comes from having a crucifying workload and working eighteen and nineteen hours out of every twenty-four."

Mike Daniels regarded her unenthusiastically.

"Are you a trained nurse?"

"No."

"Are you a trained child-care attendant?"

"No."

He didn't look like a doctor. He was a strongly built man of about thirty, carelessly dressed in slacks and a sleeveless Sea Island shirt that exposed a chest and arms that might have belonged to a professional weight lifter. His hair was thick and unruly and very dark, as were his eyes. Her first impression was that he was a purely physical personality, and then she noted the sensuality and the sensitivity in the lines of his mouth. Aggressive he may be, but it would be rash for her to make any hasty judgements.

"Then you can't possibly be of the slightest use to us here."

Serena gasped in indignation. "Why not? I'm intelligent. I can certainly look after children a damn sight better than most of the people I've seen looking after children today."

"Those children were not in Cây Thông." Mike Daniels's eyes flickered over the waist-length fall of silver-blond hair, the exquisitely cut and ridiculously short minidress, the beautifully shaped and vibrantly pink-lacquered fingernails. "I'm well aware of your motivation in offering us your help, Miss...?"

"Mrs. Kyle Anderson," Serena said frostily, aware that her title and maiden name would cut no ice with Mike Daniels and would probably only antagonize him further.

"You see yourself swanning around the

231

nursery, being an angel of mercy, though not, of course, soiling your expensively manicured hands in the process. Vietnam, to you, is a romantic adventure. Well, I'm sorry, Mrs. Anderson, but I can't accommodate you. If time is hanging heavy on your hands, as I'm sure it is, then you'll have to find some other way of occupying yourself."

Serena's right hand itched to slap his face. She controlled the impulse with great difficulty, saying through clenched teeth, her eyes blazing, "Has anyone ever told you that you are an arrogant, insufferable, ignorant, *prejudiced* bastard? I want to work at Cây Thông because there is a sea of human misery around me and I want to do something, *anything*, to help relieve it! I'm quite capable of feeding babies, and changing diapers, and washing laundry and sitting up with sick children. I've seen the children here and I know the sort of ailments they're suffering from. If I am shown, I am more than capable of simple medical tasks such as giving injections and treating skin eruptions. I have a far more realistic idea of what is involved than you seem to think I have, Dr. Daniels! And I have every intention of being here at seven in the morning and helping out with whatever task you wish to give me, even if the task is cleaning the floors!"

Before he could reply, she spun on her heel, marching from the courtyard, terrified that even a second's delay would enable him to say scathingly that if she came, she would not be admitted.

When she reached the Continental she was still seethingly angry. How *dare* Mike Daniels suggest that she would be less than useless, and that her motives were selfishly suspect! Even if he did not need her, his nursery and the children did. She had had to sidestep a rat as she had left the alley outside the nursery. She shuddered, wishing to God that she could round up every abandoned and unloved child she had seen and miraculously transport them to the open spaces and green lawns of Bedingham.

Another thought occurred to her, so startling that it took her breath away. There was no reason why at least *one* of those children shouldn't have the benefit of growing up at Bedingham. After all, they were orphans. And it was customary, where possible, for orphans to be adopted. She began to giggle to herself, imagining her father's reaction and Lance's reaction. But she didn't dismiss the idea. It was far too obvious and sensible.

"*Mon Dieu!* You're going to do *what?*" Gabrielle exclaimed incredulously as they drank Manhattans in the Continental's cocktail lounge.

"I'm going to do voluntary work at the Cây Thông orphanage, and I'm going to see if, when I return to England, I can take one of the children with me."

"You mean *adopt* one of them?"

Serena grinned. "Well, I don't think they would let me take one home under any other condition."

"I think that is a very good idea, *chérie*," Gabrielle said when she realized that Serena was serious. Her pert face was unexpectedly somber. She was missing *le petit* Gavin more and more each day and was seriously considering whether or not she should fly him out to Saigon. Only the nighttime sounds of distant gun and rocket fire deterred her. If the Viet Cong attacked the city and *le petit* Gavin were harmed, she would never be able to forgive herself.

"How did your meeting with the Vietnamese journalist go?" Serena asked, well aware that the somber expression on Gabrielle's face meant that she was thinking longingly of her son.

Gabrielle took a sip of her drink and with great difficulty turned her thoughts away from *le petit* Gavin. "I think he is going to be a very important contact," she said, lowering her voice so that no one could overhear them. "He admitted having been in contact with Dinh when Dinh was last in Saigon, and he said that he had heard rumors that a round-eye was traveling northward with Dinh when Dinh left the city."

"Did he know where they were heading? Was he able to tell you why you had been told that there would be no further information about them?"

Gabrielle shook her head, her sumptuous red hair gleaming beneath the soft lighting. "No. He did not know who the source was. But he said that he would make what inquiries he could. And he trusts me, that is the important thing, *n'est-ce pas?*"

"It is indeed," Serena agreed.

The last of Gabrielle's gravity disappeared. "You have not yet told me about this doctor who made you so angry," she said, her eyes dancing with mischief. "Is he very handsome? Is that why you are prepared to be a Cinderella and to sweep floors?"

"He is not *remotely* handsome," Serena said emphatically, conveniently forgetting Mike Daniels's hard-muscled body, and his dark eyes and dark mop of unruly hair. "He is pig-headed, obstructive, and the most *annoying* man I have ever met."

"*Alors*, to have aroused such a passionate response, I think he must be very handsome," Gabrielle said complacently. "Which is more than can be said for the men that I am at present meeting. The Vietnamese journalist was pock-marked, and Paul Dulles, Gavin's bureau chief, though he is pleasant, is certainly not the kind of man one would suicide oneself for."

Almost the first thing Gabrielle had done on arriving in Saigon had been to visit Paul Dulles. She had made up her mind before she went that, hard though it would be, she would not tell him of Gavin's disappearance. Dulles was a professional newsman and would be incapable of keeping such information to himself. All she had told him was that she was confident that Gavin was still alive, and that, as she had relations in Saigon, she intended staying in the city for an indefinite period of time.

At the thought of a man handsome enough to

235

suicide oneself for, Serena sighed. Right from the start she and Gabrielle had realized that where the opposite sex was concerned, they both had similar naturally adventurous appetites.

"Unlike Abbra," Serena had said not unkindly when she and Gabrielle had been alone for a few moments after the three of them had met at the Washington peace march. "Abbra would never even be tempted to indulge in an extramarital affair. It's impossible, in a million years, to imagine her sleeping with anyone for the sheer fun of it. She would have to be totally and irrevocably in love with someone before she would go to bed with him."

Now she said to Gabrielle, "I can hardly believe it, but I'm actually living a celibate life. It's killing me."

Gabrielle gave a grin of sympathy. She knew all about Serena's superstitious belief that if she wasn't unfaithful, Kyle would be released alive.

Gabrielle, thinking of the times she had been tempted to seek physical comfort in Radford's bed, said sympathetically, "Me too. But whenever I think of Gavin, I know that it is worth it. And even if it wasn't, who is there we could have an affair with? All the available men in Saigon are either pot-bellied journalists or clap-riddenal GIs!"

They both collapsed into laughter, and then strolled into the Continental's dining room for yet another meal of impossibly tough buffalo meat and fried rice.

Their lives soon settled into a regular routine.

Despite Mike Daniels's continuing low opinion of her, Serena continued to spend all day, every day, at the orphanage. She filed her nails short and removed her nail polish. She fastened her hair at the nape of her neck with a narrow ribbon. She forsook her stylish minidresses and high-heeled boots and sandals and began to wear serviceable jeans and T-shirts and flat-soled sneakers.

Gabrielle's days were spent in cultivating contacts with people who were Viet Cong, or whose sympathies were Viet Cong, in the hope that she would eventually find someone who would be able to give her hard information about Dinh. It wasn't an easy task. For a Vietnamese to admit to being a member of the Viet Cong or to being a Viet Cong sympathizer was to risk arrest and possibly death. However, slowly but surely, once it became known that Dinh had been her uncle, some trust was extended to her. But no one could tell her where Dinh or his companion were, or even if they were still alive.

At Christmas both she and Serena received a card and a long letter from Abbra. At the end of January, just as Gabrielle had decided that she could survive no longer without *le petit* Gavin, and was going to put arrangements in hand to have him flown out to join her, the Viet Cong launched their Tet offensive.

She and Serena were asleep in their room at the Continental where they were awakened by explosions and gunfire.

"Hell! That's near!" Serena said, sitting bolt

237

upright in bed and turning on her bedside light. "It sounds like it's right outside, in the square."

"Impossible," Gabrielle said sleepily. "What time is it?"

Serena looked at her little traveling clock. "Two-thirty."

There was more gunfire and then an explosion that shook the windows. Gabrielle's eyes widened. "*Tiens!* I think you are right. It *is* in the square!"

They both flung their bedcovers to one side, running to the window. In the darkened square below them men with guns were emerging from manholes and racing toward the top end of Tu Do Street in the direction of the American Embassy. As they watched, U.S. troops began to pour into the square from the south side, firing as they came. Bullets began ricocheting off the Continental's walls, and both she and Serena ducked hurriedly back into the room.

"What the hell is happening?" Serena gasped, struggling out of her nightdress and pulling on her jeans and a T-shirt.

"It's the Viet Cong," Gabrielle said, searching frantically for briefs and a bra. "They are inside the city and trying to take it."

For the next three days, as raging battles took place between the Viet Cong and American and South Vietnamese Army troops, Serena and Gabrielle were unable to leave the Continental. Several times Serena tried, desperate to reach the orphanage and to ensure that the staff and the children were safe, but each time she was beaten back by sniper fire.

On February 3 she finally succeeded. There was still heavy sniper fire and the sound of rocket and mortar attacks, but she ran from building to building, reaching the orphanage disheveled and breathless.

There was no tap water, and the electricity had been cut off. "God knows how we're going to survive if the fighting continues for much longer," Lucy said to her, ashen-faced with fatigue. "We're down to quinine water and whatever supplies Dr. Daniels can bring in. And every time he leaves the orphanage for water, he takes his life in his hands."

The next time Mike Daniels left the orphanage on a foraging trip, Serena accompanied him. He didn't thank her for her assistance, but afterward a grudging respect crept into his attitude toward her.

"He's no longer abominably rude to me," Serena said in amusement to Gabrielle. "Only deplorably rude."

Once the worst of the Tet offensive was over there were letters for both of them from Abbra, letters from Radford and Michel for Gabrielle, and a letter from Chuck for Serena.

"I thought you said Chuck Wilson had discouraged you from keeping in contact with him," Gabrielle said curiously.

"He did. But that was before we met." Serena slipped the letter into her lingerie drawer. Chuck Wilson was an ongoing dilemma for her. Whenever she thought of him, it was with sexual undertones. There were times when she wished she had the nerve to write to him, asking him outright if his injuries precluded him from making love. And if they didn't? What would she do then? It was a question she could never satisfactorily answer. She knew only that she couldn't shake him from her mind, and that she was glad that he had written to her.

Gabrielle was bemused by Michel's letter, and unsettled by Radford's. Michel's letter was full of details of the success of one of their songs. It was a lyric she had written in the Black Cat days, and that he had put music to, and that the band, with the singer who had replaced her, had recorded. It had reached number thirty-five in the British pop charts and had been covered almost immediately by a well-known British singer. *It's going to earn us a fortune,* Michel had written ecstatically. *Three more of our songs have already been sold to well-established singers and are due to be recorded within the next few months. You may have walked out on fame as a singer, Gabrielle, but it looks as if you're going to make it as a songwriter!*

Radford's letter had been short to the point of terseness. He simply wanted to know when the hell she was coming back.

On March 31, when President Johnson went on American television to tell the people he would not be running for reelection, Gabrielle was near the demilitarized zone. Nhu's journalist friend

240

had told her of a man who had served beneath Dinh in the North Vietnamese Army, and was now disabled with a war injury and living in his home village a few miles south of the 17th parallel. Accompanied by one of the many Vietnamese friends she had made, Gabrielle had immediately set off through the war-torn countryside in search of him.

She returned to Saigon on June 6, the day that Robert Kennedy was assassinated in the kitchens of the Ambassador Hotel, Los Angeles.

"Dear heaven," Serena said devoutly as Gabrielle entered their room at the Continental. "Where have you *been*?"

Gabrielle, looking a good eight pounds lighter than when she had started out in March, grinned wearily. She was wearing a black cotton jacket and a pair of loose black trousers with a draw-string waist. Despite their shapelessness, the trousers fitted lightly on her hips, so that even dressed as a peasant, with rough, rubber-soled sandals on her feet, she still managed to look provocative and sexy.

"Don't ask, *chérie*," she said, collapsing into a softly upholstered cane-framed chair. "Not until you have poured me a Pernod. A very *large* Pernod."

When the ice-cold drink was safely in her hand she said, "I reached the village just south of the demilitarized zone, and I spoke to the man who had served in Dinh's unit. He said that it was common knowledge that for a long period of time Colonel Duong Quynh Dinh was accom-

241

panied nearly everywhere by a fair-haired round-eye."

"And?" Serena prompted tensely.

Gabrielle shook her head. "And that was the only reliable information he was able to give me. He was posted to another unit and has not seen or heard of Dinh for many months. He doesn't know where Dinh now is, or if Gavin is still with him."

She paused and pushed a scratched and cut hand tiredly through her mop of fiery hair. "The good news is that I know that Gavin definitely *is* with Dinh, and that he remained with him after they left Saigon. The bad news is that I still don't know where they are, or how I can contact them, or why Gavin has been unable to contact me."

Serena was silent for a while and then she said awkwardly, "Did the man you spoke to give any indication as to whether Gavin was being held against his will or not?"

"No." Gabrielle's eyes were suddenly very brilliant. "But he must be, *chérie*." Two large tears began to trickle down her cheeks. "There can be no other explanation for his silence and his long absence."

Abbra's letter telling them that Lewis had died the previous October plunged them into even deeper despondency. Though they had not seen Abbra since the Washington peace march, the bond that they felt with her was as strong as ever.

"*Merde*," Gabrielle said. "*La pauvre petite. What will she do now, I wonder?*"

* * *

What Abbra proceeded to do stunned both of them so much that for several seconds neither of them could speak.

"She did *what*?" Gabrielle spluttered. She had just given *le petit* Gavin his morning cereal. He had arrived in Saigon two months previously, cared for on his flight from Paris by an Air France stewardess. Ever since his arrival Gabrielle's spirits had lifted and she was again dauntlessly confident that eventually one of the many contacts she was nurturing would bear fruit, and she would learn exactly where Gavin was being held.

Serena looked down at the letter in her hand and began to grin. "She married her brother-in-law," she said again.

"*C'est impossible!*" Gabrielle forgot all about the mess her son was making with his food. "The quiet, so-well-behaved Abbra? She has married her *brother-in-law*? A professional *football* player? It is unbelievable, *n'est-ce pas? Incroyable!*"

Serena's grin deepened. "It may be *incroyable*, Gabrielle, but that's what she has done. Still waters run deep, as my father always used to say. What shall we send her as a wedding present?"

They had sent an exquisitely carved, traditional Vietnamese wedding box decorated in mother-of-pearl. And they had sent her all their love and all their sincerest best wishes for her future happiness.

From the day that Serena had entered the doors of the Cây Thông orphanage, it had never occurred to her to leave Saigon and to return to London. With Mike Daniels's reluctant help she had obtained a residence permit, her profession listed as charity relief worker. She existed on her own private income, receiving no money for the long, arduous hours that she worked. Under Mike Daniels's grudging guidance she had learned to give medication and shots and to put in IV infusions. When she wasn't tending the children, she helped out in the kitchen, making vast amounts of fresh yogurt each day, and killing giant-size spiders and cockroaches and ants.

A few days after she had received Abbra's letter she was sitting in the office, trying to catch up on some paperwork for Mike, when Lucy came in hurriedly, saying, "There's a Vietnamese girl here, asking if we will care for her baby. Little Huong has hemorraghic fever and I must get him down to the Children's Hospital as soon as possible. Interview her for me, will you? She doesn't look the usual type. I don't think she's trying to abandon the child. I'll send her in to you."

She dashed away and Serena put her pen down and pushed the report she had been working on to one side. A second or two later a rather hesitant young Vietnamese woman entered the office, a child of about eighteen months in her arms. Serena's interest quickened. The child, a little girl, was obviously Amerasian. Though the hair was glossily black and poker straight, her eyes were blue, her skin so pale she could easily have been mistaken for a Celt.

Lucy had been right about the mother too. All too often they were approached by prostitutes wishing to permanently relinquish their inconvenient babies. It was a task that no member of the orphanage staff liked to undertake. Mike Daniels insisted that every mother be counseled against abandoning her child, and that they were all told that they would be given whatever help they needed if they would only change their mind and keep their babies.

The woman standing in front of her was obviously no prostitute. She was twenty-one or twenty-two and was dressed in a traditional silk *ao dai*. Her hair hung waist-length down her back, glossily sleek. Her face showed signs of strain but she was still stunningly pretty, and when she spoke it was in carefully phrased English.

"Excuse me," Trinh said a little uncertainly. "I was told that I must come and speak to you if I wish to leave my daughter in your care."

Serena shook her head gently. "I am sorry, but it is not our policy to care for children who have mothers able to care for them..." she began.

Trinh flushed rosily. "I do not want to leave my daughter with you permanently. I was told that you sometimes took in children of working mothers on a daily basis. You see, I have no mother, and my sister cannot help me, as she also is working. As a secretary," she added quickly, in case the phrase should be misunderstood and it should be thought that Mai was a bar girl or a prostitute. "I am a hotel receptionist, but I need someone to look after Kylie for me through the day..."

"Kylie?" It suddenly seemed very quiet. Serena could hear no street noise, no noise from the nearby creche. She looked at the child and the child looked back at her with a confident, curious, blue-eyed stare, her hair tumbling forward over her forehead in a familiar manner.

"Kylie is my daughter's name."

Serena sat very still. She had seen eyes like that before. And hair that fell the same way. The more she looked at the child, the more certain she became. There wasn't only American and Vietnamese blood running in the little girl's veins, there was a dash of Irish blood as well.

"Kylie is an unusual name," she said, dragging her eyes away from the child and back to the mother with difficulty. "Is it her full name?"

"No," Trinh said, slightly overawed by Serena's elegantly cool, gold-haired beauty. "Her full name is Huyen Anderson Kylie."

Serena let out a long sigh. Why, knowing Kyle as well as she did, had the prospect of such an eventuality never occurred to her?

"And your name?" she asked, wondering if Kyle had known about the child before he had left on his last mission, wondering which of the emotions she was feeling was uppermost, grief, or rage, or wounded pride, or disillusionment.

"Trinh," Trinh said, wondering why the English girl's manner had suddenly become so taut.

Screna drew in a deep, steadying breath. The

next few minutes were not going to be pleasant ones for either of them. "We need to talk, Trinh," she said, and all the conflicting emotions that had initially assailed her faded, and in their place she felt only stoic resignation. "We need to talk about Kylie's father."

CHAPTER ELEVEN

Gavin found Hanoi fascinating. If the price he had to pay for being there was temporary loss of his freedom, then it was a price he was happy to pay. Hanoi seemed like the real Vietnam to him, the Vietnam he had not found in Saigon. Beneath the shabbiness and the poverty it was still a beautiful city. The wide, ponderous splendor of the Red River curved protectively around it in a giant arc, and nearer to the city, some of them even in its heart, was lake after lake.

By daylight the Lake of the Restored Sword was even more beautiful than it had been at dusk. On a small verdant island a pagoda rose, drowned in magnolia blossom and honeysuckle. Gavin stood looking at it, Dinh at his side. When he had first stepped out into the crowded streets he had been afraid that he would be regarded as an enemy, an American. He had been pleasantly surprised. On their walk through the crowded city streets he had met with no hostility, only curiosity.

"There is a story about the pagoda," Dinh said as a pair of young lovers strolled past them, the girl with her head resting on the boy's shoulder, their hands tightly clasped. "It is built on the spot where a turtle arose from the water, carrying a sword with which an ancient Vietnamese hero drove out Chinese invaders."

Gavin smiled. Dinh was no longer so stiff and formal with him. They were becoming companions, friends.

"And now we will go to the school," Dinh said, turning away from the lake, walking past a bench full of old men resting and gossiping. "You will see how well prepared we are for imperialist bombing attacks."

When Dinh and Gavin entered the classroom, the girls showed the same interest and the curiosity that he had met with on the streets, though this time politely masked. Beside every desk was a trapdoor leading to an underground shelter.

"My entire class of fifty children can disappear within seconds," the teacher told them with pride.

The same meticulous protection against attack was visible in the streets. The French-built center of the city was laid out on a craft basis, entire streets devoted to ivory carving or wood carving or leatherwork. Here there were no trapdoors, but every few yards they had to sidestep a manhole cover.

Dinh removed one of the covers to reveal an underground dugout just large enough for one man. "And it is not only Hanoi that is well prepared against attack," he said as he replaced the cover. "Every village creche is similarly protected. Deep shelters have been dug beneath the cribs and the little ones can be lowered into them at a moment's notice, en masse, on slings."

"I'd like to go out to one of the villages," Gavin said as they began to cross a road thick with cyclo-pousses and handcarts. "It's the villagers who have been suffering most from the bombing, isn't it?"

Dinh nodded grimly. "I will take you, Comrade. You are going to learn more about life in the North than any western journalist has ever learned."

For the next few months Gavin was high on sheer adrenaline. When he returned to Europe he would be seen as an expert on North Vietnamese affairs. He would be able to write a book, several books. He still missed Gabrielle desperately, just as he would have missed her if he had remained in Saigon. When they had parted they had known that it would be at least a year before they would be together again. His being in the North instead of the South made no difference to their separation, now that he had learned she knew where he was, and who he was with.

"And she does," Dinh had assured him. "There is no need to worry anymore, Comrade. She will be with you in spirit and her heart and her mind will be at peace."

At Tet he shared in the celebrations as if he

were a native-born Vietnamese. The streets were vivid with red flags, the air thick with the sound and smell of firecrackers. He and Dinh shared rice cakes and then mingled with the crowds in the street, slowly but surely making their way to Lake Hoan Kiem and the Ngoc Son temple. As they crossed the Huc Bridge, surrounded by peasants dressed in their festive best, Gavin knew that if Gabrielle had been beside him, it would have the been the happiest, most memorable moment in his life.

Two weeks later they set off for Thai Binh, a northern town near the coast which had suffered a heavy bombing attack.

"When we return I am afraid that we will not see each other quite so often," Dinh said regretfully. "I am to undertake active duty again and this time in a place and on a mission that you are not to be informed of."

The jeep they were traveling in rocked and bumped over a potholed road.

"How long will you be away?" There was apprehension in Gavin's voice. Whenever Dinh was away he was replaced by an impassive-faced NVA officer whom Gavin cordially disliked. And also, his year in North Vietnam was coming to an end. He had enough copy to keep him at his typewriter for a lifetime, and his longing for Gabrielle and *le petit* Gavin was becoming unbearable.

"I cannot say, Comrade. It could be..."

His sentence was never completed. Death

came out of the air as it had come to so many thousands of others. One minute they were driving along the road leading to Haiphong with other army vehicles a few hundred yards in front of them, the next they were bombed into oblivion. Gavin could feel himself being sucked into the air, his eardrums bursting, his heart bursting, his only thought, *"Not now! Jesus, not now! Not when I'm so close to seeing Gaby again!"*

He was slammed bodily into a tree, losing consciousness. When he regained it, blood was streaming down his face, and the air was thick and acrid with smoke and debris.

"Dinh!" he shouted, pushing himself to his knees, experiencing the same terrible fear that had seized him when they had been bombed on the Ho Chi Minh Trail. *"Dinh!"*

This time there was no answer. Dinh's body was still in the burning jeep, the head at an improbable angle.

"Oh, God, no!" he sobbed, staggering to his feet. "Dinh! *Dinh!"*

He began to run toward the leaping flames. Army officers from one of the vehicles that had been in front of them reached it first. Dinh was dragged from the jeep and laid at the side of the road.

Gavin ran stumblingly toward it, half blinded by pain and blood. "He's dead," one of the army officers said cursorily, and then, turning, saw Gavin clearly for the first time.

Gavin was oblivious of the sudden change of

251

expression on the officer's face. He stared down at Dinh, tears mixing with the blood on his cheek. He had been a good friend in North Vietnam, he had been his only friend.

The army officer who had spoken to him was joined by another. They flanked Gavin, AK-47's at the ready.

"I am Australian, not American," Gavin said, his first, old fear returning. "I am a guest in North Vietnam. A journalist."

"Come," one of the officers said, motioning him toward an undamaged vehicle.

Gavin felt cold fingers beginning to close around his heart. They would, he supposed, take him back to Hanoi. In Hanoi he would be taken before Dinh's military superiors, the superiors who had authorized his presence in North Vietnam. What would happen then? Would the impassive-faced NVA officer be assigned to him on a permanent basis? Would he be told that his mission was over and would he then be escorted back down the Ho Chi Minh Trail into the South? He had no way of knowing. All he could do was climb obligingly into the army truck and hope for the best.

They did not take him to Hanoi. They continued northward to an army camp.

"I should be taken back to Hanoi," Gavin said patiently when he was first officially questioned. "The authorities in Hanoi know who I am. They have given me authorization to be in North Vietnam."

"Where are your papers?" his interrogator

252

demanded. "Where is your authorization?"

"I am a nephew by marriage of Colonel Duong Quynh Dinh, the North Vietnamese Army officer who was killed in the bombing raid," Gavin repeated, trying to keep his growing fear under control. "I am on a mission to the North to see and to report on the sufferings of the Vietnamese people."

His interrogator eyed him disbelievingly and then put a telephone call through to Hanoi. There was no quick reply from Hanoi, and Gavin was taken away and held in a cell.

"Don't panic," he told himself repeatedly, as first one hour went by and then another. "The authorities in Hanoi know who I am. They will authorize the officer here to return me to Hanoi. In Hanoi my troubles will be over."

The door of his cell opened. "Come," an unsmiling officer commanded.

He went. He was not met with a smile and an apology. "The authorities in Hanoi have ordered that you be placed under arrest," his interrogator said curtly. "You are to be taken further north, where you will be held with other enemies of our country."

It was the nightmare he had feared ever since the moment on the Ho Chi Minh Trail when he had thought that Dinh was dead. "No!" he said forcefully. "You are making a mistake! I was *invited* to the Democratic Republic of Vietnam! I am a *friend* of the Democratic Republic of Vietnam!"

"You are an Australian," his interrogator said

flatly. "You have no papers, no authorization."

"I am a *journalist!*" Gavin protested, "I am here to *serve* the Democratic Republic of Vietnam!"

None of it was any use. He was taken away, bundled into a truck, and driven north.

The camp he was taken to was small. Any hopes he had entertained of finding American pilots there were soon dashed. All the other inmates were Vietnamese. His cell was furnished with a sleeping pallet, a slop bucket, and nothing else. He tried to keep control of himself. It wouldn't be for long. There had been some confusion. When the authorities in Hanoi realized who he was, orders would be very swiftly given for his release.

No such order came. The hours merged into days, and the days into weeks. For twelve hours out of every twenty-four he was taken from his cell and put to work alongside the other inmates in nearby fields. Unlike them, he was never ill-treated, and his conviction that his captors knew perfectly well who he was, and what his status had been in Hanoi, grew. No one ever interrogated him. It was as if they knew all they needed to know about him.

The daily diet was rice and a minuscule sliver of dried fish. When rice and chicken and a flat round of dough with a candle pressed into the center were brought to him one day, he stared in amazement.

"It is Christmas," his guard said beamingly. "At Christmas there is celebration, yes?"

He wondered where Gaby and *le petit* Gavin were celebrating Christmas. Would she have been told of his arrest? Would she know that he was still alive?

Time no longer had any meaning. He had no means of keeping track of the date by writing it down, and he began to scrape a small notch on the wall for every day that passed.

Occasionally he would overhear snatches of conversation between the guards, but their conversation was almost always centered on when they could next expect leave, and very rarely on world events.

On one memorable day he overheard the guards talking of huge antiwar demonstrations that were taking place in America, on another day he even heard Joan Baez singing an antiwar song on a distant radio.

In between there was nothing. Only the stifling heat or the freezing cold of his cell, depending on the season, and backbreaking daily toil in the fields.

At the beginning of 1969 he contracted malaria and most of the year was spent in delirious spells. He was unable to faithfully notch each day that passed on his cell wall, and in periods of lucidity he panicked, unable to remember if *le petit* Gavin was two years old or three years old.

He no longer believed that Gaby still thought he was alive. How could she? How could anyone? Sometimes, late at night, he wondered if she was still singing at the Black Cat, and he conjured up her image, imagining the song she

255

was singing, the dress she was wearing.

Toward the end of the year he was given his first piece of official news. Ho Chi Minh was dead. Formal truce negotiations had begun in Paris.

There were times when he wondered if he was living in an extended dream, if any of what was happening to him was real. And then there were other times when he wondered if it was the life he had lived before Vietnam that was the dream. If Paris, and Gaby, and *le petit* Gavin were nothing more than the products of malarial hallucination.

The notches on the wall ran the entire length and breadth of his cell. Year followed year. His guards were no longer coldly polite, but were his friends, friends who did not allow him to leave the compound.

When he was told that all American troops had been withdrawn from Vietnam, he did not believe them. How could they be? How could the war be over? There were still Vietnamese prisoners in the camp. *He* was still being held prisoner. Nothing had changed and he could no longer imagine anything ever changing.

When the camp commandant came to him and told him that he was being moved from the camp to another prison camp nearer to Hanoi, he was distraught. He didn't want to leave his possessions behind. His sleeping pallet, the tin bowl from which he ate, the conical hat he had been given to shade him from the sun when he worked in the fields.

He cried when they bundled him into the back of the truck that was to take him away from everything that was familiar. Gaby. He had to think of Gaby. He always thought of Gaby whenever things became too much to bear.

He no longer knew if in the flesh the titian-haired, emerald-eyed, kitten-faced, huskily laughing image that brought so much comfort even remembered him. It was something he tried not to think about. He remembered her. He loved her now as he had always loved her. As he would always love her, until the day he died.

"Gaby," he said brokenly, passing his emaciated hand across his eyes. "Oh Gaby, Gaby, *Gaby!*"

CHAPTER TWELVE

As Christmas approached, Gabrielle found her despondency returning. She had made no new contacts, discovered no new information about Gavin's whereabouts, and it seemed very unlikely that any new information was going to be forthcoming.

It was two and a half years since she had last seen him. Sometimes she would wake in the middle of the night filled with panic, unable to remember how his face looked when he laughed, unable to recall the exact timbre of his voice. Her body ached to be held, to be made love to.

Only Serena's companionship had made the last year bearable, but now it was bearable no longer. She yearned for male company; to be able to flirt a little; to be made to feel womanly and sexy and desirable.

"It's two and a half years, Gavin," she would whisper heartbrokenly into the darkness. "Would you mind so much, *mon amour*? Would it be so very great a betrayal?"

No answer ever came. She knew that if the situation were reversed, he would never be unfaithful to her. Not in any way. It wasn't in his nature. Why, then, was it in hers? Not to be totally unfaithful. Not to fall in love with someone else and out of love with Gavin. That she would never do, it would be impossible. But surely an affair would not be so very terrible? She would toss and turn and eventually fall into a restless sleep, the dilemma unresolved.

With the coming of Christmas and the approach of the Vietnamese New Year, the American and European community in Saigon became increasingly edgy. Memories of that year's Tet, and the Viet Cong offensive that had accompanied it, were still fresh in everyone's mind, and though it was unlikely that the Viet Cong would have the resources to launch another, similar attack in Tet '69, it could not be completely ruled out.

"Perhaps you should take *le petit* Gavin home to France for Christmas and the New Year," Serena suggested tentatively. "Just in case there is another attack on the city."

258

"I will think about it, *chérie*," Gabrielle had said non-committally.

The thought of leaving Saigon terrified her. In Saigon she was able to fight the temptation to take a lover. In Saigon there was no Radford.

Serena had looked across at her, puzzled. Gabrielle was a fiercely protective mother, and she had expected the mention of another possible Tet attack to have sent Gabrielle scurrying to the nearest Air France office in order to fly *le petit* Gavin out of the country until the sensitive few weeks of Tet were safely over.

Deeply ashamed of her motive for doing so, Gabrielle had decided to risk staying on in Saigon. Two events, both on the same day, changed her mind for her.

On December 21 a grenade was thrown into a street café full of American soldiers. Gabrielle and *le petit* Gavin had been walking back from the park that lay just behind and to the left of the Roman Catholic cathedral. Though they were thirty yards away from the café, they were spattered with shards of glass and a piece struck *le petit* Gavin on the forehead, terrifying him and making a deep and ugly gash.

When they returned to the Continental, there was a letter from her mother. Her father had suffered a heart attack. It had only been mild and his condition was not serious, but her mother suggested that it might be best if she and *le petit* Gavin were to return home. At least for a little while.

"Will you able to get seats on a flight so near

Christmas?" Serena asked, a worried frown creasing her brow.

"I do not know, *chérie*," Gabrielle said with a Gallic shrug of her shoulders. "All I can do is to try."

For several hours it looked as if she was going to be unsuccessful, and then Air France called her back, saying they had two seat cancellations on a Christmas Eve flight, leaving at eight in the morning.

"And you?" Gabrielle said to Serena. "I do not know how long I will be away. It may be for quite a while. Will you be all right in Saigon by yourself? Will you stay on here?"

Serena thought of Bedingham at Christmas. Of the huge log fire that would be burning in the Adam fireplace in the yellow living room; of the enormous, gaily decorated fir tree that would be standing in the grand entrance hall; of walks over crisply frozen ground, her father's ancient spaniels at her heels; of mince pies and traditional turkey and carol singing in the little local church that was almost as old as Bedingham itself. And then she thought of the children in the orphanage. Of those whose parents had died in B-52 attacks; of the malformed who had been abandoned because they were an economic liability; of the mixed-race children whose mothers were prostitutes, and who had voluntarily relinquished them.

"Yes," she said, pushing all thoughts of Bedingham to the farthest recess of her brain. "I shall stay on. And I shall be okay. Maybe I'll move in with Lucy. She has an apartment on Phan Van Dat." But she knew she would not.

Gabrielle had packed two bags, one for herself and one for *le petit* Gavin. He was two and a half years old now and full of ebullient energy and curiosity. She couldn't imagine how he was going to endure the long, tedious flight, and she put several nursery rhyme books and a notepad and crayons into her shoulder bag hoping that they would help to keep him amused.

"I would not hurry back to Saigon," Nhu said to her somberly when she went to say good-bye to her. "I do not think there is anyone who can tell you anything further about Gavin's where-abouts. All we can do now is to wait."

It had been a dispiriting note on which to leave the city. As the Air France Boeing climbed into the sky, Gabrielle looked down on the rose-red rooftops and wondered how long the wait would be before she would do so with Gavin at her side.

When she arrived home, not only were her parents there to welcome her, but Michel as well.

"*Alors!* How on earth did you know that I was coming home?" she asked delightedly, hugging him tight.

"Your mother telephoned me," he said sheepishly.

He hadn't changed. He was still as thin and gangling and awkwardly clumsy. His bony wrists projected a good inch from beneath the bottoms of his shirt cuffs, and his tortoise-shell

261

glasses ensured that he looked more like a schoolmaster than a musician. He was laden with gifts. There were handmade Belgian chocolates for her mother, a box of Hoyo de Monterroy cigars for her father, a giant bottle of Chanel No. 5 for herself, and an armful of toys for *le petit* Gavin.

"I was afraid he would have forgotten me," Michel said, hunkering down and opening his arms wide to catch *le petit* Gavin, as Gavin gave a joyous crow of recognition and began to toddle eagerly toward him.

"He is like his mama," Gabrielle said with a happy chuckle, "He does not forget his friends."

It felt amazingly good to be back in Michel's undemanding company. Already she was thinking about songs again. In order to pass the time on the long flight from Saigon she had occupied herself by writing a lyric. It was the first one she had written in over a year and she had found the exercise deeply satisfying.

"Are you too busy writing arrangements for other people to write any arrangements for me?" she asked, knowing very well that he would never be too busy to write arrangements for her. Not ever.

He stood upright, *le petit* Gavin in his arms, saying heavily, "Gabrielle, you have no idea how *desperate* I have been for you to return to Europe so that we can write some more songs together. Radford and the band have now recorded six of your songs that I arranged. The song that made it into the top thirty has now been covered by *three* other singers and is currently at number twelve in the American charts. You have a lot of money coming to you, and an accountant who is going demented because he says you never reply to any of his letters."

Gabrielle had the grace to look a little abashed. The accountant had written to her with monotonous regularity over the last few months but somehow, in Saigon, it had seemed an intrusion, a reminder of a way of life that she had temporarily left far behind her.

"I will go and see him," she promised, picking up the cuddly toy elephant that *le petit* Gavin had dropped in order that he could secure his hold on a wooden train set more firmly.

As her mother set a place for Michel at the table, and began to bring in dishes of hot spicy food from the tiny kitchen, Gabrielle said with studied casualness, "How has the band been doing? I understand Radford soon found a singer to replace me. Is she very good?"

Michel blushed slightly. "Yes. Though not as good as you," he added hastily.

Gabrielle tilted her head to one side and waited, intrigued by Michel's embarrassed reaction.

"Her name is Rosie Devlin and she is an Irish girl. Very petite and vivacious, like you. And full of incredible energy, also like you."

"And?" Gabrielle prompted him, wondering if he was embarrassed because Rosie was having an affair with Radford and, if she was, wondering how she was going to react to the news.

263

"And I am in love with her," he finished bash-fully.

Gabrielle was aware of an incredible feeling of relief. "And is she in love with you?" she asked without giving herself time to analyze the reason for her response.

Michel's blush deepened, "Yes," he said with a happy grin. "Incredible though it may seem, and she is *very* cute and sexy, she is in love with me."

Gabrielle laughed delightedly. "And are there going to be wedding bells, *chéri*?"

"I haven't asked her yet, but I want to. I was hoping that perhaps you would have a word with her first. You know, see if a marriage proposal would be welcome..."

Gabrielle shook her head in mock despair. "I can't do that, Michel. I have never even met her!"

"But you will be meeting her," Michel said, and at his next innocent words her smile faded and all her old anxieties returned in full measure. "You will meet her tomorrow at the rehearsal room the band is using. Radford and the boys are throwing a welcome home party for you."

It was a party impossible not to attend. The rehearsal room was over a café in the rue de Charenton, not very far from the original rehearsal room where she and Radford had first met. The band hadn't changed. There had always been a great bond of affection and musical respect between herself and them, and she was touched to discover that the affection had survived her thirteen-month absence. There was a loud cheer and a cacophony of whistles the instant she and Michel entered the room.

"Welcome back to Paris. Gabrielle!"

"Great to see you, baby!"

"You been away too long, honey!"

Only Radford was silent. He stood at the far end of the room, slim and supple in hip-hugging faded denims and a T-shirt with the words BLACK LOVERS ARE BEST immodestly emblazoned across his chest.

They looked across at each other, neither of them attempting to make the first move, and as the whistles and shouts of welcome began to die down and as attention began to be focused upon them, Michel saved the moment by saying guilelessly, "Gabrielle, you must meet Rosie. Where *is* Rosie? *Rosie!*"

A vivacious, merry-eyed girl, her dark hair scooped up and secured on top of her head, a frizz of curls cascading forward forties-style over her forehead, stepped forward from behind the bass player.

"I'm very pleased to meet you," she said perkily to Gabrielle.

Her French was heavily accented with a beguiling Irish brogue, and despite teeteringly high-heeled white boots she was no taller than Gabrielle.

"I'm pleased to meet you too," Gabrielle said sincerely, warming to her immediately.

Out of the corner of her eye she was aware of Radford moving lazily forward toward her.

"Don't be worried that I may be resentful about you coming back into the band," Rosie was saying, "I've always known what the deal was, right from the beginning. However, Radford thinks there will be room enough for both of us." She began to giggle. "He says we're so similar in build and personality that we will complement each other onstage, not detract from each other."

"It's very sweet of you to take that attitude," Gabrielle said, aware that Radford was now at her side. She could no longer put off the moment she had been both dreading and looking forward to, the moment when their eyes would meet. "But I have no intention of returning to the band. Rock singing was fun for a while, but it's not really what I do best..."

"And what is it that you do best, baby?" Radford asked, and there was no mistaking the sexual innuendo in the rich dark timbre of his voice.

She turned toward him, lifting her eyes slowly up to his. She was wearing a short-skirted white cotton-piqué suit and a black cotton Italian turtleneck sweater that she had bought in Baltimore on their American tour. The jacket was thrown casually around her shoulders, and at her neck was knotted a long black and white crepe scarf, the ends falling freely down her back. A black and white leather belt with a gilt buckle cinched her waist, and on her left wrist were black and white twisted bracelets that Serena had bought her for her last birthday. She looked as coolly sophisticated as Serena at her best. Incredibly Parisian. Incredibly chic.

"I'm a nightclub singer," she said, her voice betraying none of her inner perturbation.

He was as handsome, as sensually aware, as mocking, and as confident as ever. Beneath the tight crinkle of his close-cropped hair, his eyes were hot with an expression that sent a flood tide of desire racing through her veins.

"That may be what you *think* you are," he said, one corner of his mouth curling into a crooked smile, "but what I *know* you are is one of the best female rock singers in the business. And to prove my point, I want you and Rosie to duet on the Martha and the Vandellas number 'Dancing in the Street'."

"I'm not coming back to the band," she said, grateful that there was at least one decision she was not in doubt about. "You're doing just fine as you are, without me. And I want to go back to what I feel most comfortable doing."

"Singing love songs in dime-a-dozen clubs?" he said, the humor leaving his voice, his eyes narrowing.

"The clubs don't have to be dime-a-dozen," she said, returning his gaze unflinchingly. "And they won't. Not if I have half the talent you insist I have."

"You're crazy." His nostrils flared and she knew that despite his careless dismissiveness, he was furiously, blazingly angry.

"Come on, Gabrielle," the leading guitarist said encouragingly. "We've been looking forward to this for days. Let's enjoy ourselves."

There were glasses and bottles of champagne on the lid of the nearby piano. The bass player played the opening riff of "Dancing in the Street" and grinned across at her. "It's a song just made for the two of you," he said. "Why don't you give it a blast?"

She looked across at Rosie, who was looking at her in slight consternation. Gabrielle understood why. Her refusal to sing could be interpreted as pique at being asked to share center stage with another singer. If Radford took it into his head that that was her reason for refusing to come back as a member of the band, then he might very well ask Rosie to leave it.

She gave a sudden grin. "*Ça va,*" she said, knowing that to continue to refuse was impossible, and knowing also that an informal session with the band would make not the slightest difference to the decision she had made.

Rosie's pert little face cleared with relief, champagne corks flew, Michel took his place at the piano, and Radford said to her with a smile, sure that she had changed her mind about preferring the clubs to the rock circuit, "Give it all you've got, honey," his voice thickened to a caress, "It's been too long a time without you."

This time she kept her eyes steadfastly averted from his. The undercurrents between them were so raw and live that it seemed impossible to her that the other members of the band, and Michel and Rosie, should be oblivious to them. With her fingers trembling slightly, she slipped her jacket off her shoulders, laying it on a chair, and followed Rosie. What was going to happen when the session was over? How was she going to retain self-control and self-respect? Michel began to play the first few bars experimentally, and with monumental effort she tried to think of the song she was about to sing.

"How are we going to do it?" she asked Rosie. "I'm not even sure that I know all the words."

Rosie's elfinlike face split into a grin. "We're going to do it just as it comes," she said exuberantly. "We are going to enjoy ourselves!"

From the first few bars they jelled together as if they had been singing duos for years. Even though Gabrielle had no intention of changing her mind about the decision she had made, not to return to the band, she had to admit that Radford had been right and that they would have been a sensation together onstage.

After "Dancing in the Street" they went into the Gladys Knight and the Pips number, "I Heard It Through the Grapevine", and then the Supremes' "You Can't Hurry Love" and "You Keep Me Hangin' On".

"And now I want to hear you sing one of your own songs," Rosie said, panting for breath, perspiration sheening her face. "The kind of song that you say you prefer to sing."

Before Gabrielle could even reply to her, Michel played the first few bars of a song that had been her favorite in the Black Cat days. The rest of the band stayed silent. Radford didn't move, but every line of his body was suddenly taut.

She stood for a few moments, breathing deeply after the exertion of the dancing that had accompanied the last few numbers and then, as Michel played her in again, she took hold of the mike, and closing her eyes she began to sing.

Apart from her voice, low now in register and deeply sensual, there wasn't a sound in the large, drafty rehearsal room. Watching her, Michel knew that the decision she had made was the decision that was right for her. When she sang like this, when she was totally herself, she possessed an erotic presence that was electrifying. When the last note had died away there was a pause before the band broke out into wild applause. It was a pause by her peers, acknowledging a rare talent, a stage quality so mysteriously and implacably egocentric that there was no possible name for it.

Only Radford did not join in the storm of hand-clapping and whistles and foot-stamping.

"She is superb!" Rosie said to Michel. "When she releases herself in a song she is not only a singer, she is a great dramatic artist as well."

"She has the one essential ingredient of international stardom," the bass player said in a low aside to Radford. "Every man who sees her onstage will want to make love to her."

A pulse had begun to beat at the corner of Radford's jaw. He didn't like what he was seeing and hearing because he knew damn well what it meant. She really wasn't going to come back to the band. Musically she was going to go down her own road, even if that road never led to fame and riches.

"Another!" Rosie was calling out.

"What about 'Fever'?" one of the guitarists shouted across to her.

Gabrielle shook her head. "No, not 'Fever'. Let's do 'Stormy Weather'."

This time every musician in the room reached for his instrument. The drummer did an experimental riff on the rim of his drum, and then, after a moment's pause, Gabrielle once more began to sing.

There was such deep pain in her husky, broken-edged voice that the simple words of the song became heart-wrenching.

The café proprietor had come upstairs to listen more clearly. "Now, that," he said when the song came to an end and applause burst around Gabrielle's ears like foam, "is my kind of song." He gave Radford a knowing wink and a leer. "And my kind of woman. Where the hell have you been hiding her all this time?"

Despite insistent requests from the band that they continue the session, Gabrielle walked away from the microphone and over to the chair where she had left her jacket. She was drenched in perspiration, and the intensity of emotion that had been behind the words of her last song had left her feeling emotionally drained.

Michel walked quickly after her, slipping her jacket around her shoulders, saying, "If you're not careful, you're going to catch a chill. This is Paris, not Saigon, and you don't even have a coat with you."

Radford had picked up a black leather jacket, and with his thumb hooked beneath the collar, had swung it over one shoulder.

"You and me have to talk, baby," he said, ignoring Michel.

"Yes." It would have been infantile to have refused. She knew they had to talk. They had to talk about the decision she had made about her musical future, and they had to talk about other things as well, things that she was terrified of putting into words.

In retrospect, she knew that the instant she left the rehearsal room with him the decision she had agonized for so long over had been made. There was going to be no going back. She was in utter subjection to her body and her physical needs, and she wanted one thing only. To lay naked beneath Radford's hard-muscled body, to feel herself exploding with a passion that had been kept in check for too long, to kiss and to bite, to lick and to suck and to yield.

There was a crazily ostentatious sports car parked outside the café. An Aston-Martin DB Mark 3. Radford opened the door for her and then strode quickly around to the driver's side.

"Thank Christ you've come to your senses at last," he said harshly, gunning the powerful engine into life.

She knew that he wasn't talking about music or her career or her return to Paris. There had always been a primitive telepathy between them. She didn't have to tell him by word or gesture that she had inwardly sexually capitulated to him. He already knew.

He rounded the corner of the street with a screech of the tires, not speaking to her again, not even looking at her. They raced down the rue de Charenton and across the place de la Bastille, nearly mowing down a bicyclist and narrowly avoiding a collision with a truck.

She had never been to his place, never had the remotest idea of where he lived. They swerved to a halt outside a typically grim-looking Parisian apartment block. The concierge eyed them indifferently as, still not touching, they began to run up the steep flight of uncarpeted stairs.

In the apartment she was aware of stark white walls, of several colorful rugs, of a minimum of furniture, a record player and recording equipment, and literally hundreds of records stacked along the entire length of one wall.

They didn't make it to the bed. His T-shirt was off the instant he entered the room. By the time the door slammed behind them his shoes and his socks were off and his jeans were unzipped.

She scrambled out of her panties, kicking off her shoes, lost to reason and conscience and self-respect.

"*Mon Dieu!*" she moaned as he bent her in toward him, lowering her to the floor, pushing up her skirt, "Be quick! Please, *mom amour*, be quick!"

It was like the coupling of two savage animals. Both of them had waited to sexually gratify themselves with each other for too long. There was no tenderness, not even the pretence of love. She lifted her legs up and over his shoulders, her nails scoring his flesh, drowning in a release that nearly rendered her senseless. Only later, when he carried her to the bed, did they take time to savor each other, to touch with sensuality, and to explore.

She had always been aware of his almost-pagan handsomeness. Naked, he was beautiful. His dark body gleamed the color of rich mahogany. There was a light mat of tightly curling hair on his powerfully muscled chest, and a much denser bush of hair between his thighs. As she lay beside him, running her fingertips lightly up the length of his thigh and on over the flatness of his stomach, skirting his prick, which had fallen sideways and lay large and flaccid and still throbbing on his belly, she said with devastating honesty, "I don't love you, *chéri*. I find you stunningly exciting, unbearably desirable, and I think that I must be a little in love with you. But I don't *love* you. There is a difference, *comprends-tu*?"

He understood all right. His eyes narrowed, his face suddenly expressionless. For a long moment he didn't speak, and when he did, it was to say with casual brutality, "Your husband may not be alive. He may be dead. He may have been dead for months."

She winced, and he knew a moment of harsh satisfaction.

"*Non*," she said, her voice slightly unsteady. "Gavin is alive. I know that he is."

Her fingertips were still on his flesh. His sex stirred and began to harden again. He didn't want to talk about her husband. He didn't want to do anything but make love to her again and again and again, until she forgot about Gavin Ryan, until she forgot about every other man she had ever had or had ever wanted, until she forgot about everything but him.

When they made love again he refused to allow her to rush him. He took his time, teasing and tormenting her, using every trick he knew to give her the kind of pleasure that would have her on her hands and knees begging for more. Whenever she came to the brink of orgasm he denied her, turning his attention to another part of her body, crucifyingly in control of himself.

"*Mon Dieu*," she whispered brokenly, "I can't survive much more of this, *cheri*! I am going to die!"

He was kneeling between her thighs, and she felt utterly vulnerable, utterly dominated. His tongue was hot and rough, moving in a long, agonizingly slow journey from her anus to her vagina, pushing deep inside and then, when she thought she could endure not another second, withdrawing and flicking lightly over her clitoris, sucking and nibbling and pulling with his lips at the velvety soft folds of her flesh.

"Now, oh, please, now," she gasped. She had been too long without a lover. She could not delay her climax as he was delaying his.

At the desperate plea in her voice he raised his head momentarily, a smile of triumph touching his lips, and then he thrust his tongue deep inside her. Seconds before she came he slipped a moistened finger inside her anus, and as the most intense orgasm of her life rocked through her she arched her back, giving a long, ululating cry of shock and ecstasy and total abandonment.

He resisted the almost overwhelming temptation to ask her if her husband had ever made love to her with the same shameless expertise. He doubted it. Where bed was concerned, he immodestly figured he was far better equipped and far more skillful than any Australian could possibly be.

Their affair lasted all through the spring and summer. Never once did she say that she loved him, and out of pride, never once did he say that he loved her. In bed they satisfied each other totally, and out of bed they struck the same kinds of sparks off each other that they had always struck. His fury at her refusal to come back as a member of the band was white hot, but nothing that he could do or say would make her change her mind.

She began to sing at the Chez Duprée, in the Latin Quarter. It was run by Inez Duprée, a singer who specialized in fried chicken and jazz, and Gabrielle soon established a name for herself there. She wasn't cutting records and doing tours as Radford and the band were, but she was doing what pleased her best. She was singing the songs that she wanted to sing, many of them her own, in the way that she wanted to sing them.

It was early fall when Nhu's letter arrived, informing her of Dinh's death.

I am very grieved to be writing to you with the news that your uncle has been killed up-country in a farming accident. I believe that the accident took place some time ago, but exactly when I still do not know. There is no news of the friend who was with him.

No news. There had never been any news. And now Dinh was dead. She wondered what the words *farming accident* really meant. Dinh was a soldier, not a farmer. He had never been a farmer. Was Nhu trying to tell her that Dinh had died fighting? If so, had Gavin been involved in the fighting as well? And where was he now? She put the letter down unsteadily. Wherever Gavin was, without Dinh to protect him, he would be a prisoner. As Lewis had been a prisoner. As Kyle still was. There would be no news now until the war was over.

"Oh, my love, stay alive for me!" she whispered fiercely through her tears. "Stay strong and stay alive!"

The formal truce negotiations between America and the Saigon government and Viet Cong representatives continued in Paris. Gabrielle received a letter from Abbra in which Abbra expressed the hope that perhaps the end of the war was now in sight, that perhaps soon there would be news of Gavin's whereabouts.

At the time of Tet, Communist forces carried out massive rocket and mortar attacks against

115 bases, towns, and cities in South Vietnam, and Gabrielle, intensely relieved that she had not remained in Saigon with *le petit* Gavin, waited anxiously to hear from Serena.

A letter came from her within days. The attacks in Saigon had been nothing like as bad as last year's Tet attacks, and there was good news regarding some of the children at the orphanage. In the past two months six of them had been successfully placed for adoption with families in Belgium and Luxembourg and Serena was hopeful that more would be placed in other European countries.

In June came the first piece of optimistic news since the peace talks had begun. At a meeting at Midway Island with President Thieu, President Nixon announced the planned withdrawal of 25,000 American combat troops from Vietnam.

It really was beginning to seem as if the end could be in sight. Gabrielle had written to Nhu, asking if she thought any purpose could be served by her returning to Saigon, but Nhu's reply had been disappointingly negative.

Then, in September, Radio Hanoi announced the death of Ho Chi Minh.

"I don't see why you think Ho's death is such a big deal," Radford had said to her, irritated as he always was by any mention of Vietnam and any reference to Gavin, however oblique.

"It could make all the difference in the world," Gabrielle had said, deeply thoughtful. "It could change the attitude of the North Vietnamese."

"Well, if it does, no doubt President Nixon will

tell us so," he responded sarcastically.

Gabrielle did not rise to the sarcasm. They were in his apartment and had just made love. She swung her legs from the bed, beginning to dress. He raised himself up on one arm, saying bewilderedly, "Where the hell are you going, baby? You don't have to be at the club for another three hours."

She slipped on her shoes and picked up her clutch bag, her face fiercely determined. "I cannot wait for President Nixon to discover whether Ho's death is going to make any difference to the North Vietnamese stance at the peace talks. I'm going to go there myself to find out."

"You're going to *what*?" Radford yelled, sexually satisfied lethargy vanishing as he shot upright in the bed. "You're going *where*?"

"To the peace talks," Gabrielle said composedly. "I'm going to speak to Xuan Thuy, the chief North Vietnamese delegate, and I'm going to ask him where Gavin is being held."

CHAPTER THIRTEEN

In Los Angeles, Abbra, too, wondered what political changes would result now that Ho was dead.

"That's why the North Vietnamese Army and the Viet Cong made such an all-out attempt to take the South last year at Tet," Scott said to her wryly. "It must have been obvious to them that Ho was an ill man who only had a year or so to live. I guess they wanted a decisive victory that would enable him to die happy."

The war still played a large part in both their lives. Abbra kept in regular communication with both Gabrielle and Serena, and in November, two months after Ho's death, when another massive antiwar demonstration took place in Washington, both she and Scott were among the quarter of a million participants.

"What are we going to do about this latest idea of yours?" he said to her as they flew back home to Los Angeles. "Are we going to go ahead with it?"

Her hand tightened in his. Serena had written to her, telling her of how some Cây Thông orphans had been adopted by European families. *The bureaucratic difficulties involved in the arrangements were horrendous,* she had written in her large distinctive handwriting, *but when I finally waved the children good-bye, knowing that they were going to homes where they would be loved and cherished, the satisfaction I felt was the deepest I have ever experienced.*

The letter had profoundly affected Abbra. She and Scott had been married for over a year now and though they had both been united in their desire to have a baby as quickly as possible, no baby had as yet put in an appearance.

"There is no medical reason why you shouldn't conceive," the gynecologist she had consult-

280

ed had told her. "You must be patient, Mrs. Ellis. Nature often takes her time about these things."

She still hadn't despaired of having a baby of her own, but Serena's letter opened up other possibilities. Why didn't she and Scott adopt a Vietnamese baby who had been abandoned or orphaned? If they had a baby of their own afterward, it wouldn't matter. The child they had adopted would simply be a ready-made older brother or sister for it.

She hadn't been afraid of suggesting such an unconventional idea to Scott as she would have been of suggesting it to Lewis. There had been times, in her short marriage to Lewis, when she knew that she had made very wrong assumptions about the way he was thinking or feeling. She still remembered her bewilderment and horror when he had revealed that there were some aspects of battle that he actually enjoyed. She had felt as if they were each on opposite sides of a deep chasm, a chasm that had been bridged only by her very idealistic love for him.

No such chasm had ever sprung open at her feet while she had been married to Scott, and it was unthinkable that it would ever do so. They were as mentally in tune as they had become physically in tune. On their first night in bed together he had overcome her momentary nervousness with passionate ease, making her laugh as well as arousing desire so intense that it almost bordered on pain.

Lewis had always made love to her with slow, tender deliberation. Scott's lovemaking was stunningly uninhibited. He taught her that in bed, between two people who loved each other, nothing was wrong or offensive or out of bounds if it gave mutual pleasure.

Their marriage, when it became public knowledge, gave rise to a lot of prurient speculation and gossip, but between the two of them there was never the slightest problem. Lewis's name was mentioned freely and often. His photograph stood on her desk as it had always, only now it stood alongside a photograph of herself and Scott.

On their first wedding anniversary her father-in-law had telephoned them, his voice abrupt with embarrassed awkwardness as he wished them well. Despite repeated attempts at reconciliation on their part, it was the first time he had spoken to either of them since the day they had told them of their decision to marry.

There was no such overture from Abbra's parents. The marriage was one they were totally incapable of accepting. What made things even worse, for them, was that Scott was such a public figure. There were regular articles in football magazines about him. His name was mentioned with zestful enthusiasm by television sports commentators. His photograph, with Abbra at his side, appeared regularly in the gossip columns of nationwide newspapers. It seemed to them that everyone in the country knew that their daughter had been widowed and had, within months, married her playboy football-star brother-in-law.

Abbra knew very well that her parents would be violently opposed to her adopting a Vietnamese orphan, but she was determined she and Scott would live as they wished to.

As the stewardess moved deftly through the first class cabin, removing empty glasses and serving fresh drinks, Abbra lifted her face away from Scott's shoulder, where it had been resting, and said softly, "Do you want to, darling?"

He nodded, smiling down at her, his eyes so full of love for her that her heart seemed physically to turn within her chest. "You know I do," he said, and at the husky undertone in his voice she knew that he was thinking about their previous night's lovemaking.

She smiled, a deeply happy woman, and with her hand still clasped in his, laid her head once more against his shoulder. "I'll write to Serena the minute that we reach home," she said, wondering how long it would take for all the necessary documentation to be completed. She wondered, also, how old the child that would be sent to them would be and if it would be a boy or a girl, and not caring an iota either way.

As they walked through the arrivals lounge at the Los Angeles airport, they were spotted by photographers almost immediately. Over the last year or so they had become a well-known media couple. The public liked to be reminded that some of their hard-muscled, handsome heart-throbs were also genuine Mr. Nice-Guys, and since his marriage Scott had fallen most definitely into the Mr. Nice-Guy category.

Abbra, too, had become worthy of media attention in her own right. Her novel about North Beach, and the burgeoning Beat Generation, had won a prestigious literary prize, and had established her very firmly as a young writer of great promise.

Flashbulbs popped and a journalist who was hanging around the arrival area for any story that might come his way called out, "Hey, Scott! I understand you've just flown in from attending the antiwar demonstration in Washington. How do you think your brother would have felt about that? Didn't he pick up a handful of medals before he was blown away in 'Nam?"

It was the kind of tasteless, brutal question that was regularly thrown at him by some members of the press, and though he was filled with an overwhelming desire to punch the journalist in the nose, he merely said with practised ease, "I make it a rule not to talk about my brother in airport lounges, I find it disrespectful. What do you think about the Broncos' performance this week? That new head coach of theirs is certainly hurling them from the backwoods into the twentieth century. They're a team really going places."

They were outside the arrivals lounge now, but the journalist was still hard on their heels. Suddenly there came a distant cry of "I tell you, Brigitte Bardot is aboard the New York flight that has just landed! She's traveling as Mrs. Evelyn Watson!" Their tormentor spun on his heel, almost falling over himself in his haste to run back inside the building.

"Thank goodness for that," Abbra said with a sigh of relief as they walked over to the car park. "Another minute and we would have been in 'how does it feel to sleep with your brother's widow' country."

Scott grinned. "One of these days I'm going to tell them that it feels just fine and they can make of it what they want!"

They didn't have far to drive to reach the sanctuary of their home. Although one of the first things they had done after their marriage was to buy the little beach house that Abbra had been renting, they also had a home in Westwood, less than twelve miles from the airport.

It was an elegant house, in an elegant district, and Abbra had decorated and furnished it with warmth and love. The floors were of polished beech, the rugs Oriental in soft colors of dusty rose and muted green. There were plants everywhere and comfortable sofas and chairs. On the walls were the paintings they had bought for each other over the past two years: a La Jolla beach scene that had been Abbra's first Christmas gift to him, a watercolor of the Spanish Steps that he had bought for her in Rome, an oil painting depicting a rainy evening beside the Seine, a stunning charcoal sketch of Lincoln Cathedral.

There were shelves of books, and books piled up on the glass-topped coffee tables. Poetry, and English and American classics for Abbra, biographies and spy thrillers for Scott. Beneath a

long, chintz-covered window seat were hundreds of LPs. Oscar Peterson and Sarah Vaughan
companionably piled against the Rolling Stones
and the Beatles and Chopin and Mozart.

In the kitchen there were copper pans on the
walls and jugfuls of fresh flowers and in the
bedroom there was a brass-headed bed covered
with a white damask French counterpane. The
walls were pale yellow, the carpet was creamy-
beige and ankle deep, and the windows looked
out over their flower-filled garden toward Santa
Monica and the sea.

There was a blue and white decorated guest
room that Patti had often occupied, and another
room that had stood empty for too long.

That evening Abbra opened the door onto it,
and stood looking at it thoughtfully. It had been
decorated as a nursery. Hand-painted nursery-
rhyme figures decorated the white walls. The
bassinet was a French antique that they had
bought on a visit to Gabrielle in Paris. Stuffed
toy teddy bears and tigers and elephants were
crammed onto the seat of a low-legged, Victor-
ian carved-rosewood chair which she had
reupholstered herself. Soon she would be sitting
in the chair, telling bedtime stories to her adopted son or daughter. A warm tingle of excitement
surged through her veins. She would need to buy
a small bed in case the child that they were sent
was no longer a baby. If the child was a girl, then
she would pretty up the room a little more. If it
was a boy, then she would ask Scott's advice as
to the kind of toys she should buy, toys to

supplement the waiting teddies and tigers and elephants.

It was February the following year before Serena was at last able to write to them and confirm that all the necessary documentation had been processed and that now all that was necessary was the exit visa for Fam, the five-month-old baby girl whom they were to adopt.

She was brought in to us from a village some twenty miles north of the city. Her parents both died when the village was caught in cross fire between American forces and Viet Cong. She was severely malnourished when we received her and even now is not very robust. The sooner she leaves Saigon the happier I shall be. We are suffering from a measles epidemic at the moment and several children have already died.

March came and went and still little Fam's exit visa was not processed.
Believe me, I am doing everything that I can, Serena had written in angry frustration.

Fam's travel documentation is with the Vietnamese authorities and every day I inquire I am told that the documentation will be finalized "tomorrow." I keep thinking of a few lines from Kipling:
  And the end of the fight is a tombstone white with the name of the late deceased,

And the epitaph drear: "A Fool lies here
who tried to hustle the East."
If I should meet an unexpected end, it will
be the most apt epitaph in the world for
me!

Two weeks later there was another letter, full
of rage and despair.

Dearest Abbra,
I don't know how to break the news to you,
but little Fam has died. She caught measles
three days ago and was totally unable to
withstand the disease. If only the authorities
had processed her travel documentation with
even partial efficiency she would be alive
and well and with you in Los Angeles. As it
was, we received her exit visa just two hours
after burying her.

For days Abbra felt numb. She had never held
Fam, had never even seen her, but for weeks she
had regarded her as her daughter. And now she
was dead and the little room that she had made
so pretty for her would never be hers.

"It doesn't mean the end of our plan to adopt,
sweetheart," Scott had said to her gently. "The
one thing Vietnam has, God help her, is an
abundance of orphans."

"I know," she had said quietly, "but I need to
grieve for the child I thought was going to be
ours. If I don't, who else will?"

He had given her a sad smile. "Me," he said,

pulling her lovingly into the circle of his arms and holding her close.

Toward the end of her letter, Serena had written bitterly:

Fam isn't the only victim of crass inefficiency. Do you remember Sanh? He is the little boy who was taken so very ill with hemorrhagic fever within his first few days of coming to us. He nearly died then because he was left unattended and uncared for in an overcrowded hospital ward. Shortly afterward he contracted polio. He is nine years old now and in leg irons but the most cheerful, lovable child imaginable. Last Wednesday he came down with what seemed to be a sudden toxicosis.

Unfortunately, neither Mike, Lucy, or I were there at the time. A large bomb had gone off in Cholon, killing dozens of people and injuring scores more, and we had been asked to go down there and give what assistance we could. In our absence, the Australian girl who had been left in charge took Sanh to the hospital, the same one he had previously been taken to. The minute I knew what had happened I rushed down there to see him. Once again he had been left alone and unattended, this time in a passageway full of decaying food and medical refuse. He had a temperature of 105 and was delirious. Mike came down to the hospital in a taxi and we took him immediately back to Cây Thông, where I have been nursing him night and day for the past three days. This morning, thank God, his temperature has begun to drop. I truly believe that if we hadn't removed him from the hospital, he, too, like Fam, would be dead by now.

Abbra reread the entire letter before sitting down to write back to Serena. Sanh was nine years old. She and Scott had imagined adopting a small child. A baby, or possibly a toddler. It would be strange to become overnight the parents of a nine-year-old boy, and a boy who was also crippled.

She sat for a long time, the letter in her hand, thinking. Then she pushed her chair away from her desk and went in search of Scott.

He was in the large basement room that had been converted into a gymnasium, working out. For a brief moment, as she watched him lifting weights, his arm and shoulder muscles bulging, his magnificent body gleaming with perspiration, she wondered if what she was going to suggest to him was fair. He was an athlete. Physical fitness was essential to him. If he had a son, he would surely want a son who would be able to follow in his footsteps, a son he would be able to play football and baseball with. To run and to swim and to go off on camping weekends with.

He looked across at her and grinned, putting the weights down. "What is it, sweetheart? News from Patti?"

Patti had telephoned earlier in the week to say that French translation rights were pending on Abbra's newly finished novel and that she would be in touch immediately after the deal was finalized.

Abbra shook her head. Incredibly, over the last few days she hadn't written a word and hadn't given her work a thought. "No. It's something else."

At the hesitancy in her voice he rose to his feet, throwing a towel around his neck and walking toward her. She was wearing a pair of faded denim jeans and a gentian blue, open-necked cotton shirt. Her dark, jaw-length hair fell forward softly at either side of her face; and her feet, with their pearly-pink painted toenails, were bare. He was filled with the sudden urge to make love to her, to slide her down beneath him then and there on the polished pine floor. Her eyes met his, clouded with uncertainty, and he suppressed the desire with difficulty, saying gently, realizing that something was troubling her, "Is it Fam? Are you brooding about her and unable to work?"

She looked up at him, loving him so much that her chest seemed to ache. "No, it's not Fam. I've accepted what happened to Fam. Or accepted it as much as I will ever."

Beneath the electric lights of the basement his shaggy mop of undisciplined hair was the color of old gold. A trickle of perspiration was running down his throat, and she wanted to stand on tiptoe and lick it away. As his eyes held hers, she knew with a surge of relief and shame that by doubting what his reaction to her suggestion was going to be, she was doing him a great disservice.

"I've been rereading Serena's letter. Do you remember her references to Sanh, the nine-year-old boy who is crippled by polio and who has just been so ill?"

Scott nodded, wiping his neck slowly with the towel, a slight frown touching his brow.

"Serena hasn't said so, but I imagine that a crippled nine-year-old will be far less likely to be adopted than small, healthy babies, and so..."

"And so you wondered if we might adopt him," he finished for her, his frown clearing. He had been apprehensive that she had been mentioning Sanh because the child's plight was causing her even further distress. Now that he knew what was on her mind, he slipped his arm around her shoulders, saying, "It's a good idea, sweetheart. I don't know why we didn't think of it when we first read Serena's letter."

"And you don't mind ... about his disability?"

He gave her a mock punch against her jaw. "A child of our own could be born with a physical handicap. You wouldn't expect it to make any difference to me then, would you? Besides, with the right kind of medical treatment and the right kind of care, who is to say that he will have to remain in leg irons? I don't know a damn thing about polio and its after effects, but while the adoption documentation is going through I'm going to find out all I can."

292

In May, when an estimated 100,000 demonstrators gathered in Washington to oppose the bombing of Communist base camps in Cambodia, Abbra and Scott were in Paris, visiting Gabrielle.

Feelings at the Washington demonstration were higher and more intense than ever before. Four days earlier, at an antiwar demonstration at Kent State University in Ohio, in an act that stunned America, the National Guard opened fire on the students. Four of them, two of them girls, were killed. Eleven others were injured. With the television scenes from Kent State still searing their minds, Abbra and Scott were in an unusually somber frame of mind when they met Gabrielle at the nightclub where she sang.

"It is terrible, *mes amies*," Gabrielle said as they sat at a small table in an alcove, toying with the sole Normandie that all three of them had ordered. "At the beginning of the year I thought that perhaps there would be a negotiated peace before the year was out. Now..." She gave a despairing shrug of her shoulders. "Now I am not so sure. There are times when I think that it will never end. That *mon petit fils* is going to be a man before Gavin sees him again."

Her voice had broken slightly at the mention of Gavin. Abbra felt pain shoot through her, so intense she could hardly breathe. She could only imagine what Gabrielle must be suffering. What she herself would have been suffering if there had been no confirmation of Lewis's death and if she had still been living every day, waiting for news.

"What is happening at the peace talks?" Scott asked quietly after they had sat in silence for several minutes.

"*Merde alors!*" Gabrielle said graphically, raising her eyes to heaven. "The peace talks! They are beyond belief, *mon ami*. You know, do you not, that it took seven months for them merely to reach agreement on the seating arrangements? Neither the Saigon delegate nor the National Liberation Front of South Vietnam delegates would sit opposite each other. Nothing productive is being discussed. All that is happening is that both sides spend hours each day verbally maligning each other."

"And have you managed to speak with Xuan Thuy yet?" Abbra asked, ignoring the large Neapolitan ice that had followed the sole Normandie.

Gabrielle's cat-green eyes glinted beneath the long sweep of her eyelashes. "No, not yet. But I have not given up hope. It is in the nature of a Vietnamese to be able to sit out eternity if necessary. And I am half Vietnamese. I can be just as stubborn as the embassy, just as determined. And in the end I will have my answer." She pushed her Neapolitan ice away from her, untouched. "That is what the Americans do not understand about the Vietnamese," she said with stark frankness. "They do not understand that we see time differently. And that is why they will lose the war. Americans will not endure a war that continues for ten, fifteen, twenty years. The Vietnamese will do so, *have* done so, when you consider how long it is since they first began to fight the French."

Scott nodded in agreement. An immediate rapport had sprung up between himself and Gabrielle, just as it had sprung up between the two women. When Abbra had first introduced them, Gabrielle had looked up at Scott's magnificent physique and six-foot-four-inch stature and with a naughty twinkle in her eyes had said with a husky, unchained laugh, "*Félicitations*, Abbra. *Il est magnifique!*"

Scott, in his turn, thought the petite Gabrielle an absolute delight. He admired the way she was bringing up her son by herself, the way she had turned her back on easy fame with the rock band she had once sung with in order to sing in a style true to herself, and he admired her steadfast efforts to discover news of her husband and the fierce love that was in her voice whenever she spoke of him, even though it was now four years since he had disappeared.

He knew of her affair with Radford, though Gabrielle took care that neither he nor Abbra ever met Radford. Gavin was the love of her life, and when she was with them, she wanted to talk only of him. Her tortured guilt at not being strong enough to live without physical love in Gavin's absence was often apparent, and both Scott and Abbra deeply sympathized with the terrible limbo in which she was living, and the means she had taken in order to endure it.

295

"I have visited the North Vietnamese Embassy every morning for the last eight months," she continued as the untouched ices were removed from the table and Scott ordered a round of martinis. "And every morning the routine is the same. I ring the doorbell and a Frenchwoman of about forty-five, very efficient-looking in a black skirt and a white blouse, opens the door. I ask if I may speak with Xuan Thuy. I am refused. I ask if I may speak with anyone who can give me information about my husband, and I am told that there is no one there who can give me any information. And the door is closed in my face."

"Do you think things are ever going to change?" Abbra asked as the musical trio who had been playing dance music came to the end of their number. "Do you think you ever will gain entrance?"

Gabrielle's eyes were bright with determination, "Oh, yes," she said dauntlessly. "Yesterday I saw one of the Vietnamese officials in the street and he was unable to escape me. For the first time I was able to impress upon someone in authority just who I am. Who my uncle was. He repeated only the familiar 'Madame, I am sorry. We have no information about your husband' routine, but I could see that his attitude toward me had changed." The pianist began to play the lead-in to Gabrielle's first song, and she rose from the table, saying with a wide, gamin-like smile and unquenchable optimism, "There will be news soon, *chérie*, I am sure of it."

* * *

Sanh wasn't the only Vietnamese child arriving in the country that day. A woman named Lucy Roberts had escorted seven children from Saigon, six of them babies. How she had managed, single-handedly, to feed and change and care for them on the long flight, Abbra couldn't even begin to imagine. But her attention wasn't focused on the babies. It was focused on the bright-eyed little boy who, his withered legs encased in braces, was propelling himself forward with difficulty in Lucy's wake.

"This is Sanh," Lucy said with a tired smile as they all met in the middle of the airport waiting room. "How I would have managed without his help on the plane I do not know."

"Hello, Sanh," Scott said, slipping his arm lightly around Sanh's shoulders. "Welcome to America."

Abbra's heart was beating so hard that she thought even Lucy and Sanh must be able to hear it. "Hello, Sanh," she said, stepping toward him and holding out her hand to him. "Welcome to your new home."

His hand slipped into hers, and as he looked up at her and grinned, saying in heavily accented English, "I am very glad to be here, *Maman*-Abbra," she knew that all her panic-stricken fears were groundless.

"Who told you my name?" she asked, love for him flooding through her, knowing that it was going to be all right, knowing that from now on they were going to be a family.

"*Cô* Serena," he said, his hand remaining

trustingly in hers.

Abbra smiled, grateful for Serena's thoughtful foresightedness. Although Sanh's first language was Vietnamese, his second was French, not English. It was only natural that he should, at first, refer to her as *Maman*. And *Maman*-Abbra was an ideal appellation for the first few days, when they were getting to know each other and when anything else would be touched with artificiality. Soon, she knew, the Abbra would be dropped. And soon, also, *Maman* would change quite naturally to Mom.

In April President Nixon announced that 100,000 American troops were to leave South Vietnam by the end of the year. Abbra listened to the television newscast with relief. Perhaps this time it really was the beginning of the end. She wondered if Scott had heard the news over the car radio. He and Sanh had gone to watch a basketball game and were then going on to Musso & Frank's Grill on Hollywood Boulevard. It was the only chophouse Scott knew where they served adequately burned onions with grilled liver, and he and Sanh often ate there after attending a basketball or a baseball game.

When the news program came to an end, she turned the television off, impatient for Scott and Sanh to return home. It was Sanh's tenth birthday the next day, and though Sanh did not know it, they were going to take him to a kennel that evening in order that he could choose a puppy for his birthday present.

As she turned away from the television set she saw a car enter the drive. A sleek, black, official-looking car. She stood very still, ice seeping down her spine, transported back in time to the occasions when she had been first brought the news that Lewis was missing in action, and then the news that he was dead.

What on earth was the reason for today's visit? Had they found Lewis's body? Were they coming to tell her that Lewis's body was being returned home?

The doorbell rang and with a heavy heart she forced herself to move, to walk across the room and into the hallway. She had been so happy a minute before, waiting for Scott and Sanh to return home, looking forward to Sanh's delight when they told him that he could choose a puppy for his very own. Now, if her visitors were bringing her the news that she suspected they were bringing, Sanh's birthday would be permanently marred. Instead of being a day of joyous thanksgiving, it would be a day on which she would always remember the news that came immediately prior to it.

The doorbell rang again and she put her hand on the catch. Perhaps it wasn't what she feared. Perhaps her visitors were calling about some innocuous bureaucratic matter that would be explained and over in a mere few seconds.

She opened the door wide, and the instant she saw their faces she knew that the matter they had come about was anything but innocuous.

"Mrs. Ellis? May we speak with you, please?"

She nodded, her throat dry, leading the way into the living room.

"Is your husband at home? I'm afraid that this is a matter that concerns you both."

She shook her head. They weren't the same men who had called on her on either of the two previous occasions, but they were so similar in manner and looks as to be virtually indistinguishable.

"No. Please tell me whatever it is you have to say to me."

"I'm afraid I can't do that, Mrs. Ellis, not without your husband here with you."

The officer who had so far done all the speaking looked ashen-faced. She wondered if his previous assignment had been to tell some poor woman that she was now a widow.

She was suddenly filled with a passionate desire to be rid of both him and the chaplain who was standing somberly silent at his side before Scott and Sanh returned home.

"I've received two such visits previously," she said with cool composure. "On both occasions I was informed that information couldn't be given to me unless someone was with me, and on both occasions, eventually, the information was given while I was unaccompanied. That is the way I prefer to hear difficult news, Major. By myself."

The major was beginning to look physically ill and the chaplain cleared his throat, saying placatingly, "I am afraid this time, because of the nature of the circumstances, we really must insist that your husband be present. Where is he

300

at the moment, Mrs. Ellis? Will he be long?"

"He's away for the weekend," she lied, shocking herself at the lengths she was prepared to go in order to insure that they leave before Scott and Sanh returned home.

"Then I think we will have to call again on Monday," the chaplain responded unhappily.

"No!" Her voice was so adamant that both men blinked. "I've received, alone, the worst news that any woman can receive. Nothing you can tell me today can be any more shocking than the news that has been broken to me in the past. Whatever it is, I insist upon hearing it."

She wasn't speaking to the chaplain, she was speaking to the major. His eyes held hers and then he said at last, slowly, "Okay, Mrs. Ellis. I guess there's never going to be an easy way of doing this. Will you sit down, please?"

She didn't want to sit, but it seemed pointless to prolong the proceedings by making trivial protests.

She sat. She wondered where Lewis's body had been found. How it had been found. The possibilities sickened her. But at least now he could have a proper burial.

"Mrs. Ellis." The major had seated himself in a chair opposite her, and he was leaning toward her, his eyes very grave, his hands clasped tightly and held between his knees. "Mrs. Ellis. I want you to listen to me very carefully. A month ago, as part of the negotiations that have been taking place in Paris, the North Vietnamese agreed to release three prisoners of war. No names of the men to be released were given until three days ago." He paused, and she waited patiently for him to tell her of the dead who were also, obviously, to be returned as well.

"Mrs. Ellis, when we received the names of the three men who are to be released to us, your husband's name was the first of the three."

She continued to stare at him, waiting for him to continue, to explain.

He didn't do so. She said at last, with a little helpless gesture of her hands, "I'm sorry, I don't understand. My husband" ... she corrected herself ... "my first husband is dead. He has been dead for four and a half years now. There was a witness to his death. Has his body been found? Are the North Vietnamese releasing it along with two prisoners of war? Is that what you are trying to tell me?"

The major shook his head. "No, Mrs. Ellis. What I am trying to tell you is that your husband, Captain Lewis Ellis, is alive. On receiving his name, we checked immediately with the North Vietnamese authorities. There is no doubt whatsoever. Your husband was held for three years in a jungle camp in the Ca Mau peninsula and moved north eighteen months ago. He is to be released, with two other prisoners, in a week's time."

"Lewis is alive?" the words were a stunned whisper. For a brief second of time her whole being was filled with such intense joy that she thought her heart would burst. And then, through the window, she saw Scott's car enter the drive. Lewis was alive, and her marriage to Scott was bigamous. Or illegal. Or invalid. He wasn't really her husband. He had never been her husband.

The car came to a halt and he opened the driver's door, stepping out onto the gravel. His shaggy mop of wheat-gold hair gleamed in the late afternoon sunshine. He strode round to the passenger seat door, opening it, helping Sanh to step out of the car. They were both laughing. Through the open window she could hear their laughter and she knew that she would never, ever, forget it.

"Tonight, Papa? Are we going for the puppy tonight?" Sanh was saying eagerly.

He had been with them for four months now, and already she could not imagine life without him. If her marriage to Scott was now invalid, what about Sanh's adoption? Was that invalid too? How could she live without him? How could she possibly live without Scott?

"Oh, God," she whispered as the front door opened and they came noisily and laughingly into the house. "Oh, sweet Jesus! What is going to happen to us? What are we going to *do*?"

CHAPTER FOURTEEN

Serena rose to her feet. It was impossible to keep on talking to Trinh from behind a desk. Their conversation was no longer official. It was highly personal and couldn't be conducted as if she were a person in authority and Trinh a supplicant. At this moment in time they were equals. Two women in love with the same man.

She looked out the window before beginning to speak. *Were* they both in love with the same man? Was *she* still in love with the daredevil, roustabout Irish-American that she had married in such reckless haste three years earlier? Amazingly, it was a question she had never thought to ask herself. She had simply assumed that she was. Certainly his being returned to America safe and well was one of her goals. It was concern for Kyle that had brought her to Saigon. Because of her superstitious fear that unfaithfulness on her part would affect his eventual fate, she had lived as chastely as a nun for what had begun to feel like a lifetime. So surely she was still in love with him?

Outside in a small courtyard a dozen babies lay on blankets, kicking their legs and gurgling contentedly. She stared at them unseeingly, wondering if the exquisite-looking Vietnamese girl was also in love with him. Certainly she must have been at one time. She most obviously wasn't a prostitute or a bar girl. What had Kyle told her? That he would get a divorce and marry her? And what did the girl know of Kyle's whereabouts? Did she believe that he was dead? Did she think that he had simply abandoned her? Or did she know that he was in Hoa Lo, and if so, who had told her?

She turned slowly away from the window. "What I have to say is very difficult," she began, and to her horror her voice sounded tight and brittle. She paused, trying to control it, to sound reasonable and calm. When she spoke again her voice was only slightly unsteady. "I know Kyle Anderson, the father of your little girl."

She kept her eyes resolutely away from the child. There would be time enough to look at Kyle's child. For the moment she couldn't cope with the emotions the child was arousing in her.

Trinh's whole expression and demeanor changed. "You do?" She stepped toward Serena eagerly, her eyes bright with fierce love and desperate anxiety. "You are a friend of his? A relative? Do you have news of him?"

Serena's throat hurt. She had her answer to one of her questions. The girl was still in love with him. At that moment she hated Kyle. She hated him for his irresponsibility. She had never, in a million years, expected that he would be faithful to her while he was in Vietnam. That would have been out of character. But why couldn't he have contented himself with the willing bar girls of Tu

Do Street? Why, instead, had he seduced a nice, respectable girl and probably ruined her whole life?

She said simply, knowing no other way of phrasing the words so that they sounded even remotely acceptable, "I'm his wife."

Trinh merely stared at her. For a second Serena wondered if she had overestimated the girl's seemingly excellent English.

"Do you understand me?" she said gently, wondering why she was feeling so much compassion for a girl who should, instead, be arousing in her feelings of outrage and jealous fury. "I am Kyle's wife. That is why I came to Saigon. To perhaps gain news of him, to be able to feel a little closer to him."

"No," Trinh whispered, stepping back uncertainly, her free hand stretched out as if feeling for some form of support. "No, I do not believe you. You are mistaken. You are talking of another American. Another Kyle Anderson."

On the floor near the desk was Serena's shoulder bag. Serena picked it up and opened it, taking out a dark green Gucci wallet. Silently she withdrew a photograph of Kyle. It had been taken in Scotland, only hours after their Gretna Green marriage. Kyle was laughing, his dark hair tumbling low over his brow. He was holding a can of lager in one hand and was wearing a pair of hip-hugging jeans and an open-neck shirt. Behind him were moors and the gleam of a distant loch. Serena didn't remember where they had been when she had taken the photograph.

She could only remember their laughter, their crazy elation at having pulled off a prank that was going to shock all four parents to the core. It all seemed so long ago now. A different lifetime, a different world.

She held the photograph out toward Trinh. The girl didn't take hold of it. She simply stared at it, the blood draining from her face. "No," she whispered again, her hands tightening around the child in her arms. "No, I do not believe it! I cannot believe it!"

"It's true," Serena said starkly. She withdrew a pack of cigarettes from her bag. "Would you like one?" she asked, offering the pack to Trinh.

Trinh shook her head, tears rolling mercilessly down her cheeks. "He never told me that he was married. I had no idea. I did not know. I am sorry, Madame. I do not know what to say. How to apologize to you..." Her voice broke completely, and she could not continue. Her tears were falling onto her *ao dai*, onto the bewildered child in her arms.

"Sit down," Serena said practically, moving a chair toward her.

Trinh didn't move, didn't seem capable of moving, and Serena took her lightly by the arm, pressing her down into the chair.

"It isn't up to you to apologize," she said, amazed at the maturity she was displaying and which she genuinely felt. "I believe you didn't know that Kyle was married. Do you know where he is now? Do you know that he is imprisoned in Hoa Lo?"

Trinh's head shot upward, relief replacing shocked distress in her eyes. "He is alive? Do you know for sure that he is alive? His friend wrote to me and told me that he was alive after his helicopter crashed, but that there was no news of him afterward."

"His friend?"

Tears still coursed their way down Trinh's face. "Mr. Chuck Wilson," she said thickly. "That is the name of Kyle's friend. In Saigon, they were always together."

Serena's nostrils flared. So Chuck had known about Trinh; he had probably known about Kylie, but he kept his knowledge to himself. She didn't know how she felt about his deceit. It was something she would have to think about later. She could not possibly start to assess it at the moment.

Kylie had begun to squirm in Trinh's arms and to vocally protest being held for so long, so tightly. Trinh set her down on the floor, her eyes still holding Serena's as she waited tensely for whatever information Serena could give her.

"I know that after he was shot down he was taken to Hanoi," Serena said, feeling so over-wrought that she could quite easily have burst into tears herself. "In October of the year he was shot down, the North Vietnamese released a list of names of men being held in Hoa Lo. Kyle's name was on the list. There has been no com-munication from him, but there has been no communication from the vast majority of POWs being held. Only a very small percentage has been allowed to write to their families. Kyle hasn't been one of them, but that doesn't mean that he isn't still alive."

"Oh, *Choi oui!*" Trinh gasped softly. Oh, my God!

She began to sob and Serena, feeling equally emotionally spent, walked slowly back to her desk and sat down behind it, weak-kneed.

The child, sitting happily on the floor, regarded her with a steadfast, curious gaze. Serena returned it. Every Amerasian child she had ever seen had been stunningly attractive and Kyle's child was no exception. She was ravishingly beautiful, with the kind of bone structure that indicated a beauty that would last lifelong.

Serena was tempted to rise to her feet again and to pick the child up and sit her on her knee. She resisted the temptation, unsure of how Trinh would react if she were to do so.

Trinh's sobs of relief had begun to subside, and when she was able to speak she said awkwardly, "You have been very kind to me, Madame, under the ... the circumstances." She paused, remembering that though Kyle was alive and in Hoa Lo, he was also married. He had lied to her. He had not been going to marry her. He had never intended to marry her. Her heart was breaking and she didn't know how she was going to bear the pain. She said stiffly, "I will go now. You will not want my daughter here, at Cây Thông."

She rose from the chair, bending down and scooping Kylie into her arms.

Serena regarded the pair of them thoughtfully.

She, too, had thought of the difficulties attendant on taking Kylie into Cây Thông. And she had also thought of the alternatives ... the other orphanages in the city, crammed and dirty and loveless. It was unthinkable that she should allow Kyle's child to suffer in some such institution.

She said, choosing her words carefully, "I would very much like Kylie to be cared for at Cây Thông. She would be as well cared for here as she could possibly be anywhere, and no one but us would know of the rather peculiar relationship that exists between us."

Trinh stared at her, her face troubled, and then said hesitantly, "Forgive me asking, Madame, but do you and ... and" ... she swallowed, continuing only with the greatest difficulty ... "and Kyle have children of your own?"

Serena shook her head, "No, we were married a year before Kyle came to Vietnam, but during that year we were together for only a few days."

For a moment Trinh was too stunned by Serena's frankness to be able to react, and then relief flashed through her eyes, followed by a look of triumph that she couldn't quite hide.

Serena waited, knowing why Trinh had asked her if she had children of her own, knowing what was troubling her.

"Some of the children at Cây Thông have been adopted by British and American families," Trinh continued. Serena's display of frankness encouraged her to be equally frank. "You have no children of your own, Madame. Perhaps if I left Kylie here, with you, because she's your husband's child, you would take her from me?"

"No," Serena said quietly. "I will not take Kylie from you. I do not want her for myself. I simply want to ensure that as she is my husband's child, she is suitably cared for."

She knew it was useless to say anything more. Trinh would either believe her or not. For the child's sake, she hoped very much that Trinh was going to believe her.

From outside the open window the babies could be heard, beginning to noisily demand feeding. Trinh stood silently, Kylie in her arms, struggling to come to a decision.

There was a brief knock on the rattan door, and a New Zealand girl opened it, saying, "Sorry to interrupt, Serena, but the babies are ready to be fed. As Lucy is still at the hospital, could you possibly give me a hand?"

"I'll be right with you," Serena said, rising to her feet.

When the door had closed and they were once more by themselves, Trinh said unhappily, "I do not think I have any choice. I will bring Kylie to Cây Thông to be looked after through the day while I work. And I will return for her every evening."

Serena nodded, relieved. They were not a day nursery, and the arrangement was not a usual one, but she knew that she would be able to square it with Mike Daniels.

"And nothing will be said to anyone?" Trinh asked again anxiously. "No one will know that she is your husband's child?"

"No," Serena affirmed. Christ. It was the last thing in the world that she wanted. She could just imagine Mike Daniels' reaction. Lucy's reaction. She rose from behind the desk and crossed the small room, opening the door for Trinh and Kylie.

In the doorway Trinh paused. "Thank you," she said simply. For a moment they were only a heartbeat away from friendship, and then Trinh said formally, "*Chào b*à, Madame." Good-bye. And the moment was lost.

Serena stood in the doorway, watching as Trinh walked gracefully away down the corridor, her hyacinth-blue *ao dai* fluttering softly around her legs. Kylie was in her arms, facing back over her shoulder. Her eyes met Serena's and suddenly, beneath the dark mop of hair, her face broke into a wide, mischievous smile.

At that moment she reminded Serena so much of Kyle that the blood pounded in her ears. She had encouraged Trinh to use Cây Thông as a nursery for Kylie because any other alternative had been unthinkable. But she still had no idea how she was going to come to terms with having Kyle's illegitimate daughter at Cây Thông, or of how she was going to come to terms with seeing Trinh every day, as she deposited and collected Kylie.

"When you're eventually released from Hoa Lo, you're going to have one hell of a lot of explaining to do, Kyle Anderson!" she said grimly under her breath as the hyacinth-blue *ao dai* disappeared around a corner and then, more emotionally confused than she had ever been before in her life, she hurried out into the courtyard to help feed the now-crying babies.

Kylie soon became a favorite at Cây Thông. She was the only child who was neither an orphan nor abandoned, and though some members of staff had been mildly curious about the arrangement, none of them ever suspected the truth about her paternity.

For her own mental well-being Serena took great care not to establish any sort of special relationship with Kylie. It wasn't easy. Kylie was by nature an affectionate and gregarious little girl, and Serena's gentle but firm rebuffs left her obviously hurt and bewildered. Serena steeled her heart. She could not allow mutual affection to spring between herself and Kylie. It would lead to all sorts of complications and, possibly, to untold misery. And so the rebuffs continued and eventually Kylie no longer approached Serena. But she would often stare at her, her dark blue eyes uncomprehending and miserable.

Whenever she brought Kylie to the orphanage, or picked her up, Trinh avoided Serena as assiduously as Serena avoided Kylie. The situation was one that Trinh didn't know how to handle. Kyle had lied to her, but she still loved him and she was living in the hope that despite the strangeness of their last meeting he still loved her. His wife had said herself that she and

Kyle had lived together only a few days. Perhaps that was why Kyle had not mentioned his marriage to her, because it was not truly a marriage at all. The thought had cheered her, but left her perplexed about Serena's presence in Saigon. She could imagine a woman doing such a thing only if she were very much in love. And if Kyle's wife was very much in love with him, then perhaps she would be able to persuade him to return to her when the war was over, and when he was released from Hoa Lo.

For the next year Serena rarely moved beyond the suburbs of Saigon. Mike Daniels made regular trips to the provinces, visiting regions as far apart as Da Nang and Hue in the north of the country, and Soc Trang and Can Tho in the Delta. He always returned with more orphans and more abandoned waifs, and Serena's work, trying to find loving homes for them in Europe and in America, never ceased.

Serena often thought that her relationship with Mike Daniels was very like her relationship with Trinh. It was a relationship that was going nowhere, a relationship that neither developed nor regressed. Although occasionally she thought she caught a look of interest in his eyes, his manner never changed. He tolerated her, and that seemed to be all. It was a masculine reaction that Serena had never encountered before, and it was one that infuriated her beyond bearing.

It wasn't that she lusted after him. Not the way she had with Chuck. If he had propositioned her,

314

she would have turned him down flat. But she did admire him. He was dedicated to the task of improving the lot of the sick and the destitute. As an eye specialist, his workload at the local hospital was enormous, and he took other clinics as well, clinics at the refugee camps in the city's suburbs, clinics in Cholon, clinics in the outlying villages around Saigon. And every penny he earned went into the running of Cây Thông.

Without Mike at the helm organizing the funding, and bullying and brow-beating the government and the military for whatever provisions he could get from them, Cây Thông would have been unable to survive. The children that were tended with such loving care in clean, sanitary surroundings would instead have had to fight for their survival in the unspeakably overcrowded and often rat-infested city orphanages.

But though she admired him unreservedly, he often seemed to be barely aware of her existence. Only rarely did he suggest they have a drink together at the end of the day, and when they did so their conversation was always impersonal. He knew nothing whatsoever about her private life, about her initial reason for being in Saigon. And she knew nothing at all about him. Not even if he was married, or had been married.

In 1970, at about the time she was arranging for Sanh to be adopted by Abbra and Scott, Serena told Mike of her intention to adopt not just one child, but several children.

"Ridiculous," he said shortly, not looking up

315

from the paperwork on his desk. "I haven't taken children in from the streets and from unbelievably bad provincial orphanages in order for them to run wild with drunken journalists at the Continental."

"They wouldn't be running wild with drunken journalists at the Continental," she retorted with acerbity. "They'll run wild in acres of glorious English countryside."

He put his pen down and looked up at her. "Just what the hell," he said heavily, "are you talking about?"

For once she had his attention, and she felt a stab of satisfaction. She pulled a battered cane chair near the corner of his desk and sat down. She had been nursing a sick child all night and her long pale-gold hair was scooped into a loose knot at the nape of her neck. There was no makeup on her face, and her amethyst-gray eyes were dark with tiredness. Even so, she was still the most beautiful woman he had ever seen.

"With Ho dead, and the peace talks under way, the war must be coming to an end," she said practically. "When it does, I shall return to England, to Bedingham."

"Bedingham?" he queried, his winged brows drawing together perplexedly.

"My home."

He pushed his chair away from his desk a little, leaning back in it. The sun was behind him, and she couldn't see the expression in his eyes.

"Tell me," he said briefly, his interest quickening. Serena didn't receive a piastre for her work

316

at Cây Thông, and yet she lived permanently, and with obvious financial ease, at the Continental. Her family home had to be more than a grandiosely named semi-detached villa in a London suburb.

Serena stretched out her long legs and crossed them at the ankles. They'd never been so relaxed together before. For once he was obviously prepared to give her some time and to listen to her.

"Bedingham", she said, her voice warm with love as she spoke its name, "is my ancestral home. It is in Cambridgeshire and was originally an abbey. Henry VIII put an end to its clerical life and gave it to one of my ancestors, Matthew Blyth, as a reward for services rendered."

She told him of how Bedingham had survived under Mary Tudor's reign, and then under Elizabeth's. She told him of how, in the reign of the roustabout Charles II, Bedingham had reached its apotheosis, playing host to the king and his Portuguese queen, and being lavishly extended, with west and east wings added, and elaborately formal gardens conceived and executed.

"Only in the last two hundred years or so did Bedingham run into any real problems," she finished. "And as these were financial, my grandfather very sensibly solved them by marrying the only daughter of an American railroad king."

He was grinning, the first time she had ever been aware of him doing so to her.

"And when I adopt my children, Bedingham,

with its lake and its lawns and woods, is where I am going to take them and where I am going to make a home for them."

He had moved slightly in his chair and the sun was no longer behind him. The expression in his eyes was one of frank curiosity.

"Is Bedingham yours? Have you inherited it?"

She shook her head. "No, my parents are still alive. But I've written to both my father and to my twin brother about my plans. My father says as long as his study and his library are sacrosanct, I can do what I like with the remainder of the house." A small smile played at the corner of her mouth. "Bar holding a pop concert, that is. Lance, my twin brother, is a left-wing Socialist. He says he can think of no better use for Bedingham than its becoming a home for Vietnamese war orphans. So you see, there are no objectors."

His eyes were suddenly devoid of expression. "What about Mr. Anderson?" he asked, his voice studiedly neutral. "You never mention him, but I assume that he exists. What is his opinion?"

"I haven't been able to ask him," she said, rising to her feet. "For the last four years he's been held in Hoa Lo prison, Hanoi."

The shock on his face was naked. Before he could recover from it she turned on her heel, and with an odd sense of satisfaction, swept out of his office.

Lucy had always been the person delegated to escort groups of children leaving for adoptive homes in Europe and in America, but at the beginning of 1971 Serena asked Mike if she could act as escort for the next group of children due to leave for the U.S.

"Sure," he said easily. "Any particular reason?"

Since their tête-à-tête re Bedingham and her long-term plans, and about Kyle, their relationship had slowly changed until it had reached a point where they could be safely described as being on friendly terms with each other.

She shifted the baby girl she was holding from one arm to the other. It had entered the orphanage only two days previously, and its hair had been infested with lice. She had gotten rid of the insects by powdering them with DDT, and had spent hours picking out the eggs by hand. Even now she was unsure as to whether the baby was lice-free or not.

"I have friends to see. Abbra Ellis for one. She and her husband adopted Sanh a couple of months ago and Abbra wants me to visit, to see for myself how quickly the three of them have become a family, and how happy they are."

"And two?" Mike prompted. "You said friends, plural."

Her eyes slipped away from his. "I also want to see Chuck Wilson. He was my husband's best buddy and was seriously injured trying to rescue Kyle. When I last saw him he was crippled ... confined to a wheelchair. Since then he's been undergoing intensive physiotherapy at Walter Reed Army Hospital. I'd like to see him again. To see how he is doing. And to ask him a few questions."

Chuck's letters had been maddeningly un-enlightening. He had written to her late in 1969, saying that he was moving to Washington so that he could be treated long-term at Walter Reed. He was still there, still receiving treatment, but he had never specifically said whether he had recovered the use of his legs or not.

In her own letters to him she had also evaded certain important issues. She hadn't told him about her meeting with Trinh. She hadn't asked if he knew about Kylie. And she hadn't asked the question she most wanted an answer to. Had Kyle's affair with Trinh been serious, or had it been a casual fling?

She didn't want a handwritten reply to her last question. She wanted a face-to-face situation in which he would not be able to avoid telling her the truth. And so, after months of prevaricating, she was going to see him.

"How long will you be away?"

It was a Thursday, and he had just returned from his clinic at Grall. His office had a door screen made of thick inch-square wire meshing, in order to deter any grenades that might be thrown at it, and he was leaning against it, his arms folded across his broad chest. He was wearing one of his crazily colored Sea Island Shirts and a pair of faded shorts, and with his dark hair and eyes and hard tan, he looked more like a Greek navvy than a highly skilled and deeply dedicated doctor.

"Two weeks, that's all. Maybe three." She could hear tanks rumbling down the nearby street. It was such a familiar sound that neither of them took any notice of it. "Why?" she asked mischievously, "Are you going to miss me?"

A slight grin crooked the corner of his mouth. "Stranger things have happened," he said, easing himself away from the door. "I'm going up to Qui Nhon while you're away. The situation there is god-awful. A camp with six thousand refugees and no facilities at all beyond a fly-infested shack used as a clinic. You'd better rest up as much as you can while you're in the States. When you come back, we're likely to have a lot of new inmates, all of them in a bad medical condition."

The children she was escorting were going to homes in the New York area and so, after a one-day stopover, she flew directly from there to Washington. She would visit Abbra later. After she had seen Chuck.

Once again she visited him without giving him any forewarning. The house he had rented was similar in style to his family home in Atlantic City, only instead of being built of clapboard, the Washington house was built of red brick. She rang the doorbell and her sense of *déjà vu* increased. There was no reply, but she was certain that he was home.

At the side of the house was a doorway leading through into the rear garden. She unlatched it, walking along the pathway hoared with frost, reflecting that February had not been a very sensible time of year in which to make a visit.

After the heat of Saigon, the bitter cold of Washington was almost unbearable. She pulled the collar of her hastily acquired wool coat higher around her ears and turned the corner of the house.

He sat in his wheelchair, looking out over the lawn, just as he had been the first time she had seen him. Only the flowers that were in bloom were different. Instead of a vivid blaze of black-eyed susans and chrysanthemums and calendulas and marigolds, there were snowdrops and crocuses and early-flowering Lenten roses.

She stood very still, the cold knifing through her. He was still in his chair. He was still crippled. Nothing had changed. She cleared her throat and stepped forward, and the wheelchair spun to face her.

"Goddammit!" he exploded, "Can't you pick up a telephone and warn people you intend to visit? Do you always have to appear like a genie from a lamp?"

Not only had the scenario not changed, his physical appearance hadn't changed either. He was still as heart-stoppingly handsome as she remembered. Long-lashed gray eyes; well-cut thick hair growing a trifle long; faint hollows beneath his cheekbones; a mouth finely chiseled, slightly arrogant, wholly exciting.

She stepped forward with a grin, knowing that his wrath was only pretence and that he was as pleased to see her again as she was to see him.

"If I had warned you, you might very well have run out on me."

His mouth twitched into an answering grin. "No one but you would suggest to a man in a wheelchair that he might run away!"

The empathy that had sprung up so instantly between them when they had first met was there again, easy and effortless.

They began to laugh, and she said, "What the hell are you doing out here? It's freezing! Take me inside, for God's sake, and thaw me out!"

The inside of the house was decorated in early American, the rather stern decor warmed by an open fireplace and crackling log fire. "Is the decor your choice," she asked, sitting down in a deep, red leather couch, "or did you inherit it?"

He had steered his chair toward a cocktail cabinet and was busy pouring two stiff martinis. "My choice," he said briefly.

"So Washington is permanent?" she asked, avoiding his eyes as he turned toward her with her drink.

"Yes."

He was giving nothing away. The house was obviously superbly cared for, and she wanted to ask who looked after it for him. Who looked after him. How much longer he expected to be undergoing treatment at Walter Reed. When he would be able to expect to see some results from it.

She said instead, with no preamble, "I've met Trinh, the Vietnamese girl Kyle was having an affair with."

He had positioned his chair so that it was opposite the couch on which she was sitting. He tilted his head a little to one side, nursing his martini, saying, "And you want to know if I knew about it, and if I did, why the hell I didn't tell you."

"I know that you knew about it," she said, and there was an edge to her voice that hadn't been there a moment before. "She told me that you had written to her, telling her that you saw Kyle alive on the ground after he crashed. But you're right about your second question. Yes, I do want to know why the hell you didn't tell me about it."

He looked away from her, staring into the fire. Slowly he drank his martini and then he put his glass down and turned toward her again. "To be honest, I'm not sure what my motives were. It may have been out of a sense of loyalty to Kyle, though I doubt it. After all, any dues I might have owed Kyle are more than fully paid. It may have been because of the way I felt about you. I didn't want to cause you any further hurt. And it may have been because I thought it was unimportant. Hell, she was only a Vietnamese. It was no mammoth, earth-shattering affair."

All the time he had been speaking she had been watching him very closely. Now she said quietly. "I think you're lying to me, Chuck. I think it *was* an earth-shattering affair. For him as well as for her."

Her coat lay over the arm of the couch. She was wearing a lavender-gray cashmere dress that clung provocatively in all the right places and accentuated the smoke-crystal color of her eyes.

Her hair was swept into a French knot, making her look very elegant, very sophisticated. He wanted her so much that his cock hurt.

He said tautly, "Come to bed with me and then I'll tell you all about it."

Shock flared through her eyes, and then something else, something that she couldn't hide, however hard she tried. "Okay," she said, her breath so tight in her throat that she could hardly speak, "I will."

It wasn't why she had visited him. Not consciously. She had come because she wanted to ask him about Trinh and Kyle, because she wanted to know if the treatment he had been undergoing at Walter Reed had been effective. Or so she had thought. She knew now that she had been wrong. She had visited him because he was like Kyle, and she couldn't get him out her mind. She had wanted to know if he was sexually capable. Well, she now had her answer. He wouldn't be asking her to go to bed with him if he weren't.

He said thickly, "Come on. Into the bedroom. I no longer favor rugs in front of fires."

She didn't argue. She didn't care where they did it. It had been five years since she had last made love, and she was so sexually hungry, and so horny, that when she rose from the couch she could barely stand.

He propelled his wheelchair swiftly out of the room, and across a hallway into another ground floor room. A bedroom. She followed, so possessed by physical need that she almost fell against the bed. It was higher than most beds, specially adapted so that he could transfer himself from bed to wheelchair with maximum ease.

She unzipped her dress with trembling fingers, stepping out of it, leaving it where it had fallen on the floor. He was already lying on the crisply made-up bed and his shirt was off. She didn't know how he had managed to move so quickly. She had thought she would have had to help him. Although he was as leanly built as Kyle, his shoulder and arm muscles had become powerfully developed by his having to rely on them so much. Semi-naked, he didn't look like a cripple. He looked wonderful.

She peeled off her stockings in desperate haste. She had kept her self-imposed vow of celibacy for five years, but she was totally incapable of keeping it for a moment longer. It had been a romantic, ridiculous vow that could not possibly have any effect on what was happening to Kyle in Hoa Lo. When she told him about it, she knew he would shout with laughter. She wondered if she would tell him about Chuck and didn't know.

She scrambled onto the bed beside him, hurtling into his arms. For a second she wondered if, because of his partial paralysis, she would have to be the one to take the initiative, to perhaps straddle him in order that he could enter her. He rid her of the notion within seconds.

"God, if you only knew how many years I've longed for this!" he breathed harshly, rolling her forcefully beneath him. "I've wanted you for years, lady! For years before I even met you!"

His lips were hard and hungry on her mouth, his fingertips moving down over her neck, her shoulders, her breasts. He was still wearing his jeans, and she unzipped his fly and reached inside, taking hold of him. There was nothing crippled or semiparalyzed about his erection, and she whimpered in longing.

"Quickly!" she said urgently, pressing herself up against him, not wanting him to be tender, not wanting him to take his time. "Quickly!"

He didn't disappoint her. She ground her hips beneath his, moaning with pleasure. It had been so long since she had been made love to. Far, far too long.

"Oh, God, that feels good," she panted, glorying in his size and hardness, not wanting it to come to an end, wanting it to last forever.

He raised himself up on his arms, grinning down at her, reveling in the knowledge that at that precise moment in time, she was completely at his mercy. And then his grin died away and his eyes darkened. He, too, was no longer in control. A look almost of agony crossed his face as he thrust deeper and faster.

Her hands tightened in his hair, dragging his head down to hers. His tongue drove past hers and the blood roared in her ears. She was coming and the relief was so colossal that she thought her heart was going to burst. It went on and on and she thrashed beneath him, her words and exhortations so basic and explicit that they tipped him over the edge. His own climax came, terrible in its intensity, and he arched his back, lifting his head, crying out like a wild animal.

For a long time afterward she simply lay limply beneath him, drenched in sweat, utterly satisfied, wonderfully replete.

At last she said, "Were you always capable of making love? Even before you began treatment at Walter Reed?"

He nodded, rolling his weight away from her, lying companionably at her side.

She raised herself up on one elbow and her hair tumbled free of its chignon, sliding silkily and glossily down over her shoulders and breasts. "You mean you were perfectly capable of making love when we first met?"

"Mmm mmm," he said corroboratively.

She thought of all the wasted years, the regular trips she could have made from Saigon to Washington.

"Then why the hell", she demanded indignantly, "*didn't* you?"

He began to laugh, pulling her down toward him so that her face was buried against his neck and his arms were tight around her waist. "Has anyone ever told you that you're a very fast, forward lady?"

"Not for a long time," she said wryly, thinking of the chasteness of her Saigon life-style. She ran her fingertips over his chest and said, "Have there been many ladies in the last few years, since you were injured?"

Her hand slid lower and she began to caress his limp cock.

"A few." He watched her speculatively. "There are some women who are disabled freaks. They really get off making it with cripples."

She pushed herself up again on one arm, looking down at him. "And you think that I fall into that category?"

He was stiffening again in her hand. He grinned. "No," he said. "I think you're far too way out to merely get turned on by a wheelchair!"

She giggled and lowered her head, kissing his chest and then his belly. "Tell me about the ladies you've had while I've been in Saigon," she whispered, her lips brushing his skin.

He folded his hands behind his head. "There's only been one who mattered. Things were fine until she became pregnant. Then she couldn't get an abortion quick enough." His voice had become bitter, and she paused in her ministrations, raising her head, her eyes fixed on his face. "I told her that as I was crippled in an air crash, it was hardly a condition that could be passed on hereditarily, but she obviously chose not to believe me. Or maybe she did believe me, but figured that though frolicking in bed with a cripple was okay, having one as the father of her child was definitely not as attractive a proposition." His eyes met hers, and a shadow of a smile quirked the corner of his mouth. "She's history," he said briefly. "Don't stop what you're doing."

She didn't. Desire was already stirring in her again, and this time he satisfied it as she did his, with mouth and tongue and hands.

When at last he said huskily, "I think it's time

we regained some energy with another martini," she didn't disagree.

"Make mine *very* dry," she said, stretching out in satiated languor against the tumbled pillows.

He grinned and swung his legs to the floor. His shoulder and arm muscles were still sheened in sweat, and she eyed them appreciatively. "Shaken, not stirred," he said, and rose to his feet and walked a trifle unsteadily from the room.

For a second she didn't register what had happened, and then she realized and shock hit her so hard in her chest that she gasped for breath.

"Chuck! *Chuck*!" She was out of the bed, running after him. "You didn't *tell* me! You *knew* I didn't know! When did it happen? How long ago? Why were you sitting in your wheelchair, you crazy bastard?" They were in the living room, and she was in his arms again, laughing and crying at the same time. "How could you let me go on thinking you were crippled when you can *walk*, goddammit!"

"I guess I figured you might be one of those ladies who are turned on only by disablement," he said with a grin. "And anyhow, I like surprising people."

"You've certainly done *that*," she said as he released his hold of her in order to make the martinis. "When did it happen and *why* were you in the wheelchair when I arrived?"

"To answer your first question, it's happened over a long period of time, very slowly, and to answer your second question, I was in it because

I still sometimes need it, and I was reminding myself of how much I hate it and brooding about how long it would be before I could throw it on the scrap heap." He splashed vermouth into generous measures of gin.

"And when will you be able to throw it on the scrap heap?" she asked, taking the glass he was proffering, enjoying being naked, enjoying the sight of his nakedness.

"Soon," he said noncommittally. While he had been talking he had crossed to a writing desk. "Do you want to know about Kyle and Trinh now?" he asked.

She nodded, her mood instantly changing. When she had left Saigon she had believed that this was the real purpose of her trip. Now it no longer seemed important.

He opened a drawer in the desk and took out a creased envelope. "Kyle was in the middle of writing this to you when we were called out on our last mission. A lot of his personal possessions were put in with mine, either accidentally or intentionally, I'm not sure. I sent everything else I had of his on to his folks in Boston. This I kept."

She took it from him.

Dearest Serry, Kyle had written. *This really is going to be a hell of a letter to write, but it has to be done, and I know that you will understand. I've fallen in love with a Vietnamese girl. Her name is Trinh, and she is very beautiful...* Serena's vision was suddenly so blurred that the next few lines were indecipherable. *I shall always be glad that you flew to Alabama before I left for 'Nam*, he had written in large scrawls very reminiscent of her own. *What we've had between us is something I wouldn't have missed for the world, and something I will never forget. But I have to be able to marry Trinh. I have to be able to protect her. If you knew what life was like out here, Serry, you would understand.*

She lifted her eyes from the notepaper and stared unseeingly out of the living room window. When he had written those words he couldn't have remotely imagined that when she read them, she would know exactly what it was like in Saigon.

She waited to feel betrayal, bitterness, hurt, grief. Nothing happened. She only felt sad. Sad for Kyle, in Hoa Lo; sad for Trinh; sad for Kylie.

When she finished reading it, she said quietly, "I'm glad you didn't show me it when we first met. If you had, I don't suppose I would ever have gone to Saigon. I would never have found a purpose in life, never have discovered what it is that I can do, and do well."

"And that is?" he asked.

She looked across at him and smiled. "Let's go back to bed," she said, "and I'll tell you."

"And so Bedingham is going to get a whole new lease on life," she said contentedly when they had made love again. "It's near enough to London for you to continue to receive the kind of treatment you've been receiving at Walter Reed, and it's deep enough in the countryside to be an absolute paradise for the children."

She didn't notice how very still he had become.

"What children?" he asked, and this time it was he who lay propped up on one arm, looking down at her.

"As many Vietnamese orphans as the authorities will allow me to adopt. Money isn't a problem, or at least, it's not an acute problem. I'm hoping to be able to leave Saigon with at least ten children, maybe more."

He sat upright, swinging his legs from the bed. For a long moment he remained with his back toward her, and then he twisted around, saying in an oddly offhand voice, "And you expect me to shack up with a houseful of Viets?"

She stared at him for a moment, nonplussed. "It won't be a crush," she said, uncertain as to whether he was teasing her or not. "Bedingham could house fifty children quite easily."

It was his turn to stare at her. His eyes were dark, almost expressionless, as if he were carefully beating down whatever emotion he was feeling. "You really don't understand, do you?" he said, and this time the tone of his voice left her in no doubt at all that the conversation had turned suddenly and deeply serious.

She pushed herself up against the pillows. "No. No I don't," she said in genuine bewilderment. "Tell me."

He reached across to the bedside table for his cigarettes and lighter, so obviously delaying the moment before he spoke that she no longer felt bewildered, only crazily, irrationally, afraid.

He lit a cigarette, inhaling deeply, still not speaking. It was very, very quiet. A clock could be heard ticking, but that was all. She was seized with the passionate desire to silence the clock. To halt time. A few seconds before they had been joyously happy. She wanted to go back to that moment. She didn't want him to speak. She didn't want her terrible premonition of dread to be realized.

He blew a thin plume of smoke upward and said in the tone of voice in which he might have asked her if she wanted her drink freshened, or milk in her coffee, "I never want to see another Viet as long as I live."

She closed her eyes for a moment, knowing that it was a reaction she should have anticipated, should have been prepared for. When she opened them again he was looking at her steadily, waiting for her response. There was a gleam of perspiration on his shoulders and slight scratch marks where her nails had dug deep into his flesh. The faint, polleny odor of semen still clung to their bodies and the rumpled sheets.

She said carefully, knowing that their whole future was at stake, "You feel like that only because of what happened to you in 'Nam. But there's no need to feel like that. The children didn't cause the war and the atrocities. They are not responsible. They have suffered terribly because of it, just as you have. When you see them, when you meet them, you will feel different."

His eyes held hers for a long moment. From somewhere unseen the clock continued to tick. "No," he said at last, turning away from her, reaching out for his jeans. "No. It isn't so simple. It goes too deep."

She pushed the sheets aside, kneeling toward him, saying urgently, "You don't feel hatred or revulsion toward Trinh. Why should you feel any different about the children? Why should..."

"It's no good." There wasn't the slightest trace of doubt in his voice. It was flat. Unequivocal. All emotion carefully excluded. He began to pull on his jeans. "Trinh is one of a kind. When I met her I had no feelings about the Vietnamese one way or another. And afterward, after Kyle was shot down, after I was injured" ... he shrugged dismissively ... "she was Kyle's girl. That was how I thought of her. It's how I still think of her. I don't think of her as being a Viet. I think of her simply as being Kyle's girl."

She said eagerly, "And when you meet the children you will see them as being just children, children who need love and stability and a home..."

"Then give them love and stability and a home," he said with a slight, careless shrug of his shoulders, "but don't expect me to play the role of papa-san. I don't want to live with any reminders of 'Nam. Not now. Not ever."

She swung her feet shakily to the floor and stood up, facing him across the disarrayed bed. "We could make it work," she said, her voice trembling slightly, "I know we could."

335

He shook his head, and with terrible finality she knew that she had been living in a dream world. There was going to be no future for her with him at Bedingham, just as there was going to be no future for her with Kyle.

"No," he said again. "You have a choice. The children or me."

"There is no choice," she said, and though her eyes were full of pain, her voice was as free of doubt as his had been. "It's the children. It will always be the children."

His face tightened. An expression she couldn't decipher flashed into his eyes, to be instantly suppressed. "Then it's over," he said, and walked from the room.

He didn't speak to her again. There was nothing more for him to say. She had paused at the doorway, her wool coat tightly belted, the collar already raised against the chill she would meet when she stepped outside. "I'm sorry," she had said simply. "It could have been so good between us."

His thumbs were hooked into the pockets of his jeans. He had given a slight, almost imperceptible shrug of his shoulders, his eyes telling her that it still could be if only she would give up the children.

She turned away from him, unable to make the sacrifice he was demanding, and without saying good-bye, closed the door behind her.

In the sanctuary of her motel room she retrieved

a couple of Earl Grey teabags from the bottom of her handbag and made herself a cup of tea. Then she called Gabrielle.

"Where are you telephoning from, *chérie?*" The line was bad and Serena did not hear the urgent anxiety in Gabrielle's familiarly husky voice.

"Washington. I visited Chuck," she said succinctly.

"Oh!" There was a slight pause at the other end of the line, as if Gabrielle was having difficulty in marshaling her thoughts.

Serena glanced down at her wristwatch, trying to estimate what the time was in Paris. Her brain wouldn't function and she couldn't do it, but she knew that it must be the middle of the night, which would account for Gabrielle sounding so unlike her usual exuberant self.

"I still don't know exactly what kind of treatment he's been receiving at Walter Reed," she continued, "but it has been successful. He can walk."

Gabrielle knew all about Chuck. Even though it was two years since they had lived together in Saigon, Gabrielle was still her friend and confidante. It was a role that Lance had once fulfilled, but though they exchanged occasional letters, she hadn't seen Lance for a long time. And it had been even longer since he had been the most important person in her life.

She said now, knowing that she had no need to expressly tell Gabrielle that she had broken her vow of celibacy and had made love with Chuck, knowing that Gabrielle would realize that without having to be told, "Everything was better than I could ever have hoped ... until I told him about my plans for Bedingham." She paused for a moment, aware that her voice was about to crack. When she had regained her self-control, she continued, "He said there was no way he could live with such a permanent reminder of Vietnam. He was absolutely adamant. I could have him or the children. I couldn't have both. So it's over. End of story."

"Oh, *chérie*, I am so sorry..."

"So am I," Serena said wryly. "However, onward and upward. I'm flying to Los Angeles in the morning to see Abbra and Scott and Sanh..."

"No, *chérie*," Gabrielle interrupted her, her voice cracked and raw. "I have just received a telegram from Abbra. She will not want to see you. Not just now. She will not want to see anyone."

Serena's heart began to thud erratically, "Is it Sanh? Is he ill? Has there been an accident? For God's sake, Gabrielle, what's happened?"

"No, it is not Sanh. It is Lewis."

"Lewis? I don't understand. Lewis is dead..."

"No, he is not, *chérie*," Gabrielle said, a catch in her voice. "He is alive and he is being released by the North Vietnamese. He is on his way home right at this very moment."

Like Abbra, and like Gabrielle, Serena's first reaction was one of dizzying relief that a man believed to be dead was alive. And then, in the same split second, came stupefying horror as she realized the nightmare of the situation.

"Jesus," she whispered, sitting down slowly on the edge of the bed, "what on earth is going to happen? What in the world is Abbra going to do?"

She didn't stay in Washington. She left next morning for Saigon, aboard a Pan Am Boeing.

"Nice to have you back," Mike said to her laconically when she walked into the orphanage two days later. "But why so soon?" His eyebrow quirked quizzically. "I thought you were going to stay awhile and visit friends?"

"I was," she said briefly. Later, as they sat in the Caravelle Hotel's rooftop bar, she told him about Abbra and Lewis. And about Abbra and Scott and Sanh.

He had whistled softly through his teeth, his eyes dark with compassion. For a moment she had been tempted to tell him about Chuck. She remembered the utter finality in Chuck's voice when he had said that he would never live with Vietnamese children, would never be cast in the role of a papa-san, and the temptation faded. She couldn't tell Mike about Chuck. They were a breed of men so different from one another that each would find the other totally incomprehensible.

In April President Nixon announced that 100,000 American troops would leave South Vietnam by the end of the year. Serena no longer felt that such news was an indication that end of the war was in sight. There were more refugees streaming into Saigon than ever. South Vietnamese troops, assisted by U.S. artillery, air and helicopter support, had invaded Laos in an effort to cut the Ho Chi Minh Trail once and for all. The result was official figures of 1,146 South Vietnamese troops killed in action, and 4,245 wounded. U.S. air-crew losses were lighter, with 176 dead and 1,042 wounded. The war was continuing and Serena could see no likelihood of it coming to an early end.

She spent the rest of 1971 and the first half of 1972 hitchhiking lifts on military planes and jeeps in an almost incessant round of visiting provincial orphanages with Mike. The conditions were appalling. Too many children. Too few people to care for them. Not enough food. No medical facilities. Sometimes they were able to make their trips on the Lambrettas that they both used for quick and easy movement in Saigon, but tiny babies and sick children could not be transported in that way, and endless hours were spent cajoling lifts from sympathetic army personnel.

In March 120,000 North Vietnamese troops swept across the partition line and into South Vietnam.

"This is it," Mike said to her prophetically. "This, at last, is the beginning of the end."

The invasion did not penetrate very far, but the North Vietnamese were not repulsed. Despite savage battles with South Vietnamese and U.S.

troops, they remained on South Vietnamese soil. Cities fell and were retaken and fell again, and hundreds of thousands of refugees streamed pathetically southward, toward Saigon.

In April President Nixon announced that American troop strength in South Vietnam would fall to 49,000 by July 1.

"He's obviously made up his mind that he's going to come to an agreement with Hanoi," Mike said, swabbing the wound of a child who had been injured in a grenade attack on a café. "Let's just hope he gets the hell on with it!"

It took another nine months. On January 27, 1973, the Paris peace accords were signed and the Vietnam War officially ended. President Thieu was to remain in power in South Vietnam. All American prisoners of war were to be released and returned home.

"And as far as I can see, that's all that has been achieved," Mike said bitterly. "Years of bloodshed and suffering and for what? For an agreement that could have been reached at any time. And it's the end only for America. It isn't the end for Vietnam. It won't be the end for Vietnam until she is reunited into one country again."

Serena was acting as Mike's nurse while he took a clinic in a makeshift shack in a refugee camp. Flies were clinging to her sweat-soaked hair and the child that she was holding, and that Mike was examining, was whimpering. She soothed the pain-racked child as best she could, trying to come to terms with the enormity of what had taken place in Paris.

Kyle was going to be released. He would soon be flying home. She would have to be there when he did so. Even if their marriage was over and it was Trinh he was really returning to, she would have to be there when he stepped off the plane.

Mike finished treating the child, and she carried it outside, handing it back to its anxious mother. An army helicopter was due to pick her and Mike up in ten minutes. Despite the horrific number of women and children still needing attention, they had done all they could for that day.

She stepped back inside the shack. Mike was repacking his medical bag and as she entered he paused, looking across at her, saying in a voice that was oddly abrupt, "I suppose this is the end for you as well?"

"You mean because of the POWs being returned?"

He nodded. Although it was January, it was very hot in the shack. Heat beat through the tin roof in waves. A column of red ants were narrowly skirting their feet. She thought of London and of Boston. Of Bedingham.

"No," she said slowly, "it isn't the end for me. I shall not leave Saigon, at least not for good, until I absolutely have to."

Very faintly they could hear the *whump-whump-whump* of rotor blades as the helicopter approached.

He put his bag down, saying bluntly, "I don't understand. Your husband is being released after

342

six years of God only knows what kind of hell. And you say you won't be leaving Saigon. It doesn't make any sense."

"It does when you know the facts."

"And they are?"

The helicopter was coming in to land and she had to raise her voice. "He isn't in love with me anymore. He wrote asking for a divorce shortly before he was shot down."

"And you *still* came here?"

At the incredulity in his voice she grinned. "I didn't know when I came. I didn't see the letter until a long time afterward."

"And are you still in love with him?"

She shook her head. "No. I probably never was. Not in the way that you mean. We were just kids and fellow free spirits. We never had a marriage in the real sense of the word. Just a crazy elopement followed by an impossibly grand wedding. Within hours he was winging his way thousands of miles away from me and we didn't meet again until a few days before he was due to leave the States for Vietnam."

Outside the shack, the down-draft of the helicopter's rotor blades was whipping the treetops into a frenzy.

"Then *why*?" he demanded, his eyes and voice light with relief.

"Why did I come here?" She shrugged dismissively. "A guilty conscience, I suppose. For reasons too complicated to go into at the moment, I felt responsible for Kyle's decision to join the army, and consequently I felt responsible for what happened to him out here."

"That's crazy," he said, ignoring the shouts from outside demanding that they board the waiting Huey.

She began to laugh, suddenly ridiculously happy. Within days Kyle would be free again. And after she had welcomed him home she would return to Saigon and Mike. And that was what she wanted, what, without realizing it, she had wanted for a long, long time.

"I know it's crazy, but that's how I felt then. I don't feel like that now. I know now that you can't shoulder the responsibility for other people's actions so easily."

"I didn't mean that your guilt was crazy," he yelled across to her as the Huey's copilot raced across the mud-baked earth toward them. "I meant it was crazy that your husband could possibly have fallen out of love with you!"

Her eyes danced with mischief. Her next few words were going to stupefy him. "Not really," she shouted back. "He fell in love with a Vietnamese girl. Kylie's mother."

The running copilot was within yards of the shack's open door. "Will you two numbnuts get a *move on*?" he yelled at them. "We're wasting *time* here!"

Mike ignored him. He looked like a man who had been poleaxed. "Kylie is your husband's child?"

"*We're going!*" the copilot was yelling. "*With or without you, we're going!*" He spun on his heel, sprinting back toward the Huey, ducking low as he approached it in order to avoid the spinning rotor blades.

Serena nodded, so obviously untroubled by the fact Mike found his stupefaction dissolving into dizzying relief. She hadn't been sitting out the years waiting for her husband to return to her. She wasn't going to leave Saigon now that the war was over.

"*Come on,*" he shouted, grabbing hold of her hand. "*That guy meant it when he said he would leave without us.*" And with her hand tightly holding his, he began to run with her toward the Huey.

In Saigon, Serena reminded the military of her existence and her status as a POW wife. She was told that on February 12 the first group of prisoners were being released. Kyle's name was not among the names they had been given.

"But the list isn't comprehensive, Mrs. Anderson," her casualty assistance officer said reassuringly. "Not all the POWs are being released at once. It's going to be some weeks before all the men are returned home."

By the end of the month there was still no news, though it was reported that another large batch of prisoners was going to be released in the first or second week of March.

"I'm going to do the rest of my waiting in the States," she said decisively to Mike. "He could be released at any time and without any warning. The casualty officer says that all the men are being flown via Clark Air Base in the Philippines to Travis Air Force Base in California. I want to be there when he lands."

She was in her room at the Continental, packing her suitcase, when the telephone rang and reception informed her that an army officer was on his way up to her room to see her.

Gleefully she replaced the receiver on its rest. If he was coming with the news that Kyle was among the men being released in the next week or two, then she would be in the States in plenty of time to greet him. She had a seat booked on a flight leaving Tan Son Nhut in ten hours' time. She slipped a photograph of Kylie into her valise, unable to imagine how Kyle must be feeling. He had been a prisoner for nearly six years. One of the men who had been among the first batch of prisoners to be released had been a prisoner for seven years.

There was a short knock at her door, and she ran across the room to open it. "There's no need to tell me I need to pack my bags," she said with a wide smile to the thick-set army officer facing her. "I'm already in the middle of doing so."

He gave her no answering smile. Instead, he said stiffly, "May I come in, Mrs. Anderson? I'm afraid I have bad news for you."

She stepped back into the room, her heart beginning to beat fast and light, her throat tightening. He took off his cap, holding it in the crook of his arm, saying unhappily, "Perhaps you would like to sit down, Mrs. Anderson."

"Oh, God," she whispered softly, "Kyle is

dead. That is what you have come to tell me, isn't it? He's dead."

The officer nodded. "I'm afraid so, Mrs. Anderson. It happened in late 1966. He died under torture in Hoa Lo." He hesitated, and then added with deep sincerity, "I'm sorry, Mrs. Anderson. Intensely sorry."

Nineteen sixty-six. It was so long ago that she could barely comprehend it. She doubted if Kylie had even been born by then. She said with difficulty, "And his body? Is that being returned to the States for burial?"

The officer nodded. "I have all the details." She looked so pale that he was terrified she was going to faint. "Before I give them to you, could I get you a drink? A whiskey, perhaps? Or a brandy?"

When he had gone she had telephoned Mike at the orphanage with the news. "Kyle's father has asked that Kyle be buried near their home, in a local cemetery in Boston. I'm going to fly there on tomorrow's flight as arranged. I don't know exactly when the funeral is going to take place and so I don't know when I'll be back. Trinh doesn't have a telephone, and there's no way I can get in touch with her before I leave. Will you tell her for me?"

"Yes," he said gently, wishing that she didn't have to fly to the States alone, wishing that he could be with her. "And, Serena..." It was a hell of a time to choose to tell her, but he couldn't help it. He had to tell her. He had been crazy never to have told her before. "I love you."

There was a long pause at the other end of the line, and then she said, so softly that he had to strain to catch the words. "I know, Mike. I love you too." And with tears for Kyle streaming down her face, she had replaced the telephone receiver on its rest.

It was snowing when she arrived in Boston. She knew that Kyle's parents would want nothing to do with her, and she had no intention of forcing her presence on them. She spoke to Kyle's father on the telephone, telling him that she would be attending the funeral service, but would not be coming to the house first to leave for the church and the cemetery with other family mourners. Neither would she be returning to it after the service. Royd Anderson had barely been able to bring himself to speak to her. "It's your fault," he had said harshly, his bitterness as raw as it had been on her wedding day. "It's all your fault. Goddamn you!"

She arrived at the church in a taxicab, her wool coat tightly belted against the harsh wind and still-falling snow. The church was full of mourners, and as she entered she was aware of heads swinging in her direction; of a sea of whispers; of countless hostile stares. She ignored them all, walking with self-composed dignity down to the front of the small church. Kyle's mother and father were seated in the left-hand front pew, their eyes fixed on the flag-draped coffin that lay before the altar. Neither of them looked toward her as she took her place in the right-hand pew.

The army chaplain conducting the service gave her a slight nod of his head, acknowledging her presence and her status as Kyle's widow, and then asked everyone to join with him in singing "Rock of Ages".

Serena was aware of nothing but the coffin. She knew that immediately after his death in Hoa Lo, Kyle's body had been buried in a weedy plot across the Red River from Hanoi. Now, beneath the American flag, it lay encased in bronze. There were still flecks of snow on her hair, and her face was stinging with cold. It was impossible to think that it was Kyle lying only a few feet away from her. Even after all this time, it was impossible to think of Kyle as being dead.

As the last notes of the hymn died away, the chaplain began to read the twenty-third Psalm. "Yea, though I walk through the valley of the shadow of death, I will fear no evil..."

She remembered seeing a young marine in Saigon sporting a flak jacket emblazoned with the words "Yea, though I walk through the valley of the shadow of death, I will fear no evil, for I am the meanest son of a bitch in the valley."

"...Surely goodness and mercy shall follow me all the days of my life: and I will dwell in the house of the Lord forever," finished the chaplain.

There was another hymn, and then the chaplain spoke of Kyle, of how he had been a fine, upstanding young man, a son of whom, since infancy, his parents had been nothing but proud; of how patriotism and love of his country had led him to his terrible death.

It wasn't the Kyle that Serena recognized nor, she was sure, was it one that Kyle himself would have recognized.

Pallbearers in army uniform moved forward and lifted the casket, carrying it out of the church and onto a waiting hearse. Serena and Kyle's parents followed immediately in its wake, the rest of the mourners walking behind them.

The trip from the church to the cemetery was short. Serena wished that she could reach out and take hold of Mrs. Anderson's hand, but the elder woman was gripping her black handbag tightly, her body rigid, her red-rimmed eyes steadfastly refusing to acknowledge Serena's presence.

The snow was still falling as they stood at either side of the open grave. Serena wondered where Chuck was, why he wasn't there, and was ashamed at the relief she felt at his absence.

She joined mechanically in the Lord's prayer, snow and tears mixing saltily on her cheeks. Then a bugler played taps and a uniformed officer took the flag off the coffin, folding it reverently and handing it to her. She was aware of Mrs. Anderson's grief-stricken, harrowed face, of Royd Anderson glowering at her with unconcealed loathing.

Her tears continued to fall. She and Kyle had been such heedless children when they had met and eloped. For her, life had taken shape and substance and she could barely recognize the headstrong, thoughtless girl she had once been. If Kyle had lived, no doubt, he, too, would have changed and matured. But he had not lived. He had died an early, agonizing, unspeakable death in Hoa Lo, and her heart hurt with grief.

Slowly she raised the flag to her lips and kissed it. It was not a patriotic gesture, as it would have been if she had been an American. It was, quite simply, her last good-bye to Kyle. Then she walked to where Kyle's mother was standing, and with heart-touching dignity, she handed the flag to her.

"Thank you," his mother said quietly.

Royd didn't say anything. His face was as harsh and taut as if it had been carved from stone.

Serena turned away from them, the snow lying heavy on her hair, and on the shoulders and up-turned collar of her coat. It was over. All that remained was for her to return to Saigon, where Trinh would be waiting for her.

CHAPTER FIFTEEN

When the peace treaty was signed in Paris, Gabrielle immediately made contact with the North Vietnamese official who had been feeding her tiny scraps of information ever since the summer of 1970.

"Will my husband be released with the Americans?" she demanded, her red-gold curls incandescent against the sleek, night-black mink coat that had been her Christmas present to herself.

The official's face and tone of voice was as expressionless as always. "Your husband is not an American, neither is he being held as a prisoner of war—"

"But he is a prisoner!" Gabrielle interrupted fiercely.

"He is not an American and he is not officially a prisoner of war," the North Vietnamese repeated implacably. "Because of your family connection to Comrade Duong Quynh Dinh, and because of the respect in which his memory is held, you have been given information that would normally have been forbidden. You know that your husband is alive. You know that he is being held with captured puppet troops. That is all that I can tell you, Comrade. When there is new information, then you will be informed of it."

There was no new information. On February 12 several hundred haggard but jubilant Americans were flown out of Hanoi to the Phillipines and then on to Travis Air Base, California. In March the last American troops left South Vietnam and more prisoners were released from Hanoi. A handful of civilians, some of them journalists, who had also been held prisoner by the North Vietnamese were also released. Gavin was not among them.

Gabrielle returned to the North Vietnamese Embassy. Her contact there was as immovable as ever. "I have told you everything that I can, Comrade," he said, repeating verbatim what he had told her previously. "Your husband is alive. He is being held with captured puppet troops—"

"The Peace Accords state that all South Vietnamese POWs are to be released, as well as American POWs," Gabrielle interrupted tautly. "Have they all been released yet? If not, when they are released and returned to the South, will Gavin be among them?"

"I cannot tell you, Comrade," the official said heavily. "When I have information I will give it to you. Until then, *chào ba*"

Bitterly disappointed, Gabrielle walked away from the embassy and headed back toward Montmartre, wondering for the thousandth time where it was exactly that Gavin was being held. Over the years she had managed to glean that the prison he was being held in was small, and that it was in a rural area. That was all. No matter how hard she had pleaded, no further information had been forthcoming. The Americans who had been released had come not only from Hoa Lo, but from three other prisons in Hanoi, from six prisons within a fifty-mile radius of Hanoi, and from a prison camp situated in the northern mountains, five miles from the Chinese border.

As she reached the place Blanche and the Moulin Rouge, she wondered if the northern camp could possibly be the camp where Gavin was being held. It was known to the Americans merely by the nickname Dogpatch, and though it was quite possible that it was both small and rural, for Gavin to be imprisoned there he would have had to be marched or transported by the North Vietnamese nearly the entire length of North Vietnam. She couldn't imagine them going to so much trouble when there were other prison camps nearer the point where he had been arrested. And her contact at the North Vietnamese Embassy had been adamant that Gavin was not sharing his imprisonment with captured Americans, but with captured South Vietnamese troops.

She crossed the place Blanche and began walking briskly up the steeply winding rue Lepic. She and her parents and *le petit* Gavin no longer lived in the tiny, cramped apartment in the rue Rodier. In the past few years her reputation as a nightclub singer par excellence had soared, and to her delight her bank balance had soared accordingly.

If she had wanted to, she could easily have bought an apartment in a smart residential area, but when it had come to buying an apartment of her own, which she could share with her family, she had chosen to remain in Montmartre. Although she never felt a true Montmartroise in the way that when she was in Saigon she felt a true Saigonese, when she was in Paris, Montmartre was her home and she could not conceive of living anywhere else.

She loved the village atmosphere of the hill,

the magnificent plane trees in the place Émile Goudeau, the green benches on the sidewalks, the small shops and the constant beehive of activity. She loved the translucent light that never seemed to be any different no matter what the season. The spacious apartment that she had bought was situated in a small street not far from the place du Tertre, on the crown of the hill. From the bedroom and living room windows was a magnificent view down to the boulevards of Pigalle and across the city. It was an apartment that her mother loved and that they were all exceedingly comfortable in.

She wondered how she was going to break the news to her parents and to *le petit* Gavin that for the next few weeks, possibly even the next few months, they would be living there without her. If Gavin was not being released with the Americans, then he would eventually be returned to Saigon. And she was going to be there when he was.

She walked quickly upward toward Sacré-Coeur, her high-heeled black leather boots beating a tattoo on the cobbles, her mink coat fastened high and snug around her throat. She had stayed away from Saigon far too long. First her affair with Radford had ensured that she remain in Paris, and then her escalating career had ensured that she stay. Now her career was established, and Radford was no longer her lover.

The shops and frenzied activity of the lower reaches of the street were behind her, and the atmosphere was now that of a French provincial village. She turned the corner toward the church, a small frown creasing her brows.

The decision to end the affair had been hers, but she had not found it an easy decision to make nor an easy decision to live with. Between herself and Radford there was a rapport and a physical attraction so strong that she had needed all her considerable emotional strength in order to be able to tell him that it was over. And she had found the strength because she had known that she was on the verge of betraying Gavin irrevocably. She was on the verge of falling in love.

Radford had refused outright to allow her to escape from him totally, and they still saw each other frequently, but no longer as lovers. Now she had to decide whether or not she would say a final good-bye to him before leaving for Saigon.

In the place du Tertre winter tourists strolled from souvenir stall to souvenir stall and admired the work of the only artist hardy enough to have set up an easel. One of the stalls had a display of T-shirts, and with a surge of amusement she saw that one of them was decorated with Radford's picture. Over the last two years her success as a singer had been dazzling, but Radford's success, coupled with that of the band, far exceeded hers.

He had become a cult figure, a sex symbol on par with Mick Jagger and Jimi Hendrix, and he reveled in the female adulation and hysteria that he excited. His Aston-Martin DB Mark 3 had given way to the latest Ferrari. He had bought a magnificent 18th-century house at Neuilly, as well as a London flat and a New York apartment. He had everything in the world that he wanted except one thing. And that was she.

Common sense told her that she shouldn't get in touch with him before leaving Paris, but common sense had never played a large part in their relationship. She would see him again, to say a final good-bye. After all, when she returned to Paris, she would be returning with Gavin. It would be too late for good-byes then. Radford would be in her past, where he would belong.

"...and so it is time for me to go back to Saigon," she said at the family dining table that evening.

Her father, who took less and less interest in anything other than his daily game of boules, grunted noncommittally.

Her mother's eyes flew wide open with alarm. She knew, as they all did, that just because American involvement in Vietnam was at an end, it did not mean that a long-term peaceful solution to the conflict there had been found. The present truce between North and South would not last long. Fighting would break out again as the North sought to unite Vietnam into one country. And when the fighting did break out again, it would be as fierce and as terrible as anything that had gone on before.

"Oh, *chérie*, is that necessary?" Vanh began, and was interrupted by her grandson.

"I think that is a *magnificent* idea, *Maman!*" he

357

said, forgetting all about the food on his plate as he looked across at her, his face radiant. "When can we leave? Can we leave before the next school term starts? Can we leave *this week?*"

Gabrielle suppressed a grin as her eyes met his. He was six and a half years old now and gave her so much happiness that she found it impossible to look at him without smiling. Now she said, hoping that she looked and sounded like a responsible, stern mama, "School is very important, Gavin. And Saigon is not a very pleasant place in late March. It will be humid and smelly and—"

"And I want to go with you, *Maman*," he finished simply, his eyes, so like his father's, burning hers. "A little part of me is Vietnamese, is it not? And I, too, want to be there when Papa returns."

Looking at his mop of tousled hair and his snub nose with its scattering of freckles, and the gap in the middle of his front teeth that made his grin so winning and mischievous, Gabrielle felt her throat constrict. "Of course you do, *mon petit*," she said thickly, ignoring her mother's silent plea that she say nothing further. "And of course you will come with me."

Vanh gave a small, inarticulate cry of protest and Gabrielle said gently, "It is right that he should see the city in which his mother was born, and it is also right that he is there when his papa is released from captivity."

"But the conditions!" Vanh said in distress. "Nhu says that the city is choked with refugees!

That on the streets air-conditioner and refrigerator packing boxes house up to ten children at a time! Those are not the kind of sights that a little six-year-old boy should be seeing!"

"No, they are not," Gabrielle said gravely. "Neither are they the kind of conditions that six-year-old boys should be enduring. It will not harm *le petit* Gavin to be made aware of the dreadful suffering that war entails. Such awareness is far more preferable to his playing at war, thinking it glamorous and manly."

The subject had come to a close. She was leaving for Saigon just as soon as she could arrange the flight details. And *le petit* Gavin was going to accompany her.

Breaking the news to Radford proved to be a far more highly charged affair. She had known it would be, and though he had asked her to drive to his mansion in Neuilly where, after just returning from a major tour of the States, he was supervising the building of a recording studio in the basement, she had declined.

"Meet me at La Coupole," she had suggested, and he had agreed. At La Coupole in Montparnasse it was unlikely that their sophisticated fellow diners would pester them for autographed menus.

When she entered, her mink slung carelessly around her shoulders, he was already seated, sipping a bourbon.

"*Bonjour, chéri,*" she said, kissing him lightly

359

on the temple, *"Ça va?"*

"That depends on why you want to see me," he said darkly as a waiter removed the mink from her shoulders and discreetly withdrew.

She grinned, slipping into the high-back seat across the table from him. Another waiter had approached, and she ordered a kir, saying, when they were alone again, "It is because I have something to tell you, *chéri.*"

Despite the subdued lighting, he had been wearing a pair of shades. He removed them with the panther-wary grace that characterized his every action, saying, "Unless it's to say that you've come to your senses and that you're going to move your bags and possessions down to Neuilly, I don't want to *know*, baby."

She didn't reply to him immediately. Whenever they met, it always took her a few minutes before she was able to come to terms with his dangerous, overpowering masculinity. She steadied her breathing, looking around the art-nouveau-decorated dining room, recognizing several of the other diners.

"You've been so *unavailable* lately," Radford was saying, not taking his disturbing gaze from her face, "that I've been wondering if you'd make it today. You keep so *busy* all the time."

Her mouth twitched in the beginnings of a grin. She had herself in control again, and Radford being provokingly sarcastic was a Radford that she could easily handle.

"You're not the only cat in this town with a career to think of," she said affectionately, turning to face him. "I've been singing at a new club in Saint-Germain-des-Prés. The mix there is very exciting. Jazz, African, Brazilian."

"And you?"

"And me."

"As you say, baby, quite a mix!" His voice was lazily mocking, and he flashed her a sudden smile, his teeth very white against the dark, arrogant, almost Arabic planes of his face. "But that isn't why you invited me into town, to tell me about the new club."

"No." She paused again. She was dressed starkly in a beautiful cut black wool dress. Her legs were sheathed in sheer black stockings and her shoes were black suede, ridiculously high, ridiculously insubstantial. She wore a large baroque, carved ivory bangle on one wrist, and apart from her wedding ring, no other jewelry. In the subdued lighting her short springing curls were fox-gold, her wide-spaced, tip-titled eyes as green as a cat's. She looked sexy, and stunning, and he wanted her now as he had always wanted her.

He said with sudden harshness, "Let's *cut* all this crap, Gabrielle. We're wasting time and both of us know it. The dude you've been seeing at the embassy is stringing you a line. Gavin isn't alive. Not after all this time. Even if he *was* alive, the two of you would have *nothing* going for each other. It's been too long."

She shook her head, pushing her untouched drink away from her. "You are wrong, *chéri*. He is alive. I know it in my heart and in my blood and in my bones. That is why I wanted to see you today. To tell you good-bye. I am going to Saigon with *le petit* Gavin, and I am not returning until Gavin returns with me."

His hands tightened into fists. Ever since he had heard that the American POWs were to be released, he had known what it was that she would do. He was losing her. And to a man she hadn't seen for nearly seven years. It was crazy. So dumb he could hardly believe it.

He leaned forward across the table, saying fiercely, "I'm *wild* about you, lady! Doesn't that *mean* anything? Christ! At this particular moment in time I could probably have most any woman I want. And I want *you*? I want you so much that if marriage is what you want, then we'll get married. What else can I *say* to you? What more can I do to show you that I love you just as much as your husband ever loved you, that I love you *more*, that I love you more than *anyone* else is ever going to love you!"

She knew that heads were turning in their direction, that if they weren't careful an enterprising photographer would soon be on the scene. She didn't care. She reached out, taking hold of his tightly balled fist, prising the fingers apart, interlocking her fingers with his, saying in her touching, broken-edged voice, "I am sorry, *chéri*. Truly sorry. I, too, have loved you. I have loved you too much, and that is why I have to say good-bye. Gavin came into my life first, and when I told him that I had given him my heart, I was speaking the truth. He still has my heart, just

362

as I believe that I still have his."

As she had been speaking, his face had drained of expression, hardening into an impenetrable mask. He was not going to allow them to part as friends. She had been foolish to have ever imagined that he would do so. Gently she disentangled her fingers from his and rose to her feet.

He watched her, tight-lipped and cobra-eyed. A waiter slipped her coat around her shoulders and she was grateful for its warmth. The restaurant had become suddenly cold. Almost Arctic.

"Good-bye," she said, and before he could say a word in reply, before temptation became too much for her to overcome, she turned away from him, walking quickly between white-naperied tables and out onto the boulevard du Montparnasse.

At the end of March, as another batch of haggard American POWs flew jubilantly out of Hanoi, Gabrielle and *le petit* Gavin flew into Saigon.

Serena was at Tan Son Nhut to greet them.

"Gavin! My goodness! I wouldn't have recognized you!" she exclaimed laughingly as Gavin hurtled toward her. She hugged him tight, delighted that after so many years he still remembered her.

"And me?" Gabrielle asked teasingly. "Would you not have recognized me, *chérie*?"

She was wearing a shocking-pink crossover sweater with a deep décolletage, skin-tight; three-quarter-length black pedal pushers, and high-heeled, backless patent sandals.

"Gabrielle, I would recognize you *anywhere*," Serena said truthfully, hugging her even tighter than she had hugged *le petit* Gavin.

"That is good, *chérie*, I would hate to think that I had become inconspicuous!"

They grinned at each other. Even though she had driven straight from her work at the orphanage and was wearing a T-shirt and jeans, Serena still managed to look elegant. A Christian Dior scarf covered her hair and was tied at the nape of her neck. Her short, unlacquered nails were exquisitely manicured and buffed a pearly pink.

"How is Saigon?" Gabrielle asked as they walked across to Serena's jeep. "Do the Saigonese think that the truce will last?"

"No," Serena replied briefly. "Everyone knows that it won't. The South is going to last only as long as President Thieu's ammunition lasts."

"I thought that under the terms of the peace treaty, it had been agreed that America would replace weapons and ammunition as they were expended?"

Serena slammed the jeep into gear and began to speed toward the airport's exit. "That's what the small print says, but only a fool would put any trust in it. More to the point is Article Four of the peace agreement: 'The United States will not continue its military involvement or intervene in any way in the internal affairs of South Vietnam.' America wanted out. She's now gotten out. No matter what happens in the future you can bet your life that she's going to stay out!"

They drove straight to Nhu's, where *le petit* Gavin received such a fierce embrace that he was almost smothered. From Nhu's, leaving a happily chattering Gavin behind them, Serena and Gabrielle drove to the center of the city.

"Where do you want to go first?" Serena asked as she crossed Nguyen Hue, the street of the flower sellers. "To the Continental, to check in? To the orphanage? Or to Givral for coffee and croissants?"

Givral was a little air-conditioned restaurant on the corner of Le Loi and Tu Do, across from the Continental. It baked its own croissants and baguettes, and when they had first begun living in Saigon, Gabrielle and Serena had quickly realized that breakfast at Givral was far preferable to breakfast at the Continental.

"Givral," Gabrielle said unhesitatingly. "I want to go back to all our old haunts and reorient myself as quickly as possible." She began to chuckle. "When we first arrived in Saigon, *I* was the one who showed *you* around. Now it's you who are the old hand and I am the one feeling a little like a tourist!"

"You won't feel like a tourist for long," Serena said soothingly. "Not only are all the old haunts still here, so are a lot of old faces. The debonair Paul Dulles has been recalled to Paris, but one of Gavin's old colleagues, Lestor McDermott, is still in town, and you have missed Jimmy Giddings only by inches. He left for the Philippines at the beginning of February in order to cover the POWs' arrival and from there he was sent on to the Middle East."

They were both silent for a moment, thinking of the American POWs who had returned home alive, and those who hadn't. Thinking of Kyle.

At last Gabrielle said quietly, "Was the funeral very difficult for you, *chérie*?"

Serena thought of the imposing bronze casket; the waiting frosthard ground; Kyle's mother's face, harrowed and tear-streaked; the hatred emanating from Royd Anderson and directed solely toward herself; the terrible feeling that the funeral had nothing to do with Kyle.

"Yes," she said truthfully. "It was difficult. But it was more difficult to break the news to Trinh. Mike had already told her for me that Kyle was dead, but she had refused to believe it. She was certain that I would return from the States with the news that it was all a mistake and that he was alive. Even now I'm not sure if she truly believes that he is dead."

"What will she do?"

They had parked the car and were walking across the square toward the restaurant. "I don't know. She has a family home in the city which she shares with her sister. Perhaps life will continue for her just as it has for the past six and half years. She will continue with her job, Kylie will be looked after at the orphanage, and one day, God willing, she'll meet a man she loves and who loves her, and they will get married."

Gabrielle hesitated slightly and then said a little cautiously, "And Kylie? How do you feel about Kylie, Serena?"

They sat down and ordered coffee, and it wasn't until they had done so that Serena said, "I try not to think too much about Kylie. I've tried never to have too much to do with her."

"Because you haven't wanted to become too fond of her?"

"Because I *am* too fond of her," Serena said with stark truthfulness. "It was the moment I set eyes on her. She's far more American than she is Vietnamese. She has Kyle's hair and eyes and mouth and charm. And she has other qualities of his as well. Where Kyle was recklessly devil-may-care, Kylie is impishly mischievous. She is a loving, intelligent, exuberant little girl who is very, very hard to resist."

"And will it cause any problems for you if she and *le petit* Gavin should become friends?"

Serena's somberness vanished, and she flashed Gabrielle her wide, dazzling smile. "Idiot," she said affectionately. "Of course it won't. Is that what you intend doing? Spending time with *le petit* Gavin at the orphanage?"

"I shall have to occupy myself somehow," Gabrielle said with an answering grin. "Do you think I shall make a good nurse? Or will the fearsome Dr. Daniels be as rudely and as unjustly disapproving of me as he has always been of you?"

Serena's smile widened. "You have just reminded me that there are some pieces of news that I haven't quite brought you up-to-date on. Come on, finish your coffee and we'll drive to

the orphanage. The fearsome Dr. Daniels is waiting to greet you."

Gabrielle was ecstatic when she realized what
the situation was between Serena and Mike.

"I knew it," she said complacently to them
both as they stood holding hands in one of the
orphanage's sun-filled and child-filled court-
yards. "The minute that Serena told me you were
not *remotely* handsome, and that you were pig-
headed and obstructive and the most *annoying*
man that she had ever met, I knew that she must
be falling in love with you!"

Mike shouted with laughter and the playing
children turned to look at him, intrigued.

"Is *that* what she said about me?" he asked,
still chuckling and not looking a bit put out by
the revelation.

Serena didn't give Gabrielle time to answer.
"There are times, Mike Daniels, when I *still* feel
like that," she said teasingly, "and you haven't
given Gabrielle an answer as to whether or not
she can come to Cây Thông as a volunteer
nurse."

Mike looked across at Gabrielle. At her riotous
mop of flame-gold curls, her sizzling pink
sweater and skin-tight pants and teeteringly
high, backless sandals. His grin deepened.

"I've told Serena that she was the most un-
likely-looking volunteer nurse that I had ever
seen or was ever likely to see. I take it all back.
You, Gabrielle, are *definitely* the most unlikely-
looking volunteer nurse that *anyone* is ever

368

likely to see, and the answer is yes, of course you can come to Cây Thông. I truthfully don't see how Cây Thông can possibly do without you!"

CHAPTER SIXTEEN

After the official notification of Lewis's imminent release, Abbra was inundated with advice from both the military and from her father-in-law. The overriding question was when, and by whom, Lewis should be told of her now-invalid marriage to Scott. As far as Abbra was concerned, there was no decision to make. The task of breaking the news to Lewis had to be hers. The main problem was going to be the publicity. Both she and Scott were well-known media figures. The gossip columnists were going to go crazy with delight when news of their predicament became public.

"We'll do everything possible to ensure that your husband sees no newspaper or magazine and is not approached by any reporter until after he has been apprised of the situation by yourself," her casualty assistance officer said to her.

No one from the military plucked up the nerve to ask the question that was uppermost in everyone's mind. Was she going to leave Scott and return to Lewis? Or was she going to remain with the man she had, for the past two and a half

369

years, believed to be her husband?

If they had asked her, Abbra would have been unable to give them an answer. She looked like a wraith, her face bloodless, deep circles carved beneath her eyes. She was in a private hell where no one, not even Scott, could reach her. She felt as if she were suspended in time, impaled by her memories of the past, paralyzed by the dilemma of the present, and totally unable to conceive of what the future might hold.

Her father-in-law had insisted that *he* should be the family member to first meet Lewis and to inform him of the marriage that he had always disapproved of.

"And I've been proved right!" he stormed over the telephone to Scott. "It was a disgraceful thing to do, marrying a woman who had been, who *is*, married to your brother. I knew no good would come of it! I told you both so at the time!"

Only the intervention of Abbra's casualty assistance officer ensured that, because of the abnormal circumstances, Abbra would be the only family member to immediately greet Lewis on his return to the United States.

It was Scott who came to a decision about their far greater dilemma.

"I'll go away with Sanh for a few weeks. Take him down to Mexico and the Sea of Cortez. I'll arrange with the military that similar arrangements, elsewhere, are made for you and Lewis. You can't possibly stay anywhere where the two of you are known and where you will be hounded by newsmen. He's bound to have to be hospitalized for a little while, and his debriefing could take anything from a few days to a couple of weeks, but all that can take place in a protected environment. Once it's over, I suggest you go off to a small hotel at Yosemite or Yellowstone. Somewhere miles from anywhere. Then you can tell him." His voice, so strong until then, cracked and broke as his arms tightened around her. "And then you are going to have to make your own decision, sweetheart ... Lewis or me."

She began to weep, and she wept and wept, her heart breaking, hugging her breast as though holding herself together against an inner disintegration. How could she make such a decision? It was impossible. She loved Scott. She loved Scott more than anything else in the world. Yet once she had loved Lewis. She was married to Lewis. He had survived five years of terrible captivity believing that she was waiting for him. How could she let him down? It would destroy him. And living without Scott would destroy her.

"Let's take it step by step," he said gently, stroking her hair, his own eyes full of tears that she could not see. "Lewis needs to be told of our marriage. And you need to discover just how you feel about Lewis after all this time. Only then can any decisions be made."

She had nodded and clung to him and he had said huskily, "But whatever decision you make, remember that I love you, Abbra. Only you, forever."

If it hadn't been for her casualty assistance

officer saying to her, "Lewis has seniority and so will be the first to disembark," Abbra would not have known who he was.

He was in full uniform, but he looked old, and stooped, and gaunt. She suppressed a cry of anguish, and then Lewis was being officially greeted. Flags were flying. Her legs began to shake as she became aware of the large number of photographers and newsmen covering the event.

"Don't worry," her casualty officer said, sensing her distress. "There are going to be no questions allowed."

There were none, but Lewis was given the opportunity to say a few words.

"The three of us who have been released, stand here today, proud to be American. We are American fighting men and in all the years of our captivity we have never, for one moment, forgotten it. We have kept our trust in God, our trust in our fellow countrymen, and our trust in America. Now we want to join with the rest of America in striving to obtain the release of the hundreds of men we left behind us."

There were cheers and a storm of applause and then Lewis and his two companions were swiftly led away into waiting limousines.

His speech was exactly the kind of speech that she would, once, have expected Lewis to make. But she had forgotten so much about him. She had forgotten how utterly he was a professional soldier. She wondered what he would say when he learned of her participation in the antiwar marches, and her nails dug deep into her palms. What he would say when he learned of her antiwar activities was the very least of her problems.

From the air base Lewis and his companions were brought immediately to the hospital. In a very short time they would be reunited. She would see him in the flesh. She tried to remember Hawaii and their passionate last night together before he had flown back to Vietnam. She couldn't do it. She could see only Scott's anguished face as he had said good-bye to her. The hands she remembered, hot and ardent on her body, were Scott's hands.

She began to tremble, praying for the strength to survive the next few hours. The military chaplain who had counseled her had told her that God never gave a person a burden heavier than they could bear. She clung to that thought, knowing that she had to be strong. She had to be strong for all their sakes. For Scott, for Sanh, and for Lewis ... Lewis who had suffered so much, and who she had once loved so very, very, desperately.

The casualty officer had left the room to talk to the many officials milling around in the corridor. Now she returned, saying quietly, "The men have arrived and are in the building."

"Will Lewis be coming here? To this room?" Abbra's voice was stilted, the words forced through dry lips.

"No, he's waiting for you in a room across the corridor," the officer said. "Are you ready?"

Abbra shook her head. She was going to greet Lewis exactly as she would have if she had never married Scott. After his five years of captivity, and of believing that she was faithfully waiting for him, it was the very least she could do. When his medical examinations and debriefing were completed, she was going to take him away to a small hotel in Yosemite National Park. Then, and only then, would she tell him about her and Scott.

The only thing she had asked the military to do was tell Lewis that everyone believed he was dead. Once he knew she thought he was lost to her forever, he would be a little prepared for the news that had to be broken to him.

"Then if you are ready..." the casualty assistance officer said, opening the door wide.

"Yes," she said, the blood drumming in her ears, "Yes, I'm ready."

It was only a short walk out of the room and across a corridor and into another, yet she knew that it was the longest walk she would ever take. The tension was so great that Abbra was convinced she wouldn't survive it. She felt as if she were going to faint, or have a heart attack, or die.

There were military officials in the room, and doctors. She was scarcely aware of them. She had eyes only for Lewis. His skin had taken on an unhealthy grayish-yellow cast. His hair was no longer a thick and curly brown, but grizzled, clipped short to his skull. He looked older in the flesh than he had on the television screen. Only his eyes were the same. Dark, and brown, and full of both overwhelming relief and with love ... love for her.

"Lewis," she said softly, taking a step toward him. "Oh, Lewis. What did they do to you? How did you bear it?"

He covered the distance between them in two limping strides, and her arms opened wide.

"Abbra!" He crushed her to him, burying his face in her neck, his tears of thankfulness and joy hot upon her flesh. "Oh, dear Christ! *Abbra!*"

At that moment, all that mattered was that he was alive, and that he was home. She clung to him, returning his kisses. He had endured, and he had survived, and she thanked God for it, from the bottom of her heart.

Lewis's commanding officer cleared his throat. "I know this must seem very heartless, Mrs. Ellis, but your husband still has to be medically examined. Your real reunion will have to take place a little later in the day. Perhaps even tomorrow."

Abbra tried hard not to let her relief show in her eyes. "That's all right," she said, holding Lewis's hand tightly in hers. "We've waited so long to be together again, a few more hours won't make any difference." She raised the back of Lewis's hand to her mouth and kissed it. "Good-bye for a little while, Lewis. I've been given a room in the hospital. I won't be far away."

Her voice was as smokily-soft as he had remembered it, her hair still as silk-dark, still as glossy; but there was something different about her, something he couldn't at first fathom. Then it came to him. There was an air of sophistication about her that the Abbra he remembered had not possessed. He reminded himself that she was six years older than when he had last seen her, that she was no longer a teenager, but a young woman. And however much she had changed, it wasn't an iota compared to the changes that had taken place in him.

For the next few days, though they met together for a little time each day, they were never alone. First of all came intensive medical checks. He was suffering from exhaustion, malnutrition, a glucose problem, an enlarged prostate gland. And epilepsy. He was told not to worry about the epilepsy. It could be fully controlled with drugs. He was certainly not made to feel any shame about it, rather, the reverse. As far as the medics were concerned, it indicated the very great suffering that he had undergone under torture.

After the medicals came the debriefing sessions. What other Americans had been imprisoned in the U Minh with him? Had he overheard his captors mention any American names? Any other southern camps where men who were MIA might be being held? Exactly how had he been captured? And interrogated? And treated? What information, if any, had he given to the enemy? What were the names of the men who had been his captors? Where exactly in the U Minh had his prison been located?

The questions went on and on until he was dizzy with them. He was seen by army psychiatrists, who reluctantly pronounced him stable enough to take a five-day vacation with his wife. The medical staff knew what the purpose of the vacation was and were deeply unhappy that this was the way Abbra wanted to break her news to Lewis.

"It would be far better for such emotionally traumatic news to be broken to your husband while he is under medical supervision," Lewis's psychiatrist had said to her somberly.

She had thanked him for his advice and had ignored it. She didn't want to break the news to Lewis in such clinical surroundings. She needed to be alone with him. Really alone with him. Their short periods of time together at the hospital, with medical and military staff always close by, were a nightmare that didn't grow any easier.

He was a total stranger to her, and that moment when they had first met and she had looked into his eyes and thought she had seen the old Lewis had not come again. He was a middle-aged man, deeply fatigued and physically changed almost beyond recognition. Although the physical changes had shocked her, she had been prepared for them. After such long captivity, in such horrendous conditions, it would have been ridiculous to have imagined that he would return looking no different from when they had last said good-bye.

Other changes she found harder to adjust to.

His brooding somberness, his almost manic patriotism, and his stubborn belief that the war he had fought had been a just war.

"We should be fighting in the North, where everyone is the enemy, where you don't have to worry whether or not you are shooting friendly civilians," he had said to her passionately one day. "Our biggest, most basic mistake is in the way we focus on chasing Viet Cong guerrillas. Those guerrillas have been deployed to grind down our forces until big North Vietnamese units are ready to launch major operations as at Khe Sanh and at Tet in '68."

She had wanted to cover her ears with her hands and scream. She didn't want to hear him talking about the war and about strategy and about how great a president Nixon was. She couldn't understand how he could even bear to dwell on such subjects. Surely his debriefing was bad enough. The hideous reliving of years of days and nights of sheer hell.

Apart from the physical changes, Lewis hadn't changed, she suddenly realized. She had changed. Even if she hadn't fallen in love with Scott, even if she had known that Lewis was alive, now that they were reunited she would still be having problems relating to him. She didn't know whether the realization was a shred of comfort or an added agony. She knew only that the necessity of staying within the confines of the hospital was giving her claustrophobia, that she needed Scott, needed him with all her heart and mind and body.

The small sports car she had bought when her third novel had been published had been brought to the hospital for her and left in the underground staff parking garage. Lewis knew of her plans that they take a short vacation together in Yosemite and had said enthusiastically that he thought it was the best idea anyone had come up with since he had set foot again on American soil.

He was waiting for her now, dressed in civilian clothes, his bag packed. They were going to have to leave the building by a rear service exit to avoid the newsmen who still thronged the main entrance, and she hoped that he wouldn't question their method of leaving, or begin to think there was anything odd about the way he was being kept from contact with the press.

He looked slightly more familiar to Abbra in civilian clothes. He was wearing a maroon-checked open-neck cotton shirt with a matching maroon V-neck sweater on top of the shirt, cream-colored chinos, and a pair of white leather loafers. She had bought the clothes herself and was relieved to see that though the chinos and sweater hung loosely on him, they were not grossly the wrong size.

"You look nice," she said sincerely.

He glanced at himself in the mirror. At his grizzled hair and still grayish-yellow pallor. "I look a wreck," he said truthfully, but there was also a refreshing hint of humor in his voice. "Come on. Let's leave before someone decides they want yet another goddamned urine test or blood sample."

He picked up his bag and she led the way out of the room and along the corridor and down the rear service stairs to the parking area.

He stared at the sports car in bemusement. "Whose is this? Have you borrowed it?"

She shook her head, smiling. "No. It's mine. A present to myself."

A slight frown creased his brow. "On an army pension? Wasn't that a little wasteful?"

"No," she said equably, stowing his bag in the trunk. "Because that isn't how I paid for it."

She was already behind the steering wheel, and he opened the passenger door, seating himself next to her.

"Explain," he said, his face as stern as the psychiatrist's had been when he had said he wanted them both back at the hospital in five days.

She turned the key in the ignition and slipped the car into drive. "You remember my writing? Well, I've been doing a lot of it over the last few years."

"You mean that you were able to buy this car by writing stories for women's magazines?"

For the first time since they had been reunited, she giggled. "No. I write books. I bought the car with the payment I received when my third novel was published."

His frown didn't disappear. In the rearview mirror she saw it deepen. She didn't say anything more. He had never been enthusiastic about her writing, and it would probably take him a little time to adjust to the fact that she was now a full-fledged novelist.

She drove up the ramp, speeding away quickly before any reporters or photographers should spot them. Then he said wryly, "Your driving hasn't improved with time."

"No." She managed a grin, grateful that there was humor in his voice again. They were both trying so hard to be normal with each other and it was so hellishly difficult. For him, as well as for her.

In a silence that was almost companionable they drove east toward the wild grandeur of Yosemite. At dusk, dramatically sculptured rocks and 200-foot-high giant sequoia trees came into view and she said unnecessarily, "We're nearly there."

He merely nodded, his eyes turned away from her, feasting on the wonderful views as if he could never get enough of them.

She knew why he was being so silent. He was almost as nervous as she was. She turned into the parking lot at the side of the hotel, needing Scott so badly that she didn't know how she prevented herself from crying out his name.

What was she going to do? In the name of God, how could she possibly make a choice between them? Lewis needed her in a way that Scott never would. He needed her in order to reaffirm his manhood and to help him adjust to freedom after years of unbelievably brutal captivity. Yet it was Scott who was her friend and lover, Scott whom she truly felt married to.

"You look tired," Lewis said to her as he lifted his bag from the trunk. "This whole thing must have been as big a strain for you as it has been for me."

A light evening breeze lifted her hair, blowing it softly against her face. "They told me you were dead," she said simply, and at the memory of that terrible moment her eyes became over-bright and tears glittered on her eyelashes. "For three years I believed it to be the truth."

He put his bag down and drew her into his arms. "I know, my love. I know," he said comfortingly. "But it's all over now." He tilted her chin upward with his forefinger, smiling down at her with the crooked smile that she remembered so well. "We're together again, Abbra, and we have our whole future before us."

"Lewis..."

"Come on." He picked up his bag and put his free arm around her shoulder. "Let's check in and shower and eat. We can do all the talking we have to do afterward. I want to know everything that you've been doing. What the books you have been writing are about, where you've been living, if you've seen much of my family over the years." He lowered his voice as they entered the hotel lobby. "And I want to do more than talk." In his dark brown eyes she saw again the old Lewis, the Lewis she had fallen so much in love with. "I want to make love to you," he said softly as they walked across to the reception desk. "Oh God, Abbra! How I want to make love to you!"

They ate dinner at a candlelit table in the hotel's small dining room. Abbra was never able to remember what it was that they ate, or if there were many other diners.

Lewis tried to keep the conversation light and innocuous, but nearly every subject that he touched upon was traumatic for her.

"I understand Scott is still with the Rams?" he said as her almost-untouched sirloin steak was removed.

"Yes." She was reduced to monosyllables, terrified of saying anything further for fear of where a conversation might lead.

Dessert came, and then coffee. He stretched a hand across the table toward her. "Let's leave the coffee," he said, and though his voice was carefully casual, there was a plea in his eyes that tore at her heart.

She nodded, rising to her feet, accompanying him from the room.

Where were Scott and Sanh now? How was Scott enduring their separation? How was he surviving not knowing what was taking place between her and Lewis, whether they had begun to sleep together or not? Whether she was going to return to him or not.

Their room was decorated in tones of pale yellow. The bedstead was of polished brass, and there were a half dozen goose-down pillows on it and crisp sheets and thick blankets and a yellow-hued patchwork bedspread.

She had made her decision not to tell him

about Scott until the morning, but with every passing minute it was a decision that was becoming harder and harder to abide by.

As he began to undress he said awkwardly, "I want you to be patient with me, Abbra. It's been so long ... and I feel so damn shy!"

His touchingly honest admission gave her the inner strength she needed. He was her husband, and even though they were now, in so many ways, complete strangers to each other, she still did love him. Not as she loved Scott, but then, Scott was different. Scott was lighthearted and fun-loving and made her laugh. She refused to think about Scott. She couldn't think about him. If she did, she would collapse.

She stepped out of her dress, saying truthfully, "I feel shy as well, Lewis. We're going to have to be patient with each other."

She had seen him semi-naked at the hospital, when he had been undergoing some of his medical tests, but the sight of the scars that he bore still shocked her inexpressibly.

There was a puckered scar high on his left arm where a bullet had been removed. That scar was the least terrible of all that he bore. His back was criss-crossed with the healed lacerations of repeated and prolonged whippings, and there were burn marks on his chest.

"I'm not a very pretty sight," he said, his eyes dark with anxiety as he saw her look at him and look quickly away. "I'm sorry, Abbra. If it offends you I'll..."

She didn't wait to hear what it was that he was

going to suggest. Her head spun toward him, her eyes anguished.

"*Offends* me?" Her voice was choked with tears. "Oh, Lewis! How can you possibly imagine that it *offends* me? If I look away as I did then, it's only because I can't bear to think of what they did to you ... what you suffered."

She crossed the room to him quickly, hugging him close. "I love you," she said thickly, and it was the truth. She *did* love him. She had always loved him. Even after she had fallen so very much in love with Scott, Lewis had still retained a place in her heart. And now for the next few hours, for his sake, she had to forget the terrible dilemma that she was in. She had to think only of Lewis and of his very great need.

He was gentle with her, and she remembered that he always had been. Slowly, with tender deliberation, he removed her bra and her panties.

"It's been so long, my love," he murmured as he drew her close to him. "I can't tell you how often I've dreamed of this moment, longed for it with every fiber of my being."

Her arms closed around him, and the intervening years slid away. As she closed her eyes she could almost imagine herself back in Hawaii.

"I thought I would never see you again," she whispered as his hands traveled caressingly down from her breasts to her thighs. "Oh, Lewis! When they told me you were dead, I thought I was going to die too!"

His lovemaking had always been conventional, and as he rolled her over onto her back and covered her body with his, she was grateful for it. She didn't want to be brought to screaming pitch by his tongue and his fingers. She didn't want the fevered intensity that erupted so easily and so often between her and Scott. She merely wanted to hold him close, to feel his heart beating next to hers, to savor the incredible knowledge that it was Lewis who was gaining physical release and pleasure from her body, Lewis, who she had thought was dead, and who was alive.

Afterward, still in each other's arms, they were quiet for a long time. Abbra felt a deep sense of calm and well-being. No matter what would happen between them in the morning when she told him about Scott, the lovemaking they had just experienced could not be taken away from them. Lewis would know that he was sexually capable.

She ran her hands gently over the ugly weals on his back. She had been terrified that when they went to bed she would feel as if she were committing adultery. It hadn't been like that at all. She didn't feel as if she had been unfaithful to Scott, even though she still felt far more married to him than she did to Lewis. As his weight remained comfortably on top of her and his breathing subsided, she wondered if it was because, despite all his care and tenderness, she had not been brought remotely close to orgasm. It was as if, for her, physical delight and Scott were so inextricably bound together, her subconscious mind would not allow her to respond in the same manner to other hands, no matter how familiar those hands had once been. Or how much loved.

At the thought of Scott a pang of grief stabbed through her. Scott ... She needed him so much. He always knew exactly what she was thinking; he was always so supportive to her, always so loving, always able to make her laugh and see things in perspective.

Lewis moved his head and brushed his lips against her cheek. She stirred, and though he did not read it as such, it was a movement of protest. He merely thought that his weight had become too much for her and he rolled off her and onto his back, sliding his arm beneath her shoulders.

"I love you," he said, his voice heavy with physical satisfaction and with overwhelming tiredness. "And tomorrow will be even better, my love. I promise."

She didn't say anything in return. She couldn't. She simply lay close beside him until he fell asleep and then turned on her side, waiting for the morning.

When he awoke he lay utterly rigid, sweat breaking out on his forehead, his eyes darting from one corner of the ceiling to another as he tried desperately to reorient himself.

"It's all right," she said gently, reassuring him. "You're in America and we're at a hotel at Yosemite, remember?"

Slowly he relaxed. "Yes," he said, his voice

slightly unsteady. "Of course we are. I'm sorry, Abbra, but just for a moment..."

"I know." His doctors had told her about the nightmares, of how, even if he didn't wake in the night screaming, he woke in the morning bathed in perspiration, certain he was still in Vietnam, his changed surroundings were simply a change of prison.

He shuddered and wiped a hand across his eyes and then said with a great effort at normality, "What is it we're going to do today. Visit Yosemite Valley? Or drive up and visit Glacier Point?"

She sat up and swung her legs to the carpeted floor. "I need to talk to you a little while, Lewis," she said, uncomfortably aware of her nakedness in a way she had not been the previous night. She reached for her negligee and slipped her arms into the batwing sleeves. "So much has happened since you were captured. For me as well as for you."

She rose to her feet, tying the ribbons on her negligee into a bow at her throat before turning to face him.

He had pushed himself up against the pillows. He was still naked, and in the early morning sunshine she could see that his chest and shoulders were already beginning to build up the muscle they had lost. In another few months he would be nearly as broad-chested and as toughly built as he had been when she had first met him.

She thought she saw a look of panic dart through his eyes, and then he had himself perfectly in control. "You mean about what happened after you had thought I was dead," he said somberly.

She nodded. She had been wrong in assuming that it had not occurred to him that there might have been other men in the years when she had believed herself to be a widow.

"Yes." Her lips were so dry that she could hardly force the words past them, but she had to continue. "I thought you were dead," she said quietly. "However you feel about what I am going to tell you, you must remember that, Lewis. I never even looked at another man all the months that I believed you to be alive."

His eyes held hers, so dark that it was almost impossible to read any emotion in their gold-flecked depths. "You had an affair?" he said briefly.

She nodded and he abruptly swung his legs from the bed, sitting with his terribly mutilated back toward her, not moving.

After a long moment he said, "When they told me I'd been listed as KIA, I knew ... I realized there was such a possibility." He rose slowly to his feet and faced her, as oblivious of his nakedness as she had been conscious of hers. "It doesn't matter to me, Abbra. I understand. Christ, how could I *not* understand. What is in the past is in the past. It doesn't need to affect us anymore..."

"But it does!" He was moving toward her and she knew that she had to tell him before he touched her, before he held her close in his arms.

"I ... we..." The tears were spilling down her face now, and she couldn't stop them. "We married, Lewis! I thought you were dead and ... oh, God, I can't bear it! I can't bear hurting you like this! If only I hadn't been told that you were dead! If only I hadn't believed that I would never see you again, not ever!"

He had stopped moving. He had begun to pant, to hyperventilate. His lips had gone white, and she thought he was going to faint.

"Lewis!" She rushed toward him, seizing hold of him, knowing that she had been a fool to have believed that she could handle such a nightmare situation by herself. "Lewis, please don't be ill! I've told you like this, myself, because I didn't want a stranger to tell you! Because I still love you! I still care for you!"

He rocked slightly on his heels and then his breathing began to steady as he inhaled deeply through flared nostrils.

"You love me? You married him only because you thought I was dead?"

"Yes! Yes!" Surely it was true. She couldn't possibly have married Scott if she had believed Lewis was still alive. And she *did* love him. She had always loved him.

With slow deliberation he removed her hands from his arms and walked a little way toward the window, looking out over a landscape of mountains and forest. When at last he turned to her, it seemed that the lines on his face furrowing his brow and running from nose to mouth were etched a little deeper. He was looking nearly as haggard as he had the day he had landed at Travis Air Force Base.

He forced a small, comforting smile. "Then that's all that matters. The marriage can't be valid. You're still my wife, not his."

She knew that he meant to be comforting. He believed that he had heard the worst news possible and had survived it. At the thought of what was still to come, tears rained down her face, spilling onto her hands, onto her negligee.

"Lewis, I..."

At her continuing distress his eyes darkened in concern. "What is it? Is the guy threatening you? Insisting that you return to him?"

She shook her head, struggling for the right words and failing to find them.

"Where is he now? Hasn't someone spoken with him and explained the situation? Hell, who is he? Is he someone you met through your writing?"

She shook her head again, knowing that the most terrible moment of her life was upon her. "No," she said, and she was no longer crying. She was far, far beyond tears. "No, it isn't someone you don't know, Lewis." Her eyes held his, filled with unspeakable pain, and his eyes returned her gaze, bewildered and perplexed. With a slight, almost inconsequential motion of her hand, she said simply, "It's Scott. I fell in love with Scott."

His legs buckled, and as she rushed toward him, he thrust her violently away, staggering toward the bed.

"Jesus Christ!" That was all she could hear him say *"Jesus Christ! Jesus Christ! Jesus Christ!"*

He had pushed her with such force that she stumbled and fell, sprawling on the floor. She crawled to her feet, her breath coming in harsh gasps.

"Lewis! Please! Lewis!"

She reached a hand up toward him, and he grasped hold of it, pulling her up on the bed beside him, burying his face in her neck.

"Oh, my sweet Jesus, Abbra!" He was sobbing as she was now sobbing. "Did you think you could stay married to me through Scott? Is that how much you grieved?"

His words were incoherent, and she could barely grasp the sense of them. She knew only that his reaction was not remotely the reaction she had expected, and she was almost senseless with relief. Only slowly, as he continued to talk to her, rocking her against his chest, did she realize what it was he had chosen to believe.

"Poor Scott! Christ, what he must be going through! Is that why he and Dad weren't allowed to visit? Was the virus they were both supposed to have just a lie to keep us apart until you had broken the news to me?"

She nodded, wishing that it hadn't been so easy, wishing he had realized that she had married Scott because she had fallen in love with him, that the possibility that she might still be in love with Scott had also occurred to him.

She put her hands against his chest, pushing

392

herself gently away from him. "When I went through a marriage ceremony with Scott, I went through it because I had fallen in love with him," she said, choosing her words with great care so that he should not misunderstand her.

He rose to his feet and shrugged on a dark blue terry-cloth bathrobe. Then he lit a cigarette and walked with it over to the window, leaning against the window frame, staring out over the golden beauty of the mountains.

"The North Vietnamese had a favorite way of conducting their interrogation sessions," he said, his tone of voice as unemotional as if he were asking her if they should breakfast in their room or downstairs in the hotel restaurant. "They would strap vine rope around my injured arm, just above the elbow, then the bite end would be passed over and around my right arm. When that was done they would throw me to the ground and roll me on my side, and then the vine rope would be pulled higher and tighter, drawing my elbows together behind my back. Within only seconds the pressure would be so great that my shoulders would lift out of their sockets..."

She cried out in anguish, but he did not pause or look toward her.

"My chest would feel as if it were exploding and my ribs would project like drawn bow-strings. Then, if I were lucky, I would pass out. After I had passed out, water would be thrown on me to bring me back to consciousness. They would put their questions to me again, and I would refuse to answer them again, and then straps would be put around my ankles and knees and the loop from the arm straps would be passed around my neck. The loop from the leg straps was then pulled high, drawing my heels up toward my buttocks. And then the two straps were tied together."

She was crying softly, but he still ignored her, saying conversationally, "At this point I would begin to vomit, and to choke on my vomit. I would lose control of my bladder and my bowels. I would no longer be Captain Lewis Ellis, I would be an animal. A thing. And do you know what kept me going through all those numberless sessions of torture? Through all the years of being kept for long periods in a cage measuring barely four feet by six and just high enough for me to sit in?"

He turned toward her, and in his eyes was a desperate unspoken plea. She understood then why he was telling her about what had happened to him, even though he knew that she had already been told by the doctors. It was his way of asking her to stay with him. To choose him and not Scott. It was his way of telling her how very desperately he needed her.

"You did, Abbra," he said, and his voice had lost its indifference and was raw and hoarse. "They ruptured my eardrum, they beat me with bamboo rods, and through it all only one thing kept me sane. Knowing that you were here, in America, waiting for me. I lived because I knew that if I lived, I would have you to return to. You kept me alive, Abbra. No one and nothing else.

Only you."

As their eyes met and held, she felt her heart break. There was no decision for her to make. A decision could be made only if there was a choice of actions, and she saw now that there was no choice. There never had been a choice. Her duty and her loyalty lay with Lewis.

She crossed the space between them and slid her arms around him, knowing that by doing so she was saying good-bye to Scott and to Sanh and their loving, laughter-filled, joy-filled life together.

"You did have me to return to, Lewis," she said thickly, laying her head against his chest so that he should not see the agony that was in her eyes. "You always will have me."

CHAPTER SEVENTEEN

Although Scott had said she would have to make a decision, Lewis or himself, Abbra knew that deep down Scott had been sure there was only one decision she could possibly make. Their life together had a shape and substance to it that her life with Lewis had never possessed. They had believed themselves to be married for two and a half years, and with their adoption of Sanh they had become not merely a couple, but a family.

Fresh pain knifed through her. Sanh would have to remain with Scott. The adoption would probably have to be amended so that only Scott remained as his legal guardian. She was losing not only Scott, but the little boy who had become her son as well.

For the next four days she made a superhuman effort to overcome her anguish and to help Lewis adjust to the strangeness of being both free and a tourist. They rented horses at White Wolf and trekked the back trails of the High Sierra country at an easy pace. They fished for trout, and they drove up to Glacier Point.

When it came time for them to check out of their hotel and head back for the hospital, Lewis was reluctant.

"It's the same questions time and time again. What kind of military information had my captors sought from me? What kind of military information was already in their possession? Christ, it goes on and on!"

"It won't be for much longer," Abbra said, knowing that when his debriefing and his medical checks were complete, the real difficulties would start.

They wouldn't be able to live in California. She wouldn't be able to survive knowing that Scott and Sanh were only a car ride away from her. And once Lewis was released from the hospital, he would no longer be protected from the publicity, publicity that would center, not around his curiosity value as a POW who had been released in a propaganda gesture by the North Vietnamese, but around the mistaken notification of his death and his wife's subsequent marriage to his football superstar younger brother.

"You're crazy! I don't believe you! I *won't* believe you!" Scott shouted through the telephone to her. "Jesus God! I *knew* I shouldn't have let you break the news to him alone!"

"My decision has nothing to do with my having broken the news to him by myself," she said, gripping the telephone receiver so tightly that her knuckles were white. "It is simply that it is the only decision that *can* be made. If you knew what he has suffered, Scott..."

"Christ, I've every sympathy with what he's suffered, but it doesn't mean that you have to return to him! Not when you are no longer in love with him, and you *aren't* in love with him, are you?"

It was a question she had known that he was going to throw at her. "I still love him..." she began steadfastly.

"That doesn't answer my question." His voice was remorseless. "Loving someone and being *in* love with them are two very different things. *I* love Lewis. He's my brother. And that's how I believe you love him now. As a brother. But you're not *in* love with him anymore. You can't be, because you're in love with me."

There wasn't a shred of doubt in his voice, and she knew that there was no reason for any. Everything he had said was true. But she wasn't going to change her mind about staying with

397

Lewis. She couldn't. If she did, she would never be able to live with herself.

"I've made up my mind," she said, and in her soft, smoky voice was the stubbornness that was characteristic of her.

Hearing it, his own voice took on a note of desperation. "You have to change it, Abbra! You can't leave Sanh and me. We're a *family*, for God's sake! You were never a family with Lewis. You had a total of eight days together as man and wife. Christ, Abbra! You barely *know* Lewis!"

She closed her eyes, wondering how it was possible to have cried so much and to still be able to cry more. "I'm sorry, Scott," she said brokenly. "I love you with all my heart. Good-bye, my darling."

As she lowered the telephone receiver she heard him shout, *"I'm coming to get you! I was a fool ever to have let you out of my sight!"*

She covered her eyes with her hands. She would have to inform Lewis's doctors of what had happened. They would make sure Scott wasn't allowed into the building. And when Lewis was released? She lifted her head up, her jawline strong and firm.

Lewis and his superiors had agreed that he should take a year's sabbatical before deciding whether or not to continue his career in the army. They would be able to go away somewhere together. Perhaps to the East Coast, to be nearer his father. Perhaps even farther, to London or to Paris. Wherever they went she would be able to write, that was some comfort at least. It was the one thing that no one would be able to take away from her. Not ever.

Lewis's doctors had been unified in their opinion that a meeting between Lewis and Scott would simply subject Lewis to unnecessary stress.

Despite trying to physically storm down the doors, Scott had been refused all access. Abbra remained inside the building, grateful for the privacy of the single room that she had been allocated while Lewis underwent what was described as a "reorientation" process.

Six years of his life had been lost. The world he had left behind him in 1966 was no longer the same. China was no longer regarded as an arch-enemy, but as a friend. Friendly overtures were being made by the American government to the Soviet Union. Everything was upside down, and he and his fellow prisoners had to be brought up-to-date on all the world events that had taken place during the years of their imprisonment.

There were times when it was almost too much for him. The changes inside America were the hardest for him to come to terms with. Hours and hours of newsreels took him step by step through the development of the antiwar movement. He leapt to his feet, blaspheming viciously and storming out of the room when he was shown scenes of long-haired college students burning their draft cards. The details of Watergate dumb-founded him. In his book Richard Nixon was a hero, the guy to whom he owed his freedom.

And then there were the hippies, and the amazing way homosexuality had become an accepted alternative life-style.

For hour after hour, day after day, he sat through films, read a six-year backlog of magazines and newspapers, sat in on lectures that varied in content from America's new relations with China and the Soviet Union to the change in fashion and morals to details of new military hardware.

It was dizzying and sometimes overwhelming. How could politics, fashion, morals, music, technology, even speech, change so drastically? How come the seventies were so radically different from the sixties? He watched reruns of popular television shows, episode after episode of the Waltons.

"I don't intend to watch television ever again," he said firmly to Abbra when his reorientation was over. "Nor will I ever willingly listen to today's pop music. The sixties were bad enough, but this new stuff is horrendous."

She had laughed and hugged his arm as they went out of the building by the staff exit, glad to be leaving the hospital behind them for good. At Lewis's request they were going to spend the next few days with his father in New York. The hospital authorities, eager to prevent an unpleasant confrontation between Lewis and Scott, had agreed to press announcements over the next few days indicating Lewis was still a patient and his release couldn't be expected before the end of the following week, by which time, if Lewis was agreeable, Abbra intended to be half a world away, in London.

Over the next few days, and weeks, and months, things did not grow easier. They grew more difficult. Despite the slow and steady improvement in his physical health, Lewis continued to have hideous nightmares. On their first night in London he had woken at 3:00 A. M. drenched in sweat, calling out in terror, "*Tam! Tam!*"

The next day he had shut himself broodingly away in the parlor of their hotel suite, refusing to go out with her, refusing even to have breakfast or lunch with her.

His psychiatrist had told her that there would frequently be periods when Lewis would need to be alone, and that she would have to come to terms with that need, no matter how difficult it might be for her.

On that day, their first in London, she had breakfasted alone and spent the morning wandering around the National Gallery and the National Portrait Gallery. She had telephoned him before lunch to see if he wanted to eat with her, and when he had said that he didn't, she had lunched alone at Fortnum & Mason. Afterward she had walked along Piccadilly and into Hatchards, where she had the satisfaction of seeing her latest novel prominently displayed.

Back at their hotel she had knelt beside his chair, saying concernedly, "Tell me what it is that is troubling you, Lewis. Is it your nightmare? Was the name you called out the name of one of your guards?"

He hadn't had to ask her what the name had been. "No," he said, running his hand through his hair, which was growing thick and curly again. "I was dreaming about Tam, the cleaning girl that we had at Van Binh. Do you remember me writing to you and telling you about her?"

She rested her weight back on her heels. It was so long ago, but she did remember him telling her about the village girl who had been badly mistreated by her father, and of how he had removed her from her father's care by engaging her as a general all-purpose maid.

"Was Tam the girl who asked you to teach her English?"

He nodded, the hard line of his mouth softening slightly as he remembered their teacher-pupil relationship.

Abbra looked at him, perplexed. "But when you called out her name it was because you were terrified. You were drenched in sweat. Shaking. Why? I don't understand."

His mouth hardened again as he rose to his feet and paced across to the window. "There's going to be no American victory in Vietnam, Abbra," he said, staring down into the rainwashed London street. "There's going to be a negotiated settlement that will enable America to withdraw her troops. After that, depending on what agreement is reached and how it is supervised, there may be relative stability for a little while, but it won't last. And when the North invades the South, as they will, then everyone who has ever

402

worked for Americans, as Tam did, will be in danger."

"And that was why you had the nightmare?"

"Yes," he said, "that was why."

"The press wouldn't be interested in us if you hadn't written any novels," Lewis said tightly the first time he saw a magazine article about him, Abbra, and Scott. "Christ, have you read this stuff? It's absolute filth!"

She had read so many more articles about them than he had that she was well prepared for whatever was in this one.

"It isn't so bad," she said comfortingly, dropping the magazine into a wastebasket. "It's simply what is known in the trade as a human interest story, and it's the sort of thing we have to expect."

He rounded on her savagely. "I don't have to expect it!" he said explosively. "Just because you and Scott lived your lives in a blaze of publicity doesn't mean that I have to become part of the circus as well!"

The blood had drained from her face. She knew that she dare not stay in the room with him. If she did, she would say things that would destroy everything they were trying to build together.

"I'm going out," she said tersely, and without waiting for him to reply she spun on her heel and walked swiftly from the room.

There were other difficulties as well. Although sexually he desired her as much as ever, he was a conventional lover. His caresses were always

403

the same: tender, deliberate, and unexciting. She yearned for Scott's passionate, imaginative love-making, for the laughter that they had shared in bed, for the sense of total togetherness that had always existed between them.

Sometimes her loneliness seemed so encompassing that she wondered if she would be able to survive it. Even London was no distraction. Before Lewis had left the States, his superiors had given him introductions to several U.S. Embassy officials. To Abbra's surprise he had followed the introductions up almost immediately and had quickly become a part of a social circle that she felt alien in.

Instead of partying with the wives of the friends that Lewis had made, she spent long hours wandering around art galleries and museums, her thoughts not on paintings or ancient artifacts, but on Scott and Sanh. Often, regardless of where she was, tears would stream down her face. One morning she began to cry in the middle of Piccadilly Circus, another day she began to weep while shopping in Harrods. She knew what was happening to her, knew that she heading full steam toward a nervous breakdown, and all her strength and determination were directed at staving it off.

The only person who knew her address in London, apart from her lawyer, was Patti. All through the year her letters came thick and fast, the questions in them remorseless. Why wasn't she writing? She was under contract to her publisher to deliver another book by next May.

Had she forgotten? Had she made contact with her London publisher yet? How was Lewis? Were the two of them happy in London? Were they unhappy? Was that why Abbra wasn't writing? Was it why she wasn't even writing letters? Did she want to meet and talk? If so, she would fly immediately to London.

Even worse than the questions was the information. Scott had brought Sanh to visit her. Sanh was well and happy but Scott had looked taut and strained. He was still demanding her and Lewis's London address, and she was still adamantly refusing to give it to him. It wasn't easy. On a previous visit when she had refused, his frustration had been so great that he had become violent and had smashed a door through with his fist.

Abbra had put the letter down, unable to read any further. There was no way in the world that she could see Scott again and remain with Lewis. But Sanh. Surely she could see Sanh?

"*No*," Serena had written to her firmly.

It wouldn't be fair to him to see him for a few hours or a few days and then to disappear from his life again. The traumatic relationships between you and Lewis and Scott would be beyond his understanding. Scott still writes regularly so I know that he is giving Sanh one hundred percent of his time. With Scott, Sanh is receiving all the emotional stability he needs. For you to remain in contact with Sanh, when Sanh knows that you are not in contact with Scott, would be far too difficult a situation for him to handle.

And so, because she loved him so much, and because she would have died rather than have caused him distress, she lived without her adopted son, as she lived without Scott.

The only person who did not seem to be suffering was Lewis. When they arrived in London she thought they might be there for a few weeks, perhaps even a month. But Lewis had fallen in love with the city.

He bore very few physical reminders of his imprisonment. He had always been toughly and compactly built, and through rigorous exercise his body was as hard and as muscular as it had been previously. As his hair had regrown, the gray in it no longer appeared so jarring. Instead, it merely flecked his hair, seeming to add to his physical attractiveness instead of detracting from it.

That he was still very physically attractive was obvious from the way embassy wives discreetly flirted with him. He was certainly far more popular, socially, than she was.

"Every time those women look at me, it's so obvious what they are thinking, what they are remembering," she had said after a dinner party where she had barely been spoken to by anyone other than her hostess.

Lewis had removed his dinner jacket and begun to take the cuff links out of his evening shirt. "I'm afraid that is the price you have to pay, Abbra," he had said casually, and had continued to undress, oblivious to her stunned look of disbelief.

She had known exactly what he had meant. Near social ostracism was the price she had to pay for having married Scott when she thought herself a widow. At least it was the price she was going to have to pay as long as she remained in *his* world and among his friends.

At the beginning of 1972, as his sabbatical year drew to a close, her feeling that they were growing more and more estranged increased.

"It's time we moved out of the flat and bought a house," he said to her one morning as they shared a prebreakfast cup of coffee. "I've been offered a position as an adviser at the embassy and I have decided to take it."

She put her coffee cup down a trifle unsteadily. "What sort of adviser? Why haven't you spoken to me about it? I thought you were still trying to decide whether or not to continue your career in the military?"

"Well, I've decided," he said, and smoothly changed the subject by asking if she had remembered that they were going to the theater that evening.

There were times, as 1972 dragged itself into 1973, when she wondered wildly if his new position as an adviser was actually a position with the CIA. He never spoke about what he was advising on. He never told her anything about

407

the work that he was doing. She had not made the deadline on her book, and though Abbra was afraid the publisher might cancel the contract, she could not write.

Letters still came to her, via her lawyer, from Scott. They were always the same, demanding, reasoning, pleading with her to leave Lewis and to return to him. He enclosed photographs of him and Sanh, and whenever she withdrew them from the envelope she thought that her heart would break. She loved them both so much. But she couldn't return to them, not after the solemn promise that she had given to Lewis. When the Peace Accords were signed in Paris, she had expected that Lewis's still-frequent nightmares would grow fewer and fewer. Instead, they increased, and they seemed to center more and more on the Vietnamese girl he had befriended.

His psychiatrist had warned her that some POW returnees centered all their bitterness onto one often trivial image. She wondered if that was what Lewis was doing now, of if he was deeply concerned about Tam because there had been far more to his relationship with her than he had ever admitted.

It was an intriguing supposition, but one she couldn't quite imagine. There was a puritanical streak in Lewis where sex was concerned. Despite the approaches that admiring women must have made to him, she was certain he hadn't responded to any of them. And she was equally sure that he had never been unfaithful to her while he had been in Vietnam.

Within weeks it became quite obvious that Lewis was correct and that the truce between North and South was not going to be adhered to. Almost the first people to die were nine members of an international peacekeeping commission whose helicopter was blasted out of the sky by Viet Cong guerrillas.

By the fall, small-scale Communist attacks were taking place throughout the South. In the early months of 1974 the attacks escalated in both frequency and scale. Serena's monthly letter to her from Saigon was full of the difficulties she and Mike were experiencing in arranging for the adoption of the scores of children still in their care. *We have to make the arrangements quickly*, Serena had written. *Everyone in Saigon realizes that there is very little time. That the end cannot be very far away now.*

She was still receiving letters from Scott, via her lawyer, but their tone had changed. *I love you, and I still want you back, but I'm not living like a monk anymore*, he had written in his last letter to her,

It isn't in my nature, as I'm sure you realize! But I hate it, Abbra. I don't want other women. I want you. Surely you know by now what a colossal mistake you have made. Pity isn't any reason to live with anyone. If Lewis knew that pity was your motive in choosing to remain with him, he wouldn't thank you for it. I know that you believe that what you are doing is the right and honorable thing, but you are wrong, sweetheart. It isn't. The right and honorable thing is to return to the people who love you and you love in return. Come home, sweetheart. Please.

At Christmas Patti had written to her, telling her that one of her writers, a girl Abbra had met a couple of times in Los Angeles, was going to London.

Her husband is a diplomat so you're bound to meet on the embassy circuit. I think you last met her at one of my parties. Scott remembers her, anyway. He says you liked her when you did meet, so I hope you are not going to take offence at my suggesting she keep an eye out for you...

Abbra had decided the previous year that she hated Christmas. It reminded her too strongly of children and of Sanh, and made her agonizingly aware of all the things that might have been.

"I know you don't like parties," Lewis said to her as she dressed reluctantly for a cocktail party that was being held at the French ambassador's residence, "but tonight is rather special. There'll be a lot of gossip about the deteriorating situation in Vietnam and I want to be privy to it all."

As always happened at such functions, they became almost immediately separated and swept off into different champagne-sipping groups.

"...And so in my opinion, the Communists are now ready to launch an all-out attack on the

South," the Englishman she was standing next to was saying.

She looked across the room and saw Lewis talking to a fair-haired girl who looked vaguely familiar. A small smile quirked the corner of her mouth. It was the novelist who was also agented by Patti. She wondered what on earth they were finding to say to each other.

"I'm sorry I didn't catch your name when we were introduced," the girl was saying breathlessly. "There's such a crowd in here that you can hardly hear yourself speak." She glanced around, looking for a familiar face and said, "Oh goodness, is that Abbra Ellis over there? We share the same agent. I can't imagine why she hasn't written anything recently. Do you think she's ill? She certainly looks it. The last time I saw her she was with her second husband, or the man she *thought* was her second husband. She simply *glowed* with happiness. I have never in my life seen two people so much in love..."

Lewis was no longer listening to her. He was looking across the room at Abbra.

"...and so Patti said to me, if you get a chance, *do* track her down, because she's become a positive recluse..."

"Excuse me," Lewis said curtly.

He weaved his way through the crowded room, and as he approached her, Abbra smiled at him. For the first time he was aware of how pale and strained she had become, how very much she had changed.

"Let's go home," he said briefly, taking hold of

411

her by the arm.

"But why? I thought you wanted to find out what the general feeling was about what's happening in Vietnam..."

"I think I've been very foolish," he said, steering her through the throng and toward the door, "and I need to talk to you."

He drove her home through the darkened streets in silence. Once in the luxurious warmth of their flat, he poured her a sherry and handed it to her, lighting himself a cigar.

"What is it?" she asked, bewildered. "Have you accepted a position somewhere else? Someplace you think I'm not going to like?"

She had seated herself in a chair near a small rosewood desk. He remained standing, looking at her. Despite the shadows beneath her eyes and her ivory paleness, she was very beautiful. Just as she had always been. Her dress was a narrow sheaf of black wool crepe, exquisitely and expensively cut.

He said without prevaricating, "The woman I was talking to said that she had met you in California. You were with Scott."

Abbra's fingers tightened around the stem of her sherry glass. "Yes, we met at Patti's."

His eyes held hers, their gold-flecked depths somber. "She said that you were glowing, that she had never seen a woman so much in love."

She held his gaze and said nothing. There was nothing for her to say. The time for pretence between them was long past.

"Were you in love with Scott? Have I been a

412

fool to have believed all this time that you had married him simply because you saw in him an extension of myself?"

She rose to her feet and set the sherry glass down on the desk. "I was very much in love with Scott," she said steadily. "I told you so at Yosemite. You chose not to ask me about it."

"Christ!" he said softly, crushing the barely touched cigar out in an ashtray. "And all this time you've remained in love with Scott?"

They looked at each other across the lamplit room. "Yes," she said quietly, knowing that she could lie no more, that she would never lie again. Ever.

They remained standing, yards apart, staring at each other. At last he said incredulously, "I can't believe that I've been such a fool. Because of my ego I've nearly destroyed you. And the crazy thing is, it's all been unnecessary. I *did* need you those first few weeks. But afterward, when we were in London, I realized that we barely knew each other. My interests were not yours, and your interests could never be mine. We were strangers, tied together out of deep affection and a mutual sense of duty."

The relief she felt was so dizzying, she thought she was going to faint. "You mean that you realized you were no longer in love with me?"

"I'm in love with Tam," he said, his eyes tortured. "After the way you had stood by me, I didn't see how I could possibly tell you. Or how I could possibly go back to Vietnam for her."

"But you can now."

413

"Yes."

Suddenly the terrible tension between them broke. They stepped toward each other simultaneously.

"Go back for her now, quickly!" she said, hugging him tight. "Serena says that there isn't much time."

"And you? What will you do?" he asked, his voice thick with emotion.

She was laughing and crying at the same time. "I'm going to fly back to California on the first available flight. This time tomorrow, if they will have me back, I will be with Scott and Sanh!"

CHAPTER EIGHTEEN

All through 1974, in Saigon, the unease increased. There were repeated clashes near the demilitarized zone between government soldiers and Communist troops. The truce agreed to in Paris was a truce in name only. Although no American combat troops were now on Vietnamese soil, the killing continued.

Mike and Serena, terrified of what would happen to the children in their care if and when Saigon fell and they were no longer able to look after them, worked eighteen hours a day, ceaselessly battling with bureaucratic red tape as they endeavored to finalize adoptions in America and Europe, and to obtain the necessary exit visas.

Gabrielle's bouncy vitality and infectious sense of fun had made her a favorite among the children. They were fascinated by her flaming red hair and by her ability to speak their language fluently. To both her and Serena's bemusement, although they had made no effort to encourage a special friendship between them, Kylie and *le petit* Gavin had naturally gravitated toward each other. Perhaps it was because they both looked a little different from the majority of the other children. There was a hint of Vietnamese in *le petit* Gavin, yet his hair was a cross between Gabrielle's fiery tones and his father's blondness, and freckles still sprinkled the bridge of his nose. Kylie was quite obviously Amerasian, but her vivid blue eyes and creamy skin and black hair made her look more Irish than Vietnamese.

It was a friendship that neither Gabrielle nor Serena discouraged. Now that Kyle was dead, Serena's complex emotions about Kylie were no longer so traumatic. She found herself able to spend time with her, and to make friends with her, as she had long wanted to. Her relationship with Trinh, too, had improved. They were not bosom friends, nor ever would be, but she had had the photograph of Kyle reproduced and had given it to Trinh, together with a photograph of his flower-bedecked grave which Kyle's mother had forwarded to her some weeks after the funeral. In return, when Trinh brought Kylie to the orphanage she would often bring a small bunch of flowers with her, or some homemade *chao tom*, little sticks of shrimp paste, and give them to Serena.

"Have you spoken to Trinh about her and Kylie leaving Saigon?" Mike asked Serena shortly after they had received the news that North Vietnamese forces had captured Phuoc Binh, a city that was a mere eighty miles north of Saigon.

Serena was cleaning the wound of a child who had been hit by flying glass when a bomb had exploded in a café in Cholon.

She glanced up briefly from her task. "No, but there won't be any problem about it, will there? Kylie is obviously Amerasian, and I understood that the Vietnamese wives and children of American servicemen would be given priority if it came to an evacuation."

"Trinh wasn't a wife," Mike pointed out, beginning to stitch the wound in the child's arm.

"We can testify that she was his common-law wife."

"True. But I still think you should talk it over with her. She may not even want to be evacuated. Vietnamese love their country deeply. You need to point out to her that anyone who obviously consorted with Americans is not going to be too kindly treated under a Communist regime. And that Kylie is so obviously of mixed blood that she's never going to be wholly accepted into whatever society evolves in Vietnam once it is reunited."

Trinh had shaken her head stubbornly when Serena had broached the subject. "No. Where would I go? Where would I live?"

"You would go to America, Trinh. You would be looked after, I would see to that. You speak English fluently, so that isn't a problem."

"But Vietnam is my country. Saigon is my home."

"The Communists have captured the capital of Phuoc Long province. America has done nothing to intervene, except to make a statement denouncing the action, nor will it. After Phuoc Long other provinces will fall into Communist hands. Within months, possibly weeks, the North Vietnamese Army is going to be poised to strike at Saigon."

Trinh's eyes were frightened, but she again shook her head. "No, I cannot believe it. There have been bomb attacks in Saigon, and the fighting at the Presidential Palace and at the American Embassy in 1968. But North Vietnamese troops marching down Tu Do Street? No. America would never let it happen. It is impossible."

"It *is* possible," Serena said grimly. "For Kylie's sake the two of you will have to leave, and you will need the necessary papers. I can't get them for you without your cooperation, Trinh."

"Later," Trinh said unhappily. "I cannot think about it now. It is too big a decision. Later I will give you my answer."

There was nothing more that Serena could do. Phuoc Binh had fallen to the Communists in January. By March they had attacked Ban Me Thuot, the capital of Dar Lac province, the city

417

falling to them within a day. President Thieu panicked. In a vain attempt to secure the provinces immediately around Saigon, he ordered his troops to retreat south. With that one order, half of South Vietnam was ceded to the Communists. Hundreds of thousands of refugees began to flee south, vying for space on the roads with the retreating troops.

On the twenty-first, the North Vietnamese began to assault Hue, the old imperial capital. For three days heavy artillery fire bombarded the city's outskirts and then the South Vietnamese area commander gave the order to abandon the city, fleeing with his troops by sea to Da Nang and leaving Hue's inhabitants to their fate.

Mike strode into Cây Thông's crowded nursery and said briefly to Serena, "There's an American here, asking for you. Apparently you know his wife."

Serena finished inserting an IV tube into a baby's arm, strapping it firmly so that it couldn't be dislodged.

"He must have gotten me confused with someone else."

"No, he hasn't. His name is Lewis Ellis. He intends to go down into the Delta to Van Binh, to find a girl who used to work for him in '66. He wants to know if we can give him any help."

"Lewis?" Her voice was incredulous. "Abbra's Lewis?"

"The very same," Mike said with an exhausted grin. "Though I have a feeling, judging by his desperation to find this girl, that he's Abbra's

Lewis no longer."

Stunned, Serena hurried to where Lewis was waiting. Her first impression was that he was older than she had imagined, and then she remembered the time he had spent as a prisoner in a jungle camp. He had a face she immediately liked. Strong and uncompromising, but with a warmth in the eyes that belied the straight firmness of his mouth.

"Hello," she said, stretching her hand out toward him, "I'm Serena Anderson."

His handshake was like everything else about him, strong and firm. "I'm very pleased to meet you." His voice was deep and rich and she understood why Abbra, at eighteen, had fallen so much in love with him. "Abbra has told me a lot about you."

It was no time for small talk. She said without prevaricating, "Mike tells me you want to go down into the Delta?"

"I'm going. Tomorrow. Since you and Mike know the situation here as well as anybody, I thought I'd ask your advice about the best way of doing it."

"The best way of doing it is not to do it," Mike said dryly. "There are God knows how many North Vietnamese battalions converging on Saigon. Your chances of reaching Van Binh are so slim as to be extinct."

"Nevertheless I'm going," Lewis said without the least hint of doubt in his voice. "I need to find a girl down there, Nguyen Van Tam. Once I've found her I'm bringing her back to Saigon

419

and then taking her to the States with me."

"It's been nine years," Serena said gently, inwardly rejoicing that Abbra must now be reunited with Scott. "Whatever understanding you had with Tam, you can't possibly imagine that she will be still waiting for you?"

Lewis's eyes were very dark. "No, I can't. But I can at least see her again, and give her the opportunity to leave with me if she wishes to do so."

"There's a small orphanage near Van Binh run by a small group of Catholic nuns," Mike said. "The children there are in desperate need of being brought into Saigon. There's still a chance that places can be found for them on the adoption program."

"You mean that you will come with me?" Lewis asked abruptly.

Mike nodded, knowing very well that Lewis's chances of making and surviving the trip alone were slim. He knew all about Lewis's long imprisonment in the U Minh, and as far as he was concerned, the guy had suffered enough. If the girl he was looking for was so important to him, then he was only too happy to help him in his search for her.

Within hours of their leaving the city, Gabrielle ran into the orphanage, her face radiant.

"At last, *chérie*! I have news! Real news! A journalist in Saigon who works for a Western newspaper but who is, in reality, a Communist undercover agent, has contacted Nhu. He has

420

told her that the Communists intend to take Saigon within the next few weeks and that when they do so, Gavin will be brought south with the conquering forces!"

"Oh, Gaby," Serena hugged her tight. "But how can you know that the man is genuine? That he is speaking the truth? *Why* should the army be bringing Gavin south with them?"

"Out of respect for Dinh. Because that is what Dinh intended. That, as a journalist sympathetic to the North, Gavin would be an ideal person to chronicle the historic taking of the South."

"He might have been an ideal person nine years ago, but they surely can't believe that he is sympathetic to them now? Not after they have kept him in the North so long against his will?"

Gabrielle gave a helpless shrug of her shoulders, her eyes still shining. "It may not seem to make much sense, Serena. But Vietnamese minds are not Western minds. We do not know what Gavin has said to them, or what he has agreed to. What is important is that Nhu's contact says his information is utterly reliable. When the North Vietnamese Army takes Saigon, Gavin will be with them!"

On Easter Sunday the coastal town of Da Nang fell. The chaos there was even worse than the chaos that had taken place in Hue. The city was choked with refugees who had fled from towns already captured, and hundreds of thousands, terrified of Communist reprisals, tried to escape by sea. Soldiers fought civilians in the effort to commandeer boats. Children were separated from parents and crushed and drowned in the stampede.

On that day, in Da Nang, the South Vietnamese Army reached its nadir. Leaderless and un-controlled, they stripped themselves of their uniforms and subjected the local population to a reign of terror that could not have been exceeded by the Communists themselves.

"You cannot wait any longer, *chérie*," Gabri-elle said glumly to Serena when news of the surrender of Da Nang reached them. "The adop-tion papers and exit visas of all the remaining children must be processed immediately, no matter what the bureaucratic difficulties. And you must speak to Trinh again. Arrangements must be put in hand for her and Kylie to fly to America."

"What about *le petit* Gavin?" Serena asked. Ever since the news that Gavin would be enter-ing Saigon with the North Vietnamese Army, it had been patently obvious that no matter what happened, Gabrielle would not be leaving the city.

"I want you to take him with you when you and Mike leave."

Serena nodded. Neither she nor Mike wanted to leave, but their respective embassies had left them in no doubt that when the time came for a full-scale evacuation of all non-Vietnamese personnel, they would have to be among those airlifted out of the city.

That evening she spoke to Trinh again, this

time with desperate urgency. "You must realize by now that nothing is going to stop the Communist advance, Trinh. Do you want Kylie to grow up under a Communist regime? Do you want her to risk victimization because she is so obviously half American?"

Trinh had wrung her hands, her black-sloe eyes anguished. "No, of course I do not. But I have family in Saigon. My sister..."

"I will make arrangements for your sister too," Serena said, wondering how the hell she was going to be able to keep her promise. "Pack a bag and keep it ready, and leave everything else to me."

After leaving Trinh she went straight to the American Embassy. The official she spoke to there looked at her first appreciatively, and then, when she told him what she wanted from him, pityingly.

"Lady," he said wearily, "have you any idea how many Vietnamese want to get the hell out of this city? There are one hundred and forty thousand names on our 'endangered' list, and that's just the tip of the iceberg."

"This woman was the common-law wife of Kyle Anderson, a helicopter pilot with the first Cav who died under torture in Hoa Lo," Serena said icily. "She has a child by him. Kyle died in his country's service. The least America can do is to ensure that the woman he loved, and his child, are flown to safety."

The official looked at her with interest. "How come you know so much about it?"

"Because she may have been his common-law wife, but I was married to him," she said coolly. "He wrote asking me for a divorce before he was killed. There is no doubt at all that it was a serious relationship and that Trinh and her daughter are as deserving to be evacuated as any other Vietnamese dependents of Americans."

"Phew!" the official said, regarding her with deepening interest. "I've heard quite a few stories across this desk, but this is the first time I've had a wife in here, pleading for a plane seat for her husband's mistress. It takes some believing, but as I *do* believe you, bring the necessary documents in and I'll make sure that she and her daughter are put on the list of evacuees."

"And another family member," Serena said ruthlessly. "Trinh's sister." With a wide, dazzling smile, she blew him a kiss of thanks and disappeared out of the room before he had a chance to refuse her.

It was when she returned from the embassy to the orphanage that she heard what was for her the worst news of the entire war.

Shortly after 3 P.M. a U.S. military C-5A had departed from Tan Son Nhut crammed to capacity with orphan children bound for new homes in the States. The flight had been organized by Rosemary Taylor, a young Australian adoption-agency director both Serena and Mike had great respect for.

There were 243 children loaded onto the plane, with escorts to care for them on the long flight. Within minutes of takeoff the rear cargo doors blew out and the plane began to lose height. It skidded over the Saigon River, and then crashed into rice fields, breaking in half, the tail section erupting into flames, the nose section continuing to plow over the ground for another quarter of a mile or so.

One hundred and thirty-five of the three hundred and twenty-seven people aboard the plane died. Seventy-eight of the dead were children.

"Oh, God! I can't bear to think of it!" Serena sobbed when Gabrielle broke the news to her. "Those children had so much to look forward to! A whole new life!"

Gabrielle put her arms around her, comforting her, her face ashen. It could so easily have been Cây Thông children abroad the C-5A. It could so easily have been Kylie and *le petit* Gavin.

It was now nearly three weeks since Mike and Lewis had set off in a requisitioned army truck for the Delta. No one who knew of the expedition, apart from Gabrielle and Serena, believed that they would ever be seen again. As the first week of April drew to a close, and the noose that the Communists had thrown around Saigon tightened, even Gabrielle and Serena began to lose hope.

"Even if they successfully reached Van Binh, how could they possibly evade the NVA on their return trip?" Gabrielle said despairingly. "It is not possible, *chérie*."

"It has to be possible!" Serena said fiercely. "I couldn't survive if Mike died! I wouldn't know how to go on living!"

Gabrielle said nothing, instead she walked to the nearby Catholic cathedral and, for the first time in years, prayed.

On the morning of April 8 nearly everyone in Saigon thought the end had come. A fighter-bomber flew in from the South, bombing the Presidential Palace and the giant fuel dumps west of the city. As anti-aircraft fire blasted in retaliation, Gabrielle and Serena ran out of the orphanage and into the street, certain that a full-scale attack was about to take place. Instead, all they saw was the lone bomber banking steeply and flying away from the city, and a battered truck, enormous red crosses painted on the roof of the cab and the sides, crawling toward them.

"It's Mike!" Serena shrieked. "Oh, dear God! It's *Mike!*"

She flew down the street, and the truck coughed and spluttered to a halt. Mike jumped down from the cab, grimy and weary and scarcely recognizable beneath a heavy growth of beard. She hurtled into his arms uncaringly. "I thought you were dead!" she sobbed, hugging him so tight that she nearly knocked him off his feet. "Never do this to me again! Never! Never! Never!"

As well as Lewis and a remarkably composed Tam, there were also thirteen children in the truck. All of them were tired to the point of collapse, and hungry and dehydrated.

"Let us get the children inside," Gabrielle was saying, hugging Lewis, hugging Tam, so reliev-

426

ed at seeing them that she didn't know whether to laugh or cry.

"We're flying out on a scheduled flight," Lewis said later that evening to Mike. "I've been to the embassy and I've got clearance for Tam. Rules are being bent now, thank God."

Mike didn't say anything, but he couldn't help wryly wondering if the fact that Lewis was West Point, an ex-POW, and an adviser at the American Embassy in London might not have had a little something to do with the ease with which the rules were, for him, being bent.

The next morning he drove Lewis and Tam out to Tan Son Nhut. The route was so packed with the cars of fleeing rich Vietnamese that the normally short drive took them nearly two hours.

"You're sure you've got seats reserved?" he asked Lewis anxiously. "These people are going to be willing to pay bribes of thousands in order to get on a flight out."

"Don't worry," Lewis said grimly, his arm around Tam's shoulders. "I've got everything that is necessary, and nothing on God's earth is going to prevent us flying out and putting Vietnam behind us forever!"

Tam had said very little to Mike on their arduous journey from Van Binh, but he was a good judge of people and he wasn't worried about her. She would find America strange at first, but she was a very special girl who allowed nothing to faze her. And she obviously thought that Lewis was the sun and the moon and the stars. Taking into account Abbra's marriage ceremony to Scott, a divorce between Lewis and Abbra would be quickly and easily obtained. Within months, maybe even weeks, Tam would be Mrs. Lewis Ellis. Mike thought that when she was, she would be the kind of wife that any man would envy.

As they approached the airport gates they could see barbed-wire barricades being erected. A heavy police presence was vetting every car and possibly, Mike thought, demanding bribes. When Lewis showed the pass he had been given by the embassy, there were no such demands. They were waved through without harassment, and the same treatment was accorded them once they were inside the airport building. Despite the horrendous lines and the crush at the check-in desks, Lewis's pass insured that they were swept straight through toward the exit for departures.

"I don't know what the hell is on that pass of yours," Mike said admiringly, "but I wouldn't mind having a half dozen like it!"

It was time to say good-bye. A genuine friendship, born of mutual like and respect, had sprung up between them on the perilous journey to and from Van Binh, and they shook hands warmly, clasping each other on the back.

"Make sure Serena and *le petit* Gavin get out safely," Lewis said urgently. "There's not much time left, Mike. Perhaps only days."

"I know," Mike squeezed Lewis's hand hard one last time, kissed Tam on the cheek, and then stood back as they turned and walked out through the departure exit toward their waiting plane.

The adoption work at Cây Thông was facilitated by the Australian government's decision to take an unlimited number of children, providing that they were going to Australian parents. Australian planes were available to fly the children out. Air France and Pan Am flights were still taking children whose adoption had been processed to their new homes in America and Europe. For Mike and Serena, their days were a treadmill of caring for the children, of obtaining exit visas and travel documentation for those about to leave, arranging escorts for them and transporting them out to Tam Son Nhut.

On April 17, Mike and Serena and Gabrielle were officially warned by their respective embassies that they should plan to leave the country while commercial aircraft were still operating.

"I'm not leaving yet," Serena had said fiercely, "not while there's a remote chance of getting more children out."

"What about Trinh?" Gabrielle asked. "Does she know what it is she has to do?"

The official Serena had spoken to at the American Embassy had agreed that Trinh and her sister and Kylie would leave the city when the order came for a final evacuation. Buses would pick up Americans and Vietnamese designated for departure at appointed places around the city and deliver them to various helicopter pads. From there they would be flown out to American ships, which would be waiting off shore.

Serena nodded. "Yes, she's been given documentation and the address she has to go to immediately after the signal for the evacuation is broadcast over American armed forces radio."

"And what is the signal?" Gabrielle asked curiously. As yet it was still a secret, but she knew that Lewis had informed Serena and Mike of it.

"When time has finally run out, and the North Vietnamese are only hours away, the armed forces radio will broadcast this announcement every fifteen minutes: 'The temperature in Saigon is one hundred five degrees and rising' and the announcement will be followed by Bing Crosby singing 'White Christmas'."

Gabrielle giggled. "A white Christmas in Saigon is not possible, *chérie*. Especially in April!"

On Friday April 24, the last of the children for whom Mike and Serena had been able to arrange adoptions left for America. It was Serena who drove them to the airport. A report over Radio Hanoi had announced that all Vietnamese who had worked in any capacity for the adoption of orphans would be treated as war criminals. Mike had asked every one of the Vietnamese who had worked for them either as child-care helpers or as domestics if they wanted to leave the country. All those who had said they did want to leave had been officially listed as escorts for the departing children.

The flight they were leaving on was Pan Am's last flight from Saigon. The simple task of escorting the children through the necessary security checks and into the departure lounge took on nightmare proportions. There was a panic-stricken crush of people pleading vainly for tickets, and even those who possessed tickets were pushing their way through into the departure lounge as if, at any moment, the tickets would be ripped from their hands and their departure foiled.

With admirable British coolness Serena shepherded her flock through the chaos. The majority of those who were also cramming into the departure lounge were Vietnamese who possessed French citizenship and French passports. They were the elite. The lucky ones.

As Serena said a last good-bye to the children and to the Vietnamese escorts who were leaving with them, fighter jets flew in low and fast, strafing the perimeter of the airfield.

"Oh, what is happening?" one of the Vietnamese women said tearfully, grasping hold of Serena's hand. "Are we not going to be able to leave? Is our plane going to be bombed?"

Over the sound of artillery and mortar fire, Serena assured her that the plane was going to leave and that it was going to leave safely.

Minutes later, as the fighters disappeared, the call came for all departing passengers to make their way toward their waiting plane.

Serena watched them file away, her heart in her mouth. But the fighters did not return. The giant plane taxied down the runway, lifting smoothly into the air, taking with it the last remaining orphans for whom it had been possible to arrange adoptions. They, at least, had a future to look forward to. They were going to families who would love and cherish them. The war would mar their lives no longer. She turned away, suddenly so tired she could barely stand. Almost semi-conscious with weariness, she drove back through the refugee-thronged streets toward the Continental. There, in the room that had been her home for so many years, she tumbled into bed fully dressed, asleep within seconds.

Two days later, on April 26, it was officially announced that General Duong Van Minh would take over as president of South Vietnam. There were very few foreigners left in the city now. The British Ambassador had departed, the New Zealand Embassy was empty and deserted; even a large majority of newsmen had left.

Free of the burden of ensuring that every child with an adoptive home to go to had all the necessary documentation and a flight seat, Mike had become a full-time doctor again, spending all his time trying to alleviate the suffering of the sick and often dying refugees who were still streaming into the city.

Serena spent the entire following day with Trinh. She had already spoken to Abbra on the telephone, telling her exactly what the situation was, and asking Abbra to meet Trinh and Mai and Kylie on their arrival in the United States. The happiness in Abbra's voice as she readily agreed, and as she told Serena of how she and Sanh and Scott were all reunited and living together as a family again, was radiant. Now Serena wanted to make sure that Trinh understood who Abbra was, and how to get in touch with her if there was any difficulty.

"This is a photograph of Abbra," she said, handing a group photograph of Abbra and Scott and Sanh to Trinh.

Trinh looked down at it and then up again at Serena. "Her little boy. Is he Vietnamese?"

"Yes, Abbra and Scott have adopted him. I'm sure he'll love having visitors who are also Vietnamese, and I am sure that Kylie will make friends with him just as quickly as she did with little Gavin."

"Little Gavin is not so very little anymore," Trinh said with a rare, mischievous smile. "Madame Ryan will soon have to think of another name so as not to confuse him with his father."

No matter how many times Gabrielle and Serena had requested that Trinh cease to speak to them so formally, and to address them instead by their Christian names, she had refused.

"This may be the last time we shall see each other in Vietnam," Serena said, rising to leave, suddenly serious. "Big Minh is to be inaugurated as president tomorrow and I think that once he is president, the end will come very quickly."

"But I will see you in America?" Trinh's dark eyes were anxious. If Kyle had been alive, America would have held no terrors for her. But Kyle wasn't alive, and America seemed a very strange and frightening prospect.

"Yes," Serena said unequivocally. "I shall see you in America. *Châo*, Trinh."

"*Châo*, Serena," Trinh said a trifle shyly.

Serena grinned. It had taken a long time, almost too long, but at last she had broken through Trinh's doubts and reserve and gained her friendship. Kyle would have been pleased.

The next day the sky was gray and ominous, heavy clouds threatening to unleash the first monsoon of the season. The swearing-in ceremony of General Minh took place at five o'clock. It was a televised ceremony, and Gabrielle and Serena and Mike watched it together in Gabrielle and Serena's room at the Continental.

As the general began to speak, the heavens opened, rain pouring down on the city's roofs and sidewalks.

"The situation is very critical," Minh said, trying to make himself heard over the sound of rolling thunder. "I feel a responsibility now to seek a ceasefire and bring peace on the basis of the Paris Agreements..."

Lightning cracked over the hotel, followed by a long volley of thunder. At the same time, other rumblings could be heard. Serena looked across at Mike apprehensively. "Artillery fire?" she asked.

Mike shook his head, striding to the window, no longer listening to the man who was now South Vietnam's president. "Yes, but there are planes as well. Their target seems to be Tan Son Nhut."

Before he had finished speaking they were aware of firing very near to them, coming from the direction of the Presidential Palace, and then Mike swung away from the window, saying tersely, "Get down! The planes are coming this way, strafing as they come!"

From outside they could hear screaming in the street, and then anti-aircraft fire deafened them as they threw themselves to the floor.

When the brief attack was over, Serena ran for the phone, dialing Trinh's number. The lines were dead. "I must go to her! Make sure she's okay!" she said frantically.

Mike walked across to her and removed the telephone receiver from her hand. "You will do no such thing," he said firmly. "The streets aren't safe, there's still tracer fire. Trinh knows exactly what she must do. She has her radio, she has her documentation, and she has her bags packed. You can't achieve anything by going over to her."

Serena leaned against him, knowing that he was right, hoping that now that there was no more hope for the city, the end would come swiftly.

That night Mike stayed with Serena and Gabrielle in their room at the Continental. None of them got any sleep. Tan Son Nhut was repeatedly bombed. Rocket fire lit up the night sky, and as dawn finally broke, Serena and Mike knew that the coming day was going to be the last they would spend in Saigon.

As artillery fire bombarded the outskirts of the city, Mike hurried through the now nearly deserted streets to the orphanage. There were no children there, for they had taken no more in since the last group had left for the States. He went into his office, rifling through files, selecting those that were vital, destroying those that weren't. Then he quickly packed a small bag of personal possession and headed back toward the Continental.

As he entered the room, Serena said to him, "The evacuation signal has been broadcast. It's being broadcast every fifteen minutes. Listen."

She turned the volume up on her radio. Music was playing. After a few minutes it came to an end and a calm, unruffled voice announced, "The temperature is one hundred and five degrees and rising" and then there came the soft, dulcet tones of Bing Crosby singing "I'm dreaming of a white Christmas".

"That's it then," Mike said. "Let's go."

He turned toward Gabrielle. "Are you sure you're doing the right thing staying, Gabrielle? Are you sure you will be safe?"

"*Oui*," she replied with a big smile. "In another few hours Gavin may be in Saigon. Already he is probably on the outskirts with the army. Nothing in the world would make me leave Saigon now."

Looking down at her, so petite and so heartbreakingly optimistic, Mike felt his throat tighten. "How long has it been, Gabrielle?" he asked. "How long have you and Gavin been apart?"

Her eyes met his, overly bright. "*Neuf Noëls*," she said huskily. Nine Christmases. She looked down at her son, who had been staring at the window, gazing down into the square with rapt attention. "It is time for us to say *au 'voir* for a little while, *chéri*," she said lovingly. "Stay with Serena and Mike. Keep very tight hold of Serena's hand and do not let go of it, do you promise me?"

Gavin nodded. He had already spent long days trying to persuade his mother to allow him to stay with her, but it had been hopeless. She had been adamant that he leave with Serena and Mike. Now, knowing that to argue any further was useless, and looking forward to the promised helicopter ride from the roof of the embassy to a ship of the U.S. 7th fleet far out in the China Sea, he merely said, "I promise, *Maman*," and then, as he had done when he was younger, he flung himself against her and hugged her tightly saying, "I love you, *Maman!*"

"I love you too, *chéri*." Gabrielle fought back an upsurge of tears. "*Au' voir*, take care."

The streets that had been deserted all morning were suddenly no longer deserted. Army buses and private cars and taxis began speeding through them as the remaining Americans in Saigon heeded the message that had just been broadcast to them and began heading hell-for-leather toward their prearranged pick up points.

As they did so, the Saigonese teemed out from wherever they had been sheltering, converging like lemmings on the American Embassy, determined to have one last, valiant try at hitching a helicopter ride out of their doomed city.

Mike and Serena and *le petit* Gavin didn't need transportation to reach the embassy. It was only a few blocks away. Carrying one bag of hand luggage each, they hurried up Tu Do, past the twin-spired red-brick cathedral and onto Thong Nhut Boulevard, where the embassy was situated.

Mike took one look at the crowds of desperate Vietnamese besieging the gates and walls and said grimly, "We're never going to get through. Not at this entrance anyway."

Barbed wire had been rolled along the tops of the nine-foot-high walls, and marines, M-16s at the ready, were standing behind the barbed wire, preventing anyone from scrambling over or swinging across from the nearby lamp stanchions.

"What shall we do?" Serena yelled, gripping hold of *le petit* Gavin's hand tightly. "Try the Mac Dinh Chi gate entrance?"

Mike nodded, and they battled their way through a mass of desperate humanity. Many of those haranguing the soldiers on the wall were waving pieces of paper, shouting out that they were the employees of Americans, that they had been promised evacuation. Because of their loyalty to Americans the North Vietnamese would shoot them. The marines were deaf to all

438

solicitations, she saw one marine kick his booted foot into the face of one youth who had managed to scale the wall, and another marine bring the butt of his M-16 down hard on a hand searching frantically for leverage.

As they fought their way toward the Mac Dinh Chi entrance gate her bag was wrenched from her hand. She was almost grateful to be relieved of it. There was nothing in it of great value, and without it, it was easier to forge a way in Mike's wake.

At the Mac Dinh Chi gate a marine spotted them in the crowd and yelled, "Push to the front! I'll haul you over!"

It was easier said than done. At the knowledge that a couple of privileged Americans were about to be dragged to safety while they were left behind, the crowd went wild. Serena felt blows raining down on her as Mike physically fought to make a passageway through for them.

"Gavin!" Serena gasped. "Get him to take Gavin first!"

Mike took hold of Gavin, lifting him shoulder high. The marine bent forward, took hold of Gavin's hands, and hauled him upward. As he did so, Mike tossed his bag, and Gavin's, high over the wall.

"I have passport! I have passport!" a Vietnamese woman was yelling frantically to Serena. "Tell them to let me in too! Tell them my husband, my son, both work for Americans! Both now in Bangkok! I cannot be left here alone! Tell them, Madame! Tell them!"

"I'm going to inch open the gate!" the marine yelled down to Mike. "Slip through fast. You won't get a second chance."

The gate inched open and from the pressure of the crowd around her, Serena felt as if the breath were being squeezed out of her body. Mike had pushed her in front of him and as the crowd surged forward she literally fell into the embassy compound.

"There's a woman out there with a passport! Her husband and son both worked for Americans! You have to let her in!" she yelled up to the marine. But it was too late. Mike was panting for breath, the gate firmly closed behind him, and the desperate hands clenching onto the gate's bars went ignored.

"Jesus! This is worse than anything I'd ever imagined," Serena sobbed, hugging a terrified Gavin close. "Those poor people! What on earth is going to become of them? I thought everyone who had worked for the Americans had been promised a safe passage out?"

"They had, it's a promise that's going to be impossible for the Americans to keep," Mike said, putting his arm around her shoulder and picking up his bag and *le petit* Gavin's. "Time has run out. Tan Son Nhut is unusable, and so there'll be no evacuations from there. This whole process should have been started weeks ago, not left to the last minute."

The embassy compound was thronged with Americans and third-party nationals like themselves, and with high-ranking Vietnamese. A landing zone in the embassy's parking lot had been cleared in order that helicopters could land, but so far none had arrived.

"There must be over two thousand people here," Mike said, wiping beads of perspiration from his forehead. "How many can a Huey hold? Fourteen? Sixteen?"

It was obvious that they were going to be in for a long wait before they were flown out, and they edged their way through crowds that were now orderly to find room in which they could all sit down.

As Serena was reflecting that she had been foolish not to have had the forethought to have brought some food and drink with her, she heard an American close by saying, "Christ! I thought I wasn't going to make it at all! My evacuation station was in Huu Ngoc Street, and then we were told that no one was going to show there, that we had to make our way here. If it hadn't been that they sent a bus for us, we'd never have made it. The atmosphere out there is definitely ugly!"

Serena spun toward him. "Huu Ngoc Street? Did you say Huu Ngoc Street?"

The American nodded. Panic seized hold of Serena's heart. "Were there any Vietnamese with you? Did the Vietnamese leave with you on the bus?"

The American shook his head. "There weren't any Vietnamese that I remember. Hell, why would there be? The house in Huu Ngoc was a strictly American pickup."

Serena had known that. But the official at the embassy had assured her that with the documentation that Trinh possessed, it would make no difference. And if the helicopter pickup from Huu Ngoc Street had gone as planned, it wouldn't have made any difference. But would Trinh and Mai and Kylie have been able to make it into the embassy compound? She remembered the desperate Vietnamese outside, waving passports, waving letters, waving all the pathetic pieces of documentation that they had believed would see them out of the country.

She turned to Mike, gripping hold of his arm. "You heard all that, didn't you? She couldn't have made it, Mike. I *know* that she couldn't have made it!"

Mike looked around at the crush in the compound. To search it, looking for Trinh and Mai and Kylie was practically an impossibility. It would take far too long. Especially if she wasn't there, because by then it would be too late to go in search of her.

He said briefly, "I'll go back outside and see if I can see her. She may even have returned home if she thinks it's truly hopeless. Or she may have had the forethought to go to Gabrielle at the Continental."

"Oh, God!" Serena whispered hoarsely. "Be careful, Mike! Please be careful!"

He kissed her long and hard and then, without another word, he spun on his heel, striding toward the nearest exit, aware that at that precise moment in time, he was the only man in the

442

entire city of Saigon that wanted to leave the American Embassy compound and not enter it.

The next few hours were the longest of Serena's life. At five o'clock the first of the helicopters arrived and marines began to organize the two-thousand-strong crowd into some sort of order.

At dusk Mike still hadn't returned, and her British coolness was fast beginning to desert her. She and Gavin had searched the compound time and time again, and had found no trace of Trinh, or of Mai and Kylie.

The clamor outside the gates had intensified to nightmarish proportions, and combined with it was the sound of heavy shelling in the city's outskirts.

"They're not going to be able to get us all out before the city is taken," an elegantly dressed American woman said quietly to Serena. "If I were you, I would take your place in line, otherwise you and your little boy might be left behind."

Serena didn't care if she was left behind, not if Mike was too, but she couldn't risk *le petit* Gavin being left behind. Very reluctantly she edged a way into the line that was moving slowly forward toward the foot of the stairs leading to the embassy's roof.

At about eight o'clock there was a loud explosion from the front of the embassy. Someone said that it was a hand grenade exploding, someone else said that it sounded as if a match had been dropped into the gas tank of a car. No one knew.

Serena and Gavin were nearing the top of the six flights of stairs, and she knew that if she stayed with him any longer, she was going to find herself on a helicopter, winging her way across the South China Sea, and not knowing where Mike was, or what had happened to him.

She bent down so that she was eye to eye with Gavin. "Listen, my love. I'm going back into the compound to see if I can find Mike. Whatever happens, you are not to move from here. You are to continue in the line, and if your turn comes to board a helicopter and I have not come back, you are to board it by yourself. Do you understand?"

He nodded. Although he was only nine, he already possessed his mother's unwavering common sense, and Serena knew that she could rely on him.

"These are your papers," she said, slipping his passport and identity documents into his inside jacket pocket. "Look after them very, very carefully." She kissed him lightly on the forehead. "I will see you soon. Either back here, or on an American ship far out at sea!"

He grinned. He didn't really mind being left alone. It made everything even more exciting. And he couldn't wait to board one of the helicopters and fly out into the darkness.

Serena squeezed her way back down the stairs and out into the compound. She satisfied herself that Mike and Trinh were not among those still waiting for a place in the line and then pushed her way toward the main gate. More marines

444

than ever were now manning the walls, and the shouts and pleas from those outside were deafening.

"Have you seen a New Zealander out there?" she yelled up to the marine nearest to her. "A big, broadly built man?"

The crowd outside the walls was turning very nasty and the marine didn't take his eyes away from it to look at her, but he shook his head.

Overhead in the purple-deep sky the *whump-whump-whump* of helicopter rotor blades battled against the sound of artillery and rocket fire. Serena wondered how many people there were waiting to be flown out, how many more flights would be able to be made, how many would be left behind when the last flight had departed.

Suddenly, scanning the faces of the throng in the street beyond the barred gate, she caught a glimpse of Mike.

"*That's him!*" she yelled to the marine. "*Can you see him? Has he someone with him?*"

Despite the scores of hands gripping the bars of the gate from the outside, her own fingers found a place on them.

"*Mike!*" she yelled with all her strength. "*Mike!*"

He heard her, saw her. He was carrying Kylie in his arms, and Trinh was at his side, but she could see no sign of Mai.

The marines were yelling at him, leaning over as far as they dared, hitting out at the crowd with the butts of their M-16s in order to make a way through for him. She saw him reach the gate, saw Trinh's terrified face, and then, before they could be hauled inside, the crowd turned on him. She saw one youth raise a club and bring it hard down on Mike's head, saw Mike falter, drop Kylie, and fall.

She was screaming at the marines to open the gates so that she could get to him, but their attention was centered on the mob in front of them. Trinh was sobbing, grabbing hold of Kylie.

Serena seized hold of the person nearest to her, not knowing if it was a man or a woman, a Vietnamese or an American. *"Lift me up!"* she screamed at them. *"For Christ's sake, lift me up!"*

Whoever it was obeyed her, and blessedly strong arms hoisted her high. She could no longer see Mike, but she could see Trinh and Kylie, and she shouted out, *"Pass Kylie over to me, Trinh!"*

Out of the corner of her eye she was aware that Mike's unconscious body was being hauled up the side of the wall at rifle point by two marines. He was safe. There was only Kylie and Trinh to worry about now, and Trinh was already lifting Kylie up toward her.

The little girl was screaming in terror, but Serena had hold of her. With a strength she didn't know she possessed, she lifted Kylie clear of the gate, dropping her down to safety. Then, sobbing with relief, she turned to grasp hold of Trinh's upstretched hands. Their fingers touched, grasped hold. Stones were being thrown at them now, and one of them hit Serena's left temple. She cried out in pain, blood gushing into her eye, still holding on to Trinh. A marine stretched his hand down toward Trinh, about to haul her upward and in utter rage a Vietnamese who had for hours been beseeching the marines to allow him to enter lifted a pistol high and fired at Trinh's head.

Blood spurted onto Serena's hands and arms. Shards of Trinh's skull flew upward into the night air. She fell backward and the crowd closed over her, baying for more blood. Baying for American blood.

Whoever it was who had been holding Serena lowered her exhaustedly to the ground. "I'm sorry, lady," he said awkwardly, handing her a handkerchief.

She pressed it against the cut on her face, looking at him for the first time. He was a big, burly Australian who looked as if he might be a construction worker.

"Yes," she said numbly, and then, "thank you."

She bent down, putting her arms around Kylie's shoulders, hugging her close, not knowing how much she had seen.

"It's time for us to go," a dearly loved voice said gently.

She looked up, and Mike was standing unsteadily beside her, his face ashen.

"Yes." She stood upright, her arm still around Kylie's shoulders. "Where was Mai?" she asked. "Wasn't she with you?"

Mike shook his head. "She changed her mind at the last minute. Trinh and Kylie went to the evacuation point alone."

Above them a CH-47 Chinook rose from the embassy roof, skimming over the garden of the French Embassy that was adjacent to the American Embassy, and climbing away eastward.

"Let's go," Mike said again, and heavy-hearted and somber-eyed, he led the way back toward the line leading to the stairs.

It was two in the morning before they were finally evacuated. As they sat hunched in the helicopter, Kylie no longer sobbing, but whimpering softly as Mike held her gently in his arms, Serena looked down at the city below them. The roads converging on it were full of lights. The headlights of North Vietnamese army trucks. She wondered if Gavin Ryan was in one of them, if, in another few hours, he and Gabrielle would at last be reunited. She hoped so. She hoped some happiness would come out of Saigon's hideous death throes.

She reached her hand out and lightly touched Kylie's hair. She would adopt her, of course. She wondered what Kyle would have said if he had been able to see into the future. One thing she was certain of ... he had always liked Bedingham. He would be pleased to think of his daughter growing up there.

CHAPTER NINETEEN

Despite the mayhem in the streets and the deafening noise of artillery and mortar fire that was coming from the city's suburbs, the Continental Hotel was strangely silent. There were no more journalists there, or if there were, they were conspicuous only by their absence.

Gabrielle removed all her western clothing and donned the loose black pajamas of a peasant. Then she covered her vivid red hair with a black kerchief and topped that with one of the conical straw hats that all the local girls wore. She looked at herself in the mirror and was satisfied. All the Vietnamese aspects of her features had been accentuated, and she doubted if anyone would mistake her for a Westerner.

She slipped out of the hotel, making her way to her aunt's house. Nhu, the sister of a man who had held the rank of colonel in the North Vietnamese Army, was waiting for the North Vietnamese Army's arrival without the least trace of fear.

"It will not be long now," she said, pouring Gabrielle a glass of rice wine and then turning the lamp on the table down low so as not to attract any attention from the looters who were already rampaging the streets.

"No," Gabrielle agreed, so tense with excitement that she could scarcely breathe.

They were talking of different things. Her aunt was referring to the final reunification of North and South Vietnam into one country. Gabrielle was thinking only of Gavin.

There was very little sleep for either of them. Every twenty minutes or so there would be the sound of helicopters flying in and landing in the parking lot at the embassy or on the rooftop. Then, after a short interval, they would hear them again, lifting into the night sky and wheeling eastward over the city toward the South China Sea. In the early hours of the morning there came the sound of a loud explosion from the direction of the embassy. Neither of them could imagine what it could be.

The sound of helicopters beating overhead continued, and occasionally the sounds of shouting and screaming also reached them. "It is those who worked for the Americans," Nhu said quietly, "those who are going to be left behind when the helicopters cease to come."

The helicopters came and departed with less and less regularity. Shortly after seven-thirty a Chinook 46, escorted by six Cobra gunships, flew from the roof of the embassy. After that there were no more helicopters.

Nhu looked tiredly across at Gabrielle. "They have gone," she said simply. "The Americans have finally left Vietnam."

Gabrielle's hands tightened in her lap. *Le petit* Gavin would be aboard a U.S. ship now with

450

Mike and Serena. He would be safe, and when they were reunited, he would be reunited with Gavin also.

Nhu raised the blinds on a bright, sunny morning, clean and sweet-smelling after the previous day's downpour.

"I'm going out," Gabrielle said, picking up her conical straw hat. "I'll bring back some croissants for breakfast."

"And I will stay by the radio," Nhu said, tuning it to the BBC.

Gabrielle walked leisurely toward the central square. The city was transformed almost beyond recognition. There were no cyclos racing down the streets, no Hondas, no blue and yellow taxis, no traffic at all. And there were no policemen.

Even the sidewalk outside the Continental was deserted. No flower sellers, no cigarette peddlers, no prostitutes. It was like walking on an empty stage set, waiting for the curtain to rise on the first act of a new play.

She bought some croissants, and then returned to Nhu's.

"There is nothing on the BBC," Nhu said as she made coffee. "Only news of the evacuation. Nothing about a surrender."

"Let's try Radio Saigon," Gabrielle said, adjusting the frequency. She was just in time to hear General Minh begin to speak.

"I believe firmly in reconciliation among all Vietnamese," he began emotionally. "To avoid needless bloodshed I ask the soldiers of the republic to put an end to all hostilities. Be calm

451

and remain where you are now. To save the lives of the people, do not open fire. I also call on our brothers, the soldiers of the Provisional Revolutionary Government, not to open fire, because we are waiting here to meet with their representatives to discuss the orderly turnover of the reins of government, both civilian and military, without causing senseless bloodshed to the people."

At the same time as the speech was being broadcast over the radio, Nhu and Gabrielle could also hear it being relayed over loudspeakers in the streets. Then, as General Minh finished speaking, there came the faint rumble of approaching tanks.

Despite Nhu's pleas, Gabrielle refused to stay indoors. Gavin might be with the very first soldiers to enter the city. She had to see the tanks arrive, had to be there.

Other Saigonese were also hesitantly gathering in the streets, fearful and apprehensive. Gabrielle began to walk in the direction of the Presidential Palace. The North Vietnamese would want to occupy key buildings first, and the first place they would want to fly their flag from would be the Presidential Palace.

At first there was only one tank. It rumbled majestically and undeterred down the street toward the palace and crashed through the palace gates. Small groups of bystanders gathered to see what would happen next. Minutes later, on the palace balcony, the flag of the Provisional Revolutionary Government was raised over

Saigon.

Other tanks soon followed the first one, and columns of soldiers followed the tanks, but there was no gunfire. Everything was very quiet, very orderly. Gabrielle stood for a moment watching the flag, realizing that at last, for better or for worse, Vietnam was again one country, and then she turned and began to make her way back toward the central square and the Continental.

That was where Gavin would head first. The Continental had always been the central meeting place in the city for all journalists and Europeans. He would go to the Continental in order to get his bearings, and she would be there, waiting for him.

The atmosphere in the streets was very strange. The North Vietnamese were neither being welcomed into the city as liberators, nor were they being repelled as invaders. It was as if they were simply being endured by a people who had endured much and would, no doubt, endure much more.

At the Continental Gabrielle went up to the room she had shared for so long with Serena. It looked out over the square and would give her a grandstand view of all arrivals.

Occasionally, as the long afternoon progressed, she would go back down into the street and across to Givralle where the proprietor was doing a roaring trade selling freshly baked rolls to North Vietnamese troops. With her face shaded beneath her conical straw hat, and in her black peasant pajamas, Gabrielle attracted no attention, but she was shocked at how young the majority of the soldiers were.

She went back to her room and her vigil. She saw the western journalist she had seen earlier, this time he was talking to a South Vietnamese police colonel in front of the large statue of American marines that dominated the square. As she watched, the Vietnamese turned away from the journalist, saluted the statue, and then, before the journalist could stop him, raised the pistol to his head and fired.

Gabrielle covered her eyes. Despite the lack of house-to-house fighting, or bloodshed in the streets, it was obvious that retribution would be meted out by the North Vietnamese to men who had held high rank in South Vietnam's army or police force.

The man in the square below her had decided not to face such retribution, and she knew that there would be many others who would make the same choice.

Just as dusk was approaching, a fresh convoy of trucks chugged their way up Tu Do Street and into the square. They were crammed full of *bo doi's*, North Vietnamese Army foot soldiers. All of them were dressed in baggy, dark green uniforms; all of them were wearing pith helmets. All but one. His hair was shaggy and tumbled and sun-gold.

She threw open the tall French windows, leaning perilously far out over the windowsill. *"Gavin!"* she cried, her heart full. *"Oh, mon amour! Gavin!"*

He stood in the back of the crowded truck looking around for the source of the cry. Then he looked upward. Gabrielle saw a face that at first she scarcely recognized. There were deep lines furrowing his brow and running from nose to mouth, and then she saw his eyes, and they were Gavin's eyes, warm and gray and blessedly unchanged.

"Gavin, *mon amour!*" she shouted again hoarsely.

For a second he did not recognize her, and then she ripped the black kerchief from her hair, and her sizzling red curls tumbled free. With a cry rent from his very soul he vaulted from the truck, sprinting toward the Continental's entrance.

Gabrielle was already at the room of her door, running, running, running. She raced along the corridor, narrowly missing the elderly waiters who, with no customers to wait on, had taken to sleeping in the passageways on rush mats. She raced to the head of the stairs, her heart thundering, the blood crashing in her ears. Down the stairs, running, running, running, taking them two and three at a time.

He was racing toward her. They were only yards away from each other. Only feet away.

"Oh, Gavin, *mon amour!*" she cried, hurtling into his arms, "*Tu m'es manqué*! How I have missed you!"

As soon as his lips touched hers, the long intervening years went whistling down the wind. Between them, nothing had changed. Between them, nothing ever would change.

"I love you, Gaby!" he said over and over again. "Oh, sweet Christ! How I love you!"

She was laughing and crying at the same time, touching his face with her fingertips, running them over his eyebrows, his cheeks, his mouth. "Is it really you, *mon amour*? Oh, after all this time, is it really you?"

Still kissing, still with their arms wrapped tightly around each other, they sat on the red carpeted steps of the Continental's grand staircase.

"I've never stopped missing you, never stopped loving you, Gaby," he said huskily.

Her eyes held his, so full of love that he thought he would die with happiness. "Nor me you," she said softly and truthfully. "Nor me you, *chéri*."

A long time later they moved downstairs to the empty, grandiosely furnished main lounge.

"What happened?" she asked simply. "What happened to you after Dinh was killed?"

With his arm around her shoulders, as Saigon prepared for its first night under Communist rule, Gavin told her of the life he had led for the last nine years, and which he had begun to think he would always lead.

"I was never treated badly. I was simply put to work in the fields, as were all the other prisoners in the camp I was in. There were no in-depth interrogation sessions, but whenever there was even the slightest contact between myself and any official, I always repeated that I was a friend

456

of North Vietnam. That Comrade Duong Quynh Dinh, a hero of North Vietnam and a personal friend of General Giap, had invited me into the North to chronicle the historic battles that were taking place.

"And every official seemed completely indifferent to what I said. Then, a month ago, there was a change of attitude. I was told that North Vietnam was poised to take Saigon. And that at last I could fulfil the mission Colonel Duong had assigned to me."

Gabrielle cuddled close against him. "And so you traveled south, with the troops?"

"Yes." He could still scarcely believe that it had happened, that he was no longer a prisoner, that he was free and with Gabrielle and in the Continental Palace Hotel in Saigon. "And you?" he said gently, tilting her face upward toward him. "What have you been doing in the nine years that I have been away?"

She thought of Radford, and the rock band; of her return to the kind of singing that she loved the best, and of the heady success that she had achieved with it. She thought of the long months and years she had spent besieging the Vietnamese Embassy in Paris to get information about him, the years in Saigon with Nhu and Serena. And she thought of *le petit* Gavin. None of the other things mattered. She would tell him about them all, eventually. Even about Radford. For now she would tell him about his son.

When she had finished, and when it was completely dark outside, she said, "What happens now, *mon amour*? Will we be allowed to leave the country?"

He nodded. "I've been told to report to the French Embassy. It's the only embassy still functioning. It may be a long time until there are scheduled flights, but when there are, we'll be on board one of them."

"And so it is all over," she said, raising the back of his hand to her lips and kissing it. "No more waiting. No more heartbreak."

He grinned down at her. One of the aged waiters had thoughtfully lit the lamps in the room, and in the lamplight Gavin's shaggy mop of hair was a dull, burnished gold. Incredibly, at that moment he scarcely looked any older than he had the day she had met him. "For you, and me, and for *le petit* Gavin, everything good and wonderful is just about to start," he said huskily, and then he lowered his mouth to hers, and her arms slid around his neck.

CHAPTER TWENTY

Abbra and Scott, with Sanh holding Abbra's hand tightly, stood in the arrivals hall at Orly Airport. Serena and Mike, and Kylie and *le petit* Gavin were with them. An Air France 707 from Bangkok had just landed, and Gabrielle and Gavin were aboard it.

"Oh, goodness, I wish they would hurry the

458

passengers through passport and customs!" Abbra said impatiently. "It's been on the ground for fifteen minutes now!"

Serena's mouth was so dry that she couldn't speak. Her arm was around *le petit* Gavin's shoulders, and the emotional drama of the scene that was about to be enacted was almost too much for her.

"They're beginning to come through now," Scott said tensely as a handful of passengers filed out, pushing luggage-laden trolleys before them.

"Oh, God!" Abbra whispered beneath her breath, her eyes shining. "They will be here in a minute! Oh, I can't believe it!"

An old woman came out of the swinging doors leading from the customs hall, and then a couple of teenagers. Serena felt as if she were going to die with nervous anticipation. They could be only minutes away now. Only seconds.

The doors swung open again, and this time no heavily laden luggage trolley was trundled through. Instead, Gavin and Gabrielle burst into the departure hall, holding hands.

Serena saw a fair-haired, surprisingly boyish-looking man in his early thirties, with warm gray eyes and a dazzlingly attractive smile.

"*Gabrielle!*" Abbra cried, racing forward.

Serena was hard on her heels. For a few crazy seconds they hugged and kissed, three women who had shared the same brand of suffering, who were bound closer together as friends than they would ever be with anyone else, ever.

At the same moment, Serena and Abbra remembered *le petit* Gavin. They stood aside. *Le petit* Gavin's eyes were fixed on Gavin's. Suddenly they were all very still. If there was noise in the arrivals hall around them, none of them was aware of it.

Gavin smiled at his son. "Hello, Gavin," he said tenderly. "We have a lot of time to make up for, don't we?" and he opened his arms wide.

Le petit Gavin uttered a strangled cry and then sprinted forward into his father's arms, clasping him tight, tears falling down his face.

Gabrielle looked around at her friends, her smile radiant. "I think some introductions are called for," she said, her eyes dancing with laughter at the ridiculous realization that there they were, all such good friends, and yet not everyone had been introduced. "Scott has not yet been introduced to Serena and Mike, Mike hasn't been introduced to Abbra, and Gavin has not yet been introduced to anybody!"

"Let's make all the introductions over champagne at La Closerie des Lilas," Gavin said, setting his son back on the ground but keeping firmly hold of his hand.

"A good idea!" Abbra enthused as Scott slipped his arm around her shoulders.

"A *wonderful* idea," Serena agreed in the cut-glass English accent that amused Gabrielle and Mike so much.

Mike took Serena's hand in his and Gavin's free hand encircled Gabrielle's waist. Abbra and Serena and Gabrielle looked across at each other and laughed with sheer joy. Then, their children at their side, they walked out of the arrivals hall into the Parisian May sunshine, three stunningly beautiful women, deeply and happily in love.